TERRESTRIAL
INTELLIGENCE

Also Available From New Directions,

The Companion Volume:

WORLD BEAT

INTERNATIONAL POETRY NOW
From New Directions

International

Fiction now

TERRESTRIAL
INTELLIGENCE

FROM
NEW DIRECTIONS

E D I T E D B Y B A R B A R A E P L E R

A NEW DIRECTIONS BOOK

Publisher's Note: The material in this anthology is all collected from books either published by New Directions or soon to be published by New Directions, and is copyrighted as follows, in order of appearance: Robert Bolaño, "Last Evenings on Earth," from *Last Evenings on Earth & Other Stories* © 2002 by Anagrama, and translation © 2006 by Chris Andrews; Yoko Tawada, "Where Europe Begins," from *Where Europe Begins* © 1989, 1999 by Yoko Tawada, and translation © 2002 by Susan Bernofsky; Javier Marías, "When I Was Mortal," from *When I Was Mortal and Other Stories,* © 1996 by Javier Marías, and translation © 1999 by Margaret Jull Costa; W. G. Sebald's *The Rings of Saturn* © 1995 by Vito von Eichborn GmbH & Co Verlag KG, Frankfurt, and Translation © 1998 by The Harvill Press; Can Xue's "Snake Island" from *Blue Light in the Sky and Other Stories,* © 2006 by Can Xue, and translation © 2006 by Karen Gerant & Chen Zeping; John Keene, *Annotations,* © 1995 by John Keene; Alexander Kluge "Six Stories," from *The Devil's Blind Spot & Other Stories,* © 2002 by Alexander Kluge, and translation © 2004 by Martin Chalmers & Michael Hulse; Antonio Tabucchi "Letter from Casablanca," from *Letter from Casablanca,* © 1989 by Il Saggiatore, and translation ©1986 by Janice Thresher; Yoel Hoffmann, *The Heart Is Katmandu* © 1999 by Yoel Hoffmann, and translation © 2001 by Peter Cole; Kono Taeko "Bone Meat," from *Toddler-Hunting & Other Stories,* © 1964 by Kono Taeko, and translation © 1994 by Lucy Lower; Inger Christensen, *Azorno* © 1990 by Inger Christensen, and translation © 2006 by Denise Newman; Fleur Jaeggy, "No Destiny," from *Last Vanities,* © 1994 by Fleur Jaeggy, and translation © 1998 by Tim Parks; Muriel Spark, "The Portobello Road," from *All the Stories of Muriel Spark,* © 1958 by Muriel Spark; Felisberto Hernandez, "The Crocodile," from *Lands of Memory,* © 1942, 1966 by Felisberto Hernandez, and translation © 2002 by Esther Allen; Leonid Tyspkin, *Summer in Baden-Baden,* © 1981 by Leonid Tsypkin, and translation © 1987 by Quartet Books, London; Jenny Erpenbeck "Hale and Hallowed" © 1991, 2001 by Jenny Erpenbeck, and translation © 2005 by Susan Bernofsky; Rodrigo Rey Rosa, *The Good Cripple,* © 1996 by Rodrigo Rey Rosa, and translation © 2004 by Esther Allen; René Philoctète, *Massacre River,* © 1989 by René Philoctète, and translation © 2005 by Linda Coverdale; Clarice Lispector "Three Crônicas," © 1984 by Editora Nova Fronteiro, and translation © 1992 by Giovanni Pontiero; César Aira, *An Episode in the Life of a Landscape Painter,* © 2000 by César Aira, and translation © 2006 by Chris Andrews; Victor Pelevin, "The Life and Adventures of Shed Number XII," from *The Blue Lantern & Other Stories,* © 1994 by Victor Pelevin, and translation © 1996 by Andrew Bromfield; László Krasznahorkai, *War and War,* © 2003 by László Krasznahorkai, and translation © 2006 by George Szirtes; Dubravka Ugresic, *The Museum of Unconditional Surrender,* © 1996, 1999 by Dubravka Ugresic, and translation © 1996, 1999 by Celia Hawkesworth; Enrique Vila-Matas, *Bartleby & Co.,* © 2000 by Editorial Anagrama, and translation © 2004 by Jonathan Dunne.

Manufactured in the United States of America
New Directions Books are printed on acid-free paper.
First published as a New Directions Paperbook (NDP 1034) in 2006
Published simultaneously in Canada by Penguin Books Canada Limited
Design by Semadar Megged

Library of Congress Cataloging-in-Publication Data
Terrestrial intelligence : international fiction now from new directions / edited by Barbara Epler.
    p. cm.
Includes bibliographical references.
ISBN-13: 978-0-8112-1650-0
ISBN-10: 0-8112-1650-0
1. Fiction—Translations into English. I. Epler, Barbara, 1961–
PN6120.2.T47 2006
808.83′049—dc22   2006003820

New Directions Books are published for James Laughlin
by New Directions Publishing Corporation
80 Eighth Avenue, New York 10011

CONTENTS

> "The thing is to get the nonconforming stuff
> in print when it is written and not fifteen years
> after."   —James Laughlin

Collected here are twenty-four authors from seventeen countries writing in twelve languages. All the pieces are taken from the last two decades' worth of New Directions books or from books about to appear, and although the whole is organized on a subjective pleasure principal (for enjoyment if read from start to finish), *Terrestrial Intelligence* is a ragbag to be rummaged through, and we hope the reader will feel some of our delight in the discovery of these writers.

Cohabiting in *Terrestrial Intelligence* are writers from Argentina, Brazil, Chile, China, Croatia, Denmark, Germany, Guatemala, Hungary, Israel, Italy, Japan, Russia, Scotland, Spain, the U.S., and Uruguay. Famous in their own cultures, bedecked with prizes, acclaimed at home where they are read as the new masters, these writers are the groundbreakers now: these are the real thing, not the imported wax apples: *these are the goods*. Roberto Bolaño: "his generation's premier Latin American writer. . . . Bolaño's reputation and legend are in meteoric ascent" (*The New York Times*). Javier Marías: an author of "clandestine greatness" (*The New Yorker*) and "the most subtle and gifted writer in contemporary Spanish literature" (*The Boston Globe*). W.G. Sebald: "one of the great writers of our time" (*The New York Review of Books*). Yoel Hoffmann: "Israel's celebrated avantgarde genius" (*Forward*). Muriel Spark: author of "some of the best sentences in English" (*The New Yorker*). Clarice Lispector: "the pinnacle of Brazil's impressive literary achievement" (*The Washington Post Book World*). Victor Pelevin: "A psychedelic Nabokov for the cyber age" (*Time*).

New Directions has been finding the goods since its very beginning in 1936: James Laughlin was the first American publisher of Nabokov, Borges, Mishima, Camus, Céline, Neruda,

Montale, and Paz, to name just a handful. He was also the publisher of Nathanael West, Djuna Barnes, Henry Miller, Delmore Schwartz, and Dylan Thomas. Octavio Paz said regarding New Directions books: "for us, each volume was a map, not of discovered and colonized lands, but of the unknown territories that were being explored (or invented) by the new writers appearing in the four corners of the earth. To read the ND publications was to open a window."

Terrestrial Intelligence aims to open more windows. For New Directions (as Laughlin said of Ezra Pound), it is "all about one world literature." Laughlin believed in Pound's maxim that truly new writing takes twenty years to catch on: in 1947 he is lamenting, "Bizniss stinks worse than ever. Ruin hangs like a large garbage pail over the Halloween doorway because costs are way up and sales are way down. But who knows, who ever knows, who does?" Yet he kept publishing only what he liked—"endless diversity of experiment"—and kept discovering new writers. It is good that he was still alive when W.G. Sebald's *The Emigrants* appeared: "one of the most beautiful pieces of writing which we have ever published. It's a masterpiece if ever there was one." New Directions is trying to keep on his path and, as Sebald wrote to say, when James Laughlin died, "Perhaps you know—those one truly appreciates never really depart."

Here in this book are the new new directions: what Laughlin called "the small intransigent company of experimental writers." Some are already famous in America: some are still waiting. They all deserve discovery, and perhaps it's at hand. ("But who knows, who ever knows, who does?") It's unlikely that anyone besides myself will like every single thing here, and you may pull a nettle out of the ragbag, but when we talk about great literature I think the writers collected in this book are what we mean. I find each author in the best sense—as Italo Calvino called Felisberto Hernández—"one of literature's irregulars."

Barbara Epler

TERRESTRIAL INTELLIGENCE

ROBERTO BOLAÑO

LAST EVENINGS ON EARTH
Translated from the Spanish by CHRIS ANDREWS

This is the situation: B and his father are going to Acapulco for a vacation. They are planning to leave very early, at six in the morning. B sleeps the night before at his father's house. He doesn't dream or if he does he forgets his dreams as soon as he opens his eyes. He hears his father in the bathroom. He looks out the window; it is still dark. He gets dressed without switching on the light. When he comes out of his room, his father is sitting at the table, reading yesterday's sports section, and breakfast is ready. Coffee and huevos rancheros. B says hello to his father and goes into the bathroom.

His father's car is a 1970 Ford Mustang. At six-thirty in the morning they get into the car and head out of the city. The city is Mexico City, and the year in which B and his father leave Mexico City for a short holiday is 1975.

Overall, the trip goes smoothly. Driving out of the city both father and son feel cold, but as they leave the high valley behind and begin to descend into the state of Guerrero, the temperature climbs and they have to take off their sweaters and roll down the windows. B, who is inclined to melancholy (or so he likes to think), is at first completely absorbed in contemplating the landscape, but after a few hours the mountains and forests become monotonous and he starts reading a book instead.

Before they get to Acapulco, B's father pulls up in front of a roadside café. The café serves iguana. Shall we try it? he suggests. The iguanas are alive and they hardly move when B's father goes over to look at them. B leans against the Mustang's bumper, watching him. Without waiting for an answer, B's father orders a portion of iguana for himself and one for his son. Only then does B move away from the car. He approaches the open-air eating area—four tables under a canvas awning that is swaying slightly in the gentle breeze—and sits down at the table farthest from the highway. B's father orders two beers. Father and son have unbuttoned their shirts and rolled up their sleeves. Both are wearing light-colored shirts. The waiter, by contrast, is wearing a black, long-sleeved shirt and doesn't seem bothered by the heat.

Going to Acapulco? asks the waiter. B's father nods. They are the only customers at the café. Cars whiz past on the bright highway. B's father gets up and goes out back. For a moment B thinks his father is going to the toilet, but then he realizes he has gone to the kitchen to see how they cook the iguanas. The waiter follows him without a word. Then B hears them talking. First his father, then the man's voice, and finally the voice of a woman B can't see. B's forehead is beaded with sweat. His glasses are misted and dirty. He takes them off and cleans them with the corner of his shirt. When he puts them back on he notices his father watching him from the kitchen. He can see only his father's face and part of his shoulder, the rest is hidden by a red curtain with black dots, and B has the intermittent impression that this curtain separates not only the kitchen from the café area but also one time from another.

Then B looks away and his gaze returns to the book lying on the table. It is a book of poetry. An anthology of French surrealist poets translated into Spanish by the Argentinean surrealist Aldo Pellegrini. B has been reading this book for two days. He likes it. He likes the photos of the poets. The photo of Unik, the one of Desnos, the photos of Artaud and Crevel. The book is thick and covered with transparent plastic. It wasn't covered by B (who never covers his books), but by a particularly fastidious friend. So B looks away from his father, opens the book at random and comes face to face with Gui Rosey, the photo of Gui Rosey and his poems, and when he looks up again his father's head has disappeared.

The heat is stifling. B would be more than happy to go back to Mexico City, but he isn't going back, at least not yet, he knows that. Soon his father is sitting next to him and they are both eating iguana with chili sauce and drinking more beer. The waiter in the black shirt has turned on a transistor radio and now some vaguely tropical music is blending with the noises of the jungle and the noise of the cars passing on the highway. The iguana tastes like chicken. It's tougher than chicken, says B, not entirely convinced. It's tasty, says his father, and orders another portion. They have cinnamon coffee. The man in the black shirt serves the iguana, but the woman from the kitchen brings out the coffee. She is young, almost as young as B; she is wearing white shorts and a yellow blouse with white flowers printed on it, flowers B doesn't recognize, perhaps because they don't exist. As they drink their coffee, B feels nauseous, but he says nothing. He smokes and looks at the canvas awning, barely moving, as if weighed down by a thin puddle of rainwater from the last storm. But it can't be that, thinks B. What are you looking at? asks his father. The awning, says B. It's like a vein. But he doesn't say the bit about the vein, he only thinks it.

They arrive in Acapulco as night is falling. For a while they drive up and down the seaside avenues with the windows down and the breeze ruffling their hair. They stop at a bar and go in for a drink. This time B's father orders tequila. B thinks for a moment. Then he orders tequila too. The bar is modern and has air-conditioning. B's father talks with the waiter and asks him about hotels near the beach. By the time they get back to the Mustang a few stars are visible and for the first time that day B's father looks tired. Even so, they visit a couple of hotels, which for one reason or another are unsatisfactory, before finding one that will do. The hotel is called La Brisa: it's small, a stone's throw from the beach, and has a swimming pool. B's father likes the hotel. So does B. It's the off season, so the hotel is almost empty and the prices are reasonable. The room they are given has two single beds and a small bathroom with a shower. The only window looks onto the terrace, where the swimming pool is. B's father would have preferred a sea view. The air-conditioner, they soon discover, is out of order. But the room is fairly cool, so they don't complain. They make themselves at home: each opens up his suitcase and puts his clothes in the wardrobe. B leaves his books on the bedside table. They change their shirts. B's father takes a cold shower while B just washes his face, and when they are ready they go out to dinner.

The reception desk is manned by a short guy with teeth like a rabbit. He's young and seems friendly. He recommends a restaurant near the hotel. B's father asks if there's somewhere lively nearby. B understands what his father means. The receptionist doesn't. A place with a bit of action, says B's father. A place where you can find girls, says B. Ah, says the receptionist. For a moment B and his father stand there, without speaking. The receptionist crouches down, disappearing behind the counter, and reappears with a card, which he holds out. B's father looks at the card, asks if the establishment is reliable, then extracts a bill from his wallet, which the receptionist catches on the fly.

But after dinner, they go straight back to the hotel.

The next day, B wakes up very early. As quietly as possible he takes a shower, brushes his teeth, puts on his swimsuit and leaves the room. There is no one in the hotel dining room, so B decides to go out for breakfast. The hotel is on a street that runs straight down to the beach, which is empty except for a boy renting out paddle boards. B asks him how much it costs for an hour. The boy quotes a price that sounds reasonable, so B hires a board and pushes off into the sea. Opposite the beach is a little island, towards which he steers his craft. At first he has some trouble, but soon he gets the hang of it. At this time of day the sea is crystal clear and B thinks he can see red fishes under the boat, about a foot and half long, swimming towards the beach as he paddles towards the island.

It takes exactly fifteen minutes for him to get from the beach to the island. B doesn't know this, because he is not wearing a watch, and for him time slows down. The crossing seems to last an eternity. At the last minute, waves rear unexpectedly, impeding his approach. The sand is noticeably different from that of the hotel beach; back there it was a golden, tawny color, perhaps because of the time of day (though B doesn't think so), while here it is a dazzling white, so bright it hurts your eyes to look at it.

B stops paddling and just sits there, at the mercy of the waves, which begin to carry him slowly away from the island. By the time he finally reacts, the board has drifted half way back. Having ascertained this, B decides to turn around. The return is calm and uneventful. When he gets to the beach, the boy who rents out the boards comes up and asks if he had a problem. Not at all, says B. An hour later B returns to the hotel without having had breakfast and finds his father sitting in the dining room with a cup of coffee and a plate in front of him on which are scattered the remains of toast and eggs.

The following hours are hazy. They drive around aimlessly, watching people from the car. Sometimes they get out to have a cold drink or an ice cream. In the afternoon, on the beach, while his father is stretched out asleep in a deck chair, B rereads Gui Rosey's poems and the brief story of his life or his death.

One day a group of surrealists arrives in the south of France. They try to get visas for the United States. The north and the west of the country are occupied by the Germans. The south is under the aegis of Pétain. Day after day, the US Consulate delays its decision. Among the members of the group are Breton, Tristan Tzara, and Péret, but there are also less famous figures. Gui Rosey is one of them. In the photo he has the look of a minor poet, thinks B. He is ugly, he is impeccably dressed, he looks like an unimportant civil servant or a bankteller. Up to this point, a few disagreements, but nothing out of the ordinary, thinks B. The surrealists gather every afternoon at a café by the port. They make plans and chat; Rosey is always there. But one day (one afternoon, B imagines), he fails to appear. At first, he isn't missed. He is a minor poet and no one pays much attention to minor poets. After a few days, however, the others start to worry. At the *pension* where he is staying, no one knows what has happened; his suitcases and books are there, undisturbed, so he clearly hasn't tried to leave without paying (as guests at *pensions* on the Côte d'Azur are prone to do). His friends try to find him. They visit all the hospitals and police stations in the area. No one can tell them anything. One morning the visas arrive. Most of them board a ship and set off for the United States. Those who remain, who will never get visas, soon forget about Rosey and his disappearance; people are disappearing all the time, in large numbers, and they have to look out for themselves.

That night, after dinner at the hotel, B's father suggests they go find a bit of action. B looks at his father. He is blond (B is dark), his eyes are grey and he is still in good shape. He looks happy and ready to have a good time. What sort of action? asks B, who knows perfectly well what his father is referring to. The usual kind, says B's father. Drinking and women. For a while B says nothing, as if he were pondering a reply. His father looks at him. The look might seem inquisitive, but in fact it is only affectionate. Finally B says he's not in the mood for sex. It's not just about getting laid, says his father, we'll go and see, have a few drinks and enjoy ourselves with some friends. What friends, says B, we don't know anyone here. You always make friends when you're out for a ride. The expression "out for a ride" makes B think of horses. When he was seven his father bought him a horse. Where did my horse come from? asks B. This takes his father completely by surprise. Horse? he asks. The one you bought me when I was a kid, says B, in Chile. Ah, Hullabaloo, says his father, smiling. He was from the island of Chiloé, he says, then after a moment's reflection he starts talking about brothels again. The way he talks about them, they could be dance halls, thinks B. Then they both fall silent.

That night they don't go anywhere.

While his father is sleeping, B goes out onto the terrace to read by the swimming pool. There is no one there apart from him. The terrace is clean and empty. From his table B can see part of the reception area, where the receptionist from the night before is standing at the counter reading something or looking over the books. B reads the French surrealists, he reads Gui Rosey. To tell the truth, Gui Rosey doesn't interest him much. He is far more interested in Desnos and Éluard, and yet he always ends up coming back to Rosey's poems and looking at his photo, a studio portrait, in which he has the air of a solitary, wretched soul, with his large, glassy eyes and a dark tie that seems to be strangling him.

He must have committed suicide, thinks B. He knew he was never going to get a visa for the States or Mexico, so he decided to end his days then and there. B imagines or tries to imagine a town on the Côte d'Azur. He still hasn't been to Europe. He has been all over Latin America, or almost, but he still hasn't set foot in Europe. So his image of a Mediterranean town is derived from his image of Acapulco. Heat, a small, cheap hotel, beaches of golden sand and beaches of white sand. And the distant sound of music. B doesn't realize that there is a crucial element missing from this scene's soundtrack: the rigging of the small boats that throng the ports of all the towns on the Mediterranean coast, especially the smaller ones. The sound of the rigging at night, when the sea is as still as a mill pond.

Suddenly someone comes on to the terrace. The silhouette of a woman. She sits down at the farthest table, in a corner, near two large urns. A moment later the receptionist appears, bringing her a drink. Then, instead of going back to the counter, he comes over to B, who is sitting by the edge of the pool, and asks if he and his father are having a good time. Very good, says B. Do you like Acapulco? asks the receptionist. Very much, says B. How was the San Diego? asks the receptionist. B doesn't understand the question. The San Diego? For a moment he thinks the receptionist is referring to the hotel, but then he remembers that the hotel is called something else. Which San Diego? asks B. The receptionist smiles: The club with the hookers. Then B remembers the card the receptionist gave his father. We haven't gone yet, he says. It's a reliable place, says the receptionist. B moves his head in a way that could mean almost anything. It's on Constituyentes, says the receptionist. There's another club on the avenue, the Ramada, but I wouldn't recommend it. The Ramada, says B, watching the woman's motionless silhouette in the corner of the terrace and the apparently untouched glass in front of her, between the enormous urns, whose shadows stretch and taper off under the neighboring tables. Best to steer clear of the Ramada, says the receptionist. Why? asks B, for something to say, although he has no intention of visiting either place. It's not reliable, says the receptionist, and his bright little rabbit teeth shine in the semi-darkness that has suddenly submerged the terrace, as if someone at reception had switched off half the lights.

When the receptionist goes away, B opens his book of poetry again, but the words are illegible now, so he leaves the book open on the table, shuts his eyes and, instead of the faint chimes of rigging, he hears an atmospheric sound, the sound of enormous layers of hot air descending on the hotel and the surrounding trees. He feels like getting into the pool. For a moment he thinks he might.

Then the woman in the corner stands up and begins to walk towards the stairs that lead from the terrace to the reception area, but midway she stops, as if she felt ill, resting one hand on the edge of a planter in which there are no longer flowers, only weeds.

B watches her. The woman is wearing a loose, light-colored summer dress, cut low, leaving her shoulders bare. He expects her to start walking again, but she stands still, her hand fixed to the edge of the planter, looking down, so B gets up with the book in his hand and goes over to her. The first thing that surprises him is her face. She must be about sixty years old, B guesses, although from a distance, he wouldn't have said she was more than thirty. She is North American, and when B approaches she looks up and smiles at him. Good night, she says, rather incongruously, in Spanish. Are you all right? asks B. The woman doesn't understand and B has to ask again, in English. I'm just thinking, says the woman, smiling at him fixedly. For a few seconds B considers what she has said to him. Thinking, thinking, thinking. And suddenly it seems to him that this declaration conceals a threat. Something approaching over the sea. Something advancing in the wake of the dark clouds invisibly crossing the Bay of Acapulco. But he doesn't move or make any attempt to break the spell that seems to be holding him captive. Then the woman looks at the book in B's left hand and asks him what he is reading, and B says: poetry. I'm reading poems. The woman looks him in the eye, with the same smile on her face (a smile at once bright and faded, thinks B, feeling more uneasy by the moment), and says that she used to like poetry, once. Which poets? asks B, keeping absolutely still. I can't remember them now, says the woman, and again she seems to lose herself in the contemplation of something visible only to her. B assumes she is making an effort to remember and waits in silence. After a while she looks at him again and says: Longfellow. And straight away she starts reciting lines with a monotonous rhythm that sound to B like a nursery rhyme—a far cry, in any case, from the poets he is reading. Do you know Longfellow? asks the woman. B shakes his head, although in fact he has read some Longfellow. We memorized it at school, says the woman, with her invariable smile. And then she adds: It's too hot, don't you think? It is very hot, whispers B. There could be a storm coming, says the woman. There is something very definite about her tone. At this point B looks up: he can't see a single star. But he can see lights in the hotel. And, at the window of his room, a silhouette watching them, which makes him start, as if struck by the first, sudden drops of a tropical downpour.

At first he is bewildered.

It's his father, on the other side of the glass, wrapped in a blue bathrobe that he must have brought with him (B hasn't seen it before and it certainly doesn't belong to the hotel), staring at them, although when B notices him, he steps back, recoiling as if bitten by a snake, lifts his hand in a shy wave, and disappears behind the curtains.

The Song of Hiawatha, says the woman. B looks at her. The Song of Hiawatha, the poem by Longfellow. Ah, yes, says B.

Then the woman says good night and makes a gradual exit: first she goes up the stairs to reception, where she spends a few moments chatting with someone B can't see, then, in silence, she sets off across the hotel lobby, her slim figure framed by successive windows, until she turns into the corridor that leads to the inside stairs.

Half an hour later, B goes to their room and finds his father asleep. For a few seconds, before going to the bathroom to brush his teeth, B stands very straight at the foot of the bed, gazing at him, as if steeling himself for a fight. Good night, dad, he says. His father gives not the slightest indication that he has heard.

On the second day of their stay in Acapulco, B and his father go to see the cliff divers. They have two options: they can watch the show from an open-air platform or go to the bar-restaurant of the hotel overlooking the precipice. B's father asks about the prices. The first person he asks doesn't know. He persists. Finally an old ex-diver who is hanging around doing nothing tells him what it costs: six times more to watch from the hotel bar. Let's go to the bar, says B's father without hesitating. We'll be more comfortable. B follows him. The other people in the bar are North American or Mexican tourists wearing what are obviously vacation outfits; B and his father stand out. They are dressed as people dress in Mexico City, in clothes that seem to belong to some endless dream. The waiters notice. They know the sort, no chance of a big tip, so they make no effort to serve them promptly. To top it off, B and his father can hardly see the show from where they are sitting. We would have been better off on the platform, says B's father. Although it's not bad here either, he adds. B nods. When the diving is over, and after two cocktails each, they go outside and start making plans for the rest of the day. Hardly anyone is left on the platform, but B's father recognizes the old ex-diver sitting on a railing and goes over to him.

The ex-diver is short and has a very broad back. He is reading a cowboy novel and doesn't look up until B and his father are at his side. He recognizes them and asks what they thought of the show. Not bad, says B's father, although in precision sports you need experience to judge properly. Would I be right to guess you were an athlete yourself? asks the ex-diver. B's father looks at him for a few moments and then says, You could say that. The ex-diver gets to his feet with an energetic movement as if he were back on the cliff edge. He must be about fifty, thinks B, so he's not much older than my father, but the wrinkles on his face, like scars, make him look much older. Are you gentlemen on vacation? asks the ex-diver. B's father nods and smiles. And what was your sport, sir, if I might ask? Boxing, says B's father. How about that, says the ex-diver, so you must have been a heavyweight? B's father smiles broadly and says yes.

Before he knows what is going on, B finds himself walking with his father and the ex-diver towards the Mustang and then all three get into the car and B listens to the ex-diver giving his father directions as if he were listening to the radio. For a while the car glides along the Avenida Miguel Alemán but then it turns and heads inland and soon the tourist hotels and restaurants give way to an ordinary cityscape with tropical touches. The car keeps climbing, heading away from the golden horseshoe of Acapulco, driving along badly paved or unpaved roads, until it pulls up beside the dusty sidewalk in front of a cheap restaurant, a fixed-menu place (although, thinks B, it's really too big for that). The ex-diver and B's father get out of the car immediately. They have been talking all the way and while they wait for him on the sidewalk, they continue their conversation gesturing incomprehensibly. B takes his time getting out of the car. We're going to eat, says his father. So it seems, says B.

The place is dark inside and only a quarter of the space is occupied by tables. The rest looks like a dance floor, with a stage for the band, surrounded by a long balustrade made of rough wood. At first, B can't see a thing, until his eyes adjust to the darkness. Then he sees a man coming over to the ex-diver. They look alike. The stranger listens attentively to an introduction that B doesn't catch, shakes hands with his father and a few seconds later turns to B. B reaches out to shake his hand. The stranger says a name and his handshake, which is no doubt meant to be friendly, is not so much firm as violent. He does not smile. B decides not to smile either. B's father and the ex-diver are already sitting at a table. B sits down next to them. The stranger, who looks like the ex-diver and turns out to be his younger brother, stands beside them, waiting for instructions. The gentleman here, says the ex-diver, was heavyweight champion of his country. So you're foreigners? asks his brother. Chileans, says B's father. Do you have red snapper? asks the ex-diver. We do, says his brother. Bring us one, then, a red snapper Guerrero-style, says the ex-diver. And beers all round, says B's father, for you too. Thank you, murmurs the brother, taking a notebook from his pocket and painstakingly writing down an order that, in B's opinion, a child could easily remember.

Along with the beers, the ex-diver's brother brings them some savoury crackers to nibble and three rather small plates of oysters. They're fresh, says the ex-diver, putting chili sauce on all three. Funny, isn't it. This stuff's called chili and so's your country, says the ex-diver pointing to the bottle full of bright red chili sauce. Yes, intriguing, isn't it. Like the way the sauce is the opposite of chilly, he adds. B looks at his father with barely veiled incredulity. The conversation revolves around boxing and diving until the red snapper arrives.

Later, B and his father leave the premises. The hours have flown by without them noticing and by the time they climb into the Mustang, it is already seven in the evening. The ex-diver comes with them. For a moment, B thinks they'll never get rid of him, but when they reach the center of Acapulco the ex-diver gets out in front of a billiard hall. When he has gone, B's father comments favorably on the service at the restaurant and the price they paid for the red snapper. If we'd had it here, he says, pointing to the hotels along the beachfront boulevard, it would have cost an arm and a leg. When they get back to their room, B puts on his swimsuit and goes to the beach. He swims for a while and then tries to read in the fading light. He reads the surrealist poets and is completely bewildered. A peaceful, solitary man, on the brink of death. Images, wounds. That is all he can see. And the images are dissolving little by little, like the setting sun, leaving only the wounds. A minor poet disappears while waiting for a visa to admit him to the New World. A minor poet disappears without leaving a trace, hopelessly stranded in some town on the Riviera. There is no investigation. There is no corpse. By the time B turns to Daumal, night has already fallen on the beach; he shuts the book and slowly makes his way back to the hotel.

After dinner, his father proposes they go out and have some fun. B declines this invitation. He suggests to his father that he go on his own, says he's not in the mood for fun, he'd prefer to stay in the room and watch a movie on TV. I can't believe it, says his father, you're behaving like an old man, at your age! B looks at his father, who is putting on clean clothes after a shower, and laughs.

Before his father goes out, B tells him to take care. His father looks at him from the doorway and says he's only going to have a couple of drinks. You take care yourself, he says, and gently shuts the door.

Once he's on his own, B takes off his shoes, looks for his cigarettes, switches on the TV, and collapses onto the bed again. Without intending to, he falls asleep. He dreams that he is living in (or visiting) the city of the Titans. All there is in the dream is an endless wandering through vast dark streets that recall other dreams. And in the dream his attitude is one that he knows he doesn't have in waking life. Faced with buildings whose voluminous shadows seem to be knocking against each other, he is, if not exactly courageous, unworried, or indifferent.

A while later, just after the end of the program, B wakes up with a jolt, and, as if responding to a summons, switches off the TV and goes to the window. On the terrace, half-hidden in the same corner as the night before, the North American woman is sitting with a cocktail or a glass of fruit juice in front of her. B observes her indifferently, then walks away from the window, sits on the bed, opens his book of surrealist poets and tries to read. But he can't. So he tries to think and to that end he lies down on the bed again, with his arms outstretched and shuts his eyes. For a moment he thinks he is on the point of falling asleep. He even catches an oblique glimpse of a street from the dream city. But soon he realizes that he is only remembering the dream, opens his eyes and lies there for a while contemplating the ceiling. Then he switches off the bedside lamp and goes back over to the window.

The North American woman is still there, motionless. The shadows of the urns stretch out and touch the shadows of the neighboring tables. The reception area, fully lit, unlike the terrace, is reflected in the swimming pool. Suddenly a car pulls up a few yards from the entrance of the hotel. His father's Mustang, thinks B. But no one appears at the hotel gate for a very long time and B begins to think he must have been mistaken. Then he makes out his father's silhouette climbing the stairs. First his head, then his broad shoulders, then the rest of his body, and finally the shoes, a pair of white moccasins that B, as a rule, finds profoundly disgusting, but the feeling they provoke in him now is something like tenderness. The way he came into the hotel, he thinks, it was like he was dancing. The way he made his entrance, it was as if he had come back from a wake, unconsciously glad to be alive. But the strangest thing is that, after appearing briefly in the reception area, his father turns around and heads towards the terrace: he goes down the stairs, walks around the pool, and sits at a table near the North American woman. And when the guy from reception finally appears with a glass, his father pays and, without even waiting for him to be gone, gets up, glass in hand, goes over to the table where the North American woman is sitting and stands there for a while, gesticulating and drinking, until, at the woman's invitation, he takes a seat beside her.

She's too old for him, thinks B. Then he goes back to the bed, lies down, and soon realizes that all the sleepiness weighing him down before has evaporated. But he doesn't want to turn on the light (although he feels like reading); he doesn't want his father to think (even for a moment) that he is spying on him. He thinks about women; he thinks about travel. Finally he goes to sleep.

Twice during the night he wakes up with a start and his father's bed is empty. The third time, day is already dawning and he sees his father's back: he is sleeping deeply. B switches on the light and stays in bed for a while, smoking and reading.

Later that morning B goes to the beach and hires a paddle board. This time he has no trouble reaching the island opposite. There he has a mango juice and swims for a while in the sea, alone. Then he goes back to the hotel beach, returns the board to the boy, who smiles at him, and takes a roundabout way back to the hotel. He finds his father in the restaurant drinking coffee. He sits down beside him. His father has just shaved and is giving off an odor of cheap aftershave that B finds pleasant. On his right cheek there is a scratch from ear to chin. B considers asking him what happened last night, but in the end decides not to.

The rest of the day goes by in a blur. At some point B and his father walk along a beach near the airport. The beach is vast and lined with numerous wattle-roofed shacks where the fishermen keep their gear. The sea is choppy; for a while B and his father watch the waves breaking in the bay of Puerto Marqués. A fisherman tells them it's not a good day for swimming. That's for sure, says B. His father goes in for a swim anyway. B sits down on the sand, with his knees up, and watches him advance to meet the waves. The fisherman shades his eyes and says something that B doesn't catch. For a moment he loses sight of his father's head and his arms stroking seaward. Now there are two children with the fisherman. They are all standing, looking out to sea, except for B, who is still sitting down. A plane appears in the sky, curiously inaudible. B stops looking at the sea and watches the plane until it disappears behind a rounded hill covered with vegetation. He remembers waking up, exactly a year before, in the Acapulco airport. He was returning from Chile, on his own, and the plane stopped in Acapulco. He remembers opening his eyes and seeing an orange light with blue and pink overtones, like the fading colors of an old film, and knowing then that he was back in Mexico and safe at last, in a sense. That was in 1974 and B had not yet turned twenty-one. Now he is twenty-two and his father must be about forty-nine. B closes his eyes. Because of the wind, the fisherman's and the boys' cries of alarm are almost unintelligible. The sand is cold. When he opens his eyes he sees his father coming out of the sea. He shuts his eyes and doesn't open them again until he feels a large wet hand grip his shoulder and hears his father's voice proposing they go eat turtle eggs.

There are things you can tell people and things you just can't, thinks B disconsolately. From this moment on he knows the disaster is approaching.

In spite of which the next forty-eight hours go by in a placid sort of daze that B's father associates with "The Idea of Vacation" (B can't tell whether his father is serious or pulling his leg). They go to the beach, they eat at the hotel or at a reasonably priced restaurant on the Avenida López Mateos. One afternoon they hire a boat, a tiny plastic rowboat, and follow the coastline near their hotel, along with the trinket vendors who peddle their wares from beach to beach, upright on paddle boards or in very flat-bottomed boats, like tightrope walkers or the ghosts of drowned sailors. On the way back they even have an accident.

B's father takes the boat too close to the rocks and it capsizes. In itself, this is not dramatic. Both of them can swim reasonably well and the boat is made to float when overturned; it isn't hard to right it and climb in again. And that is what B and his father do. Not the slightest danger at any point, thinks B. But then, when both of them have clambered back into the boat, B's father realizes that he has lost his wallet. Tapping his chest, he says: My wallet, and without a moment's hesitation he dives back into the water. B can't help laughing, but then, stretched out in the boat, he looks down, sees no sign of his father and for a moment imagines him diving, or worse, sinking like a stone, but with his eyes open, into a deep trench, over which, on the surface, in a rocking boat, his son has stopped laughing and started worrying. Then B sits up and, having looked over the other side of the boat and seen no sign of his father there either, jumps into the water, and this is what happens: as B goes down with his eyes open, his father, open-eyed too, is coming up (they almost touch) holding his wallet in his right hand. They look at each other as they pass, but can't alter their trajectories, or at least not straight away, so B's father keeps ascending silently while B continues his silent descent.

For sharks, for most fish in fact (flying fish excepted), hell is the surface of the sea. For B (and many, perhaps most, young men of his age) it sometimes takes the form of the sea floor. As he follows in his father's wake, but heading in the opposite direction, the situation strikes him as particularly ridiculous. On the bottom there is no sand, as he had for some reason imagined there would be, only rocks, piled on top of each other, as if this part of the coast were a submerged mountain range and he were near a high peak, having hardly begun the descent. Then he starts to rise again, and looks up at the boat, which seems to be levitating one moment and about to sink the next, and in it he finds his father sitting right in the middle, attempting to light a wet cigarette.

Then the lull comes to an end, the forty-eight hours of grace in the course of which B and his father have visited various bars in Acapulco, lain on the beach and slept, eaten, even laughed, and an icy phase begins, a phase which appears to be normal but is ruled by deities of ice (who do not, however, offer any relief from the heat that reigns in Acapulco), hours of what, in former days, when he was an adolescent perhaps, B would have called *boredom*, although he would certainly not use that word now, *disaster* he would say, a private disaster whose main effect is to drive a wedge between B and his father: part of the price they must pay for existing.

It all begins with the reappearance of the ex-diver, who, as B realizes straight away, has come looking for his father, and not for the family unit, so to speak, constituted by father and son. B's father invites the ex-diver to have a drink on the hotel terrace. The ex-diver says he knows a better place. B's father looks at him, smiles, and says OK. As they go out into the street, the light is beginning to fade. B feels an inexplicable stab of pain and thinks that perhaps it would have been better to stay at the hotel and leave his father to his own devices. But it's already too late. The Mustang is heading up the Avenida Constituyentes and from his pocket B's father takes the card that the receptionist gave him days ago. The nightspot is called the San Diego, he says. In the ex-diver's opinion, it's too expensive. I've got money, says B's father; I've been living in Mexico since 1968, and this is the first time I've taken a vacation. B, who is sitting next to his father, tries to see the ex-diver's face in the rearview mirror, but can't. So first they go to the San Diego and for a while they drink and dance with the girls. For each dance they have to give the girl a ticket bought beforehand at the bar. To begin with, B's father buys only three tickets. There's something unreal about this system, he says to the ex-diver. But then he starts enjoying himself and buys a whole bundle. B dances too. His first dance partner is a slim girl with Indian features. The second is a woman with big breasts who seems to be preoccupied or cross for a reason that B will never discover. The third is fat and happy and after dancing for a little while she whispers into B's ear that she's high. On what? asks B. Magic mushrooms, says the woman, and B laughs. Meanwhile B's father is dancing with a girl who looks like an Indian and B is glancing across at him from time to time. Actually, all the girls look like Indians. The one dancing with his father has a pretty smile. They are talking (they haven't stopped talking, in fact) although B can't hear what they are saying. Then his father disappears and B goes to the bar with the ex-diver. They start talking too. About the old days. About courage. About the cliffs where the ocean waves break. About women. Subjects that don't interest B, or at least not at the moment. But they talk anyway.

Half an hour later his father comes back to the bar. His blond hair is wet and freshly combed (B's father combs his hair back) and his face is red. He smiles and says nothing; B observes him and says nothing. Time for dinner, says B's father. B and the ex-diver follow him to the Mustang. They eat an assortment of shellfish in a place that's long and narrow, like a coffin. As they eat, B's father watches B as if he were searching for an answer. B looks back at him. He is sending a telepathic message: There is no answer because it's not a valid question. It's an idiotic question. Then, before he knows what is going on, B is back in the car with his father and the ex-diver, who talk about boxing all the way to a place in the suburbs of Acapulco. It's a brick and wood building with no windows and inside there's a jukebox with songs by Lucha Vila and Lola Beltrán. Suddenly B feels nauseous. He leaves his father and the ex-diver and looks for the toilet or the back yard or the door to the street, belatedly realizing that he has had too much to drink. He also realizes that apparently well-meaning hands have prevented him from going out into the street. They don't want me to get away, thinks B. Then he vomits several times in the yard, among stacks of beer cases, under the eye of a chained dog, and having relieved himself, gazes up at the stars. A woman soon appears beside him. Her shadow is darker than the darkness of the night. If not for her white dress, B could hardly make her out. You want a blow job? she asks. Her voice is young and husky. B looks at her, uncomprehending. The whore kneels down beside him and unzips his fly. Then B understands and lets her proceed. When it's over he feels cold. The whore stands up and B hugs her. Together they gaze at the night sky. When B says he's going back to his father's table, the woman doesn't follow him. Let's go, says B, but she resists. Then B realizes that he has hardly seen her face. It's better that way. I hugged her, he thinks, but I don't even know what she looks like. Before he goes in he turns around and sees her walking over to pat the dog.

Inside, his father is sitting at a table with the ex-diver and two other guys. B comes up to him from behind and whispers in his ear: Let's go. His father is playing cards. I'm winning, he says, I can't leave now. They're going to steal all our money, thinks B. Then he looks at the women, who are looking at him and his father with commiseration in their eyes. They know what's going to happen to us, thinks B. Are you drunk? his father asks him, taking a card. No, says B, not any more. Have you taken any drugs? asks his father. No, says B. Then his father smiles and orders a tequila. B gets up and goes to the bar, and from there he surveys the scene of the crime with manic eyes. It is clear to B now that he will never travel with his father again. He shuts his eyes; he opens his eyes. The whores watch him curiously; one offers him a drink, which B declines with a gesture. When he shuts his eyes, he keeps seeing his father with a pistol in each hand, entering through an impossibly situated door. In he comes, impossibly, urgently, with his grey eyes shining and his hair ruffled. This is the last time we're traveling together, thinks B. That's all there is to it. The jukebox is playing a Lucha Villa song and B thinks of Gui Rosey, a minor poet who disappeared in the south of France. His father deals the cards, laughs, tells stories, and listens to those of his companions, each more sordid than the last. B remembers going to his father's house when he returned from Chile in 1974. His father had broken his foot and was in bed reading a sports magazine. What was it like? he asked, and B recounted his adventures. An episode from the chronicle of Latin America's doomed revolutions. I almost got killed, he said. His father looked at him and smiled. How many times? he asked. Twice, at least, B replied. Now B's father is roaring with laughter and B is trying to think clearly. Gui Rosey committed suicide, he thinks, or got killed. His corpse is at the bottom of the sea.

A tequila, says B. A woman hands him a half-full glass. Don't get drunk again, kid, she says. No, I'm all right now, says B, feeling perfectly lucid. Then two other women approach him. What would you like to drink? asks B. Your father's really nice, says the younger one, who has long, black hair. Maybe she's the one who gave me the blow job, thinks B. And he remembers (or tries to remember) apparently disconnected scenes: the first time he smoked in front of his father; he was fourteen, it was a Viceroy cigarette, they were waiting in his father's truck for a freight train and it was a very cold morning. Guns and knives, family stories. The whores are drinking tequila with Coca-Cola. How long was I outside vomiting? wonders B. You were kind of jumpy before, says one of the whores. You want some? Some what? says B. He is shaking and his skin is cold as ice. Some weed, says the woman, who is about thirty years old and has long hair like the other one, but dyed blonde. Acapulco Gold? asks B, taking a gulp of tequila, while the two women come a little closer and start stroking his back and his legs. Yep, it calms you down, says the blonde. B nods and the next thing he knows there is a cloud of smoke between him and his father. You really love your dad, don't you, says one of the women. Well, I wouldn't go that far, says B. What do you mean? says the dark woman. The woman serving at the bar laughs. Through the smoke B sees his father turn his head and look at him for a moment. A deadly serious look, he thinks. Do you like Acapulco? asks the blonde. Only at this point does he realize that the bar is almost empty. At one table there are two men drinking in silence, at another, his father, the ex-diver, and the two strangers playing cards. All the other tables are empty.

The door to the patio opens and a woman in a white dress appears. She's the one who gave me the blow job, thinks B. She looks about twenty-five, but is probably much younger, maybe sixteen or seventeen. Like almost all the others, she has long hair, and is wearing shoes with very high heels. As she walks across the bar (towards the bathroom) B looks carefully at her shoes: they are white and smeared with mud on the sides. His father also looks up and examines her for a moment. B watches the whore opening the bathroom door, then he looks at his father. He shuts his eyes and when he opens them again the whore is gone and his father has turned his attention back to the game. The best thing for you to do would be to get your father out of this place, one of the women whispers in his ear. B orders another tequila. I can't, he says. The woman slides her hand up under his loose-fitting Hawaiian shirt. She's checking to see if I have a weapon, thinks B. The woman's fingers climb up his chest and close on his left nipple. She squeezes it. Hey, says B. Don't you believe me? asks the woman. What's going to happen? asks B. Something bad, says the woman. How bad? I don't know, but if I was you, I'd get out of here. B smiles and looks into her eyes for the first time: Come with us, he says, taking a gulp of tequila. Not in a million years, says the woman. Then B remembers his father saying to him, before he left for Chile: "You're an artist and I'm a worker." What did he mean by that? he wonders. The bathroom door opens and the whore in the white dress comes out again, her shoes immaculate now, goes across to the table where the card game is happening, and stands there next to one of the strangers. Why, asks B, why do we have to go? The woman looks at him out of the corner of her eye and says nothing. There are things you can tell people, thinks B, and things you just can't. He shuts his eyes.

As if in a dream, he goes back out to the patio. The woman with the dyed-blonde hair leads him by the hand. I have already done this, thinks B, I'm drunk, I'll never get out of here. Certain gestures are repeated: the woman sits on a rickety chair and opens his fly, the night seems to float like a lethal gas among the empty beer cases. But some things are missing: the dog has gone, for one, and in the sky, to the east, where the moon hung before, a few filaments of light herald dawn. When they finish, the dog appears, perhaps attracted by B's groans. He doesn't bite, says the woman, while the dog stands a few yards away, baring its teeth. The woman gets up and smoothes her dress. The fur on the dog's back is standing up and a string of translucent saliva hangs from his muzzle. Stay, Fang, stay, says the woman. He's going to bite, thinks B as they retreat towards the door. What happens next is confused: at his father's table, all the card players are standing up. One of the strangers is shouting at the top of his voice. B soon realizes that he is insulting his father. As a precaution he orders a bottle of beer at the bar, which he drinks in long gulps, almost choking, before going over to the table. His father seems calm. In front of him are a considerable number of bills, which he is picking up one by one and putting into his pocket. You're not leaving here with that money, shouts the stranger. B looks at the ex-diver, trying to tell from his face which side he will take. The stranger's probably, thinks B. The beer runs down his neck and only then does he realize he is burning hot.

B's father finishes counting his money and looks at the three men standing in front of him and the woman in white. Well, gentlemen, he says, we're leaving. Come over here, son, he says. B pours what is left of his beer onto the floor and grips the bottle by the neck. What are you doing, son? says B's father. B can hear the tone of reproach in his voice. We're going to leave calmly, says B's father, then he turns around and asks the women how much they owe. The woman at the bar looks at a piece of paper and reads out a sizable sum. The blonde woman, who is standing half way between the table and bar, says another figure. B's father adds them up, takes out the money and hands it to the blonde: What we owe you and the drinks. Then he gives her a couple more bills: the tip. Now we're going to leave, thinks B. The two strangers block their exit. B doesn't want to look at her, but he does: the woman in white has sat down on one of the vacant chairs and is examining the cards scattered on the table, touching them with her fingertips. Don't get in my way, whispers his father, and it takes a while for B to realize that he is speaking to him. The ex-diver puts his hands in his pockets. The one who was shouting before starts insulting B's father again, telling him to come back to the table and keep playing. The game's over, says B's father. For a moment, looking at the woman in white (who strikes him now, for the first time, as very beautiful), B thinks of Gui Rosey, who disappeared off the face of the earth, quiet as a lamb, without a trace, while the Nazi hymns rose into a blood-red sky, and he sees himself as Gui Rosey, a Gui Rosey buried in some vacant lot in Acapulco, vanished forever, but then he hears his father, who is accusing the ex-diver of something, and he realizes that unlike Gui Rosey he is not alone.

Then his father walks towards the door stooping slightly and B stands aside to give him room to move. Tomorrow we'll leave, tomorrow we'll go back to Mexico City, thinks B joyfully. And then the fight begins.

Yoko Tawada

WHERE EUROPE BEGINS

Translated from the German by Susan Bernofsky

I

For my grandmother, to travel was to drink foreign water. Different places, different water. There was no need to be afraid of foreign landscapes, but foreign water could be dangerous. In her village lived a girl whose mother was suffering from an incurable illness. Day by day her strength waned, and her brothers were secretly planning her funeral. One day as the girl sat alone in the garden beneath the tree, a white serpent appeared and said to her: "Take your mother to see the Fire Bird. When she has touched its flaming feathers, she will be well again." "Where does the Fire Bird live?" asked the girl. "Just keep going west. Behind three tall mountains lies a bright shining city, and at its center, atop a high tower, sits the Fire Bird." "How can we ever reach this city if it is so far off? They say the mountains are inhabited by monsters." The serpent replied: "You needn't be afraid of them. When you see them, just remember that you, too, like all other human beings, were once a monster in one of your previous lives. Neither hate them nor do battle with them, just continue on your way. There is only one thing you must remember: when you are in the city where the Fire Bird lives, you must not drink a single drop of water." The girl thanked him, went to her mother and told her everything she had learned. The next day the two of them set off. On every mountain they met a monster that spewed green, yellow and blue fire and tried to burn them up; but as soon as the girl reminded herself that she, too, had once been just like them, the monsters sank into the ground. For ninety-nine days they wandered through the forest, and finally they reached the city, which shone brightly with a strange light. In the burning heat, they saw a tower in the middle of this city, and atop it sat the Fire Bird. In her joy, the girl forgot the serpent's warning and drank water from the pond. Instantly the girl became ninety-nine years old and her mother vanished in the flaming air.

When I was a little girl, I never believed there was such a thing as foreign water, for I had always thought of the globe as a sphere of water with all sorts of small and large islands swimming on it. Water had to be the same everywhere. Sometimes in sleep I heard the murmur of the water that flowed beneath the main island of Japan. The border surrounding the island was also made of water that ceaselessly beat against the shore in waves. How can one say where the place of foreign water begins when the border itself is water?

2

The crews of three Russian ships stood in uniform on the upper deck playing a farewell march whose unfamiliar solemnity all at once stirred up the oddest feelings in me. I, too, stood on the upper deck, like a theatergoer who has mistakenly stepped on-stage, for my eyes were still watching me from among the crowd on the dock, while I myself stood blind and helpless on the ship. Other passengers threw long paper snakes in various colors to-ward the dock. The red streamers turned midair into umbilical cords—one last link between the passengers and their loved ones. The green streamers became serpents and proclaimed their warning, which would probably only be forgotten on the way, anyhow. I tossed one of the white streamers into the air. It became my memory. The crowd slowly withdrew, the music faded, and the sky grew larger behind the mainland. The moment my paper snake disintegrated, my memory ceased to function. This is why I no longer remember anything of this journey. The fifty hours aboard the ship to the harbor town in Eastern Siberia, followed by the hundred and sixty hours it took to reach Europe on the Trans-Siberian Railroad, have become a blank space in my life which can be replaced only by a written account of my journey.

3
Diary excerpt:
The ship followed the coastline northward. Soon it was dark, but many passengers still sat on the upper deck. In the distance one could see the lights of smaller ships. "The fishermen are fishing for squid," a voice said behind me. "I don't like squid. When I was little, we had squid for supper every third night. What about you?" another voice asked. "Yes," a third one responded, "I ate them all the time, too. I always imagined they were descended from monsters." "Where did you grow up?" the first voice asked.

Voices murmured all around me, tendrils gradually entwining. On board such a ship, everyone begins putting together a brief autobiography, as though he might otherwise forget who he is.

"Where are you going?" the person sitting next to me asked. "I'm on my way to Moscow." He stared at me in surprise. "My parents spoke of this city so often I wanted to see it with my own eyes." Had my parents really talked about Moscow? On board such a ship, everyone begins to lie. The man was looking so horrified I had to say something else right away. "Actually I'm not so interested in Moscow itself, but I want to have experienced Siberia." "What do you want to experience in Siberia?" he asked: "What is there in Siberia?" "I don't know yet. Maybe nothing to speak of. But the important thing for me is traveling *through* Siberia." The longer I spoke, the more unsure of myself I became. He went to sit beside another passenger, leaving me alone with the transparent word *through*.

4

A few months before I set off on my journey, I was working evenings after school in a food processing factory. A poster adverstising a trip to Europe on the Trans-Siberian Railroad transformed the immeasurably long distance to Europe into a finite sum of money.

In the factory, the air was kept at a very low temperature so the meat wouldn't go bad. I stood in this cold, which I referred to as "Siberian frost," wrapping frozen poultry in plastic. Beside the table stood a bucket of hot water in which I could warm my hands at intervals.

Once three frozen chickens appeared in my dreams. I watched my mother place them in the frying pan. When the pan was hot, they suddenly came to life and flew out the kitchen window. "No wonder we never have enough to eat," I said with such viciousness even I was shocked. "What am I supposed to do?" my mother asked, weeping.

Besides earning money, there were two other things I wanted to do before my departure: learn Russian and write an account of the journey. I always wrote a travel narrative before I set off on a trip, so that during the journey I'd have something to quote from. I was often speechless when I traveled. This time it was particularly useful that I'd written my report beforehand. Otherwise, I wouldn't have known what to say about Siberia. Of course, I might have quoted from my diary, but I have to admit that I made up the diary afterward, having neglected to keep one during the journey.

5

Excerpt from my first travel narrative:

Our ship left the Pacific and entered the Sea of Japan, which separates Japan from Eurasia. Since the remains of Siberian mammoths were discovered in Japan, there have been claims that a land bridge once linked Japan and Siberia. Presumably, human beings also crossed from Siberia to Japan. In other words, Japan was once part of Siberia.

In the *Atlas of the World* in the ship's library I looked up

Japan, this child of Siberia that had turned its back on its mother and was now swimming alone in the Pacific. Its body resembled that of a seahorse, which in Japanese is called *Tatsu-no-otoshigo*—the lost child of the dragon.

Next to the library was the dining room, which was always empty during the day. The ship rolled on the stormy seas, and the passengers stayed in bed. I stood alone in the dining room, watching plates on the table slide back and forth without being touched. All at once I realized I had been expecting this stormy day for years, since I was a child.

6

Something I told a woman three years after the journey:

At school we often had to write essays, and sometimes these included "dream descriptions." Once I wrote about the dream in which my father had red skin.

My father comes from a family of merchants in Osaka. After World War II, he came to Tokyo with all he owned: a bundle containing, among other things, an alarm clock. This clock, which he called the "Rooster of the Revolution," soon stopped running, but as a result, it showed the correct time twice each day, an hour that had to be returned to twice a day anyhow. "Time runs on its own, you don't need an alarm clock for that," he always said in defense of his broken clock, "and when the time comes, the city will be so filled with voices of the oppressed that no one will be able to hear a clock ring any longer."

His reasons for leaving the land of his birth he always explained to his relatives in a hostile tone: "Because he was infected with the Red Plague." These words always made me think of red, inflamed skin.

A huge square, crowds of people strolling about. Some of them had white hair, others green or gold, but all of them had red skin. When I looked closer, I saw that their skin was not inflamed but rather inscribed with red script. I was unable to read the text. No, it wasn't a text at all but consisted of many calendars written on top of each other. I saw numberless stars in the sky. At the tip of the tower, the Fire Bird sat observing the motion in the square.

This must have been "Moscow," I wrote in my essay, which my teacher praised without realizing I had invented the dream. But then what dream is not invented?

Later I learned that for a number of leftists in Western Europe this city had a different name: Peking.

7

Diary excerpt:

The ship arrived in the harbor of the small Eastern Siberian town Nachodka. The earth seemed to sway beneath my feet. No sooner had I felt the sensation of having put a border, the sea, behind me than I glimpsed the beginning of the train tracks that stretched for ten thousand kilometers.

That night I boarded the train. I sat down in a four-bed compartment where I was soon joined by two Russians. The woman, Masha, offered me pickled mushrooms and told me she was on her way to visit her mother in Moscow. "Ever since I got married and moved to Nachodka, my mother has been *behind* Siberia," she said. Siberia, then, is the border between here and there, I thought, such a wide border!

I lay down on the bed on my belly and gazed out the window. Above the outlines of thousands of birches I saw numberless stars that seemed about to tumble down. I took out my pocket notebook and wrote:

When I was a baby, I slept in a Mexican hammock. My parents had bought the hammock not because they found it romantic, but because the apartment was so cramped that there was no room for me except in the air. All there was in the apartment was seven thousand books whose stacks lined the three walls all the way to the ceiling. At night they turned into trees thick with foliage. When a large truck drove past the house, my Mexican hammock swung in the forest. But during the minor earthquakes that frequently shook the house, it remained perfectly still, as though there were an invisible thread connecting it to the subterranean water.

8

Diary excerpt:

When the first sun rose over Siberia, I saw an infinitely long row of birches. After breakfast I tried to describe the landscape, but couldn't. The window with its tiny curtains was like the screen in a movie theater. I sat in the front row, and the picture on the screen was too close and too large. The segment of landscape was repeated, constantly changing, and refused me entry. I picked up a collection of Siberian fairy tales and began to read.

In the afternoon I had tea and gazed out the window again. Birches, nothing but birches. Over my second cup of tea I chatted with Masha, not about the Siberian landscape but about Moscow and Tokyo. Then Masha went to another compartment, and I remained alone at the window. I was bored and began to get sleepy. Soon I was enjoying my boredom. The birches vanished before my eyes, leaving only the again-and-again of their passage, as in an imageless dream.

9

Excerpt from my first travel narrative:

Siberia, "the sleeping land" (from the Tartar: *sib* = sleep, *ir* = Earth), but it wasn't asleep. So it really wasn't at all necessary for the prince to come kiss the Earth awake. (He came from a European fairy tale.) Or did he come to find treasure?

When the Creator of the Universe was distributing treasures on Earth and flew over Siberia, he trembled so violently with cold that his hands grew stiff and the precious stones and metals he held in them fell to the ground. To hide these treasures from Man, he covered Siberia with eternal frost.

It was August, and there was no trace of the cold that had stiffened the Creator's hands. The Siberian tribes mentioned in my book were also nowhere to be seen, for the Trans-Siberian Railroad traverses only those regions populated by Russians—

tracing out a path of conquered territory, a narrow extension of Europe.

10

Something I told a woman three years after the journey:

For me, Moscow was always the city where you never arrive. When I was three years old, the Moscow Artists' Theater performed in Tokyo for the first time. My parents spent half a month's salary on tickets for Chekhov's *Three Sisters*.

When Irina, one of the three sisters, spoke the famous words: "To Moscow, to Moscow, to Moscow . . . ," her voice pierced my parents' ears so deeply that these very same words began to leap out of their own mouths as well. The three sisters never got to Moscow, either. The city must have been hidden somewhere backstage. So it wasn't Siberia, but rather the theater stage that lay between my parents and the city of their dreams.

In any case, my parents, who were often unemployed during this period, occasionally quoted these words. When my father, for example, spoke of his unrealistic plan of founding his own publishing house, my mother would say, laughing, "To Moscow, to Moscow, to Moscow. . . ." My father would say the same thing whenever my mother spoke of her childhood in such a way as though she might be able to become a child again. Naturally, I didn't understand what they meant. I only sensed that the word had something to do with impossibility. Since the word "Moscow" was always repeated three times, I didn't even know it was a city and not a magic word.

11

Diary excerpt:

I flipped through a brochure the conductor had given me. The photographs showed modern hospitals and schools in Siberia. The train stopped at the big station at Ulan-Ude. For the first time, there were many faces in the train that were not Russian.

I laid the brochure aside and picked up my book.

A fairy tale told among the Tungus:

Once upon a time there was a shaman who awakened all the dead and wouldn't let even a single person die. This made him stronger than God. So God suggested a contest: by magic words alone, the shaman was to transform two pieces of chicken meat given him by God into live chickens. If the shaman failed, he wouldn't be stronger than God any longer. The first piece of meat was transformed into a chicken by the magic words and flew away, but not the second one. Ever since, human beings have died. Mostly in hospitals.

Why was the shaman unable to change the second piece of meat into a chicken? Was the second piece somehow different from the first, or did the number two rob the shaman of his power? For some reason, the number two always makes me uneasy.

I also made the acquaintance of a shaman, but not in Siberia; it was much later, in a museum of anthropology in Europe. He stood in a glass case, and his voice came from a tape recorder that was already rather old. For this reason his voice always quavered prodigiously and was louder than a voice from a human body. The microphone is an imitation of the flame that enhances the voice's magical powers.

Usually, the shamans were able to move freely between the three zones of the world. That is, they could visit both the heavens and the world of the dead just by climbing up and down the World-Tree. My shaman, though, stood not in one of these three zones, but in a fourth one: the museum. The number four deprived him permanently of his power: his face was frozen in an expression of fear, his mouth, half-open, was dry, and in his painted eyes burned no fire.

12

Excerpt from my first travel narrative:

In the restaurant car I ate a fish called *omul'*. Lake Baikal is also home to several other species that actually belong in a salt-water habitat, said a Russian teacher sitting across from me—the Baikal used to be a sea.

But how could there possibly be a sea here, in the middle of the continent? Or is the Baikal a hole in the continent that goes all the way through? That would mean my childish notion about the globe being a sphere of water was right after all. The water of the Baikal, then, would be the surface of the water-sphere. A fish could reach the far side of the sphere by swimming through the water.

And so the *omul'* I had eaten swam around inside my body that night, as though it wanted to find a place where its journey could finally come to an end.

13

There were once two brothers whose mother, a Russian painter, had emigrated to Tokyo during the Revolution and lived there ever since. On her eightieth birthday she expressed the wish to see her native city, Moscow, once more before she died. Her sons arranged for her visa and accompanied her on her journey on the Trans-Siberian Railroad. But when the third sun rose over Siberia, their mother was no longer on the train. The brothers searched for her from first car to last, but they couldn't find her. The conductor told them the story of an old man who, three years earlier, had opened the door of the car, mistaking it for the door to the toilet, and had fallen from the train. The brothers were granted a special visa and traveled the same stretch in the opposite direction on the local train. At each station they got out and asked whether anyone had seen their mother. A month passed without their finding the slightest trace.

I can remember the story up to this point; afterwards I must have fallen asleep. My mother often read me stories that filled the space between waking and sleep so completely that, in comparison, the time when I was awake lost much of its color and force. Many years later I found, quite by chance, the continuation of this story in a library.

The old painter lost her memory when she fell from the train. She could remember neither her origins nor her plans. So she remained living in a small village in Siberia that seemed strangely familiar to her. Only at night, when she heard the train coming, did she feel uneasy, and sometimes she even ran alone through the dark woods to the tracks, as though someone had called to her.

14

As a child, my mother was often ill, just like her own mother, who had spent half her life in bed. My mother grew up in a Buddhist temple in which one could hear, as early as five o'clock in the morning, the prayer that her father, the head priest of the temple, was chanting with his disciples.

One day, as she sat alone under a tree reading a novel, a student who had come to visit the temple approached her and asked whether she always read such thick books. My mother immediately replied that what she'd like best was a novel so long she could never finish it, for she had no other occupation but reading.

The student considered a moment, then told her that in the library in Moscow there was a novel so long that no one could read all of it in a lifetime. This novel was not only long, but also as cryptic and cunning as the forests of Siberia, so that people got lost in it and never found their way out again once they'd entered. Since then, Moscow has been the city of her dreams, its center not Red Square, but the library.

This is the sort of thing my mother told me about her childhood. I was still a little girl and believed in neither the infinitely long novel in Moscow nor the student who might have been my father. For my mother was a good liar and told lies often and with pleasure. But when I saw her sitting and reading in the middle of the forest of books, I was afraid she might disappear into a novel. She never rushed through books. The more exciting the story became, the more slowly she read.

She never actually wanted to arrive at any destination at all, not even "Moscow." She would greatly have preferred for "Siberia" to be infinitely large. With my father things were somewhat different. Although he never got to Moscow, either, he did inherit money and founded his own publishing house, which bore the name of this dream city.

15

Diary excerpt:

There were always a few men standing in the corridor smoking strong-smelling Stolica cigarettes (*stolica* = capital city).

"How much longer is it to Moscow?" I asked an old man who was looking out the window with his grandchild.

"Three more days," he responded and smiled with eyes that lay buried in deep folds.

So in three days I would really have crossed Siberia and would arrive at the point where Europe begins? Suddenly I noticed how afraid I was of arriving in Moscow.

"Are you from Vietnam?" he asked.

"No, I'm from Tokyo."

His grandchild gazed at me and asked him in a low voice: "Where is Tokyo?" The old man stroked the child's head and said softly but clearly: "In the East." The child was silent and for a moment stared into the air as though a city were visible there. A city it would probably never visit.

Hadn't I also asked questions like that when I was a child?— Where is Peking?—In the West.—And what is in the East, on the other side of the sea?—America.

The world sphere I had envisioned was definitely not round, but rather like a night sky, with all the foreign places sparkling like fireworks.

16

During the night I woke up. Rain knocked softly on the windowpane. The train went slower and slower. I looked out the window and tried to recognize something in the darkness. . . . The train stopped, but I couldn't see a station. The outlines of the birches became clearer and clearer, their skins brighter, and suddenly there was a shadow moving between them. A bear? I remembered that many Siberian tribes bury the bones of bears so they can be resurrected. Was this a bear that had just returned to life?

The shadow approached the train. It was not a bear but a person. The thin figure, face half concealed beneath wet hair, came closer and closer with outstretched arms. I saw the beams of three flashlights off to the left. For a brief moment, the face of the figure was illumined: it was an old woman. Her eyes were shut, her mouth open, as though she wanted to cry out. When she felt the light on her, she gave a shudder, then vanished in the dark woods.

This was part of the novel I wrote before the journey and read aloud to my mother. In this novel, I hadn't built a secret pathway leading home for her; in contrast to the novel in Moscow, it wasn't very long.

"No wonder this novel is so short," my mother said. "Whenever a woman like that shows up in a novel, it always ends soon, with her death."

"Why should she die. *She* is Siberia."

"Why is Siberia a *she?* You're just like your father, the two of you only have one thing in your heads: going to Moscow."

"Why don't *you* go to Moscow?"

"Because then you wouldn't get there. But if I stay here, you can reach your destination."

"Then I won't go, I'll stay here."

"It's too late. You're already on your way."

17

Excerpt from the letter to my parents:

Europe begins not in Moscow but somewhere before. I looked out the window and saw a sign as tall as a man with two arrows painted on it, beneath which the words "Europe" and "Asia" were written. The sign stood in the middle of a field like a solitary customs agent.

"We're in Europe already!" I shouted to Masha, who was drinking tea in our compartment.

"Yes, everything's Europe behind the Ural Mountains," she replied, unmoved, as though this had no importance, and went on drinking her tea.

I went over to a Frenchman, the only foreigner in the car besides me, and told him that Europe didn't just begin in Moscow. He gave a short laugh and said that Moscow was not Europe.

Excerpt from my first travel narrative:

The waiter placed my borscht on the table and smiled at Sasha, who was playing with the wooden doll Matroshka next to me. He removed the figure of the round farmwife from its belly. The smaller doll, too, was immediately taken apart, and from its belly came—an expected surprise—an even smaller one. Sasha's father, who had been watching his son all this time with a smile, now looked at me and said: "When you are in Moscow, buy a Matroshka as a souvenir. This is a typically Russian toy."

Many Russians do not know that this "typically Russian" toy was first manufactured in Russia at the end of the nineteenth century, modeled after ancient Japanese dolls. But I don't know what sort of Japanese doll could have been the model for Matroshka. Perhaps a *kokeshi*, which my grandmother once told me the story of. A long time ago, when the people of her village were still suffering from extreme poverty, it sometimes happened that women who gave birth to children, rather than starving together with them, would kill them at birth. For each child that was put to death, a *kokeshi*, meaning make-the-child-go-away, was crafted, so that the people would never forget they had survived at the expense of these children. To what story might people connect Matroshka some day? Perhaps with the story of the souvenir, when people no longer know what souvenirs are.

"I'll buy a Matroshka in Moscow," I said to Sasha's father. Sasha extracted the fifth doll and attempted to take it, too, apart. "No, Sasha, that's the littlest one," his father cried. "Now you must pack them up again."

The game now continued in reverse. The smallest doll vanished inside the next-smallest one, then this one inside the next, and so on.

In a book about shamans, I had once read that our souls can appear in dreams in the form of animals or shadows or even dolls. The Matroshka is probably the soul of the travelers in Russia who, sound asleep in Siberia, dream of the capital.

19

I read a Samoyedic fairy tale:

Once upon a time there was a small village in which seven clans lived in seven tents. During the long, hard winter, when the men were off hunting, the women sat with their children in the tents. Among them was a woman who especially loved her child.

One day she was sitting with her child close beside the fire, warming herself. Suddenly a spark leapt out of the fire and landed on her child's skin. The child began to cry. The woman scolded the fire: "I give you wood to eat and you make my child cry! How dare you? I'm going to pour water on you!" She poured water on the fire, and so the fire went out.

It grew cold and dark in the tent, and the child began to cry again. The woman went to the next tent to fetch new fire, but the moment she stepped into the tent, this fire, too, went out. She went on to the next one, but here the same thing happened. All seven fires went out, and the village was dark and cold.

"Do you realize we're almost in Moscow?" Masha asked me. I nodded and went on reading.

When the grandmother of this child heard what had happened, she came to the tent of the woman, squatted down before the fire and gazed deep into it. Inside, on the hearth, sat an ancient old woman, the Empress of Fire, with blood on her forehead. "What has happened? What should we do?" the grandmother asked. With a deep, dark voice, the empress said that the water had torn open her forehead and that the woman must sacrifice her child so that people will never forget that fire comes from the heart of the child.

"Look out the window! There's Moscow!" cried Masha. "Do you see her? That's Moscow, *Moskva!*"

"What have you done?" the grandmother scolded the woman. "Because of you, the whole village is without fire! You must sacrifice your child, otherwise we'll all die of cold!" The mother lamented and wept in despair, but there was nothing she could do.

"Why don't you look out the window? We're finally there!" Masha cried. The train was going slower and slower.

When the child was laid on the hearth, the flames shot up from its heart, and the whole village was lit up so brightly it was as if the Fire Bird had descended to Earth. In the flames the villagers saw the Empress of Fire, who took the child in her arms and vanished with it into the depths of the light.

20

The train arrived in Moscow, and a woman from Intourist walked up to me and said that I had to go home again at once, because my visa was no longer valid. The Frenchman whispered in my ear: "Start shouting that you want to stay here." I screamed so loud that the wall of the station cracked in two. Behind the ruins, I saw a city that looked familiar: it was Tokyo. "Scream louder or you'll never see Moscow!" the Frenchman said, but I couldn't scream any more because my throat was burning and my voice was gone. I saw a pond in the middle of the station and discovered that I was unbearably thirsty. When I drank the water from the pond, my gut began to ache and I immediately lay down on the ground. The water I had drunk grew and grew in my belly and soon it had become a huge sphere of water with the names of thousands of cities written on it. Among them I found her. But already the sphere was beginning to turn and the names all flowed together, becoming completely illegible. I lost her. "Where is she?" I asked, "Where is she?" "But she's right here. Don't you see her?" replied a voice from within my belly. "Come into the water with us!" another voice in my belly cried.

I leapt into the water.

Here stood a high tower, brightly shining with a strange light. Atop this tower sat the Fire Bird, which spat out flaming letters: M, O, S, K, V, A, then these letters were transformed: M became a mother and gave birth to me within my belly. O turned into *omul'* and swam off with S: seahorse. K became a knife and severed my umbilical cord. V had long since become a volcano, at whose peak sat a familiar-looking monster.

But what about A? A became a strange fruit I had never before tasted: an apple. Hadn't my grandmother told me of the serpent's warning never to drink foreign water? But fruit isn't the same as water. Why shouldn't I be allowed to eat foreign fruit? So I bit into the apple and swallowed its juicy flesh. Instantly the mother, the *omul'*, the seahorse, the knife and the volcano with its monster vanished before my eyes. Everything was still and cold. It had never been so cold before in Siberia.

I realized I was standing in the middle of Europe.

JAVIER MARÍAS

WHEN I WAS MORTAL

Translated from the Spanish by MARGARET JULL COSTA

I often used to pretend I believed in ghosts, and I did so blithely, but now that I am myself a ghost, I understand why, traditionally, they are depicted as mournful creatures who stubbornly return to the places they knew when they were mortal. For they do return. Very rarely are they or we noticed, the houses we lived in have changed and the people who live in them do not even know of our past existence, they cannot even imagine it: like children, these men and women believe that the world began with their birth, and they never wonder if, on the ground they tread, others once trod with lighter steps or with fateful footfalls, if between the walls that shelter them others heard whispers or laughter, or if someone once read a letter out loud, or strangled the person he most loved. It's absurd that, for the living, space should endure while time is erased, when space is, in fact, the depository of time, albeit a silent one, telling no tales. It's absurd that life should be like that for the living, because what comes afterwards is its polar opposite, and we are entirely unprepared for it. For now time does not pass, elapse or flow, it perpetuates itself simultaneously and in every detail, though to speak of "now" is perhaps a fallacy. That is the second worst thing, the details, because anything that we experienced or that made even the slightest impact on us when we were mortal reappears with the awful concomitant that now everything has weight and meaning: the words spoken lightly, the mechanical gestures, the accumulated afternoons of childhood parade past singly, one after the other, the effort of a whole lifetime—establishing routines that level out both days and nights—turns out to have been pointless, and each day and night is recalled with excessive clarity and singularity and with a degree of reality incongruous with our present state which knows nothing now of touch. Everything is concrete and excessive, and the razor edge of repetition becomes a torment, because the curse consists in remembering *everything*, the minutes of each hour of each day lived through, the minutes and hours and days of tedium and work and joy, of study and grief and humiliation and sleep, as well as those of waiting, which formed the greater part.

But, as I have already said, that is only the second worst thing, there is something far more wounding, which is that now I not only remember what I saw and heard and knew when I was mortal, but I remember it in its entirety, that is, including what I did not see or know or hear, even things that were beyond my grasp, but which affected me or those who were important to me, and which possibly had a hand in shaping me. You discover the full magnitude of what you only intuited while alive, all the more as you become an adult, I can't say older because I never reached old age: that you only know a fragment of what happens to you and that when you believe yourself capable of explaining or recounting what has happened to you up until a particular date, you do not have sufficient information, you do not know what other people's intentions were or the motivations behind impulses, you have no knowledge of what is hidden: the people closest to us seem like actors suddenly stepping out in front of a theater curtain, and we have no idea what they were doing only a second earlier, when they were not there before us. Perhaps they appear disguised as Othello or as Hamlet and yet the previous moment they were smoking an impossible, anachronistic cigarette in the wings and glancing impatiently at the watch which they have now removed in order to seem to be someone else. Likewise, we know nothing about the events at which we were not present and the conversations we did not hear, those that took place behind our back and mentioned us or criticized us or judged us and condemned us. Life is compassionate, all lives are, at least that is the norm, which is why we consider as wicked those people who do not cover up or hide or lie, those who tell everything that they know and hear, as well as what they do and think. We call them cruel. And it is in that cruel state that I find myself now.

I see myself, for example, as a child about to fall asleep in my bed on the countless nights of a childhood that was satisfactory or without surprises, with my bedroom door ajar so that I could see the light until sleep overcame me, being lulled by the voices of my father and my mother and a guest at supper or some late arrival, who was almost always Dr. Arranz, a pleasant man who smiled a lot and spoke in a low voice and who, to my delight, would arrive just before I went to sleep, in time to come into my room to see how I was, the privilege of an almost daily check-up and the calming hand of the doctor slipping beneath your pajama jacket, the warm and unrepeatable hand that touches you in a way that no one else will ever touch you again throughout your entire life, the nervous child feeling that any anomaly or danger will be detected by that hand and therefore stopped, it is the hand that saves; and the stethoscope dangling from his ears and the cold, salutary touch that your chest shrinks from, and sometimes the handle of an inherited silver spoon engraved with initials placed on the tongue, and which, for a moment, seems about to stick in your throat, a feeling that would give way to relief when I remembered, after the first contact, that it was Arranz holding the spoon in his reassuring, steady hand, mistress of metallic objects, nothing could happen while he was listening to your chest or peering at you with his flashlight fixed on his forehead. After his brief visit and his two or three jokes—sometimes my mother would lean in the doorway waiting until he had finished examining me and making me laugh, and she would laugh too—I would feel even more at ease and would begin to fall asleep listening to their chatter in the nearby lounge, or listening to them listening for a while to the radio or playing a game of cards, at a time when time barely passed, it seems impossible because it's not that long ago, although from then until now enough time has elapsed for me to live and die. I hear the laughter of those who were still young, although I couldn't see them as young then, I can now: my father laughed the least, he was a handsome, taciturn man with a look of permanent melancholy in his eyes, perhaps because he had been a republican and had lost the war, and that is probably something you never recover from, having lost a war against your compatriots and neighbors. He was a kindly man who never got angry with me or my mother and who spent a lot of time at home writing articles and book reviews, which he tended to publish under various pseudonyms in the newspapers, because it was best not to use his own name; or perhaps reading, he was a great francophile, I mainly recall novels by Camus and Simenon. Dr. Arranz was a jollier man, with a lazy, teasing way of talking, inventive and full of unusual turns-of-phrase, the kind of man children idolize because he knows how to do card tricks and comes out with unexpected rhymes and talks to them about soccer—then it was Kopa, Rial, Di Stefano, Puskas and Gento—and he thinks up games that will interest them and awaken their imaginations, except that, in fact, he never has time to stay and play them for real. And my mother, always well-dressed despite the fact that there wasn't much money in the home of one of the war's losers—there wasn't—better dressed than my father because she still had her own father, my grandfather, to buy her clothes, she was slight and cheerful and sometimes looked sadly at her husband, and always looked at me enthusiastically, later, as you get older, not many people look at you like that either. I see this now because I see it all complete, I see that, while I was gradually becoming submerged in sleep, the laughter in the living room never came from my father, and that, on the other hand, he was the only one listening to the radio, an impossible image until very recently, but which is now as clear as the old images which, while I was mortal, gradually grew dimmer, more compressed the longer I lived. I see that on some nights, Dr. Arranz and my mother went out, and now I understand all those references to good tickets, which, in my imagination then, I always thought of as being clipped by an usher at the soccer stadium or at the bullring—those places I never went to—and to which I never gave another thought. On other nights, there were no good tickets and no one mentioned them, or there were rainy nights when there was no question of going for a walk or to an open-air dance, and now I know that then my mother and Dr. Arranz would go into the bedroom when they were sure I had gone to sleep after having been touched on my chest and on the stomach by the same hands that would then touch her, hands that were no longer warm, but urgent, the hand of the doctor that calms and probes and persuades and demands; and having been kissed on the cheek or the forehead by the same lips that would subsequently kiss the easy-going, low voice—thus silencing it. And whether they went to the theater or to the movies or to a club or merely went into the next room, my father would listen to the radio alone while he waited, so as not to hear anything, but also, with the passage of time and the onset of routine—with the levelling out of nights that always happens when nights keep repeating themselves—in order to distract himself for half an hour or three quarters of an hour (doctors are always in such a hurry), because he inevitably became interested in what he was listening to. The doctor would leave without saying goodbye to him and my mother would stay in the bedroom, waiting for my father, she would put on a nightdress and change the sheets, he never found her there in her pretty skirts and stockings. I see now the conversation that began that state of affairs, which, for me, was not a cruel one but a kindly one that lasted my whole life, and, during that conversation, Dr. Arranz is sporting the sharp little moustache that I noticed on the faces of lawyers in parliament until the day Franco died, and not only there, but on soldiers and notaries and bankers and lecturers, on writers and on countless doctors, not on him though, he was one of the first to get rid of it. My father and my mother are sitting in the dining room and I still have no consciousness or memory,

I am a child lying in its cradle, I cannot yet walk or speak and there is no reason why I should ever have found out: she keeps her eyes lowered all the time and says nothing, he looks first incredulous and then horrified: horrified and fearful, rather than indignant. And one of the things that Arranz says is this:

"Look León, I pass a lot of information on to the police and it never fails; basically, what I say goes. I've taken a while to get around to you but I know perfectly well what you got up to in the war, how you gave the nod to the militiamen on who to take for a ride. But even if that wasn't so, in your case, I've no need to make anything much up, I just have to stretch the facts a little, to say that you consigned to the ditch half the people in our neighborhood wouldn't be that far from the truth, you'd have done the same to me if you could. More than ten years have passed, but you'd still be hauled up in front of a firing squad if I told then what I know, and I've no reason to keep quiet about it. So it's up to you, you can either have a bit of a rough time on my terms or you can stop having any kind of time at all, neither good nor bad nor average."

"And what are your terms exactly?"

I see Dr. Arranz gesture with his head in the direction of my silent mother—a gesture that makes of her a thing—whom he also knew during the war and from before, in that same neighborhood that lost so many of its residents.

"I want to screw her. Night after night, until I get tired of it."

Arranz got tired as everyone does of everything, given time. He got tired when I was still at an age when that essential word did not even figure in my vocabulary, nor did I even conceive of its meaning. My mother, on the other hand, was at the age when she was beginning to lose her bloom and to laugh only rarely, while my father began to prosper and to dress better, and to sign with his own name—which was not León—the articles and the reviews that he wrote and to lose the look of melancholy in his clouded eyes; and to go out at night with some good tickets while my mother stayed at home playing solitaire or listening to the radio, or, a little later, watching television, resigned.

All those who have speculated on the afterlife or the continuing existence of consciousness beyond death—if that is what we are, consciousness—have not taken into account the danger or rather the horror of remembering everything, even what we did not know: knowing everything, everything that concerns us or that involved us either closely or from afar. I see with absolute clarity faces that I passed once in the street, a man I gave money to without even glancing at him, a woman I watched in the subway and whom I haven't thought of since, the features of a postman who delivered some unimportant telegram, the figure of a child I saw on a beach, when I too was a child. I relive the long minutes I spent waiting at airports or those spent lining up outside a museum or watching the waves on a distant beach, or packing my bags and later unpacking them, all the most tedious moments, those that are of no account and which we usually refer to as dead time. I see myself in cities I visited a long time ago, just passing through, with a few free hours to stroll around them and then wipe them from my memory: I see myself in Hamburg and in Manchester, in Basle and in Austin, places I would never have gone to if my work hadn't taken me there. I see myself too in Venice, some time ago, on honeymoon with my wife Luisa, with whom I spent those last few years of peace and contentment, I see myself in the most recent part of my life, even though it is now remote. I'm coming back from a trip and she's waiting for me at the airport, not once, all the time we were married, did she fail to come and meet me, even if I'd only been away for a couple of days, despite the awful traffic and despite all the activities we can so easily do without and which are precisely those that we find most pressing. I'd be so tired that I'd only have the strength to change television channels, the programs are the same everywhere now anyway, while she prepared me a light supper and kept me company, looking bored but patient, knowing that after that initial torpor and the imminent night's rest, I would be fully recovered and that the following day, I would be my usual self, an energetic, jokey person who spoke in a rather low voice, in order to underline the irony that all women love, laughter runs in their veins and, if it's a funny joke, they can't help but laugh, even if they detest the person making the joke. And the following afternoon, once I'd recovered, I used to go and see María, my lover, who used to laugh even more because my jokes were still new to her.

I was always so careful not to give myself away, not to wound and to be kind, I only ever met María at her apartment so that no one would see me out with her anywhere and ask questions later on, or be cruel and tell tales, or simply wait to be introduced. Her apartment was nearby and I spent many afternoons there, though not every afternoon, on the way back to my own apartment, that meant a delay of only half an hour or three quarters of an hour, sometimes a little more, sometimes I would amuse myself looking out of her window, the window of a lover is always more interesting than our own will ever be. I never made a mistake, because mistakes in these matters reveal a sort of lack of consideration, or worse, they are acts of real cruelty. I met María once when I was out with Luisa, in a packed movie theater at a première, and my lover took advantage of the crowd to come over to us and to hold my hand for a moment, as she passed by without looking at me, she brushed her familiar thigh against mine and took hold of my hand and stroked it. Luisa could not possibly have seen this or noticed or even suspected the existence of that tenuous, ephemeral, clandestine contact, but even so, I decided not to see María for a couple of weeks, after which time and after my refusing to answer the phone in my office, she called me one afternoon at home, luckily, my wife was out.

"What's wrong?" she said.

"You must never phone me here, you know that."

"I wouldn't phone you there if you'd pick up the phone in your office. I've been waiting a whole fortnight," she said.

And then, making an effort to recover the anger I had felt a fortnight before, I said:

"And I'll never pick up the phone to you again if you ever touch me when Luisa is there. Don't even think of it."

She fell silent.

You forget almost everything in life and remember everything in death, or in this cruel state which is what being a ghost is. But in life I forgot and so I started seeing her again now and then, thanks to that process by which everything becomes indefinitely postponed for a while, and we always believe that there will continue to be a tomorrow in which it will pe possible to stop what today and yesterday passes and elapses and flows, what is imperceptibly becoming another routine which, in its way, also levels out our days and our nights until they become unimaginable without all their essential elements, and the nights and days must be identical, at least in their essence, so that nothing is relinquished or sacrificed by those who want them and those who endure them. Now I remember everything and that's why I remember my death so clearly, or, rather, what I knew of my death when it happened, which was little and, indeed, nothing in comparison with all that I know now, given the constant razor edge of repetition.

I returned from one of my trips exhausted and Luisa didn't fail me, she came to meet me. We didn't talk much in the car, nor while I was mechanically unpacking my suitcase and glancing through the accumulated mail and listening to the messages on the answering machine that she had kept for my return. I was alarmed when I heard one of them, because I immediately recognized María's voice, she said my name once and was then cut off, and that made my feeling of alarm subside for a moment, the voice of a woman saying my name and then breaking off was of no significance, there was no reason why Luisa should have felt worried if she had heard it. I lay down on the bed in front of the television, changing channels, Luisa brought me some cold meat and a shop-bought dessert, she clearly had neither the time nor the inclination to make me even an omelette. It was still early, but she had turned out the light in the bedroom to help me get to sleep, and there I stayed, drowsy and peaceful, with a vague memory of her caresses, the hand that calms even when it touches your chest distractedly and possibly impatiently. Then she left the bedroom and I eventually fell asleep with the television on, at some point I stopped changing channels.

I don't know how much times passed, no, that's not true, since now I know exactly, I enjoyed seventy-three minutes of deep sleep and of dreams that all took place in foreign parts, whence I had once again returned safe and sound. Then I woke up and I saw the bluish light of the television, the light illuminating the foot of the bed, rather than any actual images, because I didn't have time. I see and I saw rushing towards me something black and heavy and doubtless as cold as a stethoscope, but is was violent rather than salutary. It fell once only to be raised again, and in those tenths of a second before it came crashing down a second time, already spattered with blood, I thought that Luisa must be killing me because of that message which had said only my name and then broken off and perhaps there had been many other things that she had erased after listening to them all, leaving only the beginning for me to listen to on my return, a mere foreshadowing of what was killing me. The black thing fell again and this time it killed me, and my last conscious thought was not to put up any resistance, to make no attempt to stop it because it was unstoppable and perhaps too because it didn't seem such a bad death, to die at the hands of the person with whom I had lived in peace and contentment, and without ever hurting each other until, that is, we finally did. It's a tricky word to use, and can easily be misconstrued, but perhaps I came to feel that my death was a just death.

I see this now and I see the whole thing, with an afterwards and a before, although the afterwards does not, strictly speaking, concern me and is therefore not so painful. But the before is, or rather the rebuttal of what I glimpsed and half-thought between the lowering and the raising and the lowering again of the black thing that finished me off. Now I can see Luisa talking to a man I don't know and who has a moustache like the one Dr. Arranz wore in his day, not a slim moustache, though, but soft and thick and with a few gray hairs. He's middle-aged, as I was and as perhaps Luisa was, although she always seemed young to me, just as my parents or Arranz never did. They are in the living room of an unfamiliar apartment, his apartment, a ramshackle place, full of books and paintings and ornaments, a very mannered apartment. The man is called Manolo Reyna and he has enough money never to have to dirty his hands. It is the afternoon and they are sitting on a sofa, taking in whispers, and at that moment I am visiting María, two weeks before my death on the return from a trip, and that trip has still not begun, they are still making their preparations. The whispers are clearly audible, they have a degree of reality which seems incongruous now, not with my current non-tactile state, but with life itself, in which nothing is ever quite so concrete, in which nothing ever breathes quite so much. There is a moment, though, when Luisa raises her voice, like someone raising their voice to defend themselves or to defend someone else, and what she says is this:

"But he's always been so good to me, I've nothing to reproach him with, and that's what's so difficult."

And Manolo Reyna answers slowly:

"It wouldn't be any easier or any more difficult if he had made your life impossible. When it comes to killing someone, it doesn't matter any more what they've done, it always seems an extreme response to any kind of behavior."

I see Luisa put her thumb to her mouth and bite it a little, a gesture I've so often seen her make when she's uncertain, or, rather, before making a decision. It's a trivial gesture and it's unseemly that it should also appear in the midst of a conversation we were not party to, the one that takes place behind our backs and mentions us or criticizes us or even defends us, or judges us and condemns us to death.

"Well, you kill him, then; you can't expect me to do anything that extreme."

Now I see that the person standing next to my television set—still on—and wielding the black thing is not Luisa, nor even Manolo Reyna with his folkloric name, but someone contracted and paid to do it, to strike me twice on the forehead, the word is assassin, in the war a lot of militiamen were used for such purposes. My assassin hits me twice and does so quite dispassionately, and that death no longer seems to me just or appropriate or, of course, compassionate, as life usually is, and as mine was. The black thing is a hammer with a wooden shaft and an iron head, a common-or-garden-variety hammer. It belongs in my apartment, I recognize it.

There where time passes and flows, a lot of time has gone by, so much so that no one whom I knew or met or pitied or loved remains. Each one of them, I suppose, will return unnoticed to that space in which forgotten times past accumulate, and they will see only strangers, new men and women who, like children, believe that the world began with their birth and there's no point asking them about our past, erased existence. Now Luisa will remember and will know everything that she did not know in life or at my death. I cannot speak now of nights and days, everything has been levelled out without resort to effort or routine, a routine in which I can say that I knew, above all, peace and contentment: when I was mortal, all that time ago, in that place where there still is time.

W. G. Sebald

chapter 6 of **THE RINGS OF SATURN**
Translated from the German by Michael Hulse

Not far from the coast, between Southwold and Walberswick, a narrow iron bridge crosses the river Blyth where a long time ago ships heavily laden with wool made their way seaward. Today

there is next to no traffic on the river, which is largely silted up. At best one might see a sailing boat or two moored in the lower reaches amidst an assortment of rotting barges. To landward, there is nothing but grey water, mudflats and emptiness. The bridge over the Blyth was built in 1875 for a narrow-gauge rail-

way that linked Halesworth and Southwold. According to local historians, the train that ran on it had originally been built for the Emperor of China. Precisely which emperor had given this commission I have not succeeded in finding out, despite lengthy research; nor have I been able to discover why the order was never delivered or why this diminutive imperial train, which may have been intended to connect the Palace in Peking, then still surrounded by pinewoods, to one of the summer residences, ended up in service on a branch line of the Great Eastern Railway. The only thing the uncertain sources agree on is that the outlines of the imperial heraldic dragon, complete with a tail and somewhat clouded over by its own breath, could clearly be made out beneath the black paintwork of the carriages, which were used mainly by seaside holidaymakers and travelled at a maximum speed of sixteen miles per hour. As for the heraldic creature itself, the *Libro de los seres imaginarios*, to which reference has already been made, contains a fairly complete taxonomy and description of oriental dragons, of those that inhabit the skies and of those that dwell on the earth and in the seas. Some are said to carry the palaces of the gods on their backs, while others are believed to determine the course of streams and rivers and to guard subterranean treasures. They are armour-plated with yellow scales. Below their muzzles they have beards, their brows beetle over their blazing eyes, their ears are short and fleshy, their mouths invariably hang open, and they feed on pearls and opals. Some are three or four miles long. Mountains crumble when they turn over in their sleep, and when they fly through the air, they cause terrible storms that strip the roofs off houses and devastate the crops. When they rise from the depths of the sea, maelstroms and typhoons ensue. In China, the placating of the elements has always been intimately connected with the ceremonial rites which surrounded the ruler on the dragon throne and which governed everything from affairs of state down to daily ablutions, rituals that also served to legitimize and immortalize the immense profane power that was focused in the person of the emperor. At any moment of the day or night, the members of the imperial household, which numbered more than six thousand and consisted exclusively of eunuchs and women, would be circling, on precisely defined orbits, the sole male inhabitant of the Forbidden City that lay concealed behind purple-coloured walls. In the latter half of the nineteenth century, the ritualization of imperial power was at its most elaborate: at the same time, that power itself was by now almost completely hollowed out. While all court appointments, rigidly controlled as they were by an immutable hierarchy, continued to be made according to rules that had been perfected down to the last detail, the empire in its entirety was on the brink of collapse, owing to mounting pressure from enemies both within and without. In the 1850s and 1860s, the Taiping rebellion, launched by a messianic Christian-Confucian movement, spread like wildfire across all of southern China. Reeling with privation and poverty, the people—from starving peasants and soldiers at large after the Opium war to coolies, sailors, actors and prostitutes—flocked in undreamt-of numbers to the self-appointed Celestial King, Hung Hsiu-ch'üan, who in a feverish delirium had beheld a glorious future in which justice prevailed. Soon a steadily growing army of holy warriors was making its way northwards from Kwangsi. It overran the provinces of Hunan, Hupeh and Anhwei, and in early 1853 was at the gates of the mighty city of Nanking, which was overwhelmed after a two-day siege and was declared the celestial capital of the movement. Fired by the prospect of a golden age, the rebellion now flooded wave upon wave across the whole vast country. More than six thousand citadels were taken by the rebels and occupied for a while; five provinces were razed to the ground in battle after battle; and more than twenty million died in just fifteen years. The bloody horror in China at that time went beyond all imagining. In the summer of 1864, after a seven-year siege by imperial forces, Nanking fell. The defenders had long since exhausted their supplies, and had abandoned all hope of attaining in this life the paradise which had seemed within reach when the movement began. Broken by hunger and drugs, they were on their last legs. On the 30th of June the Celestial King took his own life. Hundreds of thousands followed his example, either out of loyalty to him or for fear of the conquerors' revenge. They committed self-slaughter in every conceivable way, with swords and with knives, by fire, by hanging, or by leaping from the rooftops and towers. Many are even said to have buried themselves alive. The mass suicide of the Taipingis is without historical parallel. When their enemies broke through the gates on the morning of the 19th of July, they found not a soul alive. But the city was filled with the humming of flies. The King of the Celestial Realm of Eternal Peace, according to a dispatch sent to Peking, lay face-down in a gutter, his bloated body held together only by the silken robes of imperial yellow, adorned with the image of the dragon, which, with blasphemous presumption, he had always worn.

Suppressing the Taiping rebellion would almost certainly have proved impossible had not the British army contingents in

China taken the imperial side after the resolution of their own conflict with the Emperor. The armed presence of the British dated back to 1840, to the beginning of the so-called Opium war. In 1837 the Chinese government had taken measures to prevent opium trading, whereupon the East India Company, which grew opium poppies in the fields of Bengal and shipped the drug mainly to Canton, Amoy and Shanghai, felt that one of its most lucrative ventures was in jeopardy. The subsequent declaration of war began the opening-up, by force of arms, of the Chinese Empire, which for two hundred years had remained closed to foreign barbarians. In the name of Christian evangelism and free trade, which was held to be the precondition of all civilized progress, the superiority of western artillery was demonstrated, a number of cities were stormed, and a peace was extorted, the conditions of which included guarantees for British trading posts on the coast, the cession of Hong Kong, and, not least, reparation payments of truly astronomical proportions. In so far as this arrangement, which from the outset the British regarded as purely interim, made no provision for access to trading centers within China itself, the need for further military campaigns could not be ruled out in the longer term, especially in view of the existence of four hundred million Chinese to whom the cotton fabrics produced in the Lancashire mills might have been sold. It was not, however, until 1856 that an adequate pretext for a new punitive expedition presented itself, when Chinese officials in the port of Canton boarded a freighter to arrest some members of the all-Chinese crew who were suspected of piracy. In the course of this operation, the boarding party hauled down the Union Jack, which was flying from the main mast, probably because at that time the British flag was not infrequently flown as a cover for illegal trafficking. But since the boarded ship was registered in Hong Kong and was flying the Union Jack rightfully, the incident, laughable in itself, provided the representatives of British interests in Canton with the occasion for a confrontation with the Chinese authorities which was presently and deliberately pushed so far that there was felt to be no alternative but to occupy the port and bombard the official residence of the prefect. At very nearly the same time, as luck would have it, the French press was running reports of the execution, on the orders of officials in Kwangsi province, of a missionary named Chapdelaine. The description of this painful procedure culminated in the claim that the executioner had cut the heart from the breast of the dead abbé, and cooked and eaten it. The cries for retaliation and punishment which promptly filled France chimed perfectly with the endeavours of the warmongers in Westminster, so that, once the necessary preparations had been made, there was witnessed the spectacle of a joint Anglo-French campaign, a rare phenomenon in the age of imperial rivalry. This enterprise, which was dogged by the greatest of logistical difficulties, entered its crucial phase in August 1860 with the landing of eighteen thousand British and French troops in the Bay of Pechili, barely a hundred and fifty miles from Peking. Supported by a Chinese auxiliary force recruited in Canton, they captured the forts of Taku that stood surrounded by deep ditches, immense earthworks and bamboo palisades amidst saltwater marshes at the mouth of the Peiho River. After the fortress garrison had unconditionally surrendered and attempts were being made to put an orderly end, by negotiation, to a campaign that had already been concluded from a military point of view, the allied delegates, despite the fact that they had the upper hand, became ever more lost in a nightmarish maze of diplomatic prevarication dictated partly by the complex requirements of protocol in the dragon empire and partly by the fear and bewilderment of the Emperor. In the end, the negotiations foundered on the mutual incomprehension of emissaries from two fundamentally different worlds, a gap which no interpreter could bridge. While the British andFrench side viewed the peace they would impose as the first stage in the colonization of a moribund realm untouched by the intellectual and material achievements of civilization, the Emperor's delegates, for their part, endeavored to make clear to thesestrangers, who appeared to be unfamiliar with Chinese ways, the immemorial obligations toward the Son of Heaven of envoys from satellite powers bound to pay homage and tribute. In the end, there was nothing for it but to sail up the Peiho in gunboats and advance on Peking overland. Emperor Hsien-feng, who was debilitated despite his youthful years and suffered from dropsy, shirked the impending confrontation, departing on the 22nd of September for his retreat at Jehol beyond the Great Wall amidst a disorderly array of court eunuchs, mules, baggage carts, litters, and palanquins. Word was conveyed to the commanders of the enemy forces that his majesty the Emperor was obliged by law to go hunting in autumn. In early October the allied troops, themselves now uncertain how to proceed, happened apparently by chance on the magic garden of Yuan Ming Yuan near Peking, with its countless palaces, pavilions, covered walks, fantastic arbours, temples and towers. On the slopes of man-made mountains, between banks and spinneys, deer with fabulous antlers grazed, and the whole incomprehensible glory of Nature and of the wonders placed in it by the hand of man was reflected in dark, unruffled waters. The destruction that was wrought in these legendary landscaped gardens over the next few days, which made a mockery of military discipline or indeed of all reason, can only be understood as resulting from anger at the continued delay in achieving a resolution. Yet the true reason why Yuan Ming Yuan was laid waste may well have been that this early paradise—which immediately annihilated any notion of the Chinese as an inferior and uncivilized race—was an irresistible provocation in the eyes of soldiers who, a world away from their homeland, knew nothing but the rule of force, privation, and the abnegation of their own desires. Although the accounts of what happened in those October days are not very reliable, the sheer fact that booty was later auctioned off in the British camp suggests that much of the removable ornaments and the jewelry left behind by the fleeing court, everything made of jade or gold, silver or silk, fell into the hands of the looters. When the summerhouses, hunting lodges, and sacred places in the extensive gardens and neighbouring palace precincts, more than two hundred in number, were then burnt to the ground, it was on the orders of the commanding officers, ostensibly in reprisal for the mistreatment of the British emissaries

Loch and Parkes, but in reality so that the devastation already wrought should no longer be apparent. The temples, palaces, and hermitages, mostly built of cedarwood, went up in flames one after another with unbelievable speed, according to Charles George Gordon, a thirty-year-old captain in the Royal Engineers, the fire spreading through the green shrubs and woods, crackling and leaping. Apart from a few stone bridges and marble pagodas, all was destroyed. For a long time, swaths of smoke drifted over the entire area, and a great cloud of ash that obscured the sun was borne to Peking by the west wind, where after a time it settled on the heads and homes of those who, it was surmised, had been visited by the power of divine retribution. At the end of the month, with the example of Yuan Ming Yuan before them, the Emperor's officers felt obliged to sign without further ado the oft-defferred Treaty of Tientsin. The principal clauses, apart from fresh reparation demands that could scarcely be met, related to the rights of free movement and unhindered missionary activity in the interior of China and to negotiation of a customs tariff with a view to legalizing the opium trade. In return, the Western powers declared themselves willing to uphold the dynasty, which meant putting down the Taiping rebellion and crushing the secessionary movements of the Moslem population of the Shensi, Yunnan and Kansu valley regions, in the course of which between six and ten million people were made homeless or killed. Charles George Gordon, by nature shy and Christian-spirited, though also an irascible and profoundly melancholy man, who was later to die a famous death in the siege of Khartoum, took over the command of the demoralized imperial army and within a short period transformed them into so powerful a fighting force that when he left the country he was invested with the Chinese Empire's highest decoration in recognition of his services, the yellow jacket.

In August 1861, after months of irresolution, Emperor Hsien-feng lay in his Jehol exile approaching the end of his short and dissipated life. The waters had already risen from his abdomen to his heart, and the cells of his gradually dissolving flesh floated like fish in the sea in the salt fluid that leaked from his bloodstream into every available space in the body tissue. Through his flickering consciousness, Hsien-feng followed the invasion by foreign powers of the provinces of his empire by perfect proxy, as his own limbs died off and his organs flooded with toxins. He himself was now the battlefield on which the downfall of China was being accomplished, till on the 22nd of the month the shades of night settled upon him and he sank away wholly into the delirium of death. Because of the precisely ordained procedures to which the Emperor's body had to be subjected before being placed in its coffin, procedures which were linked to complex astrological calculations, transfer of his corpse to Peking could not be arranged before the 5th of October. It then took three weeks for the cortège, more than a mile long, to make the journey, in evenly falling autumn rain, up hill and down dale, through black valleys and gorges and across bleak mountain passes blurred to sight by icy-grey blizzards. The catafalque, which time and again threatened to topple over, was borne on a huge golden bier on the shoulders of a hundred and twenty-four hand-picked pallbearers. On the morning of the 1st of November, when the cortège reached its destination, the road leading to the gates of the Forbidden City had been strewn with yellow sand and screens of blue Nanking silk were positioned on either side to prevent the common people from looking upon the countenance of the five-year-old child Emperor T'ung-chih, whom Hsien-feng had named as his successor to the dragon throne in the last days of his life and who was now being taken homeward on a padded palanquin behind the mortal remains of his father, together with his mother Tz'u-hsi, who had risen from the ranks of concubines and even now had assumed the illustrious title of Dowager Empress. Following the return to court in Peking, the struggle for the powers of regency during the interregnum which inevitably ensued since the heir to the dragon throne was not yet of age, was soon resolved in favour of the widow, whose craving for power was insatiable. The princes who had acted as Hsien-feng's viceroys during his absence were accused of conspiracy against the legitimate ruler, a crime for which there was no defence, and they were condemned to be dismembered and cut into slices. When this sentence was commuted and the traitors were granted permission, offered to them in the form of a silken rope, to hang themselves, it was seen as a token of merciful clemency in the new regime. Once Princes Cheng, Su-shun and Yi had availed themselves of this prerogative, seemingly without any hesitation, the Dowager Empress was the uncontested locum of the Chinese Empire, at least until the time when her son became old enough to rule himself and began taking measures that ran counter to the plans she had nurtured to extend and perfect her power, plans of which many had already been but into practice. Given this turn of events, it was tantamount to providential, from Tz'u-hsi's point of view, that, a scant year after coming to the throne, T'ung-chih was so weakened—by smallpox or by some other disease he had picked up, as rumor had it, from the dancers and transvestites of Peking's streets of sin—that when the planet Venus crossed before the sun in the autumn of 1874, a grim omen, there were fears for his life at the age of barely nineteen. And indeed T'ung-chih did die, a few weeks later, on the 12th of January 1875. His face was turned to the south and for the journey into the beyond he was enrobed in the vestments of eternal life. The funeral obsequies had scarcely been completed in the prescribed form when the wife of the departed Emperor, seventeen years old and several months pregnant according to various sources, poisoned herself with a massive dose of opium. The official version, that her mysterious death was due to the unassuageable grief that had overwhelmed her, could not entirely dispel the suspicion that the young Empress had been got out of the way in order to prolong the regency of the Dowager Empress Tz'u-hsi, who now consolidated her position by having her two-year-old nephew Kuang-hsu proclaimed heir to the throne, a manoeuvre which flew in the face of tradition since Kuang-hsu was of the same generation as T'ung-chih in the lineage of descent, and thus, under an incontrovertible Confucian rule, unentitled to proffer the services of reverence and mourning which were owed the dead man that his spirit might be appeased. The way the Dowager Empress, in other respects extremely conservative in her views, contrived to flout the most venerable precepts when it became necessary, was one sign of her craving for absolute power, which grew more ruthless with every year that passed. And like all absolute rulers, she was concerned to display her exalted position to the world at large and to herself by a lavishness beyond comparison. Her private household alone, managed by senior eunuch Li Lien-ying,

standing to her right in this picture, went through a truly appalling annual sum of six million pounds sterling. The more ostentatious the demonstrations of her authority became, however, the more the fear of losing the infinite power she had so insidiously acquired grew within her. Unable to sleep, she roamed the bizarre shadow landscapes of the palace gardens, amidst the artificial crags, the groves of ferns, and the dark arborvitaes and cypresses. In the early morning she swallowed a pearl ground to powder, as an elixir of invulnerability. She took the greatest of pleasure in lifeless things, and by day would sometimes stand for hours at the windows of her apartments, staring out upon the silent lake to the north, which resembled a painting. The tiny figures of the gardeners in the distant lily fields, or those of the courtiers who skated on the blue ice in winter, did not recall to her the natural occupations and feelings of human kind, but were rather, like flies in a jamjar, already in the wanton power of death. Travellers who were in China between 1876 and 1879 report that, in the drought that had continued for years, whole provinces gave the impression of expiring under prisons of glass. Between seven and twenty million people—no precise estimates have ever been calculated—are said to have died of starvation and exhaustion, principally in Shansi, Shensi and Shantung. A Baptist preacher named Timothy Richard, for example, noted that one effect of the catastrophe, which grew more apparent week by week, was that all movement was slowing down. Singly, in groups and in straggling lines, people tottered across the country, and the merest breath of air might suffice to topple them and leave them lying by the wayside forever. Simply raising a hand, closing an eyelid, or exhaling one's last breath might take, it sometimes seemed, half a century. And as time dissolved, so too did all other relations. Parents exchanged children because they could not bear to watch the dying torment of their own. Towns and villages were surrounded by deserts of dust, over which trembling mirages of river valleys and forested lakes often appeared. Sometimes at first light, when the rustling of leaves dry on the branch penetrated their shallow sleep, people imagined, for a fraction of a second in which wishful thinking was stronger than what they knew to be the case, that it had started to rain. Though the capital and its environs were spared the worst consequences of the drought, when the ill tidings arrived from the south, the Dowager Empress had a daily blood sacrifice offered in her temple to the gods of silk, at the hour when the evening star rose, lest the silkworms want for fresh green leaves. Of all living creatures, these curious insects alone aroused a strong affection in her.

The silk houses they were raised in were among the finest buildings of the summer palace. Every day that came, Tz'u-hsi walked the airy halls with the ladies of her retinue, clad in white pinafores, to inspect the progress of the work, and when night fell she particularly liked to sit all alone amidst the frames, listening to the low, even, deeply soothing sound of the countless silkworms consuming the new mulberry foliage. These pale, almost transparent creatures, which would presently give their lives for the fine thread they were spinning, she saw as her true loyal followers. To her they seemed the ideal subjects, diligent in service, ready to die, capable of multiplying vastly within a short span of time, and fixed on their one sole preordained aim, wholly unlike human beings, on whom there was basically no relying, neither on the nameless masses in the empire nor on those who constituted the inmost circle about her and who, she suspected, might go over at any time to the side of the second child Emperor she had installed. Kuang-hsu, who was fascinated by the mysteries of modern machines, spent most of his time taking apart the mechanical toys and clocks sold by a Danish tradesman in his Peking shop, and it was still possible to distract his awakening ambition by promising him a real railway train which he would be able to ride across his own country but the day was not long remote when his would be the power which she, the Dowager Empress, was ever less able to relinquish the longer she possessed it. As I imagine it, the little court train with the image of the Chinese dragon that later served the line from Halesworth to Southwold was originally ordered for Kuang-hsu, and the order was subsequently cancelled in the mid-1890s when the young Emperor began to espouse, in opposition to Tz'u-hsi, the causes of the reform movement under whose influence he had fallen, causes that ran counter to her own purposes. What we do have on authority is that Kuang-hsu's attempts to wrest power to himself ultimately led to his being imprisoned in one of the moated palaces in the Forbidden City, where he was forced to abdicate and make over the power of government, without reservation, to the Dowager Empress. For ten years Kuang-hsu languished in exile on his paradisical island until in the late summer of 1908, the various ailments that increasingly troubled him since the day of his deposition—chronic headaches and backache, renal cramps, hypersensitivity to light and noise, weak lungs, and severe depression—finally overcame him. One Dr Chu, who was familiar with western medicine and was the last to be consulted, diagnosed Bright's disease but also noted a number on inconsistent symptoms—palpitations of the heart, an empurpled complexion, a yellow tongue—that suggests, as has since been speculated, that Kuang-hsu was being gradually poisoned. Visiting the patient in his imperial apartments, Dr Chu noticed moreover that the floors and all the furnishings were thick with dust, as if the house had been long since deserted, an indication that no one had attended to the Emperor's needs for years. On the 14th of November 1908 at dusk, or, as they say, at the hour of the cockerel, Kuang-hsu, racked with pain, departed this life. At the time of his death he was thirty-seven years old. Strangely enough, the seventy-three-year-old Dowager Empress, who had destroyed his body and his spirit with such persistent intent, outlived him by less than a day. On the morning of the 15th of November, still in reasonably good health, she presided over the grand council's deliberations upon the new situation, but after her midday meal, which in defiance of her personal doctors' warnings she had concluded with a double helping of her favourite pudding—crab apples with clotted cream—she was stricken with an attack resembling dysentery, from which she did not recover. She died at about three o'clock. Already draped in her shroud, she dictated her farewell to the Empire which now after the near half century of her regency was in the throes of dissolution. Looking back, she said, she realized that history consists of nothing but misfortune and the troubles that afflict us, so that in all our days on earth we never know one single moment that is genuinely free of fear.

The denial of time, so the tract on Orbius Tertius tells us, is one of the key tenets of the philosophical schools of Tlön. According to this principle, the future exists only in the shape of our present apprehensions and hopes, and the past merely as memory. In a different view, the world and everything now living in it was created only moments ago, together with its complete but illusory pre-history. A third school of thought variously describes our earth as a cul-de-sac in the great city of God, a dark cave crowded with incomprehensible images, or a hazy aura surrounding a better sun. The advocates of a fourth philosophy maintain that time has run its course and that this life is no more than the fading reflection of an event beyond recall. We simply do not know how many of its possible mutations the world may already have gone through, or how much time, always assuming that it exists, remains. All that is certain is that night lasts far longer than day, if one compares an individual life, life as a whole, or time itself with the system which, in each case, is above it. The night of time, wrote Thomas Browne in his treatise of 1658, *The Garden of Cyrus*, far surpasseth the day and who knows when was the Aequinox?—Thoughts of this kind were in my head too as I walked on along the disused railway line a little way beyond the bridge across the Blyth, and then dropped from the higher ground to the level of the marsh that extends southward from Walberswick as far as Dunwich, which now consists of a few houses only. The region is so empty and deserted that, if one were abandoned there, one could scarcely say whether one was on the North Sea coast or perhaps by the Caspian Sea or the Gulf of Lian-tung. With the rippling reeds to my right and the grey beach to my left, I pressed on toward Dunwich, which seemed so far in the distance as to be quite beyond my reach. It was as if I had been walking for hours before the tiled roofs of houses and the crest of a wooded hill gradually became defined. The Dunwich of the present day is what remains of a town that was one of the most important ports in Europe in the Middle Ages. There were more than fifty churches, monasteries and convents, and hospitals here; there were shipyards and fortifications and fisheries and merchant fleet of eighty vessels; and there were dozens of windmills. All of it has gone under, quite literally, and is now below the sea, beneath alluvial sand and gravel, over an area of two or three square miles. The parish churches of St James, St Leonard, St Martin, St Bartholomew, St Michael, St Patrick, St Mary, St John, St Peter,

St Nicholas and St Felix, one after the other, toppled down the steadily receding cliff-face and sank in the depths, along with the earth and stone of which the town had been built. All that survived, strange to say, were the walled well shafts, which for centuries, freed of that which had once enclosed them, rose aloft like the chimney stacks of some subterranean smithy, as various chroniclers report, until in due course these symbols of the vanished town also fell down. Until about 1890 what was known as Eccles Church Tower still stood on Dunwich Beach, and no one had any idea how it had arrived at sea level, from the considerable height at which it must once have stood, without tipping out of the perpendicular. The riddle has not been solved to this day, though a recent experiment using a model suggests that the enigmatic Eccles Tower was probably built on sand and sank down under its own weight, so gradually that the masonry remained virtually intact. Around 1900, after Eccles Tower had also collapsed, the only Dunwich church that remained was the ruin of All Saints. In 1919 it, too, slipped over the cliff edge, together with the bones of those buried in the churchyard, and only the square west tower still rose for a time above those eerie parts. Dunwich reached the high point of its evolution in the thirteenth century. Every day, in those times, the ships came and went, to London, Stavoren, Stralsund, Danzig, Bruges, Bayonne and Bordeaux. A quarter of the great fleet that sailed from

Portsmouth in May 1230, bearing hundreds of knights and their horses, several thousand foot soldiers, and the entire royal entourage, came from Dunwich. Shipbuilding, and the trade in timber, grain, salt, herring, wool and hides, were so profitable that the town was soon in a position to build every conceivable

kind of defence against attack from the landward side and against the force of the sea, which was ceaselessly eroding the coast. One cannot say how great was the sense of security which the people of Dunwich derived from the building of these fortifications. All we know for certain is that they ultimately proved inadequate. On New Year's Eve 1285, a storm tide devastated the lower town and the portside so terribly that for months afterwards no one could tell where the land ended and the sea began. There were fallen walls, debris, ruins, broken timbers, shattered ships' hulls, and sodden masses of loam, pebbles, sand and water everywhere. And then on the 14th of January 1328, after only a few decades of rebuilding, and following an autumn and Christmas period that had been unusually tranquil, an even more fearful disaster occurred, if such were possible. Once again, a hurricane-force north-easterly storm coincided with the highest tide of the month. As darkness fell, those living around the harbour fled with whatever belongings they could carry to the upper town. All night the waves clawed away one row of houses after another. Like mighty battering rams the roofing and supporting beams adrift in the water smashed against the walls that had not yet been levelled. When dawn came, the throng of survivors—numbering some two or three thousand, among them gentry such as the FritzRicharts, the FitzMaurices, the Valeins and the de la Falaises as well as the common people— stood on the edge of the abyss, leaning into the wind, gazing in horror through the clouds of salt spray into the depths where bales and barrels, shattered cranes, torn sails of windmills, chests and tables, crates, feather beds, firewood, straw and drowned livestock were revolving in a whirlpool of whitish-brown waters. Over the centuries that followed, catastrophic incursions of the sea into the land of this kind happened time and again, and, even during long years of apparent calm, coastal erosion continued to take its natural course. Little by little the people of Dunwich accepted the inevitability of the process. They abandoned their hopeless struggle, turned their backs on the sea, and, whenever their declining means allowed it, built to the westward in a protracted flight that went on for generations; the slowly dying town thus followed—by reflex, one might say—one of the fundamental patterns of human behaviour. A strikingly large number of our settlements are oriented to the west and, where circumstances permit, relocate in a westward direction. The east stands for lost causes. Especially at the time when the continent of America was being colonized, it was noticeable that the townships spread to the west even as their eastern districts were falling apart. In Brazil, to this day, whole provinces die down like fires when the land is exhausted by overcropping and new areas to the west are opened up. In North America, too, countless settlements of various kinds, complete with gas stations, motels and shopping malls, move west along the turnpikes, and along that axis affluence and squalor are unfailingly polarized. I was put in mind of this phenomenon by the flight of Dunwich. After the first serious disaster, building began on the westernmost fringe of the town, but even of the Grey Friars monastery that dates from that time only a few fragments now remain. Dunwich, with its towers and many thousand souls, has dissolved into water, sand and thin air. If you look out from the cliff-top across the sea towards where the town must once have been, you can sense the immense power of emptiness. Perhaps it was for this reason that Dunwich became a place of pilgrimage for melancholy poets in the Victorian age. Algernon Charles Swinburne, for instance, went there on several occasions in the 1870s with his companion Theodore Watts-Dunton, whenever the excitement of London literary life threatened to overtax his nerves, which had been hypersensitive since his early childhood. He had achieved legendary fame as a young man, and many a time he had been sent into such impassioned paroxysms by the dazzling conversations on art in the Pre-Raphaelite salons, or by the mental strain of composing his own verse and tragedies, overflowing with wonderful poetic bombast, that he could no longer control his own voice and limbs. After these quasi-epileptic fits he often lay prostrate for weeks, and soon, unfitted for general society, he could bear only the company of those who were close to him. Initially he spent the periods of convalescence at the family country estate, but later, ever more frequently, he went to the coast with the trusty Watts-Dunton. Rambles from Southwold to Dunwich, through the windblown fields of sedge, worked like a sedative upon him. A long poem entitled *By the North Sea* was his tribute to the gradual dissolution of life. Like ashes the low cliffs crumble and the banks drop down into dust. I remember reading in a study of Swinburne that, one summer evening, when he was visiting the churchyard of All Saints with Watts-Dunton, he thought he saw a greenish glow far out on the surface of the sea. The glow, he is reported as saying, reminded him of the palace of Kublai Khan, which was built on the site later occupied by Peking at the very time when Dunwich was one of the most important communities in the kingdom of England. If I remember rightly, that same study told how Swinburne described every last detail of the fabled palace to Watts-Dunton that evening: the snow-white wall more than four miles in length, the arsenals crammed with bridles, saddles and armour of every sort, the storehouses and treasuries, the stables where row upon row of the finest horses stood, the banqueting halls that could accommodate more than six thousand, the private apartments, the zoo with its unicorn enclosure, and the hill, three hundred feet high, that the Khan had caused to be raised on the north side, in order to command an unrestricted view. Within the space of a year, Swinburne reputedly said, this new landmark, the slopes of which were strewn with green lapis lazuli, was planted with the rarest and most majestic of mature evergreen trees, which had been dug up complete with roots and earth from where they originally grew and transported, often over considerable distances, by specially trained teams of elephants. Never before, Swinburne is said to have claimed that evening in Dunwich, nor ever since, had anything more beautiful been created on earth than that artificial hill, which was green even in midwinter and crowned by a palace of peace, in a similar hue of green. Algernon Charles Swinburne, whose life was coterminous to the year with that of the Dowager Empress Tz'u-hsi, was born on the 5th of April 1837, the eldest of the six children of Admiral Charles Henry Swinburne and his wife, Lady Jane Henrietta, daughter of the third Earl of Ashburnham. Both families traced their ancestry to that remote time when Kublai Khan was building his palace and Dunwich was trading with every nation that could then be reached by sea. As long as anyone could remember, the Swinburnes and the Ashburnhams had been members of the royal entourage, prominent commanders and warriors, lords of vast estates, and explorers. Curious to relate, one General Robert Swinburne, great uncle to Algernon Swinburne, became a subject of His Apostolic Majesty and was invested a Baron of the Holy Roman Empire, presumably on the strength of his pronounced ultramontane leanings. When he died he was governor of Milan, and his son, until his death in 1907 at the age of eighty-seven, held the office of chamberlain to Kaiser Franz Josef. This extreme manifestation of political Catholicism in one branch of the family may conceivably have been a first sign of decadence. That aside, however, the question remains of how a family so adept at life should have produced a scion forever on the verge of a nervous breakdown, a paradox which long puzzled Swinburne's biographers as they eagerly teased at his family descent and hereditary make-up, till at length they agreed to describe the poet of *Atalanta in Calydon* as an epigenetic phenomenon sprung from the void, as it were, from beyond all natural possibility. It is certain that Swinburne, by reason of his physical appearance alone, must have seemed a complete aberration. He was small of sta-

ture, and at every point in his development he had remained far behind a normal size; he was quite startlingly fine-limbed; yet even as a boy he had an extraordinarily large, indeed outsize, head on his shoulders, which sloped weakly away from his neck. That truly unusual head, which was made the more striking by his bushy, fiery-red shock of hair and his piercing, watery-green eyes, made Swinburne, as one of his contemporaries noted, an object of amazement at Eton. On the day that he started school—it was the summer of 1849, and Swinburne had just turned twelve—his was the largest hat in all Eton. A certain Lindo Myers, together with whom Swinburne later crossed the Channel from Le Havre in the autumn of 1868, on which occasion a gust of wind blew the hat off Swinburne's head and swept it overboard, writes that after they docked in Southampton it was not until the third purveyor of hats that they found headgear to fit Swinburne, and even then, Myers adds, the leather band and the lining had to be removed. Despite his extremely ill-proportioned physique, Swinburne dreamt from early youth, and particularly after reading newspaper accounts of the charge at Balaclava, of joining a cavalry regiment and losing his life as a *beau sabreur* in some equally senseless battle. Even when he was a student at Oxford, this vision outshone any other conception he might have of his own future; and only when all hope of dying a hero's death was gone, thanks to his underdeveloped body, did he devote himself unreservedly to literature and thus, perhaps, to a no less radical form of self-destruction. Possibly Swinburne would not have survived the nervous crisis which became more serious as time went on, had he not increasingly submitted to the regime of his lifetime companion, Watts-Dunton. Watts-Dunton was soon attending to the entire correspondence, dealing with all the little matters that were continuously putting Swinburne into the utmost panic, and thus made it possible for the poet to eke out almost three more decades of pallid afterlife. In 1879, more dead than alive following a nervous attack, Swinburne was taken in a four-wheeler to Putney Hill in south-west London, and there, at number 2, The Pines, a modest suburban town house, the two bachelors lived henceforth,

carefully avoiding the least excitement. Their days invariably followed a routine devised by Watts-Dunton. Swinburne, Watts-Dunton reportedly said with a certain pride in the tried and tested correctness of his system, always walks in the morning, writes in the afternoon and reads in the evening. And, what is more, at meal times he eats like a caterpillar and at night he sleeps like a dormouse. Now and then a guest who wished to see the prodigious poet in his suburban exile was invited to lunch. The three would then sit at the table in the gloomy dining room, Watts-Dunton, who was hard of hearing, making conversation in booming tones while Swinburne, like a well-brought-up child, kept his head bowed over his plate, devouring an enormous helping of beef in silence. One of the visitors to Putney at the turn of the century wrote that the two old gentlemen put him in mind of strange insects in a Leiden jar. Time and again, looking at Swinburne, this visitor continued, he was reminded of the ashy grey silkworm, *Bombyx mori*, be it because of how he munched his way through his food bit by bit or be it because, out of the snooze he had slipped into after lunch, he abruptly awoke to new life, convulsed with electric energy, and, flapping his hands flitted about his library, like a startled moth, clambering up and down the stands and ladders to fetch the one or other treasure from the shelves. The enthusiasm which seized him as he was thus engaged found expression in rhapsodic declamations about his favourite poets Marlowe, Landor and Hugo, but also in not infrequent reminiscences of his childhood on the Isle of Wight and in Northumberland. In one such moment, in utter rapture, he apparently recalled sitting at his old Aunt Ashburnham's feet as a boy, listening to her account of the first grand ball she went to as a girl, accompanied by her mother. After the ball they drove many miles homeward on a crisp, cold, snow-bright winter night, when suddenly the carriage stopped by a group of dark figures who, it transpired, were burying a suicide at a crossroads. In writing down this memory that goes back a century and a half into the past, noted the visitor, himself long since deceased, he beheld perfectly clearly the dreadful Hogarthian nocturne as Swinburne painted it, and the little boy too, with his big head and fiery hair standing on end, wringing his hands and beseeching: Tell me more, Aunt Ashburnham, please tell me more.

CAN XUE

SNAKE ISLAND

Translated from the Chinese by KAREN GERNANT AND CHEN ZEPING

You could say that Uncle San is the only relative I have left. Whenever I think of my small, remote, depressing home village, a shiver runs down my spine. Called "Snake Island," it's situated on hilly land. When I was a child, I always wanted to learn the derivation of its name, because we didn't have any more snakes there than any other place. An older youth had told me there used to be snakes here. Sometimes several of them hung from a tree. Uncle San's family lived at the end of the village. As if their house had ostracized itself, it was located next to paddy fields, about a hundred paces from other people's homes. Back then, Uncle San was always carrying radishes to sell in a distant town. He generally set out in the morning, and didn't return until almost midnight. The poverty there was appalling. It was said that because of the poor quality of the land, the harvests were always poor. For the most part, beginning in the winter, all of the villagers ate only red potato gruel; they did that right up until the new rice was ready to harvest.

I hadn't gone home for more than thirty years. Even Father's death couldn't call me back. My mother had died earlier, and I was the only child. It was Uncle San who buried Father. At the time, he sent me a scrawled letter: the gist of it was that the funeral had been taken care of and I didn't have to go back.

One line in the letter was engraved on my heart: "The sooner you forget this hopeless village, the better off you'll be." Even though Uncle San was a farmer, he'd been rather well educated. People called him "The Scholar." For years, I'd wondered: I'd been gone for more than thirty years. Why hadn't any of my fellow villagers (including my old father) come to see me even once? It was a long way away—that was one reason—but it certainly wasn't so far away that one couldn't make the trip. It was just a little more than a day's journey by train. It appeared that they were all like me—all part of the blood lineage of Snake Island.

The letters my father wrote me always emphasized that the villagers now lived well: no one was starving; the young people were leaving and going all over the world. He never suggested that I come back for a look; instead, he told me that one room in our house had been destroyed by mountain floods. Now our house had only one room left, so if I went back, there'd be no place for me. I'd just be able to stay with Uncle San. It was as if he was offering me an excuse for not going home, and yet that wasn't all of what he was implying. Perhaps he and Uncle San were standing their ground about something? What could it be? After Father died, no one wrote me letters about what was going on in the village. My contact was completely broken. I knew that Uncle San was still living; twenty years younger than my father, he was in good health.

Destiny always likes to play tricks on people. Just as I had almost forgotten my home village, one day (I still remember it was my birthday), my boss called me into his office.

"Recently, you haven't been very enthusiastic about your work," he said, motioning to a hard chair—indicating that I should take a seat.

"I'm sorry. I wish you'd tell me if I did something wrong."

"Actually, it's no big deal. It's just that I heard someone say that you haven't gone home for thirty years. As soon as I heard that, I felt ashamed of myself. I haven't shown enough concern for my employees. No wonder you've begun to lose enthusiasm for your work. So now I've made a big decision (it wasn't easy to make this decision, because this is a busy time for the company): I'm giving you two weeks off, so that you can go home and see your father."

"My father passed away a long time ago."

"Really? You didn't even tell me such an important thing. I say you—ah, you're really too tolerant and quiet. I can imagine how much you suffered at that time. If that's true, there's even more reason that you should go home for a visit. Go back and take care of your poor father's grave to comfort the old man. You'll go tomorrow."

Even though I didn't much want to go, one had better do as one's superior orders. And so I—this uninvited guest—went home.

But my hometown looked completely wrong. The strange thing was that no matter how I combed through my memory, no matter how I stared at the scenery, I couldn't call back that old village. As soon as I got off the bus, I thought I'd recognize the mountain road that went through our village—that twisting cobblestone road that I'd taken countless times from childhood to young adulthood. But—where was the road? Even the mountain had disappeared. In the open country stretching to the horizon was a walled community of bungalows in garish colors. There weren't even many trees near the houses. Wondering if I'd come to the wrong place, I went to ask a farmer's wife.

"Snake Island?" She squinted, responding in the village dialect that I hadn't heard in ages: "This is it."

"Where?"

"All around. Who are you looking for?"

"My third uncle."

"Oh, you're from Xu Liang's family. Aren't you already dead?"

"Me? Dead?!"

"Your grave is at one end of the village. It never crossed my mind that you would come back."

She drew closer, and pinched my back with two of her fingers, as if to make sure there was really a person underneath the clothes. She was still exclaiming, "I never dreamed. I never dreamed." Suddenly letting go of me, she dashed away. Her figure flashed through the paddy field, but she didn't rush toward those bungalows: she disappeared behind them.

Taking the only road, I went into the village. The first home was an ugly two-room grass hut. I was doubtful that anyone actually lived there, so I just walked past. I stopped at the door of the third home, where I saw two little girls, roughly seven or eight years old, plaiting straw sandals. I supposed they were about the same age as my grandchildren. They both ignored me. All I could do was brazenly ask, "Is anyone home? I'm looking for someone." Finally, the one who was a little thinner looked up, but said, "Go away."

My only option was to go on and knock on the door of the fourth home, but this door wasn't actually locked. As soon as I knocked, the wind blew the door open. I took in the furnishings at a glance. An old man was asleep on the bed in the inner room. In the gloomy interior, his long snow-white hair was striking. I was surprised at how elegant this gaffer was—actually wearing his hair long.

"Grandpa, I'm looking for Xu Sanbao."

The old man twisted around on his bed, indicating that I should approach him.

I realized he was ill. His chest was heaving. The sound of his coughing was muffled, and he was in tears.

"Looking for Sanbao?" He said huskily, "Good. In the end, someone has come looking for him. He hasn't waited all these years for nothing. Good."

"I'm from Xu Liang's family. I've just come home."

"Xu Liang's family. Good. Before long, I'm going to go over to the other side—where you guys are. You—you're looking for Sanbao? That's really difficult."

I thought this old man was already gaga. To continue here would just be a waste of time, so I left him and went on looking. I walked past several homes. I saw a middle-aged man in one of them. He was sun-drying mung beans on the ground. I didn't recognize him at all.

"Could you please tell me where Sanbao's home is?"

"You're from Xu Liang's family? Ha! It's really so!"

"Did someone tell you I'd come?"

"Naturally, naturally. Welcome. The news of your return has circulated all through the village." With some exaggeration, he sketched a big circle with his hand.

But he didn't invite me into his home. He just stood outside talking with me. I saw a woman shake her head inside: it was the same woman I had just run into in the field. I asked again where Sanbao lived. The middle-aged man looked embarrassed. He hemmed and hawed, and finally told me, "Sanbao doesn't have a home anymore. Ever since that tragedy, lots of people have been homeless. Now everyone has grown used to it. You're the only one who doesn't know. In fact, this happened years ago." As he said this, his wrinkled face showed the changes he had seen.

"So where is he?" I asked.

"You have to change your mental concept of the village. To give you a simple example, when you came to the village today, did you run into dogs? No. Do you see any dogs anywhere? Hey. You ask where he is. This question is asked only by people unfamiliar with our circumstances. Aside from the village, where else can he go?"

"Then, where is he now?" I asked patiently.

"You'll run into him!!" he said indignantly. Abandoning me, he went inside.

I asked at several homes. If those people weren't extremely impatient, then they gave irrelevant answers. I was exhausted from carrying my suitcase. Just then, I recalled that my grave was at the end of the village. Gritting my teeth, I walked once more toward the other end of the village where I put my suitcase down under an emaciated camphor tree and then sat on a rock to rest. I gazed ahead: linked together with the paddy fields were a lot of grave mounds, but not one of them had a tombstone. How would I know which one was mine? Probably I wouldn't even be able to locate my father's grave. In spite of that thought, I still dragged myself over there. The graves were almost all alike. It seemed there was no way to distinguish them. Some of them were actually open, with the person's dry bones flung around next to them. Lingering too long here, I felt the gloomy air rising and so I left in a hurry. By this time, I'd concluded: *That farm woman completely fabricated the story that my grave was at the end of the village. So, is this really Snake Island? If it isn't really Snake Island, then how could those two people just now have known who I am? I can't leave this unfinished. I have to wait in the village—wait right until Uncle San shows up.* I opened my bag, took out bottled water and sausages, and started eating my lunch. My thoughts were all mixed up.

Once more, I carefully took stock of the village. I recalled what the middle-aged man had said about a disaster. Truly, there wasn't one little thing about my surroundings that reminded me of my hometown. I had evidently come to a different village, yet the people in this village somehow all knew me. Had there really been a disaster here? If so, was the history of Snake Island buried in these unkempt graves?

I intended to go back to the village and make inquiries at one home after another. I had to get everything straight. On this trip home, I also had to spruce up my parents' graves. If I couldn't fulfill even this responsibility, what would I be able to tell my boss? And so, after getting a second wind, I approached a home whose outer wall was golden yellow. I put my suitcase down at the door and craned my neck to look inside. Suddenly someone clapped me on the shoulder from behind.

"Haha! It's really you! What a strange world! Interesting, interesting. I'm one who doesn't believe in evil. What's the common saying? Right: 'Continue undeterred by the dangers ahead.' Now you've finally come to the right person!"

This was an old man with a gray goatee. He was another person I definitely didn't recognize. Yet I wasn't prepared to ask him probing questions. The old man sat down on a stone stool in the courtyard, and motioned to me to sit beside him. After a while, a young woman came out—probably his daughter or daughter-in-law. The woman asked the old man if the guest would be eating with them. Glaring at her, the old man answered fiercely, "Do you have to ask? We'll have a good meal. Tonight, we still have something to do."

The woman didn't argue and went back inside.

I began examining this face across from me. I looked and looked, and still couldn't call up any memory of him. The man saw me staring at him, and began laughing, revealing his yellow teeth. I didn't know what he was laughing about. Then, my neck began itching strangely. I slapped it hard, and killed two mosquitoes. In the ditch in front of the house were swarms of mosquitoes. I couldn't sit still. I took a towel out of my bag and wound it around my neck. I put my hands in my pockets. Even so, the noxious mosquitoes attacked them through the cloth of my pockets. I looked at the old man again. He was sitting there without moving. He wasn't aware of these mosquitoes at all. That woman came out again just then and gave the old man a pipe. The old man started smoking. I was bitten two more times on the face. I really couldn't stand this. All I could do was stand up impolitely and walk around. At the same time, I also warned myself: under no circumstances should I ask improper questions, in order to avoid angering the old man. But I didn't ask anything and he didn't say anything. It was awkward. After he finished smoking, he finally opened his mouth. "I'm telling you, only at night can you meet up with him."

"Is it Uncle San you're talking of?"

"Who else?"

"Can you take me?"

"Sure thing. I'll take you there, but then you'll be on your own. I cannot go in. I've tried all kinds of times, and each time, I've been driven out. Once, a guy was hewing in my direction with a two-pronged hoe. He hit a tree trunk. Now, that tree still bears a scar the size of the rim of a bowl. It's that camphor tree that you saw over there."

"Who are those people?"

"I think they are people like you. They have marks on their faces. When I saw you just now, I thought of that incident right away. How many people now still remember to go back to their hometowns? Only people like you."

His words made my hair stand on end. I was vaguely aware that the place he wanted to take me to was that stretch of unkempt graves. Did Uncle San live in the midst of the unkempt graves? Why did everyone here consider me a dead man? As I was still mulling this over, he clapped me on the shoulder and invited me in for dinner. He looked quite affable, and I relaxed a little.

Their son came for dinner, too. With a nod at me, he gloomily sat down next to me. The women came in and out carrying bowls. Besides the daughter-in-law (not, after all, a daughter), there were two middle-aged women whose positions in the family I couldn't figure out. They seemed to be relatives. The food was bubbling and abundant; it filled the large platters. There was also wine. It was hard to imagine that in such a barren place one could eat such a sumptuous spread. Head down, the son was concentrating on eating. The two middle-aged women seemed on edge. They kept staring at me, not eating much. The old guy was shouting at me to drink some wine—this was a homemade wine that tasted rather bitter. After two cups of it, I was quite dizzy, but the old guy didn't let me off: as he kept plying me with wine, he served me some delicious wild duck. All styles of dishes were heaped up on my plate. I kept murmuring, "This is too much. It's really too much. . ." After another cup of wine, I thought the sky was spinning around, and then I was dazed. It seemed that the old guy's voice was coming from far away as he recited a line from a poem: "When the hero leaves, he doesn't look back."

When I woke up, I discovered that I was still hunched over the table strewn with cups and dishes, but the others had all disappeared. I looked outside: it was already dark. I thought I'd better spend the night in the village. I stood up and walked around the interior. I looked inside each room, and didn't see even one person. Just then, I noticed that my suitcase had been brought in and set on a chair. Crickets were singing incessantly in the kitchen. I thought, I shouldn't question this family's intentions and hospitality, even though they are a little odd. It seemed that I should stay in their home tonight. After making this decision, I walked out to the courtyard. In the moonlight, there was nothing but paddy fields as far as the eye could see. All the villagers were sound asleep. In the courtyard, someone was sitting on that rock that I'd sat on during the day. I walked over, and saw that it was that old man.

"You'd better go on your own. I can't help you. Just now, the wine gave me enough enthusiasm to go over there once. But I was thrown out again. I hurt both legs when I fell. Aiya! Aiya!"

He bent over and began groaning with pain.

I didn't know what to do: I didn't know if he had broken his legs. I asked where his son and daughter-in-law had gone. Did he want me to go and tell them to come back? The old guy gestured dismissively, and said, "Absolutely not." He moaned again for a while, then seemed a little calmer.

"My son is young and aggressive. He's still over there fighting with them. All of those guys are wielding hoes. We didn't take anything with us, though. We went empty-handed. Your Uncle San's weapon is a large sickle. Just seeing that sickle was enough to make me run for my life. How would I—a handful of old bones—be able to resist him? Listen, my son has come back. It really upsets me that this guy is so useless."

I heard hurried footsteps outside circling around to the back of the house.

"He's embarrassed to come in the front door. He's ashamed of himself."

"Did you say Uncle San was wielding a large sickle?"

"Yes! He's over there—where you went in the daytime. I don't think he would hurt you. Why not go and try your luck now?"

When I reached the graveyard, all was quiet. I couldn't find the camphor tree that was my landmark. I thought, *If I just stay here and don't move, Uncle San will probably find me.* I looked up: in the moonlight, the undulating grave mounds were like a herd of cattle. As I thought of the old man's description of the fighting that had just occurred, I was afraid to walk on any farther.

I sat at the edge of the graveyard for a long time. Nothing happened. Had that old man perhaps just been talking rubbish? I thought and thought, but it didn't seem so. I forced myself to go on waiting. It was probably almost midnight. I sat awhile on the rock, and then stood up and walked. In my eyes, the village became completely unreal. Those tile roofs pitched at random heights and those mottled outer walls had seemed awfully vulgar in the daylight; now, by starlight, they revealed their incomparable timelessness. I suddenly felt that perhaps the person I was meant to find wasn't Uncle San (it was likely that he'd been dead for a long time), but this strange old man and his son that one couldn't get close to. And even the old man's daughter-in-law and the two middle-aged women, and the crazy old guy that I'd encountered at the fourth home. And the farmwoman, the first one I'd seen, and her husband whom I'd run into later. Even the two little girls I'd bumped into at the third home. Were they from a different world? Or was it perhaps I myself who was difficult to understand? In the eyes of so many people, wasn't I already dead? How should people interact with a ghost? Did they tacitly believe that the only way to deal with a ghost like me was to reject me? Somewhere, far away from here, a dog began barking. It seemed that lots of dogs were barking in unison. That sound was familiar: it was the barking I remembered from childhood. So, I'd come to the wrong place. This wasn't my hometown: this village was a trap set next to my hometown. First, I had to suffer through the night, and then look for that village of mine. After coming to this decision, I walked toward the old man's home.

When I got back there, I noticed that the door was already closed. Probably everyone inside was already sound asleep. I went over and rapped on the bedroom window. I rapped twice. But there wasn't any movement inside. "They closed the door on me," I said sorrowfully to myself. I sat down on the stone stool in the courtyard. My head against the trunk of the dead tree next to me, I felt distressed. "How does it happen that even trees can't grow here?" I asked myself drowsily. Although my eyes were closed, I could still see those big stars in the sky. I could also hear the crazed barking of dogs in the distance. I couldn't get to sleep in this odd position. I felt terribly uncomfortable. Probably it was well after midnight when the door clanged wide open. I saw the father and son run out. After they left, the door still stood open. I took advantage of the opportunity to slip inside the house, and fell onto the wooden sofa in the hall and went to sleep. The wooden sofa was short. I curled up, hoping for a good sleep before the two of them came back. I was awfully tired. In a fog I noticed that the whole room was brilliantly lit. I also noticed that the women were already in full swing in the kitchen, sharpening knives and boiling water. I struggled several times to wake up without succeeding. But finally the women noticed me. The three of them stood next to the sofa, watching me wordlessly. I sat up, but they didn't say anything. They were still watching me as they wept sorrowfully.

"Haven't they come back yet?" I asked.

"Why are you here?" The three of them said in a tone of prolonged weeping.

I supposed that for some reason they were greatly disappointed in me, and that because of this, they were being hateful toward me. Probably I shouldn't have stayed in their home. Probably just now they'd been hoping I'd gone to fight in the graveyard with the old man and his son. Now, if I hurried, I should still get there in time. Really, how could I have forgotten my responsibility in coming here? If I didn't find Uncle San and my boss asked about him, I wouldn't have an answer. In the eyes of my superior, I'd be done for. As I stood up and walked to the door, the three women let out sighs of relief. They commented quietly, "He still has a sense of responsibility, after all."

It wasn't actually very dark outside; it was probably almost dawn. I looked back at the little house: the inside really *was* illuminated by lamplight. I didn't know what the women were so busy with. When I reached the graveyard, the old man and his son were lying on the ground moaning. When the old man saw me leaning over him, he waved and said, "Over there. Go over there. You're one of them. I can't ward those guys off, and neither can my son."

"There isn't anything over there. Leave them alone. Why ask for trouble?"

At this, the old man stopped moaning and sneered, "We aren't convinced. Who can be sure that they can win every time?

Open your eyes and look carefully. Isn't your uncle over there? Look: he's slipped over next to the vegetable plot. Hey: old fellow, your nephew is here! Ha! This trick is really effective: he's getting out of the way."

While the old man was talking, his son got up and walked home without a word. Just then, the old man suggested that he go with me into the graveyard, so he could show me my grave. I cheerfully agreed. Supporting him with my hand, I walked toward those undulating grave mounds. The old man said feverishly, "Since we're together, those devils are all getting out of the way." As he walked, he asked me if saw my uncle, and I said I didn't. Disappointed, he rebuked me for not looking hard enough. The old man told me to stop in front of a grave mound that had been excavated, so I faced that large, pitch-dark hole.

"Is this my grave?"

"Yup. Everyone knows this. The one next to it is your uncle's. Your father's is behind them. Look, everyone is still together in death. This is wonderful."

He sat down on the muddy ground and started smoking. It was as though all his injuries had healed. I wanted to tell him that I certainly hadn't died. I was a living person, not a ghost. But I couldn't open my mouth: what use would it be to explain? He believed only his own experience. Now he and I were walking among the graves, and nothing was happening; but before he and his son had been knocked to the ground so they couldn't move. What could be more convincing than that? But then, why were the ghosts afraid of me?

"I live and work in the city. I certainly didn't know that I had a grave in my hometown." I was trying to engage him in conversation.

"That's because you didn't come back and look around. As soon as you came back, everything was clear." He said calmly, "But your uncle is a tenacious old guy. Each time, he has to knock me down. . . . Did you notice the difference between our village and the outside world?"

"What difference?"

"It's like this: stand up and look around. Do you see? The

quick and the dead each occupy one half. That old camphor tree is the boundary. We each have our own territory. For several decades, we've always had to struggle fiercely against each other. During the day, you also saw that not even trees could grow in this village. The harvests aren't good, either. The dead struggle for the territory with the living. Just now, we were fighting fiercely. As soon as you got here, they all turned meek. They aren't used to your scent yet. If you stay here long enough, they'll get used to it. It's really difficult. This time, you didn't come back until we had sent you numerous telegrams."

"You sent me telegrams?"

"Didn't you know that? Your boss received all of them. He's my younger son."

He began laughing hollowly. The village was floating before my eyes. Concealed in these farmhouses were so many secrets. They converged in an ocean of nothingness, and sailed toward me like boats, as if to crush me. Probably nothing could ever really be forgotten. Nothing. I thought of my bespectacled boss: he did resemble the old man's gloomy older son. I was a son of this "Snake Island," and my hometown, after all, hadn't forgotten me. I'd lived all along in its primordial memories. Who was this old man before my eyes? In such a large village, he was the only one who had welcomed me, but I hadn't even asked his name. I sat next to my grave thinking of these things. In this strange night without end, I lost my grip on myself. But who the hell knew what tomorrow would bring? Thinking these thoughts, I didn't have any more misgivings. The night wind carried the sound of the old man's son shouting through his tears, "Papa . . ." His voice was hoarse and indignant. I couldn't see the old man's expression, but I knew he was indifferent.

"Add it up. How many years have you been away from home?"

"Thirty-one years. I never thought I'd come back. It's really quiet in this graveyard!"

"They've all gone into hiding, probably because they aren't used to you. Just now, it was as lively as a marketplace. I come here every night to while away the time. It's commonplace for me to scrap with them. Anyhow, the old don't sleep much. No fooling: beginning this year, I haven't slept yet. Look, your uncle is coming again. He looks humiliated. Generally, they blow hot and cold when they see strangers, but you're certainly not an outsider. You're one of them. This is a little strange. Hey, where are you going? Don't run around aimlessly!"

I was running in circles among the grave mounds. I wanted to shake off the old man, and go and see Uncle San. I thought to myself, it was the old man blocking my field of vision that kept me from seeing Uncle San. I ran without stopping, but in fact there wasn't anything going on in this graveyard. A thin mist was in the air. Probably some of the graves were newly excavated, for I could smell the mud. At this moment, the graveyard didn't give me an eerie feeling at all. Rather, it made me feel at home. What's more, no matter where I looked, I couldn't see any ghosts. The old man stood there all alone. It seemed he was listening attentively to some sound. I ran a large circle and returned to his side. All at once, I figured something out: I said to him brusquely, "You're my uncle, aren't you?"

"Doesn't make much difference to you now, does it?"

I thought about it, and then answered, "No, it doesn't."

The night was endless. As I smelled the fresh earth, a profound weariness spread from my bones all through my body. When we were young, we had thrown ourselves into fleeing from this place. We'd run far away—into the midst of strangers. Simultaneously, here at this place—my hometown as tenuous and wispy as smoke—a process that couldn't be reversed was taking place. My hometown had experienced such misfortune that long ago it had changed beyond recognition. Even more likely, none of its former appearance had ever existed, and what did exist were merely illusions transmuted by the River Lethe. In the grip of illusions, naturally I couldn't recognize Uncle San. To be blunt about it, who could recognize those people and events that he had downright forgotten? As I was mulling this over, I saw from Uncle San's profile that he was going into a trance: he was beginning to wobble.

That night, in Uncle San's small, narrow bedroom, while enduring the mosquitoes' attacks, he and I began a rambling talk.

Outside, it was dark. Uncle San's son was snarling angrily in the courtyard. I don't remember exactly what we talked about. It was that kind of heart-to-heart exchange, yet most of what we said was rather incoherent. Even though we confided in each other for a long time, Uncle San's former appearance wasn't restored at all. Slowly, the stubborn feeling I had of wanting to match my recollections with the present grew hazy. This old man before me had become a mottled portrait, a call from the ancient past difficult to discern . . .

JOHN KEENE

from ANNOTATIONS

NOTES, INSCRIBED INITIALLY IN THE NARROW, RUNNING MARGIN

Such as it began in the Jewish Hospital of St. Louis, on Fathers' Day, you not some babbling prophet but another Negro child, whose parents' random choices of signs would disorient you for years. It was a summer of Malcolms and Seans, as Blacks were transforming the small nation of Watts into a graveyard of smoldering metal. A crueler darkening, as against the assured arrival of dusk. Selma-to-Montgomery. Old folks liked to say he favored the uncle who died young, an artist. In that way, a sense of tradition was upheld, one's place in the reference-chain secured. Digression. Brick houses uniform as Monopoly props lined the lacework of street for miles. Before there was Arlington, there was Palm, indeed a dimmer entity which burns in one's memory like iodine. "Baltimore Law." They eventually settled on a single-family detached, in the Walnut Park section of the city, after months of wrangling with the agent, as it was quite naturally assumed that they, like others who worked for a living, would eventually own their own property. The red cement porch, which Daddy painted at least one time, beneath the gray-green-ish, slate-shingled eaves. The draperies had not yet begun to rot, nor had the ottoman relinquished a leg to leaning. Some of them were working at the post office then, though many were unionized auto-plant or factory workers. Cleverness in conformity often goes unnoticed. The block opened out onto the immense Calvary Cemetery that we had heard to be the haunt of vampire mummies, who would lie in wait beneath the headstones for children who failed to say their prayers. In the mirror, an admirer. You dreamed of romping there when older with the tougher boys, smoking cigarettes, copping feels, jumping out from behind trees, playing like an agent from "Dragnet." Crossing the street was considerably more forbidding. Four, in hand. A home in which to watch the seasons pass, to grow old within a chosen "community." Now names of most neighbors have shifted past his consciousness like afternoon shadows across the living room floor. Everyone, except the neighbors, marveled at the size of the basement. Then no one used heroin because they lacked for "family values," even though they spoke so blithely of our "ghetto." Pruitt-Igoe. Words, wildly uttered, acts unmitigated, emergence of their search for validation. Many backyards wore a chain-link garter that stretched out to the alleyway, and so whenever the rudipoots shattered their wine or soda bottles into smithereens of glass, it always fell to us to sweep them up. Now-or-Laters. Snoopy, the second in a cavalcade of pets, would parade regally about the screened-in back porch. Daddy soaked then bathed him in a pan of gasoline to strip his coat of mange, so that when we spoke of him at all, it was as "under quarantine." Children often see with a clarity that adults ignore. Around the corner, down the hill, three blocks or so, until the fields of St. Catherine Labouré unreeled before us, as in the scenes in that movie usually broadcast during the "sweeps" preceding Christmas, the projector that lit up the cinema of our childhood dreams. Desire is, among other things, a function of repetition, or so the very patterns of your life have led you to believe. No better place existed to fly kites or box-crates, except Penrose Park, where, one supposed, the nuns never chanced to set habit.

You assembled the frame and tail according to the package's confusing directions, which required more than the recommended ten minutes. Junie aided him in getting his aloft, before it tangled and then plummeted with the others. The genius lies in the execution. The Ville, whose village. Shivering, you stood on the sunlight's skirt, yet they laughed as they looked right through you. Shrieks of all sizes and colors would distort the evening air, rendering it opaque and virtually unreadable. Who would not beg to stay out past curfew, when the excitement usually began. "Catch the ball, boy, catch the ball!" as it rearranged the contours of our face. "Tag" became the game of choice, though we occasionally improvised with "Batman" or with "Johnny Quest." Against form. Before the final closing of eyes and the "good night's sleep," the irrepressible march of twilight.

A Chain of Incidents, Antecedents, the Very Events Themselves

Memory, that vast orchard of myriad, variegated moments, appears to undergo an endless replanting. In the summer the heat would troll across the city like an immense seine, gathering every living and inanimate thing in its folds. This entails no notion of the "subject." Being of Southern blood, nearly all of them could bear it, though not without some cavils and some grudging. Chatillon-DeMenil. Ardor, or another, made the man next door shoot his wife, though at the beginning there was little violence and still the white flight had begun. Contingency spells the death of certitude. Of course everyone had relatives in Arkansas and Mississippi who were on their way, since Negroes just two years before had finally won jobs at the Jefferson Bank. The impact of this pebble of history is barely felt nowadays, particularly by the generation that has benefited most. From West Florissant one could quickly reach the highway heading south to the riverfront, where the Arch and the riverboats reveled. Mill Creek Valley. Few of the homes had central air, a fact made obvious by a simple street review, as almost every other window distended with those plastic, wheezing boxes. This note: Baden sat less than a half-hour's walk away. Somnambulant majority. Like his mother he was said to possess a "viper's tongue," a trait leaving all but the older teachers wary. Her family had washed north in several tides, the main ebbing occurring shortly after the First World War. Whether they came by train or by carriage bears important historical implications. *Aos pés da cruz.* By his time several of the city's schools had been integrated, but the decisive court order lay decades away, and then how often would his parents repeat to him that Sumner High School, founded in 1875, was the "first comprehensive Black high school this side of the Mississippi." St. Louis was spared the riots of that era, despite the anger burgeoning in the projects. Many of the protesters lived within a few miles of where the slaves had been manumitted, a fact particularly evident in Wellston. Well, you needn't. Please print on the dotted line. This, as does each of these flares of intellection, takes note of the structural aspects of signification. Uncle Clarence and Aunt Emma stood guard before an armory of toys, a few of which were older than the century. Like most of the father's family, they represented a higher social class and the products of vibrant miscegenation. Years before, someone, in a spirit one might now term enterprising, had sold the family farm in St. Charles that would have been their birthright. Portage des Sioux. You spoke up, as was usual, but they simply chose to ignore you, interested instead in their game of spades, with its rising, idle chatter. The kitchen of his body in which the fires of history were blazing. In the sword tree there were Osage whom we mistook for Cherokees, which seemed not an uncommon occurrence. Certain actions need no convincing. Veronica, who could tell better stories than one might find in library books, thus assumed the role of play-mommy, teaching you how to sing and fight and whom to call "meshugenah." Out of earshot, one heard talk of depression, accompanied by the occasionally unsubtle comment on her weight. Loneliness is solitude unfulfilled by its own presence. Their eyes fled this text, or perhaps its context, one infers, out of a fear of contamination. Mild and muddy springs, hot and humid summers, brief and balmy autumns, how they sabotaged one's readiness for winter. We were admonished to wear caps to prevent an attack of heatstroke, since our heads, small lots of blacktop, proved extraordinary attractors of sun. Ring-A-Levio. Still, he grew dizzy and dropped to his bed of sedge, which they dismissed as so much unnecessary drama. White reflects, relax. "Speak when you are spoken to and tuck in your lower lip, and save a big kiss for Maman," which each, like well-reared little boys, would have done without the threat of a "whupping." Night, a knowing not. Then you noticed the motorboat moored in the Deans' backyard, and went home and dreamt that some-one might eventually sail her. The thought alone is often worth the promise. Perhaps out near Lake St. Louis, or in Illinois on Lake Carlyle, or more likely on the Missouri or the Lake of the Ozarks, though the important point was that they could at least afford to. Religion then was but one current in the river of our lives. Poinciana. By adolescence, most of these reflections had lost their color, which adulthood later restored from its dull and pallid palette.

LANGUAGE, KNOWLEDGE, A TEEMING RIVER OF IMPLICATIONS

A small yet insubordinate squadron of impressions had laid siege to his consciousness since infancy. Everything reposed beneath a glaze of dew, which was each morning's way of announcing its arrival. The slow greening of the daylight through the shutter slats, or evening, when the gangway grew sullen with darkness. Chances are. Shadows appeared to creep across the floor, until you focused to discover them ants. Photographs will substitute for a fully-sketched description. Waterbugs and spiders were re-ally more common, rapelling down the tiles like mountaineers. In the jar, the aphids asphyxiated. With a view to pleasing the adults, you told no one. Moreover he could claim two godfa-thers, to everyone's amusement, of whom one had served quite honorably in Vietnam. The violent tenor of the recollections, perhaps resulting from a delayed effect, far exceeded what everyone had expected. Your tongue, but a bat in its cavern of reassurance, would take flight when you least expected it. Montgomery, My Lai. Many of the children, except those whose parents were considered "strivers," would walk to the neighborhood school. They first launched his punt at a Montessori Academy, which was thought to enhance a youngster's chances in life. There we could play with Legos of innumerable colors, a pint-sized oven that actually baked, and the other kids, including Patty, who soon became enamored of the red-haired boy. This was before one gained a sense of the "body" and could picture oneself "in affliction." Double talk. Eventually they took turns reading the "Negro" poets from those yellow-papered books whose covers had long ago disappeared. Usually we would sit and talk, or watch the TV set, or on warmer evenings walk several blocks with the dogs or alone for a "breath of fresh night air." Nice work, if you can get it, and you might get it if you lie. At the corner store, nickle candy and a sody pop, but only if you had been sterling. There never was, consequently, any incentive to steal, since this course of action had not been fostered alongside some greater moral lassitude. Pilfer, for a pal. Occasionally we heard shooting, but most often it was shouting, which a battle of fists or blades would readily resolve. Our ears hammer impressions into audible jewels. Further down the boulevard sat the unimposing branch library, further still the artist's studio. His wife, an artist in her own right, had sculpted the papier-mâché painting of Kali, which hung for years like a totem above the sofas. Chain Of Rocks. You drew not only numerous studies of people, but a series of scenes to accompany them, yet they still denied that a child was capable of such work, convinced instead that you had traced or forged. Treemonisha. Just as well, heedlessness or laughter, a sure forgetting. The subsequent art teacher showed a mastery of the art of drawing lips and eyes, and thus encouraged us all to indulge in more identifiably "African" forms. Use a pen or pencil and answer all questions. A simpler example: a V with a circle on top, or a colorless ice-cream cone. Eugene Field House. Few things compared to culling lightning bugs live, since your Mason jar theater became their nightstage. Roaches comprised a different category altogether, like the stains that created a rusty crust upon the motel sheets, or that car that leapt the curb to cut the corner. "Em, eye, crookaletta, crookaletta, eye, crookaletta, crookaletta, eye, humpback, humpback, eye," and thus one could always avoid utter embarrassment in any blackboard bee. The result, a fathoming beneath the flourish of so many notes, a veritable exigesis. Music is the obvious analogue, that inimitable California poet tells us, which, in the context of the life that you have lived so far, is as much truth as trope. Yes and no. Yet, whenever the ice-cream truck would come by, the first impulse was to run to the window and perform the dance of seven wails. Who would not relent, before such shameless displays of talent. These episodes ceased however temporarily, in the presence of "company," and at the family reunions, when all small ones were expected to be on their "absolute best behavior." Eventually the blight of crime and drugs would subsume the entire area, forcing a capitulation to the prerogatives of personal safety. And so, as his cousin said more eloquently than the mayor and the experts, when officials speak of "Urban Renewal," it's the Black folks that got to go.

Arrived at By Rites, By Rituals, A Final Line of Defense

In that house then, on that morning, as many in those families were Catholics, they were observed to interact in rhythms common to their faith and class, leaving abstract yet indelible imprints on the etching-plate of others. There who could ever truly "be a boy," given the demands of such games of truth. Magnificat. The grandparents' church sat on a street named Cote Brilliante, where the shade stood as still as the spire. They had become Presbyterians, a sect commensurate with a certain social standing. This preoccupation with the religious aspect points to a fuzzy, metaphysical nature. Natural Bridge. Several liquor stores sat in walking distance of that narrow, Negro crossroads, having reared and raised the men who owned them. Oh now, go to it, jazzmen. The excommunicated, like the divorced, were denied the most blessed sacrament, yet we refrained from overt comment on them as we had learned our contempt to be un-Christian. The paralyzing force of such inflexibility soon endeared you to certain Protestants, which only the testimony of succeeding years demonstrated the power to dispel. Underlining this were nuns who bore the names of exalted men, who taught their lessons in frowns and furrowed chins. In the end this disquieting descant left each child more unsure than before. His heart is a grotto bearing witness to others' kindnesses. A sudden musicality of phrase, as when one hears the windowpanes humming. Louis the Conqueror, not High John. Although in our sepia book of saints we were usually drawn to the visage of St. Martin de Porres, your city had received its name from the patron saint of France. Pronounced phonetically, after the British fashion. Religion now plays such an ambiguous role in American children's development. "Pass the plate, don't keep us late," which confirmed that he had originally been a Baptist. The priest, whose voice engraved these messages into our callow youth, would homilize before leading the whole congregration in song. Though his claps seldom managed to keep the beat, we thought them to be heartfelt. Nave of doves. A stranger terror lurked within the confessional, which was unlighted and reeked of sweat. Dance of the infidels. Aleikam salaam one replied to the man who peddled oils, incense, revolutionary tracts, and slender, mimeographed volumes of poetry. And so by the end of the Detroit riots they had chosen completely new names, thereby casting off another aspect of their heritage. Isis, Icarus, Iscariot, Idris. "I discovered that I could never remember how my favorite songs went," she wrote as if in anticipation of your "problem." Sunday-school lessons and softly spoken psalms had lodged in that crystalline realm of the mind which the swirl of adolescence would dissolve. To reach the building on Kingshighway required a half-hour drive from home, yet you could always sneak in through the side doors if late or you forgot your tithe, or beg for doughnuts if the culprits were gas and cigarettes. Something, however, points to behavior that is indisputably trifling. In the interim he flipped through the bulletins, which were troves of vital information. Memories, like cataracts, sometimes blind us to the present. All the cats come in. He prayed, kneeling solemnly on the rug's sandpapery surface, but his prayers remained wholly unanswered. A call, as always, upon the authority of the ancestors, at a pitch such as might befit a cantilene. Innumerable the issues they hid before the children, thinking them simply incapable of coping. Cousins who were Jehovahs argued that Jesus died on a tree, enlisting anecdotes and apocrypha as their proof. At Mass no one caught the spirit like those "Pennycostals" do. More baffling was why they called the holy bread the "host," why it could not touch our hands, and why it resided hidden in the "sepulcher." Would it melt in the mouth or turn to flesh again, and then how on God's earth could someone swallow? Dim body, dazzling body. When the fun began it was frequently bedtime. Volubility unchecked in an imaginative child is a sure prescription for disaster. Although he tried to cloak these comments in a voiceless whisper, his voice dispersed the silence like a well-cast stone.

Texts, Context, A Fear of Contamination

Education, they counseled us, is the one true key, yet the school was less known for its floors of tidy classrooms than for its gym with collapsible bleachers and that polished, hardwood floor. Promise-harness. The committee, comprising the clergy and the most prominent lay members, rechristened the complex after the first Black Catholic bishop, which provided even the most taciturn with an engaging topic of discussion. Simply naming, while powerful, never proves enough. He was usually charily chosen for the kickball teams, or last for any sport requiring aggression. A palpable terror, a shortness of breath.

Consolation lay in the reading contests and the sketching assignments, when we could excel far beyond the expectations of both teachers and friends. My teeth cast a gleaming net for you, a white and wordless reply. Cardinal Ritter. "Poetry" served then as the recitative of bible-men and the pimp who stayed on the corner, or the huckster who with brio sold them a faulty vacuum cleaner. In those days we could recall the names and life stories of the major Black inventors almost as readily as our multiplication tables, though in truth a disjuncture persisted between their paradigms and how we perceived them, which neither teachers nor other adults sought to bridge. No one really slept at naptime. After the wedding, marked by a holy sacrament which he believed he understood, he and the other children brought Mrs. Orange her namesake fruit. In fourth grade, following a premise that defied "equality," the classes cleaved into two distinct and ability-based homerooms, which garnered for the smaller, brighter class a rancor it little deserved. "Freedom School." Thus that year proceeded by way of experimental groupings and methods, which sounds nothing short of radical in the context of education today. Many the nuns who scored the names of saintly men in their heads until each was resurrected by reflex, and who, in daily sweeps past their desks, left a near-visible trail of camphor. With your hair cut so short, the older boys renamed you "Shine," rubbing your head as though it were their own personal talisman. "Sensitive." Yet who did not desire to follow their model, for they were more real than his idols. What little boys do. Behavior enough to gain us mention in the newspaper, where he spoke of his desire to be popular, or in the parlance of those days, the "Caped Crusader." Ivanhoe, Pip, and Peter Pan led the list of childhood favorites, though it was hard to identify with that bespectacled, British "John." His father would not hesitate to mine him for that single ore of truth, since this, he had convinced himself, was a father's chief occupation. If you therefore were one who regularly lied, then your recollections might consist of the sum total of your childhood fictions. He waited but the invitations never materialized, so he learned to create small diversions for himself. A cleansing

thus ensued, an art of remembering developed, a renewal undeniably the result. "Straight-A, Straight-A, nothing but a sissyboy
who's scared to play," they screamed burning tracks across the
playground, their faces brown, blazing globes of glee, as he
crumpled near the swingset like a raveling, forgotten husk-doll.
Repression's effects assume manifold forms. One option proposed seriously was that of skipping a grade, though they feared
that might warp her emotional development. In other words,
neither parent had expected such a fragile character, though
they bore the verdict better once they had bought it. Some children are badly suited to this world, though their elders rarely
gather this fact until the dawn of the teen years, when the complement of options has shrunk to zero. Baldwins reclined between a Jong, several Cozzens, and two Morrisons, but Mich-
ener's *opera* had long held sway of the bookshelf. Neither Bolivia
nor Paraguay has an ocean port, you learned from encyclopedias
at the great-aunt's house. A few of them so old that they crumbled between the fingers, others crinkled with that odor of never
having been fully opened. The genius lay in the execution, or at
least in how she kept the deception from becoming apparent.
Ebony and *Black Enterprise* graced the marble coffee table, though
Jet garnered everyone's initial review. Our generation possesses
only a cursory sense of the world that our ancestors braved,
though the burdens of history bear unmovably upon us. Homer
G. Phillips. Rollerskating in the summer around Steinberg
Rink, or else in one of many indoor halls, and when he was old
enough to wield a racket, tennis in O'Fallon Park. Sugarloaf
Mound. One assessment: the chill cast the courts in a crepuscu-
lar light. Stan, who coached the older, lither players, sported a
thick, beguiling mustache, while coiled hairs spilled from the V-
neck of his jersey, leaving us with a sensation that we were yet
unable to name. Ruby, my dear. "Swing, baby, lemme hear that
ball sing and dance, serve, but not so much racket string, you
got it, now, whoa, don't fling it." By perfecting a strategy, we
learned gradually, we could organize and master almost any
game, a lesson as applicable and valuable outside the court as
on it.

ALEXANDER KLUGE

SIX STORIES

Translated from the German by MARTIN CHALMERS & MICHAEL HULSE

A CASE OF LOVING WHAT IS REMOTE

"Fantasy is aroused by those very women who lack fantasy."
—THEODOR ADORNO, *Minima Moralia*

We are told of Marcel Proust that "he dragged his body along behind him like a St. Bernard dog." The vessels and the juices often felt out of sorts. Even in the late afternoon, Proust was in doubt whether he would go to the soirée at all. He was also deeply afraid of being bored, of meeting people he did not want to listen to and who would not listen to him.

But then, making a decision in a moment, he had had himself dressed, and had made his appearance at the soirée; and as midnight approached the teller of tales was encircled by aristocrats, and specially invited newspaper men, and warmed to the occasion. In the grounds, where the parkland came up to the pavilions, tables and buffets were set up as on parade, steaming fragrances. To protect them from the November air, everyone present was clad in furs, and grog was served.

Proust, in hibernal mood, had been fired with enthusiasm by something he had happened to read that morning. Lively interest was the only thing that could keep the autumnal coughing at bay. He had started talking of Friedrich Schiller, a subject that took Parisian society by surprise, the name being unfamiliar to most present. He could measure the success of his performance from the expression of the Princesse de Parme, reading it like a gauge that registers the intensity and pitch of sound. For seventeen seconds the princess had paid attention, and this prompted a hope that he might arouse her interest again. And so, uninterrupted by those who stood around, Proust talked on, discoursing on Schiller's plots.

The deeds of William Tell came from the very "jaws of hell," he declared. A huntsman by trade, not an artisan or farmer like other Swiss, Tell was an adventurer, a mystical hunter, who shot at the Landvogt and alleged tyrant as he would shoot at an especially noble game animal. What interested him was not the conclusion of peace, the Rütli oath, or matters of camaraderie, but accuracy of aim. A fine shot was an older thing than the new-fledged aristocracy, and Gessler, the *Landvogt* or governor, had merely achieved aristocracy. *Don Carlos*, said Proust, was extremely odd, and needed rewriting altogether. What ludicrous words the Marquis de Posa was made to utter to the king. He described himself as "the representative of the human race." What authority could confer such power on a man? The king's jealousy of his heir apparent, the obsession of Princess Eboli who loves the heir, the tender emotion Queen Elizabeth feels for Don Carlos, to whom she was once betrothed—what an explosive, emotionally charged foursome! Quite enough to kill Don Carlos. It might also have sufficed to save him. How quickly can a play two hundred and fifty pages long, eight hours in performance, be rewritten and adapted into French, so as to be a success in the winter season?

Speaking only half in jest, Proust grew ever more agitated. At that hour he was outstripping the body that strove to tyrannize him, but that was now showing him obedience like an animal should for its master, this animal that so often puts the brakes on him.

As we have said, the Princesse de Parme had listened for seventeen seconds; then she had turned away, to new impressions. The impact of her attentiveness stayed with Proust for eons.

This extempore performance by Proust was heard by one Monsieur Octave, a relative of the Verdurins. He was living with Rachel, the lover of St. Loup, and was a man who had married advantageously under false pretences. A journalist, he had a telephone contact at *Le Figaro*, which is to say that no editor at that newspaper had ever received him, but whenever a feature was dropped he might manage to place this article or that in its pages. He found it difficult to repeat what the genius had said about Schiller in his monolog. He had recognized the value of what Proust had said only by watching the faces of the other listeners. They (all of them aristocrats) had retained not a word. For centuries it had been bred into them, however, to translate a passing interest into a facial expression which (even after the French Revolution had stripped them of their power) signaled permission to continue speaking, indeed even to deliver an overlong monologue.

I am the representative of humanity, was the way Monsieur Octave formulated it the next morning. The statement had none of the wit that had made the Marquis de Norpois laugh out loud.* Marcel Proust really did maintain that the final scene of *Nathan the Wise* (Proust mistakenly ascribed Lessing's play to Schiller) should be performed first. In that scene, while the Knight Tem-

*Octave mentioned that Friedrich Schiller had been made an honorary citizen of the French Revolution. But on the other hand, the aristocratic nature of the group to whom Marcel Proust was speaking canceled out any emancipatory tones. It was only when the word "freedom" was deleted from them, declared Proust, that Schiller's plays unfolded their true power. Thus Octave; but in fact Proust had observed how surely the emotional energies of Don Carlos and the Marquis de Posa meshed, and how ridiculous the effect was in a love relationship if one of the partners said: Till now I have loved you, but now I am in love with Freedom and must leave you. This could be said in a relationship if one remained concrete, exchanging one partner for another, but the loved one could not be exchanged for a statue of liberty.

plar (a spirit), Saladin (a Moslem), and Nathan (a Jew) were discussing peace, the location of the scene itself in the heart of Jerusalem would be destroyed by a bomb. This would clear the stage for a new play.* The very thought delighted the Marquis de Norpois, a diplomat. Where there is a place of such distinction, he said, there is also space for a stroke of genius.

But how was this to be transformed into an interesting *Figaro* article? The swiftness with which a pack of arrogant, leering egocentrics at an amusing soirée decided whether the hasty statements of a fiery-eyed man, a writer, were right or wrong, with the writer behaving much like a pedigree racehorse forever triumphing in the final furlong, cannot be reconstructed the following morning in a journalist's brain governed by quite other interests. Thus a cobbled-together item was published in *Le Figaro* which claimed that Friedrich Schiller was comprehensible only when translated into French, but that this involved changing the plots of his plays, so that the Marquis de Posa finally received the ministerial position at the Spanish court that he had craved ever since the Battle of Lepanto; and peace with the Moslems of the Levant was due to the Sultan Saladin and a celebrated Jew by the name of Nathan. This had been asserted at a soirée by the Jewish writer Proust, to the applause of a gathering of aristocrats. The aristocrats, however, traced their bloodline back to a child couple who landed in Marseilles in A.D. 37, who were themselves evidently the progeny of the liaison between Jesus Christ and Mary Magdalene, and thus of blue blood, that blue blood from which all the French nobility was descended.

Proust slept in and missed that number of *Le Figaro*. His body was exacting revenge on him for the extravagance of his monologues, and the remoteness of his trans-Rhenish interests, though of

---

*Proust did in fact say that the scene concerned the power of three rings given by a father to his sons. But discussion among the three protagonists led to the suspicion that all three rings in their possession were fakes ("the true ring was presumably lost"). One of the three fake rings, however, did contain so much explosive emotional power that the impressive opening scene was the result, maintained Proust: all the protagonists were dead on the spot.

course he had captivated his society audience with them. Sleep, indolence.

THE THOUSAND EYES

The tempestuous development of the Soviet Union's secret services and terror agencies* up to 1937 had painful after-effects for more than 15 years.**

The evolution of the terror apparatus had favored less the INWARDLY HARDENED EXECUTOR WITH STRONG NERVES type than the SENSITIVE SCOUT. This second group of semi-intellectual file clerks was more likely to have escaped the internal persecutions and purges than the activist type, who'd bloodied his hands in whichever phase of the revolutionary or counter-revolutionary (braking) process had just become obsolete.

Shortly after Stalin's death, at the beginning of the power struggle that was concluded with Beria's fall, one of these SENSITIVE SCOUTS, Sergei M. Vorolov, was also expelled from headquarters. Beria is shot, Molotov named director of a distant power station. Vorolov becomes the forester of an enormous forest area north of Novgorod. With the same meticulous precision he'd employed in the offices on Red Square, he now worked his way through the vast northern-jungle-like landscape of Holy Russia, supported by seven forestry workers. He couldn't

---

*"Terror agency" and "secret service" are part of the same department, but are organized separately.

**In a terror agency a generation lasts about three years (one tenth of the generational interval in life). The time before these three years in control of a post is used for preparation, for GOAL ORIENTATION. The following years until retirement from the agency are taken up with defensive battles against successors. But that corridor of freedom, the years in which the functionary is in power, is a known quantity. But in Beria's department, of all places, there was a minor official (responsible for a single function in the library), who held out from 1917 to 1958, but only because he never left his subordinate position. In the crisis phase of 1937 there were MONSTERS OF POWER who ruled only for seven days.

shoot. Lumber shipments from this remote district, not directly linked by road with the main transport routes of Russia, were not provided for in the Plan. So, armed only with his urban intelligence, he lived here alone on his piece of public property. At night he slept badly, and by day his capacities were not truly fully occupied.

Around the shacks, which made up the foresters' settlement, there lived a nation of ants 22 million strong (in fact there was a total of 140 nests, and therefore many nations, some of them, such as the blood-red slave-making ants, very hostile to others). Vorolov felt himself observed. It was not the individual ant that scared him, but the mighty collective. The creatures have one complex eye on each side of the head (compound facet red eyes), supplemented by three ocelli on the forehead. What do these five eyes see? What do 22-million-times-five eyes see, above all at night when they don't rest?

If one starts from the small number of sight lines, then one underestimates the ants' powers of vision, says Vorolov. Also, each individual insect doesn't have much of a brain, so not much memory. What, however, if such numerous pinpoints were to be linked up in a network? Does that produce a super eye, that looks at me at night, that follows my steps on my walks along my forest paths, which are after all necessary, if I want to keep my muscles, my body intact?

Vorolov has a Bakelite wall-mounted telephone of the successful 1931 type, and if the forests are not too damp, its connections reach a long way, especially in the dry winters. So at times he is in contact with the science cities and the academies. He can ask the biologists questions. He finds out that the five-eyed visual apparatuses of the ants are incapable "of adjusting to shifting distances of an object." The grid, which they "see" or "scan," is a "blurred restless picture." From that the ants draw their "conclusions." The insect eye does have a high-speed resolution capacity. The creature can distinguish 300 impressions per second.

My dear Vorolov, you cannot even see the eyes of the ants which you suspect are out there, said the biologist Iglovsky, to whom Vorolov was talking on the telephone. And the insects can only see a couple of yards. They are not in a position to observe you through the windows of your hut.

— But, yes, yes. Their glances add up to glowing points. Each set of five eyes multiplied by a thousand.
— Nonsense. What you see is woodland. Some bushes.
— How can you judge that over the telephone, Iglovsky?
— It's your imagination. The imagination of a city-dweller. You're seeing city conditions. But it's only forest.

It's only my imagination, Vorolov tells himself. I'm seeing ghosts. Even as he repeated that to himself, he didn't believe it. Over the long evenings the lonely forester's senses became befuddled. SENSITIVITY CHARACTERIZES A POSSIBILITY, INTELLIGENCE DESCRIBES A RESULT. Neither was any use in interpreting the phenomenon outside.*

But outside—that was Vorolov's impression, particularly early this morning, with thunderstorms approaching from the east—a THOUSAND-EYED UNDERSTANDING was spreading in waves. With the color-sensitive eyes on their foreheads the creatures analyzed the direction of movement of linear polarized light. Thus in the evenings they see the position of the sun long after the sun has disappeared over the horizon. And in the early morning they know on the basis of the polarization pattern of the horizon that the sun is returning over Siberia.

For a while Vorolov thought they were looking at him. That made him afraid. But now he knows they are not interested in him, they are preoccupied with minute changes in light and

*Vorolov had never himself seen the more than one thousand inhabitants of the USSR whom he had kept under surveillance during his service; he merely read what the files reported about them. The eyes of those he'd observed could not look back from the files.

register the racing shadows as they hurry along their routes through the forests, which they are never able to appreciate as a whole. That makes him feel lonely. Had he been hoping for an opponent, with whom he could talk in some way?

What longing! After all, during the 15 years in his office he had had such rich contact with all zones of Soviet society, because nowhere else is there such a concentration of sensual variety for a keen mind as in the files of the NKVD! He would like to go home. Home to the information which so many informers report to the organization. Return was denied to him. Like the regime of which he had been part, the man was deleted from the planning, the official staff hierarchy of headquarters.

If one looks with a steady human eye at a forest, the details of the forest floor or the six foresters' huts, or indeed at the path that leads south and which at some point therefore arrives at the rivers and roads of Russia or even the capital, then after a while one sees nothing at all any more. At most premonition, that most fleet-footed of eyes, runs away down the path to the human beings.

THE MIX-UP

For all five US Armies advancing into the heart of Germany, Major Arnold Patterson was the officer responsible for the gathering up of children whose parents were missing. A considerable number were collected. The children (from camps and from orphanages, if it was certain they were offspring of those who had been persecuted) were brought together in huts close to a military airfield outside Rheims. The rescue of the children had been accompanied by press coverage in the United States.

In early May the children were air-lifted to London, and welcomed at a grand hotel by British children's nurses. The mites were undressed in an opulently furnished suite, their things deposited in the anteroom, the children concentrated in the bath-room in orderly fashion, hot water run. They have to be cleaned up, that was the view of the capable nurses.

A relative or a friend of the family had been established for each of the children; indeed in some cases missing parents had been rediscovered. The London hotel was a stopover.

The children splashed about in the water and forgot the miseries of the past in this sociable grouping. What a shock for the supervisory staff that, separated from their clothes and documentation in the anteroom, the LITTLE ONES could afterwards no longer be identified. Interrogation was in vain. Not a single child knew who his relatives were. Not one was able to name their parents.

— The supervisory staff resorted to deception, to cover up the mistake?
— Yes, in panic. The press made the situation potentially explosive.
— They arbitrarily allocated the children to the addresses to which the children were to be brought?
— Somehow. The black-haired ones to South America, the fair-haired ones to Boston or the north of England. The addresses were spread all over the world.
— So that none of the addressees, not even those parents who had re-emerged, could be certain that the consignment they received was really their own child?
— No one could know.
— Most of the children had been separated from their parents immediately after birth?
— Yes, it was a matter of saving the children. Well-meaning Germans had torn persecuted parents and their children apart.
— And their feelings don't tell the parents which child is theirs?
— One woman maintained that the child sent to her was not hers. She searched, and found another in the batch. It later turned out she was mistaken. In this case the blood types were a help.

It was a homecoming for the children nevertheless. They never subsequently had doubts that they had been found the proper home: that was the view of the head of the supervisory staff, who had only reached the grand hotel in London after the disaster. She had handed in a report to the ministry. Afterwards she was pleased with her decision.

The mixed-up children

The Homeward Voyage of the Presumptuous

For inhabitants of distant planets the Pacific Ocean appears as the "Earth's eye." The watery desert has not yet been completely researched by the meteorologists. In August its surface is struck by typhoons.

Select ships from all the U.S. Navy's squadrons had participated in the naval review marking the capitulation of Japan. The mass of the ships lay scattered, just as the final phase of operations had required. But the mighty armada was now to be assembled once again and brought home eastward across the Pacific in three columns. This was the obsession of the commander-in-chief, Admiral "Bull" Halsey, and his staffs, who had hatched and fostered the plan.

In the conditions of 1945 such a naval force, concentrated into a column yet dispersed over the sea, could not be tracked by the human eye, though it did draw a current of radio contacts, communicative high spirits, across the ocean.

The opinion of naval meteorologists (some sailing with the fleet, some transmitting their messages from fixed bases) was divided. On one side were those who advised caution, on the other those who wished the ships *bon voyage*, because it was only the *edges* of the big typhoons which could affect such a spread-out fleet. It would take a hellish coincidence, said the chief meteorologist on Hawaii, for the typhoons to make common cause against the home-comers. The weather, he said, has no reason, and no will either.*

---

*Until the very last, the Japanese leadership had placed hopes in supernatural influences concealed in the elements and the weather. Just as the Mongol invasion centuries before had been repelled by gods hidden in the tempest, which had scattered the Khan's fleet. That did not happen in time off Okinawa. Typhoons and the landing of US troops were about eight weeks apart. Giving their own suicide assault elites the symbolic names of the anticipated weather gods hadn't done any good.

On the fleet staff of the US Navy there were still Congressional auditors, who in the midst of the war had the task of ensuring that the values of economy and thrift were maintained. One of these controllers, Mr. Allen Murphy, thought the concentration of the whole fleet—as a kind of beauty parade—constituted an unnecessary risk. Why offer fate (the uncertainties of a great ocean) three great columns, when each ship could also sail to its home port on its own. There is no insurance coverage for war fleets, he said. The risk should be spread. No one paid any attention to the man.

The pessimistic weather researchers of the University of California at San Diego were also ignored. They voted against the Atlanticists of the East Coast universities, who tended to underestimate the dangerous peculiarities of the Pacific. Shortly afterwards there was an increase in data which pointed to immediate risk. Admiral Halsey rejected any change to the planned return. His forces, consisting of such diverse ships (aircraft carriers, supply ships, hospital ships, battleships, submarines, minesweepers, troop transports, etc.) with very different speeds, could not be redirected from one hour to the next.

So it came to pass that three extreme low-pressure zones—whirling typhoons—descended on the returning fleet. Despite four years of naval warfare the power of the elements had remained unknown.* For three days and nights the spirits of the great ocean struck at the presumption of the naval commanders. According to Mr. Murphy, the auditor, in these seventy-two hours the US Navy suffered greater material losses than during all the naval battles against Japan. The affair was hushed up.

---

*Typhoons had hit individual ships and small squadrons; the reports of the effects had not been filed centrally. The commanders themselves, always on the largest ships, had not experienced any of the catastrophes.

Little Dog Laika

In the wastes of the cosmos the little dog Laika, a stray Moscow mongrel bitch of great robustness, circled the globe for a time. Full of trust in the keepers and trainers, who had signaled to her

"They had firmly believed they could bring the dog back down again."

that if she only obeyed, then continued life would be guaranteed by the daily provision of food and personal attention.

This expectation was not fulfilled in practice. Secured inside a device which, industrially speaking, was 87 billion times more expensive than her animal body, LAIKA circled the earth for two weeks, the capsule emitting mechanical signal beams and transmitting data from the canine body.

LAIKA'S masters, a combination of astro-engineers and dog handlers, had firmly believed that they could bring the dog back down again. Their good will was undeniable not least for research reasons, because they wanted to retrieve the capsule's instrument data.

Recovery proved to be impossible. In the emotional balance—the subjective world according to Karl Marx—the dog's slow demise turned out to be a capital way of annihilating all galactic plans.

No one (even outside the Soviet Union) any longer believed the makers of grand utopian schemes (e.g., for the conquest of nearby planets or nearby stars) if they couldn't even fetch an ordinary dog back from orbit. In fact, they couldn't even supply the little thing with morphine, which would have granted her a gradual death of reflected splendor under the stars. Instead the engineers at Mission Control in CITY OF THE STARS (no one dared break off the acoustic contact) listened to the little dog's efforts to draw breath. Its vitality prolonged the crisis. The animal did not depart from life in orbit without resistance.

THE DEVIL IN THE WHITE HOUSE

"There he is nice and plump at the heart of power."

You're making a mistake there, replied Nigel MacPherson, in charge of security at the White House that month. Satan never grows fat. He seeks out the leanest bodies, pure mental power.

— And you think that you recognized him in the immediate vacinity of the President?

— (*Points at the group photo*): That's him. As soon as he knew we had recognized him, he was gone. Not even a puff of smoke, which from vivid medieval accounts we assumed is the sort of thing the Devil leaves behind when he disappears.

— No stench?

— Nothing. He disappeared from my side, one moment he was there, the next he was gone.

— The President is supposed to have been hopping mad. Every day he's looking for the Evil One. And here he was, standing five yards away from him. Recognized too late, not exorcised.

— I'm interested in something else. Where is he now? Once he has decided on a plan, the Devil doesn't abandon it. We know that much about him.

— You think that the superpower headquarters exerts a magical attraction for him?

— What could be more attractive?

— And he's not put off by the proximity of the God-fearing President? The fiercest pursuer of evil? He's not afraid of being caught?

— You mean, because the President can "see evil"? Because he has a sixth sense for when the Tempter is standing in the same room? But evidently he didn't notice the "assistant," who sneaked onto the staff.

— He'd taken the shape of an assistant known to the staff?

— His corpse had been lying in a barn near Philadelphia for weeks.

— And didn't come back to life, when the Devil disappeared?

— These powers are ruthless.

— So the Devil is not only the Evil One, Satan, but also quite concretely a murderer?

— He is the enemy of mankind.

— And what does he want in the White House?

— Presumably to mess up the threads of world politics.

— But what happens in the world is only influenced in an indirect way by decisions made at such a center of power.

— That's true. Because when things happen the real conditions are too numerous to be directed.

— But then wouldn't it be better for the Devil to get involved in the *real conditions?* That's where the bombs are planted, that's where they explode.

— It could be that the Devil is still following older ideas of power. It's hard to learn as quickly as the world changes.

— But one assumes that Satan knows everything for eons in advance.

— Hence also the idea to trap him in the White House, perhaps pump him for information. That's why they've been waiting for him to turn up again.

— In a different shape?

— He's always changing his shape.

— As a dog he wouldn't be allowed into the Oval Office?

— He has to take on the shape of an adviser.

— You can't tell from looking at an adviser, whether he's a lobbyist for an arms company, or an honorable man, or the Devil.

— How is it possible, theologically speaking, to really determine whether someone is the Devil, if he's a master of every disguise?

— We'd have to use torture. If the person concerned withstands the torture, then it's the Devil, and if he doesn't, then we've accused the wrong guy.

— What makes you think that the Devil would always assume the shape only of an adviser or a minister? He could also take the shape of the President himself.

— Not of a God-fearing President.

— It's strange, but I'm finding this hypothetical discussion with you (as long as the Devil hasn't returned to the White House) something of a relief. I find it reassuring in a way that such an ancient steersman of the world is present at the center of power, even if he wants to do evil; at least he knows what he's up to.

— You think that the decision-makers of the world only stir up things they can't control, "like hitting an anthill with a stick"?

— Exactly. Someone well-informed, using that stick, is still better than someone who's naive.

— What further security measures should we take to make the

White House safe? How can we be certain of excluding Satan from the center of power?

— But we don't even know what effect banishing the Devil from there will have. Where will he go? Isn't he more dangerous as a guerrilla than in the proximity of the ruler?

— We would have to know more about his nature.

— I have the feeling, a good feeling, that he isn't concerned about the world, about our planet at all, but that he's a powerful spirit in the universe. The disappearance of the assistant in the middle of a meeting then would still be mysterious, but it would fit better with the fallen archangel.

— Do you mean that if we strain good will as severely as we do, as a superpower, then that would entail risks? That excessive hoarding of "good will" is explosive?

— So that it might be a good thing if some of that were constantly being undermined by a metaphysical force.

— Do you consider the Devil to be a critical spirit?

— We know too little about him. Our files are incomplete.

— How on earth did you find out that the assistant in your group photo was the Tempter in another form?

— A tip from the German Intelligence Service.

— From Germany?

— Yes, information from the "old Europe."

ANTONIO TABUCCHI

LETTER FROM CASABLANCA

Translated from the Italian by JANICE M. THRESHER

Lena,

I don't know why I begin this letter talking to you about a palm tree when you haven't heard anything from me for eighteen years. Perhaps because there are many palm trees here. I see them from my hospital window waving their long locks in the torrid wind along the blazing avenues that disappear in whiteness. In front of our house, when we were children, there was a palm tree. Maybe you don't remember it because it was pulled down, if my memory does not fail me, the year what happened took place—in 1953, therefore, I think in summer. I was ten years old.

We had a happy childhood, Lena. You can't remember it, and no one could talk to you about it. The aunt with whom you grew up can't know about it. Yes, of course, she can tell you something about Papa and Mama, but she can't describe for you a childhood she didn't know and which you don't remember. She lived too far away, up there in the north. Her husband was a bank clerk. They considered themselves superior to the family of a signalman, a level-crossing keeper, and they never came to our house.

The palm tree was pulled down following a decree by the Minister of Transport which maintained that it impeded the view of the trains and could cause an accident. Who knows what accident that palm tree, grown so high, could cause, with a tuft of branches that brushed our second-floor window? From the signalman's house, what might be slightly annoying was its trunk, that trunk thinner than a lamp post: it certainly could not impede the view of the trains. Anyway, we had to pull it down, nothing could be done about it, the land wasn't ours. One night at supper Mama, who from time to time had grand ideas, decided to write a letter personally to the Minister of Transport, signed by all the family, a kind of petition. It went like this:

Dear Mr. Minister: In reference to the circular number such-and-such, protocol such-and-such, concerning the palm tree situated on the small piece of land in front of the signal house number such-and-such on the Roma-Torino line, the family of the signalman informs Your Excellency that the above-mentioned palm tree does not constitute any obstacle to the view of the trains in passage. We beg you, therefore, to leave the above-mentioned palm tree standing, it being the only tree on the land apart from a pergola of vines and it being much loved by the children of the signalman, especially for keeping the baby company. Being by nature delicate, she is often confined to bed, but at least she can see the palm tree through the windowpane rather than only air, which would make her sad. And to bear witness to the love that the children of the signalman have for the above-mentioned tree, sufficeth it to say that they have christened it and do not call it "palm tree," but call it Josephine, owing this name to the fact that when we took them once to the cinema in the city to see *The Talking Dead* with Totò, they saw in the film the famous French Negro singer of the above-mentioned name who danced with a most beautiful headdress of palm leaves, and since, whenever there is a wind, the palm tree moves as if it is dancing, our children call it Josephine.

This letter is one of the few things that remain to me of Mama. It is the rough copy of the petition we sent. Mama wrote it in my composition notebook and so, by fortuitous chance, when I was sent to Argentina, I took it, in her handwriting, along without knowing it, never imagining the treasure that that page would become for me later.

Another thing that remains to me of Mama is a photo, but you can hardly make out that it is of her. It's a photograph that Signor Quintilio took under the pergola of our house around the stone table. It must be summer. Seated at the table there are Papa and Signor Quintilio's daughter, a thin girl in a flowered dress with her hair in long braids. I am playing with a wooden gun, pretending to shoot at a target. On the table there are some glasses and a bottle of wine. Mama is coming out of the house with a soup tureen. She was just entering the photograph when Signor Quintilio clicked. She came in by chance and in motion. For this reason she is a little out of focus and in profile, and it is difficult to recognize her, so much so that I prefer to picture her as I remember her. I remember it well, that year. I am speaking of the year in which the palm tree was pulled down. I was ten years old, it was summer (the event happened in October). A person possesses perfectly the memory of when he was ten years old, and I will never be able to forget what happened that October. But Signor Quintilio—do you remember him? He was the bailiff at a farm about two kilometers from the signal house, where in May we used to go to pick cherries. He was a happy, nervous little man who always told jokes. Papa made fun of him, because under fascism he had been Vice-Federal, or something of the kind, and he was ashamed. He would shake his head, saying that it was water under the bridge, and then Papa would begin to laugh and give him a slap on the back. And his wife— do you remember her? Signora Elvira, that big, sad woman. She suffered terribly from the heat. When she came to dinner with us, she brought a fan. She sweated and panted, then she sat outside under the pergola, asleep on the stone bench with her head leaning on the wall. Nothing woke her, not even passing freight trains.

It was splendid when they came Saturday after supper. Sometimes Signorina Palestro came too, an old maid who lived alone in a kind of dependent villa on the farm, surrounded by a battalion of cats. She had a mania for teaching me French because as a girl she had been tutor to the children of a count. She always said, "*Pardon*," and "*C'est dommage*," and her favorite exclamation, used in all situations to underline an important fact or simply if her glasses fell, was "*Eh, lá, lá!*" Those evenings Mama sat down at the little piano. How she held herself at that piano was a testimony to her upbringing, to her well-to-do girlhood, to her chancellor father, to summers spent in the Tuscan Apennines. What stories she told us about her vacations! And then she had graduated in domestic science.

If you knew, during my first years in Argentina, how much I wished I had lived those vacations! I wanted those summers so much and I imagined them so vividly that sometimes a strange witchcraft came over me, and I remembered vacations spent at Gavinana and at San Marcello. We were there, Lena, you and I, as children. Only you, instead of being you, were Mama as a little girl, and I was your brother and I loved you very much. I remembered when we went to a stream below Gavinana to catch tadpoles. You—that is, Mama—had a net and a funny big hat with a brim like those of the Sisters of St. Vincent. You ran straight ahead, chattering, The tadpoles are waiting! Run! Run! What fun!" and it seemed to me to be the funniest rhyme, and I laughed like crazy. Bursts of laughter prevented me from following you. Then you disappeared into the chestnut wood near the stream and shouted, "Catch me! Catch me!" At that point I did my very best and caught up with you. I took you by the shoulders, you gave a little cry, and we fell down. The ground was sloping and we began to roll over, and then I embraced you and whispered to you, "Mama, Mama, hug me tight, Mama," and you hugged me tight. While we rolled over, you had become Mama as I knew her. I smelled your perfume, I kissed your hair, everything intermingled—grass, hair, sky—and at that moment of ecstasy the baritone voice of Uncle Alfredo broke in: "Now then, *niño*, are the *platinados* ready?" They were not ready, no. I found myself in the wide-open jaw of an old Mercedes' back seat with a box of tacks in one hand and a screwdriver in the other. The floor was studded with blue spots of oily water. "What a dreamer this boy is!" Uncle Alfredo said good-naturedly, and gave me an affectionate slap.

It was 1958 and we were in Rosario. Uncle Alfredo, after many years in Argentina, spoke a strange mixture of Italian and Spanish. His garage was called "The Motorized Italian," and he repaired everything, but mainly tractors, old Ford carcasses. As an emblem (nest to Shell's shell) he had a neon leaning tower of Pisa which, however, was only half-lit because the gas in the tubes was used up, and nobody had ever had the patience to replace it. Uncle Alfredo was a corpulent man, full-blooded, patient, a gourmet, with a nose furrowed by many tiny blue veins, and a constitutional tendency to hypertension—everything exactly the opposite of Papa. You would never have guessed they were brothers.

Ah, but I was telling you about those evenings after supper at our house, when visitors came and Mama sat down at the piano. Signorina Palestro went into ecstasies over Strauss waltzes, but I liked it much better when Mama sang. It was so difficult to make her sing. She acted coy, she blushed. "I don't have a voice anymore," she said smiling, but then she gave in at the insistence of Signora Elvira. She, too, preferred ballads and songs more than waltzes. And finally Mama surrendered. Then there was a great silence. Mama began with some amusing little songs in order to enliven the atmosphere—something like "Rosamunda" or "Eulalia Torricelli." Signora Elvira laughed delightedly, somewhat breathlessly, emitting the cluckings of a brooding hen and lifting her enormous bosom, while she cooled herself with her fan. Then Mama executed an interlude at the piano without singing. Signorina Palestro requested something more challenging. Mama raised her eyes to the ceiling as if searching for inspiration or ransacking her memory. Her hands caressed the keyboard. It was a dead hour for trains, there were no disturbing noises. From the window wide open to the marsh came the sound of crickets. A moth battered its wings against the net, trying in vain to enter. Mama sang *Luna rossa, All'alba se ne parte il marinaro*, or a ballad by Beniamino Gigli, *Oh begli occhi di fata*. How lovely it was to hear her sing! Signorina Palestro's eyes were shining, Signora Elvira even stopped fanning herself—everyone was watching Mama. She wore a rather filmy blue dress. You were sleeping in your room, unaware. You haven't had these moments to remember in your life. I was happy. Everyone applauded. Papa overflowed with pride. He circled around with the bottle of vermouth and refilled the guests' glasses, saying, "Please, please, we're not in a Turk's house."

Uncle Alfredo always used this curious expression, too. It was funny to hear him say it in the middle of his Spanish sentences. I remember we were at the table. He liked tripe *alla parmigiana* very much and thought that the Argentinians were stupid because they appreciated only the steaks from their cattle. Helping himself abundantly from the big steaming soup tureen, he told me, "Go on and eat, *niño*, we're not in a Turk's house." It was a phrase from their childhood, Uncle Alfredo's and Papa's. It went back to who knows what ancient time. I understood the concept: this is a house of abundance, and the owner is generous. Who knows why the contrary was attributed to the Turks? Perhaps it was an expression that dated from the Saracen invasions. And Uncle Alfredo really was generous with me. He brought me up as if I really were his son. He had no children of his own. He was generous and patient, just like a good father, and probably with me plenty of patience was necessary. I was an absent-minded, sad boy. I caused a lot of trouble as a result of my temperament. The only time I saw him lose his patience it was terrible, but it was not my fault. We were having dinner.

I had precipitated a disaster with a tractor. I had had to execute a difficult maneuver to get it into the garage. Maybe I was inattentive—at that moment Modugno was singing "Volare" on the radio, and Uncle Alfredo had turned it up to full volume because he loved it and I scraped against the side of a Chrysler going in and did a lot of damage.

Aunt Olga wasn't bad. She was talkative, grumbling Venetian who had remained stubbornly attached to her dialect, and when she spoke, you understood almost nothing. She mixed Venetian with Spanish—a disaster. She and my uncle had met in Argentina. When they decided to marry, they were already elderly.

In fact, you couldn't say they had married for love; let's say it had been convenient for both of them—for her, because she gave up working in the meat-canning plant, and for Uncle Alfredo, because he needed a woman to keep his house in order. However, they were fond of each other, or at least there was liking, and Aunt Olga respected him and spoiled him. Who knows why she came out with that sentence that day? Maybe she was tired or out of sorts, but she lost her patience. I am sure it was not how she really felt. Uncle Alfredo had already reprimanded me about the tractor earlier, and I was mortified enough: I was keeping my eyes on my plate. Aunt Olga, point-blank, but not in order to hurt my feelings, poor thing, almost as if she were confirming something, said, "He's the son of a madman—only a madman could do that to his wife." And then I saw Uncle Alfredo get up, deliberately, his face white, and give her a terrible backhanded slap. The blow was so violent that Aunt Olga fell from her chair, and in her fall she grabbed the tablecloth, pulling it with all the dishes after her. Uncle Alfredo left slowly and went down to the garage to work. Aunt Olga got up as if nothing had happened and began to pick up the dishes, swept the floor, put on a new tablecloth because the other one was a mess, set the table, and appeared at the stairwell. "Alfredo," she shouted, "dinner's ready!"

When I left for Mar del Plata I was sixteen years old. Sewed inside my vest was a roll of *pesos*, and in my pocket a business card from the Pensione Albano—"hot and cold running water"—and a letter to its proprietor, an Italian friend of Uncle Alfredo's, a friend of his youth. They had arrived in Argentina on the same ship and had always kept in touch. I was going to attend a boarding school run by Salesian Italians who had a conservatory, or something of the kind. My aunt and uncle had encouraged me. By this time I had finished the grammar school. I was not cut out to be a garage mechanic, this was evident, and then Aunt Olga hoped that the city would change me. One evening I had heard her say, "Sometimes his eyes scare me, they're so frightened. Who knows what he saw, poor boy? Who knows what he remembers?" I'm sure my way of doing things was a little distressing. I admit I never talked, I blushed, I stammered, I often cried. Aunt Olga complained that the popular songs with all those stupid words ruined me. Uncle Alfredo tried to arouse my interest by explaining camshafts and clutches to me, and in the evening he tried to persuade me to go with him to the Caffè Florida, where there were many Italians playing cards. But I preferred to stay by the radio listening to music. I adored the old tangos of Carlos Gardel, the melancholy sambas of Wilson Baptista, the popular songs of Doris Day, but I liked all music. And perhaps it was better for me to study music, if that was my inclination, but far away from the prairie, in a civilized place.

Mar del Plata was a bizarre and fascinating city, deserted in the cold season and crowded in the vacation months, with huge white hotels, twentieth-century style, that in the off season emitted sadness. In that period it was a city of exotic seamen and of old people who had chosen to spend their last years of life there and who tried to keep each other company by taking turns making dates for tea on the terraces of the hotels or at the café concerts, where shabby little orchestras caterwauled popular songs and tangos.

I stayed two years at the Salesian conservatory. With Father Matteo, an old, half-blind man with deathly pale hands, I studied Bach, Monteverdi, and Palestrina at the organ. The classes of general culture were held by Father Simone for the scientific part and Father Anselmo for the classical part, in which I was particularly gifted. I studies Latin willingly, but I preferred history, the lives of the saints and the lives of illustrious men. Among those particularly dear to me were Leonardo do Vinci and Ludovico Antonio Muratori, who had gotten his education by eavesdropping under the window of a school, until one day the teacher had discovered him and told him, "Come into the classroom, poor boy!"

In the evening I returned to the Pensione Albano. Work awaited me because the monthly allowance that Uncle Alfredo sent me was not enough. I slipped on a jacket that Señora Pepa made me wash twice a week and stationed myself in the dining room, a pale blue room with around thirty tables and pictures of

Italy on the walls. Our clients were pensioners, small business-men, and the occasional Italian immigrant to Buenos Aires who could permit himself the luxury of spending fifteen days at Mar del Plata. Signor Albano ran the kitchen. He knew how to make *pansoti* with walnuts and *trenette al pesto*: he was Ligurian, from Camogli. He was a follower of Peron. He said that he had lifted up a nation of lice. And then Eva was enchanting.

When I found steady work at the "Bichinho" I wrote Uncle Alfredo not to send me my allowance anymore. It wasn't that I was earning enough of a salary to fritter it away, but, well, it was enough for me, and it didn't seem fair that Uncle Alfredo was fixing tractors in order to send me a few *pesos* every month. "O Bichinho" was a restaurant-nightclub run by a plump, cheerful Brazilian, Senhor João Paiva, where you could have supper at midnight and listen to native music. It was a place with preten-sions of respectability and considered itself superior to other more shady nightclubs, even if whoever went there to look for company found it easily, but only discreetly and with the com-plicity of the waiters, because the prostitution was not at all blatant. Everything had a respectable appearance—forty tables with candles. At two tables toward the back, near the coatroom, there were two young women, each sitting alone in front of a plate that was always empty, sipping an apéritif as if waiting for her order to arrive. And if a gentleman entered, the waiter guided him skillfully and asked him discreetly, "Do you prefer to dine alone or would you like a little company?" I was an expert at these games because my job was at the rear of the room, while Ramón attended to the tables near the platform for the show. To make those propositions you needed tact, good manners. It was necessary to understand the client in order not to offend him. And who knows why by intuition I immediately understood the clients? In short, I had a flair for it, and at the end of the month my tips were greater than my salary. Besides, Anita and Pilar were two generous girls.

The high point of the show was Carmen del Rio. Her voice was no longer what it had been, of course, yet she still consti-tuted an attraction. With the passing years the hoarse timbre that gave charm to her more desperate tangos had weakened, had become more limpid, and she tried in vain to regain it by smoking two cigars before her performance. But what was spectacular about her and what she knew would send the public into a frenzy was not so much her voice as a combination of resources: her repertory, her movements, her make-up, her costumes. Behind the platform curtains she had a little room crammed with rubbish and a majestic wardrobe with all her clothes from the Forties when she was the great Carmen del Rio. There were long chiffon dresses, marvelous white sandals with very high cork heels, feather boas, tango singers' shawls, one blonde wig, one red one, and two raven black ones parted in the middle and with large chignons with white combs, as in Andalusia. The secret of Carmen del Rio was her make-up. And she knew it. She spent hours making herself up. She did not neglect the smallest detail: the tinted base, the long false eye-lashes, the glittering lipstick she had used in earlier days, the very long fatal fingernails painted vermillion.

She often called me because I helped her. She said that I had a very light touch and exquisite taste, I was the only person in the nightclub whom she trusted. She opened her wardrobe and wanted me to advise her. I went over the repertory for the evening. For the tangos she knew what to wear, but for the sentimental songs I chose. Usually I went for the light, filmy, pastel dresses—I don't know, apricot, for example, which was enchanting on her, or a pale indigo that seemed to me unbeatable for "Ramona." And then I did her nails and eyelashes. She closed her eyes and stretched out in the easy chair, surrendering her head to the head-rest, and whispering to me as if in a dream, "Once I had a sensitive lover like you. . . . He spoiled me like a baby. . . . His name was Daniel. . . . He was from Quebec. . . . Who knows what became of him. . . ." Close up and without cosmetics Carmen looked her age, but under the spotlight and after my make-up job she was still a queen. I overdid the base and the grease-paint, naturally, and for face powder I insisted on a very pink Guerlain, instead of the too-white Argentine brands which gave prominence to her wrinkles. And the result was sensational. She was most grateful to me. She said that I pushed back the clock. And for her perfume I converted her to violet—much, very much, violet—and on principle she had protested, because violet is a vulgar perfume for schoolgirls. She didn't know that it was just this contrast that fascinated the public: an old defeated beauty singing tango made up like a pink doll. This was what created the pathos and brought tears to the eyes.

Then I went to do my work at the rear of the room. I circulated among the tables with a light step. "More *carabineros a la plancha, señor?*" "Do you like the rosé wine, *señorita?*" I knew that while she was singing, Carmen was searching for me with her eyes. When with the boss's gold cigar lighter I lit the cigarette which some client had just finished inserting between his lips, I held the flame burning a minute at heart level. It was an agree-upon signal between Carmen and me. It meant that she was singing divinely, that she went right to the heart. And I observed that her voice vibrated even more and gained warmth. She needed to be encouraged, the splendid old Carmen. Without her, "*O Bichinho*" would have been nothing.

The night Carmen stopped singing there was panic. She did not give up of her own accord, obviously. We were in her dressing room, I was doing her make-up, she was stretched out in the armchair in front of the mirror. She was smoking her cigar, keeping her eyes closed, and all of a sudden the powder began to get sticky on her forehead. I realized that she was sweating. I touched her: it was a cold sweat. "I feel bad," she murmured, and said nothing else. I put my hand on her chest, took her pulse, and couldn't feel it any longer. I went to call the manager. Carmen was trembling as if she had a fever, but she did not have a fever. She was icy. We called a taxi to take her to the hospital. I helped her out the back way so the public wouldn't see her. "*Ciao*, Carmen," I said to her, "it's nothing. I'll come to see you tomorrow," and she attempted a smile.

It was eleven o'clock. The clients were having supper. On the platform the spotlight made a circle of empty light. The pianist played softly in order to fill the void. Then from the room came a little impatient applause. They were demanding Carmen. Senhor Paiva, behind the curtain, was very nervous. He sucked his cigarette anxiously, called the manager and told him to serve some champagne gratis. Probably the idea was to keep the public in a good mood. But at that moment a little chorus chanted, "Car-men! Car-men!"

And then I don't know what came over me. It wasn't something I thought about. I felt a force drive me into the dressing room. I turned on the make-up lights around the mirror. I chose a very tight-fitting sequined dress with a slit up the side, of the deliberately showy sort, some white shoes with very high heels, black elbow-length evening gloves, a red wig with long curls. I made up my eyes heavily, with silver, but for my lips I chose an opaque apricot lipstick. When I stepped on the platform the spotlight struck me full force. The public stopped eating. I saw faces staring at me, many forks remaining suspended in the air. I knew that public, but I had never seen it from up front, arranged in a semi-circle like this. It was like a siege.

I began with *"Caminito verde."* The pianist was an intelligent type. He immediately understood the timbre of my voice, provided me with a very discreet accompaniment, all in low notes. And then I nodded to the stage hand and he put on a blue disc. I grasped the microphone and began to whisper into it. I let the pianist do two intermezzos to prolong the song because the public didn't take its eyes off me. And while he played I swayed slowly about the platform and the cone of blue light followed me. Now and then I moved my arms as if I were swimming in that light and stroked my shoulders, with my legs slowly spreading apart and my head swaying so my curls caressed my shoulders, as I had seen Rita Hayworth do in *Gilda*, and then the public began to applaud excitedly. I understood that it was going well and I launched a counter-offensive to not let the enthusiasm die down, attacking another song before the applause ended. This time it was *"Lola Lolita la Piquetera,"* and then a Buenos Aires tango of the Thirties, *"Pregunto,"* that sent them into delirium. It was applause Carmen won only when she was at her very best. And then an inspiration came to me, a whim. I went to the pianist and made him give me his jacket. I put it on over my dress and as a joke, but with much sadness, I began to sing the love ballad of Beniamino Gigli, "*Oh begli occhi de fata*," as if it were addressed to an imaginary woman for whom I was pining. And little by little, while I was singing, that woman whom I was evoking came to me, called up by my song. At the same time I slowly took off the jacket. And while I was whispering into the microphone the last line, "*della mia gioventù cogliete il fiore*," abandoned by my lover, but now my lover was the public, who were staring at me with rapture. And I was myself once more, and with my foot I pushed away the jacket that I had let fall to the platform. And then, before the enchantment ended, rubbing the microphone on my lips, I began to sing "*Acércate más*." An indescribable thing happened. The men got up on their feet applauding, an old man in a white jacket threw me a carnation, an English officer at a table in the first row bounded up on the platform to try to kiss me and I escaped to the dressing room. I felt I was going crazy with excitement and joy. I felt a kind of shock all over my body. I shut myself inside, I panted, I looked at myself in the mirror. I was beautiful, I was young, I was happy. And then I was overtaken by a new whim. I put on the blonde wig, I put around my neck the blue feather boa, letting it drag on the floor behind me, and I returned to the platform in little elf-like steps.

First I did "*Que será será*" in the Doris Day manner, and then I attacked "*Volare*" with a chá-chá rhythm. Wiggling, I invited the public to accompany me by beating time to the rhythm with their hands. And when I sang "Vo-la-re!" a chorus answered me "Oh-oh," and I sang "Can-ta-re," and they sang "Oh-oh-oh-oh." It was like the end of the world. When I returned to the dressing room, I left surging behind me excitement and noise. I collapsed there, in Carmen's easy chair, crying with happiness, and I heard the public chant, "Name! Name!" Senhor Paiva came in, speechless, beaming, his eyes shining. "You've got to go out and tell them your name," he said. "We can't calm them down." And I went out again. The stagehand had put in a pink disc that flooded me with a warm light. I took the microphone. I had two songs that surged in my throat. I sang "*Luna rossa*" and "*All'alba se ne parte il marinaro.*" And when the long applause died away, I whispered into the microphone a name that came spontaneously to my lips. "Josephine," I said. "Josephine."

Lena, many years have passed since that night, and I have lived my life as I felt I had to live it. During my travels around the world I have often thought of writing to you and never had the courage to do it. I don't know if you have ever known what happened when we were children. Perhaps our aunt and uncle weren't able to tell you anything. There are things that cannot be told. anyway, if you already know or if you come to know, remember that Papa was not bad. Forgive him as I have forgiven him.

From here, from this hospital in this far-away city, I ask you a favor. If what I am willingly about to face should turn out badly, I beg you to claim my body. I have left precise instructions with a notary and with the Italian Embassy so that my body may be returned home. If this is the case you'll receive a sum of money sufficient to execute this and an extra sum as recompense—I've earned enough money in my life. The world is stupid, Lena, nature is vile, and I don't believe in the resurrection of the flesh. I do believe in memories, however, and therefore I am asking you this.

About two kilometers from the signal house where we spent our childhood, between the farm where Signor Quintilio worked and the town, if you take the little road between the fields that once had the sign saying "Turbines" (because it led to the suction pump for the reclaimed land), after the locks and a few hundred meters from a group of red houses, you come to a little cemetery. Mama rests there. I want to be buried next to her and to have on the tombstone a photograph (enlarged) of me when I was six years old. It's a photograph that remained with our aunt and uncle. You must have seen it many times: It's of you and me.

You are very small, a baby lying on a blanket. I am sitting beside you and holding your hand. They dressed me in a pinafore and I have curls tied with a bow. I don't want any dates. And don't have an inscription put on the stone, I beg you, only the name. But not Hector. Put the name with which I sign this letter, with the brotherly affection which binds me to you, your

Josephine

YOEL HOFFMANN

THE HEART IS KATMANDU
Translated from the Hebrew by PETER COLE

1.

At age 43, Yehoahim seldom ate cucumbers. Sights distracted him (how Ehud Vazana washes his Ford Fiesta under the poplar tree while small birds chirp over his head, et cetera).

People come and say things to him like *Erlakan. Erlakan?* He thinks, Why, that's the name of the primary substance. He lifts his blue-gray eyes (like the eyes of Prince what's-his-name in *War and Peace*) to the sky.

2.

Yesterday, for instance, he ran into Batya.

Behind her he saw the coast of Acre and the refineries and nevertheless he asked in an ordinary manner: "How are you?"

How *are you?!* (he thought later). For how might she be? The five toes of each foot (hers and mine), and together that makes twenty. . . .

Incredibly, a large mastiff crosses the street, and this (Yehoahim thinks) is the right side whereas Lilith* (who was reborn as Batya) is the left and the measure of judgment, which is devoid of mercy, although she said "Fine," and said "thank you."

3.
Batya walks up Moriah Street, whereas Yehoahim buys a paper (*HaAretz*) and casts a spell on the Discount Bank.

At the corner of Ocean Boulevard, he orders an espresso with milk, and from where he sits (from the edge of his head) a chimney opens out and his thoughts run through it like the Orient Express.

4.
It is extremely important to know *what* Yehoahim is thinking.

The mantle of the world is double. It encircles the outermost stars, and when it returns it encircles the skulls.

Sometimes (when the stars are pale before the day) the flesh is transparent. Then one can see how the organs within lean toward each other over and over. And when a person says something (Oy, for example), enormous flames of fire on the sun answer him.

It's four in the afternoon, and now the mastiff is standing where Rose of the Carmel Street begins.

Time inches along. One minute pushes up against the next, as in the workers' strike by the factory gate.

5.
German immigrants pass by the café, and also the large letter *tzaddik*.**

*Lilith—Adam's wife before Eve, a seducer of men, from whose nocturnal emissions she bears an infinite number of demonic sons.

** The eighteenth letter of the Hebrew alphabet

And because it is late afternoon, the trees' shadows are longer now. But what (Yehoahim thinks) is a shadow.

A shadow (he thinks) is like a thought. The upside-down reflection of something larger.

I (he thinks) am the shadow's shadow. And therefore he no longer cares, and says, "Hey, Itzik."

6.

Itzik holds out one of his hands (the other he keeps in reserve) and says "What's up?"

The mastiff's back is lit with a reddish glow. Cranes fly south (to warmer climes) and some of the angels over Itzik's head (his gabardine pants are held in place by a yellow belt made of suede) fly off a short distance and return, like children whose mother is calling them home for dinner.

7.

Itzik says: "Yesterday I ran into Shula" (though actually he says: These two hands I'm waving might be three).

Yehoahim says: "Didn't she get married?" (And actually he says: If the sea rose up to the edge of the mountain and everything.)

Variatzia the waitress comes and goes during this conversation, her heels clicking against the floor (*Derabbanan . . . derabbanan . . .*).*

A great wind rises up from the wadis and whistles through the end-of-the-season sales.

8.

What is suffering for? (Yehoahim thinks).

Take a roof. Take a mountain. Take a tree.

What? What?

* *"Of our rabbis" (Aramaic),* as in Kaddish Derabbanan—*the Rabbis' kaddish.*

9.
Should I assemble myself (he thinks) out of memories?

For I wasn't like that, and like that, and like that. Someone, after all, named me Yehoahim, and then said to himself: "This is Yehoahim."

Where is my father—whose name, Ephraim, I barely remember?

In some strange way he watched them moving his bed toward the last window.

10.
It turns out that birds do in fact say "chirp," Yehoahim thinks.

He tells himself the story of the dead woman: There was a woman who was born very late. Seventy years, perhaps, after she came into the world. People asked her: Where have you been all this time, et cetera.

Meanwhile, the colors of the sky are shifting, and on the table Itzik unfolds a lease.

11.
In the small room, he says, you'll be able to have guests over.

The hoopoe, Yehoahim thinks.

The lease is written out, line after line, and in all sorts of places Yehoahim needs to set down his initials.

He writes YH YH YH and between the Y and the H he places a period.

The mastiff is now standing on the other side of the street (in the world, if you like).

12.
Hallelujah!

The sun finally sets and, as though at a concert, an invisible director turns on the street lights.

Variatzia the waitress gathers the coffee cups and wipes off the table with a damp cloth.

Maybe because of the cloth, or the motion of her hand, or her fingernails, which are red, Yehoahim is suddenly filled with joy.

13.
At night, strange figures come to Yehoahim:
There's a lion, and though behind it one can see the sea, one cannot call it a sea lion.
A cook, or a woman cook. The woman who warmed his first milk.
A toy rhinoceros.
If he turned over in his sleep, he did so weightlessly, with the motion of a book lying open in a field as a gust of wind comes across it.

14.
The first foot that Yehoahim puts down onto the floor is the foot of morning (from which the sight of the window is formed, along with the sun behind it).

Edith Piaf sings *je ne regrette rien*. Yehoahim takes an umbrella out of the closet and walks from corner to corner like the chapters in a history book (Napoleon's conquests, et cetera).

15.
In the kitchen there stands a clay pot, and in it—a philodendron.
No one knows its first name, but it has a discernable shape—a leaf . . . a leaf . . . a leaf . . . a leaf. It continues today what was started yesterday.

O the sun (Yehoahim thinks), *le soleil*. The dermatologist.

16.

Suddenly, for no reason, his heart breaks.

His red heart which has seen all sorts of things—streets, candles burning in the night, countless feet—this heart gives way out of loneliness and fear.

There is no longer anything to hold on to (Yehoahim thinks) and he weeps like a jackal, or an owl, or a legendary river that sweeps along what it sweeps along, with neither purpose nor end.

17.

Now he is thinking:

I had a dog and the dog died.

I had a woman and she went away.

I have seen cadavers. The empty shell of a man, and I have heard the terrible sound lying beneath the world.

He lies in bed and counts his limbs: Ten. Two. One. In a little while (he thinks) his heart will go still.

[. . .]

70.

Because it's eleven and the sky is so sexual, he calls Batya.

The words "his mouth" and "her mouth" are extremely disturbing because they don't have the sound of a language so much as of an act, like that wringing out that occurs, at the end, in washing machines.

Nevertheless, as in a novel, when it says "he said" or "she said" they speak, but because of Oblivion it's impossible to know just what they speak of. Maybe Time (like history. For example, tomorrow at six).

71.

When he steps out of the phone booth he sees other women.

A woman who is entirely white, and it's possible to know

from the look of her thighs. An Egyptian woman who walks like a large bird. A woman upside-down, and a woman for whom the glass is broken again and again.

This walking across the earth's crust while the toenails are polished with various colors as though there had never been a tremendous explosion which, to this very day, distances the heavenly bodies with small handbags containing a mirror and rouge, and so on, and what is said like Listen, or I'm telling you, and all the while the body is made of light years (Yehoahim thinks).

(A logical question disturbs his spirit: *Within* his shoes is a person barefoot?)

72.
At night the shutter creaks in the empty room.

Yehoahim passes through his heart into what is beneath the heart: now he is dead, and he asks for a glass of water but no one hears him.

Deeper still, beneath this death, he is an infant, and beneath that infant he's an infant again but he, this infant, has nothing to grasp.

*Zeig mir, Zeig mir,** someone calls out. But what is there to show?

73.
Suddenly (at two thirty) he sees that happiness is located beneath death and the infant. Like a hanger (he thinks). Like fox fur. Like a mountain. Like aftershave. Like trousers. Like walking out through the front gate of the school. Like the burnt side of things (toast, for example).

74.
In the morning he has a dream: His father, Ephraim, comes to him, but the space of the dream is the space of touching.

* *Show me, show me (German)*

He thinks (in the dream): Dreams are airier. How could the dead be embodied in flesh?

This thought drives his father (bit by bit) from the space of the dream, and he's awakened, because the inner talk about dreams has driven him toward the Great Dream.

Here (he thinks) my wife left me, and, all morning long sea winds come from the beach at Atlit.

(Pfff! he says to himself just as the world was created.)

75.

He looks through the books he brought to the new apartment and finds a novel.

A woman is sitting in the guest room and waiting for a letter, but someone comes in and announces that the hunting dog has been hurt. The woman thinks "this is an evil omen" and looks through her desk for the forbidden letters. In the meantime, the veterinarian arrives and he, too, desires her, and through the French doors she sees that a carriage is approaching and so forth.

76.

And what (he thinks) if the carriage is carrying a letter, or the window through which one sees in the book shatters and the sound of glass comes to *these* very ears?

What passes between worlds that *here* there is pain, and there the memory of pain that took on the form of words?

Now his life, too, seems like a story, except that *here* there occur the same eruptions that take place on the surface of the sun, and he hears the sound of this burning, like the song which is of this world *alone:* "Frère Jacques."

77.

And what (he thinks) do I want?

A woman. A large woman. A very large woman who will

block out every horizon until nothing is left but a single leg in the world.

Take (he thinks) a bookbinder. He binds and binds and binds and binds, and before his death he remembers a cup of tea that he drank.

This (he thinks) is the mystery of the world. A man whose name is Buchbinder, who drinks a cup of tea. Afterward, he sucks on a lemon and adjusts the yarmulke on his head.

(In sorrow he drives the sphere of Earth.)

78.
In the morning as well it isn't too late to bring back the night, and therefore Yehoahim turns the big map over and brings Dr. Neurath back to bed.

The sound *Svetlana* is also gathered from end to beginning as though in a time tunnel, and the heart, ahh, the heart carries an entire herd of Brahman cattle into sleep.

Now Batya (today at six) enters from below, in the way that people enter dreams, and she is like a beloved for whom a Taj Mahal is built.

Someone from Revlon is distributing an essence of flowers. Woe to the god who's a traveling salesman.

79.
Between sleep and sleeplessness he pictures Batya offering him her toes like Dunkirk when the straits fill up with ships and the dress (the atmosphere we breathe in) is crumpled on the floor— a floor that exists for acts such as this—while the body (like an iceberg) rises up from the water and already on its surface there are white bears and seals and young seals clinging to their mothers and penguins who, like short philosophers, march back and forth in front of invisible desks.

[. . .]

96.
Silently, he tries out a conversation:

—Hello
—Hello

Or:
—How are you
—Fine, thanks

Or:
—Einstein
—Darwin (or Freud)

Or:
—*Please!*
—*Please!*

97.
And what (he thinks) will that place bring forth when he comes
with his white shirt and Batya sits in her batik dress at the back
of the Bank Café, by Lebanon Gate Road*?

*forms will change into the formless and everything human will turn
divine. a huge bird will hover over the street like an old battleship.*

Because loneliness strikes he lays out solitaire cards on the table,
and the numbers (one to thirteen) close in on him like the fences
of a concentration camp.

98.
Four in the afternoon, and the white shirt is already wrinkled,
but the air is filled with tiny angels known as zephyrs.
　　The shoreline is going red, and even though Friday is still far

* *a street in Haifa*

off, the voice of the muezzin, sick with longing, comes with the wind from Kabbabir.

These (Yehoahim thinks) are the legs I will lead to the Bank Café, a grasshopper like me, alas, and he cries over the sink into the stainless steel.

Something ascends through this inner fire and burns toward the ceiling: Life, which is frighteningly only for once.

99.
Like a cow he lifts up a prayer. Like a goat whose one eye is green and the other a murky white, or like an albatross, or masts of a sailboat, ahh, that once they fed him and carefully cut up a piece of bread, as his mouth was still small, and toys (like a tin duck) surrounded him as though an old man had arranged his life within hours that were sweet as sugar cane.

100.
The unbelievable: He walks step by step toward the Bank Café, in infinite space, across the crust of a star.

101.
Five to six.

On the other side of the street, Batya walks toward the Bank Café because of the fog and the down quilts people keep in the inner rooms, or their viscera. Though her beauty is external, what nourishes it comes from the dark.

By the supermarket, flesh responds to flesh, as the butcher sees her from behind the glass and the cleaver he's holding dies of love.

102.
As in the comics, one could draw a bubble over her head and write in the words "in a little while I'll see him" or "I don't know if" and so on.

She, Batya, has no interest in the sun, and therefore she brings up the moon, which, though grammatically masculine is actually feminine, in accordance with the laws of revelation and concealment.

A little while before the moon goes pale over the insurance office, windows open and shut because Batya is thinking.

[. . .]

113.

Now Yehoahim is following Batya step for step as though he were a camel and the roofs of the central Carmel were the tops of mountains at the edge of the desert. Display windows send back reflections for an instant and return to their toys' tranquility: large bottles of perfume or rows upon rows of eyeglasses. Only the moon, that member, is fat because it's the middle of the month.

114.

In front of the door to the house, Batya looks at Yehoahim for a moment and sticks the key into the keyhole.

The key fits (Yehoahim thinks). Like mountain and valley. Like light and dark. Like a kiosk and the daily paper. Like a leg and the hair along it.

She sets the key down on the table in the hall and, in the same motion, from below to above, strips off her batik dress.

Now Yehoahim can see the buttocks and spine as though he had turned into the legs of a horse.

115.

He remembers something from the *Bhagavad-Gita*. A thousand suns or something of that sort. *Tsinder, Tsinder*, he thinks. The skin is everything. And the beauty of the naked and hairy woman before him sets his heart on fire, so he will go to her, as one does when heroin goes to the head or awe comes through the great churches filled with depictions of lechery.

She undoes the buckle on the belt, and the pants fall to the floor, thank god.

116.
the naked body connects directly to the skies. as stardust it shines dimly like gold. as flesh it moves like huge waterplants.

The sound of the tapping on flesh is the sound of the one hand, for there is no longer any division between body and body, ah, this love for ourselves, like suddenly turning a light on and seeing.

[. . .]

121.
World, world, he thinks, and even though another word after this word is called for, once again he thinks only *world, world.*

Batya (*world, world*) brings out the coffee and puts it (*world, world*) by the bed.

This is love, he screams, like the man Munch painted. An entire person stoops over the bed and they call him Batya.

122.
It's raining outside now and Batya takes in the laundry: A shirt. A towel. Underwear, et cetera. Something about the sight and scent of the laundry reminds him of the Garden of Eden: Snakes went about on all fours. The sounds of a flute and a woman stretching strings, like those of a violin, between two apple trees, and hanging transparent dresses from them.

(Do you know Mira? Batya asks, as though a vase had just fallen.)

123.

Suddenly, all at once, the words *Petah Tikvah** saw through the space of the room like a cicada in August.

Or also the word *Hoffnung* and *hope*, because there are also grasshoppers that make a sound and some of them rub their hands together like merchants at the diamond exchange.

This, Batya thinks, is love, and her down quilt is torn clouds.

[. . .]

131.

"Hey," says Batya (where she should have said "Listen," and therefore his heart goes out to her) . . . "Hey," she says, and Yehoahim almost shouts "I hear you," as the children of Israel shouted at the foot of the mountain and took it upon themselves to observe the entire Torah, and he, too, wants to observe the commandments (for example, the commandment regarding good morning when rising to brush one's teeth after she comes out of the bathroom) like an extremely religious person who follows the scent of the toast and coffee into the kitchen that they call Mecca.

132.

Things happen, like the water dripping from the broken faucet. Gestures. A gust of air. Thoughts. A bird or the shadow of a bird. Books, and Heaven help us.

Yehoahim utters his name (silently) in order not to lose it, and Batya does something internal that cannot be disclosed.

---

* *a city near Tel Aviv—literally, The Gateway to Hope (Hebrew)*

133.

How, they're thinking like a Greek chorus, how can we bring this love into the world? Sometimes, after all, one drags one's feet and looks for aspirin or an eye is swollen (they think together) or the soul wants to be elsewhere . . .

It's already 9:00, and, as on one's birthday when an extra candle is lit for the coming year, they clasp hands, their fingers meshing (ten altogether), and each finger meets in the other's hand another one like it, like two women sitting at a café and reminiscing about Bucharest.

134.

Stay a little longer, Batya says.

Munch's mother is on the wall, beneath her a glass fawn that someone blew in Venice. The palm being held is warmer than the other, like the lit side of the earth, and time is being formed (despite what Einstein thought) from rest.

The two of them recall other loves, and the heart, thank god, beats with the other's, like going together to a museum and stopping, now here, now there.

135.

My wife left me, Yehoahim says.

He sees the empty house and Nitza-the-closet but now the pain has grown dull, as though it were coming from the other side of the wall.

Batya runs the fingers of her free hand over Yehoahim's chin, and makes the sound of a B-flat.

(Imagine, for a moment, the death of God. That great body ceases to breathe and nevertheless we're all within it.)

[. . .]

137.
Two (he says to himself) two, two . . . what good is it all and
we're still two?

He goes back to the place where it all began, before he was
born and before the birth of the world. Before there were even
the silhouettes of mountains, and how is it possible to cut
through something that's empty?

What brought about (he thinks) all this multiplicity, so that
in the end a man walks along, his name (Rosenberg) clinging to
him as though there were no world at all?

138.
Suddenly (what do you mean, suddenly? at a quarter to ten)
Batya says I love you, and a tremendous happiness fills his heart.

Now he understands the great mystery: everything is split in
appearance only, and he can contain even Munch's mother.

139.
Also (he thinks) inside the eye. And also inside the liver. And on
newsprint. In granola and yogurt too. And in gardens. And beyond gardens, in lightning and flashes during the night. And in
endless darkness when one exits the galaxy and not even the
sight of a star exists and one remembers only a single toy (a dog-
gie doll, or cat).

140.
Take a word (Yehoahim says to himself). Take a word like son,
thy son, thine only son, in that scene where Abraham drew the
knife like "yes" or "let there be," or like "Jehovah," just so long
as you don't make a mistake, for if you make a mistake creation
will take everything back, as when one regrets a momentous act
and reverts to no-thing. I can't afford to make a mistake, he
thinks to himself, and, therefore, his lips mouth the only word
that holds all of these worlds: Batya.

141.

Batya removes the earring from her right ear. The silver gives me an infection, she says. The desk lamp shines on the roots of her hair, and Yehoahim sees that some are white.

Ever since I saw you, she says, last year, I've hoped that you would call me.

What a peculiar word, Yehoahim thinks, hoped, hoped. I hoped too, he says, but doesn't know what.

142.

All my life, Batya says, I've looked for someone who would understand this. Now she takes off the other earring, and Yehoahim sees the hole in the lobe.

Things are distant, he thinks, truly distant. Like lights you see from within a train and you know that people are eating dinner out there, but *you* will never know this.

[. . .]

144.

This, then, is happiness, he thinks. And as a result his heart breaks in folds like a mountain when the lava rises. Like the splinters of chairs on a café patio after a bomb has gone off, now half of him is dead and the other half is looking at death. He realizes that he has to go, but his feet are very cold, like Socrates' when the poison had gone halfway through him.

I'm going out on the balcony, Batya says, and he sees her go out to a place where there isn't any balcony, and there she stands, three stories up in the air over the sidewalk.

145.

Yehoahim puts on the clothes he'd put on the chair, shirt and pants, and Munch's mother stares at him from the wall.

On the counter he sees a letter, and since the paper is crumpled up, he reads only "I also saw the Grand Canyon and believe me . . ." (and he sees a woman standing at the edge of the huge canyon).

Suddenly he is thirsty, but Batya's on the balcony and it's dark in the kitchen and the spirit of God is hovering over the face of the waters.

146.
At ten-thirty Yehoahim drinks lemonade and Batya wraps—in white paper—a tomato and a cucumber that he needs for breakfast.

All theories (he thinks to himself) of creation can be refuted, for space itself was created from a kitchen table, and time—from the motion of two hands.

Do you want some olives? she asks, and something in his soul cries out: Yes! Yes! Yes! Yes!

147.
Now, as in a novel being written by a woman writer from Finland who was stricken with polio, Yehoahim stands at the door, holding a paper bag in one hand and an umbrella in the other.

Of all possible questions, Batya chooses to ask: "Will I see you tomorrow?"

You'll see . . . Yehoahim thinks. Rays of light will strike me, be broken, and progress in a straight and broken line toward the two lenses you're carrying inside your eyes. The image of light will rise like an electric current toward your head and *there* you'll see me, deep within.

148.
In the stairwell Yehoahim notices graffiti. Someone has written "God is hairy," and through the latticework on the first floor he sees a strip of sky full of stars.

The stars . . . he thinks, but his thoughts reverse themselves, in the way one turns a coat inside out, and now it's the stars that are thinking.

Man (they think) is only a kind of chop meat, and, nevertheless, at times, he says things like: "Where are you, Eurydice?"

[. . .]

KONO TAEKO

BONE MEAT

Translated from the Japanese by LUCY LOWER

It was last fall, but the woman could not seem to take it into her head to dispose of the belongings the man had left behind when he deserted her.

A day or two before, it had been raining. Four or five days later she noticed his umbrella and her own lying by the window. She had no recollection of putting the umbrellas there, so perhaps the man had done it. In her panic over being deserted, however, perhaps she had forgotten what she herself had done. She opened them, and found they had dried completely. The woman carefully adjusted the folds of each, wound around the strap, and hooked the metal ring over the button. But after standing her own umbrella in the umbrella rack inside the shoe cupboard, she wrapped the man's umbrella in paper, along with another of his she had found there, tied them up with a string, and put them away in the closet.

It was, perhaps, around the same time that she threw away the man's toothbrush. One morning, as she was about to pick up her own toothbrush, her eyes fell on his lying beside it. The bristles at the end of the transparent, light-blue handle were bent outward from hard use. Once, he had come home with an assortment of six toothbrushes for the two of them which he had bought on sale. She also recalled having bought them toothbrushes two or three times. Whether the toothbrush that remained was one of the six the man had bought, she didn't know. But as she picked it up she remembered his purchase and, seeking an excuse for discarding it in the painfully worn-out bristles, dropped it in the wastebasket. Next, she threw in three or four old blades from his safety razor. She also removed the blade still clamped in the razor, on which were hardened bits of soap mixed with the man's whiskers, and discarded it. But the razor she wrapped in his dry towel, together with several small boxes of unused blades, and put them away in his underwear drawer.

That drawer was the top one in the woman's wardrobe. Previously, the man's clothes had hung inside together with hers, but before leaving he had collected them quickly. However, the woman later noticed a faded gray lizard-skin belt which he no longer wore, and that too she put in his underwear drawer.

There were other things of his that ought to have been put away. Two or three of his shirts were probably at the laundry, and she intended to go pick them up and put them in the drawer too, though she hadn't done it yet. She couldn't imagine he had gone to get them. . . . Atop the wardrobe lay his four clothing boxes, a couple of which seemed full; she put them in the closet in place of her own.

The man's pillow stayed where it was for quite some time. Each night when the woman laid out the quilts, she first took the man's pillow out of the bedding closet, holding it by the opening of its oversized pillowcase, and put it back when she had finished taking out the quilts. And in the morning when she put the quilts away, she took it out once again. This continued for several weeks before it occurred to her to pack it away. She washed the case and set the pillow in the winter sun, choosing as bright a day as possible; then, replacing it in its cover and putting it into a nylon bag, she laid it on top of the man's clothing boxes in the closet.

The woman knew perfectly well that the man would not be

back. How many times had she been unable to refrain from saying things like "I'd be better off without you!" and meaning them. And one day when she had again been unable to restrain herself, the man had replied "So it seems, doesn't it?" and left. The remorse she felt afterward had been painful. She acutely regretted having become accustomed to speaking in that way, and having said those words once again the day the man took her up on them. But what made it so painful, in retrospect, was that she had no right to regret, considering the man's attitude for some time past as well as his adroitness in taking advantage of her words. And the pain drained her of the energy to pursue him.

The woman no longer wanted even to ask the man to come pick up his things. His reply was certain to be: "Do whatever you like with them." And, in fact, perhaps what he had left there he cared nothing about. As their relationship had begun to deepen and he stayed at her place for long intervals, he had little by little brought over personal things he needed. But even after he was virtually living with her, he didn't move out of his own lodgings, where he must have still had a dresser and a desk, several boxes of clothing, ski equipment, and bedding. He had taken away the everyday clothing he had kept for convenience in her wardrobe; furthermore, it seemed that he was rising to a higher position at work. Surely he felt no attachment to the worn-out things he had left behind.

The woman, however, was at a complete loss as to how to dispose of them. Aside from putting them away, she simply could not decide what to do with the objects the man had left lying about. If she called him to come for them, it would be equally disagreeable whether he told her to throw them out or said: "Are they still there? Well, just send them over." Even if someone else would see to it, getting in touch with the man like that was itself distasteful. Yet it was also disagreeable to take it upon oneself to throw away someone else's belongings—still quite useful things—or to have them carted off by a junk dealer. Besides, she couldn't give these things, which the man had abandoned along with herself, to someone else.

She regretted she had not had him take all of his belongings when he left. She regretted it with all her heart.

The first hints that the man was beginning to think of a life in which she had no part appeared even before his work took a turn for the better. His decision to abandon her had been reflected in both his private and public aspects; even the clothing he wore was all newly made. She felt the sympathy of a fellow-sufferer for the old clothes that he took no more notice of, and yet felt scorned by the very things she tried to pity. And thus the woman found even more unbearable these troublesome leftover belongings.

She had several times considered taking the man's underwear, which filled the top drawer of the wardrobe, and his woolen clothes that lay mixed with her own in the tea chest on the lower shelf in the closet, and making a single bundle of them, but the mere thought of it made her feel weary and feverish. If one were to open them and look, there might also be just enough room to put the man's underwear and woolen clothing in his suitcase which was on the tea chest, or in the four clothing boxes that she had put in place of her own on top of her suitcase on the upper shelf. The man's rucksack and canvas shoes, also on the upper shelf, might well fit into one of these too. But she didn't feel like opening any of them. She always felt that the things the man had left weighed upon her.

She was terribly envious when she thought of the man's delight as he abandoned her and his belongings with the single comment "So it seems." She had decided that the best method of dealing with the perplexing problem of the man's belongings was herself to abandon them entirely, along with her own, and move to a new place. But she didn't have the money to move to a new place or to buy all the necessary things for it. Although the woman would have liked to abandon it all, she could not, and even her own belongings and the place itself became repugnant to her.

The woman could only trust that circumstances would arise in which her lack of money presented no obstacle. She felt she would like to burn it all—the man's things, and her own, and the place. If she too were to burn up with them, she thought, so much the better. But she merely hoped for it, and made no plans. Strangely, for a woman who wanted even herself to be destroyed in the conflagration, she was inclined to be wary of fire. She always recalled one late winter night in her childhood, when there was a fire close by and she saw an old man from the burning building, with a padded jacket slipped on over his flannel nightshirt, being swept along in the crowd, barefoot on the asphalt where water streamed from the fire hoses.

Now she was even more careful. She was tortured by the fear that if she were to start a fire accidentally it would seem like arson. When she went out, especially, she felt she had to check for fire hazards two or three times, all the more so if she was in a hurry. Once, after she had locked the door and taken a few steps, she suddenly became uneasy. Unlocking the door and reentering, she checked the outlets and gas jets. She held an already wetted ashtray under the faucet in the kitchen and ran more water in it until the ashes floated. Reassured, she went out, but she hesitated as she was about to drop the key into her handbag. She couldn't help recalling an impression she had had just now. When she picked up the ashtray she had been reminded of how she had smoked half a pack of cigarettes the man had left behind. Ordinarily, the woman smoked only her own brand. When she ran out, even if the man had some, she found it unsatisfying to make do with a brand not her own, and she would take the trouble to go and buy some. However, the day the man left, or perhaps the next day, when her cigarettes ran out, she was so distressed that she did not want to go. Her eyes fell on the half-empty pack the man had left, and in her agitation she thought, Oh good—any brand, as long as there are cigarettes. All that the woman had disposed of among the things the man had left behind was the discarded toothbrush, the old razor blades, and the cigarettes. A moment before, when she had held the ashtray in her hands, she had the dreamlike feeling that everything would, happily, burn to ashes like the cigarettes. She felt then, suddenly, that when she had first locked the door she had already taken care of all possible fire hazards. Having gone out a second time, she found herself worrying that she might now have unthinkingly contributed to an outbreak of fire. And again she had to use her key.

Winter was almost over, and from time to time a springlike sun shone. The woman recalled how, last year about the same time on just such an afternoon, she and the man had gone out together. Where they had gone and with what purpose, she had forgotten, but she retained a vivid impression of the window of a shop where they had stopped to buy bread on the way home, and of various sorts of bread in steam-clouded cellophane wrappers.

As she waited for her bread, the woman looked again at the loaves heaped in the window and noticed a glass case next to them. In it were a number of whole chickens glowing in an electric rotisserie, roasting as they revolved. She took the bread and, glancing around at the man, moved toward them.

"Are you going to buy some?" the man said.

"I thought I might," she replied.

"Are the ones here good?"

"Hmm, I've never bought any from here before. . . ."

Inside the glass case each row of four chickens, richly glazed, rose, turned, and sank back down. As they rose again, with hardly a trace of the severed necks, they seemed to be lifting their wings high. The row of plump breasts rose, then began dropping out of sight, and the bones that peeped out from the fat legs as they rose made the chickens appear to be falling prostrate, palms up, withdrawing in shame.

The woman stood waiting for the man to speak and watched the movement of the chickens. The man, too, seemed to be watching them and said, finally: "Would you mind not buying any? Lately they're fattening chickens with female hormones. It seems a man shouldn't eat too much of it."

The woman wondered if he weren't thinking of American chickens. She had been present when one of his friends, home from the United States, had spoken about cooking for himself there. He said that he had often bought small fried shrimp that were sold cheaply at the market, and salted and ate them. He had often bought halves of roast chicken cheaply too. "They weren't so tasty, though. They're fattened with hormone injections," he had said, pantomiming an injection. The woman didn't remember for certain whether he had said simply "hormones" or "female hormones," nor did she know whether Japanese chickens were so treated or not, but she wondered if the man weren't misremembering that comment. She didn't say anything, though. She realized she could hardly claim they didn't often have roast chicken.

"I see. Well, shall we have oysters? On the half-shell?" Although that too they certainly had often enough.

"Yeah, that would be better," the man agreed this time.

They went into a department store. What with the heat from the steam that clouded the inside of the bread's cellophane wrapper, and the store's intemperate heating system, the woman breathed a sigh of relief when she stood before the cool abalone-filled glass water tank of the shellfish stall in the basement. Pointing to the oysters in the glass case next to it, where frost had crystallized on the horizontal bars, she asked for ten of them. The clerk picked out ten of the larger ones and put them in a short, wide oilpaper sack, and then on a rear table wrapped it up in two sheets of paper. As she took the parcel, the woman could feel the same bulk and weight as always.

She had become skilled at opening the oyster shells. In the beginning the man had opened them, and she had enjoyed watching him do it. But he relied on strength alone to break open the shells, always leaving their contents in a sorry state, so the woman learned from someone else and undertook the task herself. With the rounded side down and the hinge toward her, she held one firmly on the cutting board, tilted at an angle away from her. The brownish color and rippled surface merged so that it was hard to tell the seam from the shell. Searching for the point near the middle of the edge where the inside of the shell peeked through, or, if she couldn't find it, somewhere in that area, she inserted the knife forcefully, blade turned outward, taking care not to damage the oyster, then turned the blade sideways, slipped another small knife between the shells, and with the tip of that blade scraped downward, cutting the hinge. Then the top shell would loosen abruptly and she would catch a whiff of the seashore. But if the top shell had not been cut loose completely she once again turned the blade in the opposite direction and sawed upward. That usually did the trick.

That evening, too, the woman opened the oyster shells in this way and laid them on a plate of ice cubes. She added lemon wedges and carried it to the table.

"Go ahead and have some," the man said, taking one from the center of the large plate, dropping it with a clatter on the small plate before him, and trickling lemon juice over it.

"Mm," she replied, but did not reach for one.

"No, really," the man continued, lifting the edge of the oyster he was about to eat with his fruit fork.

"Mm," she again replied, but took pleasure in not reaching for one.

She watched the man's hand, clenched so tightly around the fruit fork that it appeared even more delicate, as he maneuvered it right and left, trying to cut loose the hinge muscle. He seemed to have done it neatly. As he lifted the oyster to his mouth, seaweed still clinging to its shell, he worked it slightly with his fork and the sound carried the smell, taste and freshness of the seashore.

"Is it good?" the woman asked. The man nodded, laid aside the shell, and with the same hand took another from atop the ice on the large plate. He placed it on his small plate and the woman squeezed lemon juice over it.

When he had progressed to his third and laid the shell on the table, the woman transferred one of the shells he had discarded to her own plate.

"Have some of these," said the man, indicating the large plate.

At this, she took even greater pleasure in not doing so, and instead scraped with her fork at the bit of muscle left by the man. At last she got a tiny piece of white meat on the tip of her fork, and rubbed it against her lips. She liked to hold the morsel of meat pressed firmly to her lips and feel her tongue become instantly aroused with the desire to have its turn. The hinge muscle lay in a slight hollow of the shell, and she had still not taken quite all of the meat the man had left there. She again moved her fork toward it, urged on by lips and tongue that had already finished off the first piece. As her hand holding the fork responded violently to the impatience of the urging, she found herself struggling with the bit of meat. This made it that much more difficult to get loose; once loosened, more difficult to get hold of; and when at last she lifted it to her lips, her hand trembled. Holding both her fork and the empty shell aloft in her hands, she savored the eager rivalry of her lips and tongue for the meat.

The woman did not yet lay aside the shell. All that was left of the oyster was a brownish arc in low relief, where some flesh was still attached. She sliced at it with her fork and, bringing the shell to her mouth, tipped it up. The woman felt that all the parts of her mouth were contending for the taste, the smell, the freshness of the seashore. So it seemed, from the intensity of the rivalry in there. But it also felt to her as if all of these many parts stirred simultaneously with the pleasure of gratification. Before her, she could see nothing but the glistening inside of the shell, with its matchless white, pale purple and blue, and yellow. All the parts of her mouth reverberated at once with pleasure when she put that last brownish ridge of meat to her lips, because it seemed that this fresh glistening flowed in, too, with a rush.

"Ah, that's good," the woman sighed, at last putting down the shell.

"That's because you're only eating the best part," the man said.

"True. . . ." Nodding emphatically, she took the next shell that lay beside the man's plate.

"Shall I give you one?" the man suggested after a few minutes, speaking of the oysters on the bed of ice. "Or maybe I'd better not."

"Let me have just one," the woman said, holding her fork in one hand and a shell with a bit of meat attached in the other.

"For you, that'll be plenty." He pointed to the shell in her hand.

"Don't say that—please give me one," she said.

The man quickly picked one off the ice and laid it with a clack on the small plate in front of her.

"Try it and see," he said. The woman, with this departure from the usual order of things, felt somewhat at a loss. He went on: "They don't seem to be as good as usual. I was hungry, so at first I didn't realize it."

The woman put down the shell she was holding and, cutting loose the oyster the man had laid on her plate, she sucked it from its shell. In an instant the entire cold, slippery thing slid through her mouth that had leapt so at just the tiny morsel of meat.

"How is it?" the man asked.

"Well, I can't really tell," she replied. What she could tell was that it was not nearly so good as the taste of the hinge muscle scraped from the empty shell or the other bit of meat that had given her such ecstasy. And it seemed distinctly inferior to the flavor, the smell, the freshness of the seashore called up in her mind by the voluptuous sound the man made when he raised the shell to his lips and sucked out the oyster. Even the flavor evoked by that sound amounted to little more than imagining a long-past and much-faded sensation. For the woman, the whole raw oyster always tasted the same. She could by no means tell by tasting one whether tonight's oysters were as good as usual.

"They don't seem quite so good to me," the man said.

The woman noticed that it was unusually bright and sunny for a winter's day. "Are they diseased, I wonder?"

"No, you could tell right away. The taste is completely different."

The man took another from the large plate. He loosened the oyster, but did not squeeze lemon over it; picking it up in its shell, he raised it to his mouth with an air of examination.

"Maybe it's just me. They look all right, don't they?" he said. He laid one from the large plate on the woman's plate and one on his own. There remained one more on the large plate. When she had finished hers, the woman ate that one too.

She gathered the empty shells on the large plate of melting ice and carried it to the drainboard. She washed the knife she had used in the preparation, put it in the dish drain, and picked up the cutting board from where she had left it. As she was rubbing it clean under running water at the faucet, something broad and sharp pricked her palm. She shut off the water and felt the board to see what it was, then took the board to the man.

"Look here," She took his wrist and placed the palm of his hand on the board. He withdrew it immediately.

"What happened? It's so rough," he said, touching it again lightly with his fingertips.

"This is where I opened the oysters. When I stick the knife in hard, the edges on the bottom are crushed and cut into it. It always happens." The woman spoke as though in a dream. It did happen every time, but for once, instead of smoothing it with pumice as usual, she couldn't resist bringing it to show him, because she felt dissatisfied that the scene they always played when they ate oysters on the half-shell had not been followed. The man took her hand and stroked it. She wished she might feel that on another part of her body.

"Do you think it's all right?" she asked.

"It's a cutting board. So it can't help getting bloody sometimes."

That evening, however, which ended without the usual fulfillment of the scene she associated with the taste, was the last time they ate oysters together. Before too many more days passed, spring was upon them and the raw-oyster season was over. The summer passed and autumn came, and by the time the air again began to turn cold, the man had already left.

This year as the days turned more and more springlike, the woman had grown very thin, The man's belongings, as always, remained with her. To him they were invisible, but they weighed upon her whenever she was at home. These troublesome belongings of his, and her own which for lack of money she could not abandon, and the place, became all the more unbearable to her, and she frequently saw herself being swept along the crowded late-night street flooded by the fire hoses, barefoot, with something thrown quickly over her nightgown.

It was about this time that the man's stored belongings, which weighed so on her conscious mind, gradually began to obtrude on her vision. It was as though the top drawer in the wardrobe had changed into some semitransparent material, so that the man's underwear within it shone white and what seemed to be his socks shone black. Little gauze-covered windows appeared here and there in the thick paper sliding doors of the closet, and the bulky shapes of his suitcase, the umbrella package, his clothing boxes, his rucksack, and his pillow showed through. From within one of the drawers he had used in the desk, too, a plastic box began to be visible.

The woman herself thought that she must be terribly weak. At meals, she must try to eat as much as possible. She must gain some weight. She must get stronger. If she didn't, perhaps the wardrobe drawer, the closet door, and the drawer in the desk would turn to glass. Perhaps too the man's suitcase and clothing boxes would become glass cases, and his rucksack and canvas shoes would become like the nylon pillow cover, or a cellophane bag. At this rate, she might very well find herself being swept along barefoot in the night in the crowded street flooded by water from the fire hoses, with only something slipped on over her nightgown. It might happen, she thought, if she didn't eat a lot at mealtimes and recovered from this weakness.

But when she tried to carry out her resolution, the woman realized that she ate even less. It had always been a peculiarity of hers that when she was excited—pleasantly or unpleasantly—she would become strangely hungry. She seemed to give way to the excitement and gorge herself whenever she had been aggravated into saying "I'd be better off without you!" and meaning it, and especially during her agitation after the man left her. But she had by now lost the energy and the momentum of the excitement, and her appetite no longer asserted itself even in that form. No matter what was set before her, after one or two bites she could not proceed.

Since girlhood, the woman had hardly been what could be described as plump. However, from about the time the man began gradually bringing in his personal belongings, she had started to gain a little weight.

Their tastes concurred, and they both liked dishes with bones or with shells. The woman was poor, and the man's prospects, up until about the time he abandoned her, had not looked good, so in order to serve such dishes often, they had to economize on their other meals. Even so, it was mostly the bones or shells which went to the woman. But although she seldom ate richly, she began to gain weight.

The woman recalled this odd phenomenon as not odd in the least. The man would attack a boiled tuna tail avidly and set the plates rattling, and although the woman called what little was left a "bone-tail," the flavor that could be drawn from each hollow in it made her want to exclaim: "Are there such flavors in this world!" Likewise, the sight of the scarlet-wrapped slender morsel of flesh bursting from the single lobster claw granted her made her want to sigh. All those varied bone and shell dishes began to give her the feeling that a sense of taste had been awakened throughout her body; that all her senses had become so concentrated in her sense of taste that it was difficult for her even to move. And when she awoke the next morning, she felt her body brimming with a new vitality. It would have been odd had she *not* gained weight.

Even after she had noticed a change in the man's behavior and had become critical of him (though not yet to the point of being unable to refrain from saying "I'd be better off without you!"), the two of them continued tao enjoy these dishes with bones or shells. Whether because of that or because their relationship had not yet deteriorated too badly, she continued to gain weight.

The day the man had said that males probably shouldn't eat too much chicken, she had deffered to him, although afterward he still brought home roast chicken any number of times. In the intervals between roast chickens, the woman sometimes fixed boiled tuna tail as before, or bought the head of a coastal sea bream and boiled it. Because of the season, that night was the last time they had oysters on the half-shell, but during the summer they often ate abalone. The man liked the whole abalone, and seemed to enjoy begrudging the woman the least morsel. For her part, she took intense pleasure in savoring the meager flavors of the big shell itself.

The woman had never been critical of him when they had dishes with bones or shells, because at those times he never made her anxious or brought her troubles to mind. He coveted meat even more fiercely than before, and she even more wholeheartedly savored the tiny bits of bone meat. They were a single organism, a union of objectively different parts, immersed in a dream. Sometimes both would sigh simultaneously from the excess of flavor, and then laugh so much that they had to put down the food they were holding.

The woman, now grown thin, realized that she longed only for the taste of those dishes. It was not only herself and his belongings that the man had deserted, but that taste as well. However, her sense of taste did not yet seem to understand that it had been abandoned. When she ordered one of the old dishes with bones or shells and something else was brought out, she rejected it at once, saying "No, not that!" The woman began to wonder if this weren't how a mother, abandoned with a young child by her husband, must feel. And like the mother, she now took pity on the young child's unreasonableness, now scolded it, at times hugged the still uncomprehending child and cried; she even thought of killing the child and then committing suicide. Once, at her wit's end with the unreasonableness of her own sense of taste, she raptly imagined the man to be standing just beyond the grillwork partition devouring a chicken thigh, then tearing the stripped bones apart at the joint and throwing the pieces in to her, so that suddenly she felt she heard the sound as it hit the floor. If she could be sure that she would be able to share it, she thought, she wouldn't mind being swept along the crowded asphalt street barefoot where water streamed from the fire hoses, with only something slipped over her nightgown. Then, becoming aware of the semitransparent top drawer of the wardrobe, she stared at it, trembling. She lacked the courage to look around at the desk drawer, which of course must have become transparent, or at the little gauze-covered windows that must have appeared here and there in the thick paper doors.

"You going to burn this?" The voice seemed to belong to one of the children in front of the large cooperative trash incinerator.

"Yes, I am."

"Give it to me!"

"I can't do that, I have to burn it. Throw it in, please. I'll buy you an even fatter red pencil. That's right—that's the way."

"Are you going to burn the clothing box?"

"The box? Yes, I am."

"Shall we help you?"

"Well, thank you. But you mustn't open it. I don't want the contents to get scattered around. Just burn it that way."

"OK. Everything in here can burn, huh?"

"Yes. Can you burn these up for me? I have a lot to bring over here."

"Bring all you want."

"That's great."

"Shall we help you carry it over?"

"Would you mind?"

"Of course not."

The words echoed pleasantly in her ears. It was an exhilarating feeling. Tomorrow when she awoke, she would no longer be troubled by anxiety over the semitransparent drawer or all the little gauze-covered windows in the thick paper doors, or whether they might be getting even worse. It was months since the woman had felt calm, and so exhilarated; the thought put her completely at ease.

Just then, there was a knock at the door.

"Aren't you the one who used the incinerator today?"

The woman realized that she hadn't checked on how the

schoolchildren who had helped her had left things, but she knew it was part of the dream, so it was all right. Trying to keep from awakening and interrupting her dream, she kept her eyes shut, the quilt pulled up around her head, as she rose and went to the door.

"Won't the people who use it later have a hard time? Leaving a mountain of bones that way. We're supposed to clear out what's left unburned. Why, there are oyster shells alone to fill a bucket."

To fill a bucket—what fraction of the oysters they had eaten together would that be? But there weren't very many from that last time, so when might these shells be from?

The siren of a fire engine wailed somewhere continuously. But what caused her dream to recede was less the siren than the words she had just heard in her dream. From the ashes of the man's belongings, that there should be so many bones and shells! "Is that so? Is that so?" she said nodding, and the siren, to which was added a furiously ringing bell, filled her ears. Was what she had been told in the dream perhaps prophetic? The bell stopped, and just then the siren arrived blaring under her window. But the woman, her eyes closed, nodding "Is that so? Is that so?" simply snuggled deeper into the quilt as it seemed to begin to smolder.

INGER CHRISTENSEN

from AZORNO

Translated from the Danish by DENISE NEWMAN

I've learned that I'm the woman he meets on page eight.

It was Azorno who told me. Come to think of it, I've never dared to ask him why he's called Azorno.

We were supposed to meet just to the right of the main entrance, under those big trees, where people waiting won't get in anyone's way. I was wearing a white hat, and when I went in through the turnstile everything fell completely silent.

The man waiting for me wasn't Azorno.

In a split second my blood, my thoughts, nerves, and senses were swept back ten years and I think I felt like a diver who finds himself at the bottom of the ocean one minute and on solid ground the next unable to hear whether the others are saying he is dead or alive because he's encapsulated in a silence as vast as if he'd brought the ocean up with him and it surrounds him now like a huge bell which no one could pass through without drowning.

The next second was very painful, or rather I felt it as pain. I wanted to avoid meeting the past, and so I turned quickly and tried to get out the way I'd entered, through the turnstile, but of course it only turns one way which it did right then. Azorno came whirling through, grabbed me and swung me around, laughing. Then we walked on into the gardens with our arms around each other.

And I saw that there was no longer anyone under the big trees whose shadows peacefully slid over and passed us while Azorno spoke about the imagery of certain artists, about water and waterlilies, parasols and white clouds and fabrics, a wealth of the kind of luminous, tangible things that are supposed to evoke the intangible, and which now suddenly had assembled in one specific place in the world, resting around me like a bell, Azorno said, a silence.

By this time we had come to the wide tulip beds. Do you know Azorno? I can't recall if I've seen you together, but of course you could have met each other in places I don't go.

All the tulip plants were the same pale green, but the groupings had faint suggestions of other colors as well, and I understood that they would bloom in a specific pattern according to the vision of the landscape gardener, the vision he must have had one cold winter's day when Tivoli was covered with snow.

While I chatted about the flowers, the weather and the long winter, Azorno had begun, without my noticing, to tell me about Sampel's new novel. I calmly continued to speak about the way tulips grow, for no one, not even Azorno, could deny that to retell a novel seems like gossiping about other people's private lives. Anyway, the book is supposed to be excellent. Have you ever read Sampel?

I think I'd been telling about a bouquet of multicolored tulips that Katarina once gave me, when suddenly we both became silent, and we kept walking down past the lake and all the way around it, until we came back to the tulip beds, where we sat down at a table and ordered two Dubonnets.

I was a little sorry that we hadn't spoken about the lake. It was the same pale green as the tulips, but it wasn't from the reflection of the trees since they hadn't come into leaf yet, and it wasn't from the sky either, since of course that was blue.

Azorno began talking about Sampel's novel again and eventually I realized that he was serious, because he took my hand, and while he was playing with it a little awkwardly, maybe with a slightly studied awkwardness, he slowly revealed that he had wanted to meet me here to tell me that a couple of days ago he learned that I was the woman who the main character in Sampel's novel first meets on page eight.

After reading these two typewritten pages, I had to slide them back quickly under the many papers spread over the writing table that all, whether written on or not, lay blank side up. I heard footsteps in the long tiled gallery, heard Randi scold the dog in German, and heard with increasing clarity the squeaking castors under the heavy tea cart, which was so heavy that it really needed two people to push it from the kitchen down through the gallery to the different rooms. Still, Randi used it every day.

I opened the door and right away the dog began chewing on the raised threshold. Randi gave the dog, named Goethe, a cookie and he immediately ran in and sat in the big blue armchair.

I understood that this was a trick that they enjoyed, and I smiled.

So this was the sunroom I'd heard so much about.

This was where Randi had tea every afternoon with Goethe, or with Goethe and others, as today with Goethe and me, or maybe the other day or last year with Goethe and Azorno.

All the way down through Germany I'd been longing for the sunroom that I'd heard so much about.

It proved a remarkable answer to my expectations: sure enough there were seven very high windows, three in the south wall that stretched the width of the house, with, by the way, Lake Zurich immersed in the landscape far below; two to the west, overlooking lower-lying houses with their parks, gardens, groves, and small ponds or pools, and one to the east with an unobstructed view of blue mountains floating in the distance.

I had now firmly resolved to find out the truth about the letter or that part of the letter that I'd just read and on which we now turned our backs while we drank tea.

Finally, there was a window to the north since the house was a

little wider in the corner between the gallery and the sunroom—
the sunroom that I'd heard so much about first and foremost because of this very window to the north.

Because of its design this room could catch sunlight from the
earliest to the latest hours, even on the longest and lightest summer day.

It had rained the whole way down through Germany and it
was still raining. The windows to the north and west were
nearly black with rain, and those to the south and east grew
steadily grayer with rain.

Even so, the sunroom shone with such a radiance that it dissolved all my longings into perfect calm.

I have to mention right away that the darkest spot in the room
was the blue armchair with Goethe, but this was also the only
dark spot. Everything else was dazzling, and if it had any color, it
was of the same color as the tulip beds before they came into
bloom, a pale green. By the way, I think the furniture was made of
ivory. But of course it might have been just painted white.

These observations may seem superficial, like a set of paren-
theses in the previously mentioned perfect calm, which I still
must have looked as if I were enjoying, but at the same time,
they may also be understood as a deep and irritating development, a kind of itch arising precisely in response to the very per-
fection of the calm.

When I looked at Goethe I had to admit he was smiling.

And how that dog could smile!

In fact, it may not even have been the sunroom that was having such a strong effect. That strong effect was certainly something we have all experienced before and in very different places.
And that's why this dog in the blue armchair could sit there boldly
sharing his anxious awareness that perfect calm brings always a
painful silence.

—The sunroom has always made a strong impression on
everyone, Randi said; the dog barked and I took a cookie, and
managed to say that I had read the letter.

—As we always did in the old days, I added, smiling while
the rain whizzed in my ears.

—What letter?

—Well, that's what I wanted to ask. Who is the letter from, or is it one that you're writing?

Randi had stood up.

—It's about Azorno, I said.

Randi leafed through the papers on the desk.

—I didn't write it, she said then.

—I know Azorno very well, I said.

—Possibly in the same way I know Sampel, said Randi.

Goethe barked. Randi gave him a cookie, and he jumped up on my lap and stretched his muzzle down the length of my thighs. I settled beneath him and looked welcoming.

Actually, it didn't matter which of us knew Azorno and which of us knew Sampel. But it of course would be very interesting if the letter were from the author himself, since then it would be all about an author's close relationship to his two main characters.

—It's from Xenia. Randi let the letter slide back among the many sheets of paper that were spread over the writing table.

—I don't think I know her.

And then Randi told me all about Xenia.

It grew into a very long and also a very sad story which I am completely incapable of retelling, mainly because I have to object to Randi's way of presenting it. She didn't speak of Xenia, but about Xenia's approach to life.

The sunset ended somewhere far beyond the rain and the mountains, and the sunroom appeared more and more radiant. By the way, I don't think Randi was even trying to get close to the truth, if for a moment I consider the truth to be the factual circumstances.

The end of the whole story was the frightening revelation that the story itself was precisely the cause of my having been asked to drive as fast as possible down through Germany, because Randi, on account of this whole story etc., needed me, etc., etc.

—What do you mean? I asked.

—Well, said Randi, I wanted to ask you to save Xenia.

—What do you mean? I said, sounding more foolish than before.

—Well, Randi said, you have to help her understand that she's caught in a daydream.

—What do you mean? I said helplessly.

—Well, Randi said, you have to explain everything to her, tell her that I was with Sampel the other day, and that he told me *I'm* the woman who meets the main character in his novel on page eight.

I almost said, What do you mean, but stopped myself.

—And do you know who the main character is, the man? continued Randi, it's Azorno and Sampel wants to introduce me to Azorno now, on the first Sunday in May; she smiled. Goethe barked and ran anxiously back and forth in front of the door to the gallery.

—But what? I asked, do you want me to do?

—Just anything, tell her something or other, be with her, entertain her, something or other, anything. . . . Want to come along while I take the dog downstairs?

I stood up and went over to Randi and she put her arm around my shoulders and we walked through the gallery.

—You know what I mean, she said. I want you to just keep her away from both Sampel and Azorno, at least keep her away from them until I've had enough time with Azorno to get an impression of him.

We went down the wide stone staircase in the center of the house and I could hear Goethe scratching at some door downstairs; it turned out to be one that led from an inner courtyard out to the garden. Randi opened the door; the rain blew in for a moment and we sat down on a stone bench in the colonnade. A fountain splashed in the courtyard with a different tone than the rain.

—She has always been quite a liar, Randi said.

Goethe now rushed in with a bone, shook off the rain and started chewing the bone. I was picking at an old sandstone sculpture, a little greenish mannequin with oversized ears and waves down the chest as on a washboard to signify frizzy hair.

—Xenia's always been quite a liar, Randi said.

I promised to do what I could, mostly because I couldn't stand thinking how meaningless my whole trip down through

Germany would have been otherwise, with all my longing to see the sunroom that I'd heard so much about, and then having it rain the whole time.

So I promised to do what I could, and we went upstairs again and she kindly and absently showed me the many carved wooden chests along the gallery walls. She didn't open them, and we didn't go back to the sunroom.

I didn't ask her about anything specific. She said she'd bought the big bouquets of flowers the day before.

I glanced at a couple of the many photographs and paintings that hung on the walls.

Randi said they all had a story.

Then we took a quick tour through some of the many carefully furnished rooms, all unusable because of their dead smell.

In the kitchen we stopped suddenly, as though Randi had just realized where we were, and I ended up sitting at a very large table with a red-checked cloth.

Randi took out a salad left over from the previous day. The greens had turned brown at the edges and had yellowish spots and creases, and the tomatoes were unusually pale.

She opened a can of asparagus and a can of shrimp, drained the liquid, and added them to the salad.

Then she stood there tossing it as though she were about to fall asleep.

I searched for something to talk about.

Goethe rattled his metal bowl and a chunk of rye bread rolled out and landed next to my toe.

Randi chopped an onion, some tomatoes, and a couple of hard-boiled eggs that were blue or violet or almost black. She threw it all into the salad bowl.

—There, she said.

The original salad was now nearly hidden. She gave it a little toss, then spread out her arms, and laughed.

The whole situation felt artificial, when the last thing in the world we wanted was to act like strangers to each other.

Now she took out a bigger bowl made of ceramic and glazed

in two shades of brown that flowed into each other in a speckled pattern. She poured in plenty of oil, shook in a good amount of vinegar, sprinkled in some salt and pepper, and crushed a few cloves of garlic.

Then she took the bowl in her arms, stirring and continuing the motion herself in a dance across the wide floor.

—I am so glad you came, she said.

—So happy, she said, setting down the bowl and kissing me on the forehead.

She snipped a head of lettuce into strips, letting them fall into the dressing.

—Too bad I didn't throw away the old salad, she said.

—It doesn't matter, I said, now you almost can't see the brown spots.

—Actually it should marinate a while, Randi said, but we can't do that today.

I must have looked confused because she quickly added: I mean since you have to leave so soon. She laughed. To meet Xenia.

—I wish I knew Xenia, I said.

—You can take along her letter, said Randi, heaping salad onto my plate.

She immediately went off to get it as I sat there chewing on a piece of hard bread. It took a long time. So the idea was that I should take off as soon as we had eaten.

And that's what happened, and when I was out sitting in the car, Randi said, I hope to see you again soon.

Goethe barked, and I started the car and called, I'll do what I can.

I drove slowly down through the increasingly populated areas near Uetliberg, where the rain had stopped and the trees shone in the lights, making my way onto broader and longer roads, where the rain had stopped and the asphalt shone in the headlights, and finally I let myself be pulled with the current into the city, where the rain . . . where the lights were lit.

I had almost reached downtown when I realized that I was in

the wrong lane, and that coincidence was the reason I decided to drive south rather than north. I followed a sign that said Thalwil-Zug-Luzern and drove around the right side of Lake Zurich.

The road was smooth and sang in the mild evening air. Houses glided by, but mostly it was flat wide fields gliding by and transforming themselves far out in the semidarkness into mountains where the rain had presumably also stopped and the invisible shone in the headlights. I rolled the window down and sang in the mild evening air.

I particularly remembered the river in Luzern . . . that sang in the mild evening air.

I was going to stay in Lucerne, but I didn't feel like sleeping yet, so I drove on through a landscape that slowly rose and fell in the darkness, down toward the lights of Brienz, where the rain had long since stopped, and where, from my hotel room, I could see the lights around Lake Brienz and remembered the lights around Lake Vierwaldstadt, and the lights around another lake whose name I couldn't remember, but which also sang in the mild evening air. There I lay by the open windows and slept and dreamed.

The next morning I discovered that I had come too far west of Passo S. Gottardo 2109. So I drove due east, up over Sustenpass 2224, but when I finally approached the Gotthard area, I was so confused by the views and ravines, bridges and tunnels, glaciers and streams, memorial markers for generals apparently of Russian descent, and by the cows on the roads, by the flowers among the rocks called alpeflora, and in Andermatt, by the police officers, to such a degree that I drove across Oberalppass 2044 instead of across Passo S. Gottardo 2109 and had to continue down through Tschamut and Sedrun with the headwaters of the Rhine far below me, until I reached a slightly larger town called Disentis/Muster 1133 where I stopped to ask directions and was told that I had to turn due south and drive up over Passo del Lucomagno 1917, which I then did, and so at last I found the road that could take me much more quickly over Passo S. Gottardo 2109, Biasca 293, where the lush Tessin Valley, with its river and vineyards, began to stretch down toward

Bellinzona 241, with a scent of Italy beginning approaching via Lugano 334 and becoming fully present in the hot, crisp, spicy landscape around the border at Chiasso and Como 201. And now, as you can see, I'm in Rome.

And my dearest Katerina, I know you won't be sad or angry when I send you my letter about how I ended up with Xenia's letter which I am also sending. You know me!

And you know Xenia.

You once gave her a bouquet of multicolored tulips.

As for me, I have carefully read Xenia's letter here at the Hotel Rome (Via Napoli 3, tel. 484-409-471-565) many times and have arrived at the completely personal conviction that it's a little too well-written to have very much to do with the truth.

Probably, if the truth were to come out, Xenia's letter should be called Randi's letter. She's always been quite a liar; I mean Randi, which means Xenia.

And if the truth is to finally come out, there is one matter about which there can be no two opinions: Yesterday I was here with Azorno in Rome. It was the first Sunday in May, and unbelievably hot at noon.

It was the first Sunday in May and the air was unusually cool. I had just said good-bye to Azorno and wasn't sure in which direction to walk, now that I was alone after three uninterrupted days with Azorno who always decides which direction to take, alone in deciding, determining, ensuring how Sunday would go and in which direction I myself would go since I had said good-bye to Azorno at track 2 and now stood outside Copenhagen's Central Station looking at posters in the travel agency windows, the blue of the sea and sky, particularly the sea which was a lake lined with houses, all the white houses in all the completely overwhelming green with its broad, lush plains that brought out the gleaming letters of Tessin, Lugano, Bellinzona, flowers, flowers, flowers.

The air was unusually cold, time stood unusually still and I was hungry and went down to the hot dog cart near the main entrance to Tivoli, two, grilled. Inside Tivoli people were beginning to stroll down toward the lake and around it. Here and there they stopped, possibly to comment on the landscape gardener's vision. Or they loudly expressed their wonder and disappointment over the soundless fountain. I couldn't see that, either. The ticket collectors behind the turnstiles behind the woman with the hot-dog-colored hair who sold regular and grilled to a long line of customers who lined up with other customers in front of the turnstiles in front of the ticket collectors in front of Tivoli with the silent fountain, which I thus could not see and on which I therefore will not comment.

However I will gladly comment on the previous sentence: it is not a sentence.

The woman with the hot-dog-colored hair said that personally she never eats hot dogs.

On the way back I bought a bouquet of multicolored tulips that has been in my dining room ever since, reaching out and stretching in all directions. I actually thought they would stay completely straight since of course I never let a single light ray disturb me in this room here where I sit and meditate several times a day while eating.

I started on this letter as soon as I put the tulips in water.

First, I cleaned up after Azorno, the cigarettes, his bathrobe, his newspaper, a book. Then I put the tulips in water.

So then I started on this letter right away. Although at first I meditated in order to find a suitable beginning for the letter. That is, I began meditating without eating at the same time.

When I realized after a bit that I was meditating without eating anything at the same time, it occurred to me how improper or at least unusual for me this was and therefore risky, so I went right out and made a cup of coffee and two pieces of French bread with raspberry jam and brought it in here to the dining room on the little white tray I always use when I'm alone, and started on this letter right away.

By this time the tulips have been in water for awhile and a few have already bent and stretched in all directions although I have never let any rays of light disturb me in this room where I sit and eat several times a day while I meditate.

After I had eaten the two pieces of French bread with raspberry jam I started right away on this letter.

It's now been several days since I started on this letter and I should have told you right away that it was specifically this bouquet of multicolored tulips that got me to start right away on this letter.

After I had at last bought them on the way back.

After I had put them in water.

It's now several days later, and as I've been writing and eating while meditating at the same time, they have reached and stretched out in all directions and I have searched my memory to recall whether I have ever given you a bouquet of multicolored tulips.

But of course I have never even given you a bouquet of plain tulips.

Of course I have never given you a bouquet of any kind.

And my dearest Xenia, you can be completely sure that I never will.

Have I ever given you anything at all?

No. I know that you're allergic to gifts. You can't stand flowers. They wither up, turn pale, sicken, droop, and I understand you so well. Believe me, I understand you so well.

Now I have thrown out the tulips and ought to really start the letter over, but I think that would be going too far, and perhaps these prefatory lines have filled a certain function after all.

Dare I hope that they have helped you understand that I have never, at any point, believed you could have written that incidentally very fine account of the young woman with the white hat whom Azorno meets in Tivoli and who shows a somewhat unusual interest in the tulip beds.

Ludicrous that it could have been you. Ludicrous. Only a person who had never known either you or your very highly allergic style could come up with something so ludicrous. Believe me, I know you too well to fall for this sort of thing. Believe me, I know you too well.

And therefore, I see no reason to rescue you.

On the other hand, now that the tulips have long since been thrown away, I would like you to meet me here at my place to talk over how we can rescue Louise.

You do not know her, true, but her account of the car trip through the Alps is in itself enough to tell you that something is wrong. Only a person who knows she is going to write it down would drive in that way.

Or, the only kind of person who writes in that way is one who no longer knows how she is driving.

To put it briefly, I'm afraid that she is wandering about.

I'm afraid she is no longer aware of what she writes or to whom she is writing.

Believe me, I know how dangerous it is to dream of Azorno. Believe me, I know how dangerous it is. I have certainly known Azorno long enough to know that these are not dreams that come true.

But of course I'm writing first and foremost to you, to assure you that I am very willing to keep you informed about these rumors and their possible course.

About their course, naturally, one can only guess. That Louise says that Randi says that you, my dearest Xenia, started them, is something you shouldn't worry about. Not in the least. Louise has, of course, always been quite a liar.

Other factors may, of course, have come into play and maybe you, with your intimate knowledge of these types of symptoms, will be in a position to establish whether there is anything at all in Louise's letter to suggest that she may be allergic to the sun.

In that case we would probably come closer to the truth if we just forgave her everything. One would need only to hint at it, for example, to use a matter-of-fact phrase, when declaring her missing. I think it would sound fine and caring in Italian: she has, as I mentioned, taken lodgings in Rome where she is feared to be wandering about due to sunstroke.

[. . .]

FLEUR JAEGGY

NO DESTINY

Translated from the Italian by TIM PARKS

Then she hated her. Marie Anne had spent all afternoon pruning, more than was necessary. She gave herself up to her rage.
Cleaning mainly. The soil was soft, it had rained. And looked
dirty. Her garden was in a courtyard, the sun couldn't get at the
earth. Uncertain, the heat stopped at the outside wall. A small
thing, that garden. Damp. White in winter. Dirty white. In
spring it was dirtier still, the cold and decay wouldn't leave that
patch of soil alone. In summer it was dry. And the years were
slipping by. Marie Anne sits in the garden pushing the pram
against the wall with her foot. Then pulling it back with a piece
of string. So the baby could move about a bit. The little girl
looked dumbly around. Marie Anne had hated her from the moment she appeared in the world. She appeared along with a hundred other newborns, there was a tag, and that was her daughter.
Normal. She wasn't blind, her hearing was good. Her friend
Johanna wanted to have the child. She was a half-caste. "If you
don't like her, why not give her to me?" Johanna had gone on
and on. And even the people she worked for—Johanna was a
maid—would have liked to have the girl. If you don't like her, let
us look after her. We'll adopt her. Marie Anne had seen the nice

house Johanna's employers had. And the nice garden. The white wicker chairs, so elegant and uncomfortable. They showed her the girl's room too. A little bed that looked like cream and strawberry ice. In another room there were toys. The toys of Johanna's employers' little girl that died. No one had touched them since. Sometimes, in the evening, the mother rocked the rocking horse. You can't play with a dead child's toys. That's what her husband said. A sensible fellow, he would have liked to play with his dead daughter's dolls himself. The dolls laughed at this man and woman who couldn't forget their baby. They were still intact. The little girl hadn't had time to smash in their faces or pull off their legs or maybe an arm. It saddened the wife: this lack of wear and tear precluding renewal. Premature toys. Even the dolls' clothes were intact. Ironed. Their hair too. Lots of soft little wigs in their boxes. Blond, black, with curls even, like Johanna's. Their daughter never combed them. But perhaps she's doing it now. In her cute little grave she combs and combs their hair, like Lorelei. The wife wonders about that. But the husband said it was impossible and that she mustn't think of such things. That deep down he thinks of himself. His daughter was growing in her grave. She would have been five now. And it made no difference that it was a heap of dust doing the playing. They wouldn't have any other children. And they felt extremely pleased now to be showing their daughter's room to Marie Anne. Marie Anne looked everything over with stubborn amazement. She felt generous praising it all, she thought it would please the woman that someone was saying she had done up her dead daughter's room so well. The wallpaper was red cherries and white irises with leaves. There was even a little table with a mirror for the child. Where she would look at herself while Johanna braided her hair. Everything arranged as if she were already a little woman. The child's clothes were still in the closet. All pink. The little shoes at the bottom. Ready to run. Some of them white. Some in blue calfskin. On the top shelf were some little straw hats. It was summertime. Johanna was so hot she couldn't work. In the evening, before going to bed, she would sit by the window with her legs spread wide. Even the lawn was sweating. Voices came form far away. Even they sounded sweaty. No color to the sky. When it's very hot, it gets like an infected sheet, and she saw bad luck in that sheet. But then she went to sleep almost at once, a heavy sleep. She didn't like her life that much. Marie Anne said that was because she didn't like men. What Johanna liked was bending down for hours and hours wiping the floor. Then going to sleep. She was still good-looking. There was nothing she really liked. Unless maybe the people she worked for. Because they were sad. They hid it. When she served them at table they pretended to be happy. You don't have to laugh to pretend you're not sad, she thought. They were never vulgar. Their laughter is instructive. When Johanna laughs she's vulgar. She laughed for joy when Marie Anne's baby was born. Everybody in the hospital heard her. But Johanna wasn't Marie Anne's husband. Even though they'd once been to bed together. Johanna couldn't give Marie Anne a baby. Perhaps everything had happened after Marie Anne had been to bed with Johanna. Towards dawn she went out for a walk. And nine months later Johanna had laughed at the hospital. Nine months had passed. In her head she thought of herself as the father. When Marie Anne said: "I don't want her, take her away," the baby had been in her arms, where a nurse had put her. Then Johanna had begun to think of being both mother and father to the girl. "Give her to me, give me the baby," she had asked, over and over. And now her employers kept asking too. Johanna knew her employers would win. The child would grow up rich and respectable. She would be her maid, as she had been the dead child's. Marie Anne looked round and found she liked the room. "It would be just fine for my baby," she said, "that's for sure." And at the same time she was thinking of the room where her daughter slept now, a narrow room with no windows. But if you left the door open it did get a little grey light from the kitchen window. Johanna had given her the crib, the little undershirts, and all the rest. Johanna went into the shops and asked for clothes for her daughter: "I had a little girl a few days ago," she told them. The assistants congratulated her. She only bought the best and went proudly back to Marie Anne's, where the mother spent all day in the garden, pruning—and cursing.

Hearing those curses, Johanna feared what the heavens might do. She held the baby tight. To hide her from the heavens. Johanna's employers kept inviting Marie Anne to visit. They invited her to lunch. Marie Anne behaved like a lady almost. She watched how the wife served herself and then did the same. She smiled sweetly at the woman's husband. She said a few things about herself, concealing the worst. Johanna had even given her some evening clothes. Black dresses, stylish. One day the woman's husband gave her a pearl necklace. Another day the wife gave her a gold bracelet with a diamond. All things that would have belonged to the little girl who had died. But now they must grace the mother of a child who was alive and might become their child. For it looked as though Marie Anne would give up her daughter. Who lay in her pram in the garden, pushed with a kick and jerked back with a string. The child could hardly have imagined what a splendid future was to be hers. Her mild eyes turned, it seemed, to the void, in an unbearable way. It was still too soon. One supposes. At that age you don't think about your destiny.

More months went by. Marie Anne wore more and more jewelry. Johanna doesn't say "Give your little girl to me" anymore. By now the little girl has been promised to her employers. She watches her employers embrace Marie Anne. They had tears in their eyes. They went into the toy room and, crouching down, all three of them began to play. Marie Anne got on the woman's husband's back and the woman laughed, holding a doll in her hand. Like a battle ax. Johanna brought them drinks. They celebrated. They put wigs on their glasses. That night the dolls were no longer a cult of the dead, but dolls to disembowel, pull to bits with pleasure. They dressed and undressed them, even the wife took off her dress. They played at being happy. Happiness bit into them like a burning blade. They shook hands to settle the deal. Marie Anne gave a look of triumph. She gave her word of honor. She laid it down before them. It was a spring day and getting late. Marie Anne wasn't in the habit of speaking a great deal, dragging things out, that is. To her mind the origin of speech, and creation, was the curse. Now Marie Anne had promised. "My daughter will be yours."

The wooden horse was still rocking at dawn. Johanna claimed it rocked for days. While the dolls sat still and gazed.

At home, Marie Anne went to her child. She was asleep. She watched her for a long time. Next morning she took her into the muddy garden. Marie Anne couldn't find anything else to prune. She held the pruning shears in her hands. And didn't know who to use them on. She looked at her child. She won't have a nice destiny. I won't leave her to those people. She won't have a nice house. Why should that little girl she hated have a better life? She wrote a letter to Johanna's employers. "I've changed my mind. It was a joke." Goodbye. The wife hung herself five minutes later. Like the rocking horse, her body swung back and forth. The child has grown up. Marie Anne hates her. Yesterday they walked by the couple's big house and she told the girl everything. She had been promised to that house. The girl is fifteen now and she often walks by that house. People say she's a little dumb. But she's not. She's just looking at her destiny. Or rather, at where destiny passed her by.

Muriel Spark

THE PORTOBELLO ROAD

One day in my young youth at high summer, lolling with my lovely companions upon a haystack, I found a needle. Already and privately for some years I had been guessing that I was set apart from the common run, but this of the needle attested the fact to my whole public: George, Kathleen and Skinny. I sucked my thumb, for when I had thrust my idle hand deep into the hay, the thumb was where the needle had stuck.

When everyone had recovered George said, "She put in her thumb and pulled out a plum." Then away we were into our merciless hacking-hecking laughter again.

The needle had gone fairly deep into the thumby cushion and a small red river flowed and spread from this tiny puncture. So that nothing of our joy should lag, George put in quickly,

"Mind your bloody thumb on my shirt."

Then hac-hec-hoo, we shrieked into the hot Borderland afternoon. Really I should not care to be so young of heart again. That is my thought every time I turn over my old papers and come across the photograph. Skinny, Kathleen and myself are in the photo atop the haystack. Skinny had just finished analysing the inwards of my find.

"It couldn't have been done by brains. You haven't much brains but you're a lucky wee thing."

Everyone agreed that the needle betokened extraordinary luck. As it was becoming a serious conversation, George said,

"I'll take a photo."

I wrapped my hanky round my thumb and got myself organised. George pointed up from his camera and shouted,

"Look, there's a mouse!"

Kathleen screamed and I screamed although I think we knew there was no mouse. But this gave us an extra session of squalling hee-hoo's. Finally we three composed ourselves for George's picture. We look lovely and it was a great day at the time, but I would not care for it all over again. From that day I was known as Needle.

One Saturday in recent years I was mooching down the Portobello Road, threading among the crowds of marketers on the narrow pavement when I saw a woman. He had a haggard, careworn, wealthy look, thin but for the breasts forced-up high like a pigeon's. I had not seen her for nearly five years. How changed she was! But I recognised Kathleen, my friend; her features had already begun to sink and protrude in the way that mouths and noses do in people destined always to be old for their years. When I had last seen her, nearly five years ago, Kathleen, barely thirty, had said,

"I've lost all my looks, it's in the family. All the women are handsome as girls, but we go off early, we go brown and nosey."

I stood silently among the people, watching. As you will see I wasn't in a position to speak to Kathleen. I saw her shoving in her avid manner from stall to stall. She was always fond of antique jewellery and of bargains. I wondered that I had not seen her before in the Portobello Road on my Saturday morning ambles. Her long stiff-crooked fingers pounced to select a jade ring from amongst the jumble of brooches and pendants, onyx, moonstone and gold, set out on the stall.

"What do you think of this?" she said.

I saw then who was with her. I had been half-conscious of

the huge man following several paces behind her, and now I noticed him.

"It looks all right," he said. "How much is it?"

"How much is it?" Kathleen asked the vendor.

I took a good look at this man accompanying Kathleen. It was her husband. The beard was unfamiliar, but I recognised beneath it his enormous mouth, the bright sensuous lips, the large brown eyes forever brimming with pathos.

It was not for me to speak to Kathleen, but I had a sudden inspiration which caused me to say quietly,

"Hallo, George."

The giant of a man turned round to face the direction of my face. There were so many people—but at length he saw me.

"Hallo, George," I said again.

Kathleen had started to haggle with the stall-owner, in her old way, over the price of the jade ring. George continued to stare at me, his big mouth slightly parted so that I could see a wide slit of red lips and white teeth between the fair grassy growths of beard and moustache.

"My God!" he said.

"What's the matter?" said Kathleen.

"Hallo, George!" I said again, quite loud this time, and cheerfully.

"Look!" said George. "Look who's there, over beside the fruit stall."

Kathleen looked but didn't see.

"Who is it?" she said impatiently.

"It's Needle," he said. "She said 'Hallo, George'."

"*Needle*" said Kathleen. "Who do you mean? You don't mean our old friend *Needle* who—"

"Yes. There she is. My God!"

He looked very ill, although when I had said "Hallo, George" I had spoken friendly enough.

"I don't see anyone faintly resembling poor Needle," said Kathleen, looking at him. She was worried.

George pointed straight at me. "Look *there*. I tell you that is Needle."

"You're ill, George. Heavens, you must be seeing things. Come on home. Needle isn't there. You know as well as I do, Needle is dead."

I must explain that I departed this life nearly five years ago. But I did not altogether depart this world. There were those odd things still to be done which one's executors can never do properly. Papers to be looked over, even after the executors have torn them up. Lots of business except, of course, on Sundays and Holidays of Obligation, plenty to take an interest in for the time being. I take my recreation on Saturday mornings. If it is a wet Saturday I wander up and down the substantial lanes of Woolworth's as I did when I was young and visible. There is a pleasurable spread of objects on the counters which I now perceive and exploit with a certain detachment, since it suits with my condition of life. Creams, toothpastes, combs and hankies, cotton gloves, flimsy flowering scarves, writing-paper and crayons, ice-cream cones and orangeade, screwdrivers, boxes of tacks, tins of paint, of glue, of marmalade; I always liked them but far more now that I have no need of any. When Saturdays are fine I go instead to the Portobello Road where formerly I would jaunt with Kathleen in our grown-up days. The barrow-loads do not change much, of apples and rayon vests in common blues and low-taste mauve, of silver plate, trays and teapots long since changed hands from the bygone citizens to dealers, from shops to the new flats and breakable homes, and then over to the barrow-stalls and the dealers again: Georgian spoons, rings, earrings of turquoise and opal set in the butterfly pattern of true-lovers' knot, patch-boxes with miniature paintings of ladies on ivory, snuff-boxes of silver with Scotch pebbles inset.

Sometimes as occasion arises on a Saturday morning, my friend Kathleen, who is a Catholic, has a Mass said for my soul, and then I an in attendance, as it were, at the church. But most Saturdays I take my delight among the solemn crowds with their aimless purposes, their eternal life not far away, who push past the counters and stalls, who handle, buy, steal, touch, desire, and ogle the merchandise. I hear the tinkling tills, I hear the jangle of loose change and tongues and children wanting to hold and have.

That is how I came to be in the Portobello Road that Saturday morning when I saw George and Kathleen. I would not have spoken had I not been inspired to it. Indeed it's one of the things I can't do now—to speak out, unless inspired. And most extraordinary, on that morning as I spoke, a degree of visibility set in. I suppose from poor George's point of view it was like seeing a ghost when he saw me standing by the fruit barrow repeating in so friendly a manner, "Hallo, George!"

We were bound for the south. When our education, what we could get of it from the north, was thought to be finished, one by one we were sent or sent for to London. John Skinner, whom we called Skinny, went to study more archaeology, George to join his uncle's tobacco farm, Kathleen to stay with her rich connections and to potter intermittently in the Mayfair hat shop which one of them owned. A little later I also went to London to see life, for it was my ambition to write about life, which first I had to see.

"We four must stick together," George said very often in that yearning way of his. He was always desperately afraid of neglect. We four looked likely to shift off in different directions and George did not trust the other three of us not to forget all about him. More and more as the time came for him to depart for his uncle's tobacco farm in Africa he said,

"We four must keep in touch."

And before he left he told each of us anxiously,

"I'll write regularly, once a month. We must keep together for the sake of the old times." He had three prints taken from the negative of that photo on the haystack, wrote on the back of them, "George took this the day that Needle found the needle," and gave us a copy each. I think we all wished he could become a bit more callous.

During my lifetime I was a drifter, nothing organized. It was difficult for my friends to follow the logic of my life. By the normal reckonings I should have come to starvation and ruin, which I never did. Of course, I did not live to write about life as I wanted to do. Possibly that is why I am inspired to do so now in these peculiar circumstances.

I taught in a private school in Kensington for almost three months, very small children. I didn't know what to do with them but I was kept fairly busy escorting incontinent little boys to the lavatory and telling the little girls to use their handkerchiefs. After that I lived a winter holiday in London on my small capital, and when that had run out I found a diamond bracelet in the cinema for which I received a reward of fifty pounds. When it was used up I got a job with a publicity man, writing speeches for absorbed industrialists, in which the dictionary of quotations came in very useful. So it went on. I got engaged to Skinny, but shortly after that I was left a small legacy, enough to keep me for six months. This somehow decided me that I didn't love Skinny so I gave him back the ring.

But it was through Skinny that I went to Africa. He was engaged with a party of researchers to investigate King Solomon's mines, that series of ancient workings ranging from the ancient port of Ophir, now called Beira, across Portuguese East Africa and Southern Rhodesia to the mighty jungle-city of Zimbabwe whose temple walls still stand by the approach to an ancient and sacred mountain, where the rubble of that civilization scatters itself over the surrounding Rhodesian waste. I accompanied the party as a sort of secretary. Skinny vouched for me, he paid my fare, he sympathized by his action with my inconsequential life although when he spoke of it he disapproved. A life like mine annoys most people; they go to their jobs every day, attend to things, give orders, pummel typewriters, and get two or three weeks off every year, and it vexes them to see someone else not bothering to do these things and yet getting away with it, not starving, being lucky as they call it. Skinny, when I had broken off our engagement, lectured me about this, but still took me to Africa knowing I should probably leave his unit within a few months.

We were there a few weeks before we began enquiring for George, who was farming about four hundred miles away to the north. We had not told him of our plans.

"If we tell George to expect us in his part of the world he'll come rushing to pester us the first week. After all, we're going on business," Skinny had said.

Before we left Kathleen told us, "Give George my love and tell him not to send frantic cables every time I don't answer his letters right away. Tell him I'm busy in the hat shop and being presented. You would think he hadn't another friend in the world the way he carries on."

We had settled first at Fort Victoria, our nearest place of access to the Zimbabwe ruins. There we made inquires about George. It was clear he hadn't many friends. The older settlers were the most tolerant about the half-caste woman he was living with, as we found, but they were furious about his methods of raising tobacco which we learned were most unprofessional and in some mysterious way disloyal to the whites. We could never discover how it was that George's style of tobacco farming gave the blacks opinions about themselves, but that's what the older settlers claimed. The newer immigrants thought he was unsociable and, of course, his living with that nig made visiting impossible.

I must say I was myself a bit off-put by this news about the brown woman. I was brought up in a university town to which came Indian, African, and Asiatic students in a variety of tints and hues. I was brought up to avoid them for reasons connected with local reputation and God's ordinances. You cannot easily go against what you were brought up to do unless you are a rebel by nature.

Anyhow, we visited George eventually, taking advantage of the offer of transport from some people bound north in search of game. He had heard of our arrival in Rhodesia and though he was glad, almost relieved, to see us, he pursued a policy of sullenness for the first hour.

"We wanted to give you a surprise, George."

"How were we to know that you'd get to hear of our arrival, George? News here must travel faster than light, George."

"We did hope to give you a surprise, George."

At last he said, "Well, I must say it's good to see you. All we need now is Kathleen. We four simply must stick together. You find when you're in a place like this, there's nothing like old friends."

He showed us his drying sheds. He showed us a paddock where he was experimenting with a horse and a zebra mare, attempting to mate them. They were frolicking happily, but not together. They passed each other in their private play time and again, but without acknowledgment and without resentment.

"It's been done before," George said. "It makes a fine strong beast, more intelligent than a mule and sturdier than a horse. But I'm not having any success with this pair, they won't look at each other."

After a while, he said, "Come in for a drink and meet Matilda."

She was dark brown, with a subservient hollow chest and round shoulders, a gawky woman, very snappy with the house-boys. We said pleasant things as we drank on the stoep before dinner, but we found George difficult. For some reason he began to rail me for breaking off my engagement to Skinny, saying what a dirty trick it was after all those good times in the old days. I diverted attention to Matilda. I supposed, I said, she knew this part of the country well?

"No," said she, "I been a-shellitered my life. I not put out to working. Me nothing to go from place to place is allowed like dirty girls does." In her speech she gave every syllable equal stress.

George explained, "Her father was a white magistrate in Natal. She had a sheltered upbringing, different from the other coloreds, you realise."

"Man, me no black-eyed Susan," said Matilda, "no, no."

On the whole, George treated her as a servant. She was about four months advanced in pregnancy, but he made her get up and fetch for him, many times. Soap: that was one of the things Matilda had to fetch. George made his own bath soap, showed it proudly, gave us the recipe which I did not trouble to remember; I was fond of nice soaps during my lifetime and George's smelt of brilliantine and looked likely to soil one's skin.

"D'yo brahn?" Matilda asked me.

George said, "She is asking if you go brown in the sun."

"No, I go freckled."

"I got sister-in-law go freckles."

She never spoke another word to Skinny nor to me, and we never saw her again.

Some months later I said to Skinny

"I'm fed up with being a camp-follower."

He was not surprised that I was leaving his unit, but he hated my way of expressing it. He gave me a Presbyterian look.

"Don't talk like that. Are you going back to England or staying?"

"Staying, for a while."

"Well, don't wander too far off."

I was able to live on the fee I got for writing a gossip column in a local weekly, which wasn't my idea of writing about life, of course. I made friends, more than I could cope with, after I left Skinny's exclusive little band of archaeologists. I had the attractions of being newly out from England and of wanting to see life. Of the countless young men and go-ahead families who purred me along the Rhodesian roads, hundred after hundred miles, I only kept up with one family when I returned to my native land. I think that was because they were the most representative, they stood for all the rest: people in those parts are very typical of each other, as one group of standing stones in that wilderness is like the next.

I met George once more in a hotel in Bulawayo. We drank highballs and spoke of war. Skinny's party were just then deciding whether to remain in the country or return home. They had reached an exciting part of their research, and whenever I got a chance to visit Zimbabwe he would take me for a moonlight walk in the ruined temple and try to make me see phantom Phoenicians flitting ahead of us, or along the walls. I had half a mind to marry Skinny; perhaps, I thought, when his studies were finished. The impending war was in our bones: so I remarked to George as we sat drinking highballs on the hotel stoep in the hard bright sunny July winter of that year.

George was inquisitive about my relations with Skinny. He tried to pump me for about half an hour and when at last I said, "You are becoming aggressive, George," he stopped. He became quite pathetic. He said, "War or no war I'm clearing out of this."

"It's the heat does it," I said.

"I'm clearing out in any case. I've lost a fortune in tobacco. My uncle is making a fuss. It's the other bloody planters; once you get the wrong side of them you're finished in this wide land."

"What about Matilda?" I asked.

He said, "She'll be all right. She's got hundreds of relatives."

I had already heard about the baby girl. Coal black, by repute, with George's features. And another on the way, they said.

"What about the child?"

He didn't say anything to that. He ordered more highballs and when they arrived he swizzled his for a long time with a stick. "Why didn't you ask me to your twenty-first?" he said then.

"I didn't have anything special, no party, George. We had a quiet drink among ourselves, George, just Skinny and the old professors and two of the wives and me, George."

"You didn't ask me to your twenty-first," he said. "Kathleen writes to me regularly."

This wasn't true. Kathleen sent me letters fairly often in which she said, "Don't tell George I wrote to you as he will be expecting word from me and I can't be bothered actually."

"But you," said George, "don't seem to have any sense of old friendships, you and Skinny."

"Oh, George!" I said.

"Remember the times we had," George said. "We used to have times." His large brown eyes began to water.

"I'll have to be getting along," I said.

"Please don't go. Don't leave me just yet. I've something to tell you."

"Something nice?" I laid on an eager smile. All responses to George had to be overdone.

"You don't know how lucky you are," George said.

"How?" I said. Sometimes I got tired of being called lucky by everybody. There were times when, privately practicing my writings about life, I knew the bitter side of my fortune. When I failed again and again to reproduce life in some satisfactory and perfect form, I was the more imprisoned, for all my carefree living, within my craving for this satisfaction. Sometimes, in my impotence and need, I secreted a venom which infected all my life for days on end and which spurted out indiscriminately on Skinny or on anyone who crossed my path.

"You aren't bound by anyone," George said. "You come and go as you please. Something always turns up for you. You're free, and you don't know your luck."

"You're a damn sight more free than I am," I said sharply. "You've got your rich uncle."

"He's losing interest in me," George said. "He's had enough."

"Oh well, you're young yet. What was it you wanted to tell me?"

"A secret," George said. "Remember we used to have those secrets."

"Oh, yes we did."

"Did you ever tell any of mine?"

"Oh no, George." In reality, I couldn't remember any particular secret out of the dozens we must have exchanged from our schooldays onwards.

"Well, this is a secret, mind. Promise not to tell."

"Promise."

"I'm married."

"Married, George! Oh, who to?"

"Matilda."

"How dreadful!" I spoke before I could think, but he agreed with me.

"Yes, it's awful, but what could I do?"

"You might have asked my advice," I said pompously.

"I'm two years older than you are. I don't ask advice from you, Needle, little beast."

"Don't ask for sympathy then."

"A nice friend you are," he said, "I must say after all these years."

"Poor George!" I said.

"There are three white men to one white woman in this country," said George. "An isolated planter doesn't see a white woman and if he sees one she doesn't see him. What could I do? I needed the woman."

I was nearly sick. One, because of my Scottish upbringing. Two, because of my horror of corny phrases like "I needed the women," which George repeated twice again.

"And Matilda got tough," said George, "after you and Skinny came to visit us. She had some friends at the Mission, and she packed up and went to them."

"You should have let her go," I said.

"I went after her," George said. "She insisted on being married, so I married her."

"That's not a proper secret, then," I said. "The news of a mixed marriage soon gets about."

"I took care of that," George said. "Crazy as I was, I took her to the Congo and married her there. She promised to keep quiet about it."

"Well, you can't clear off and leave her now, surely." I said.

"I'm going to get out of this place. I can't stand the woman and I can't stand the country. I didn't realize what it would be like. Two years of the country and three months of my wife has been enough."

"Will you get a divorce?"

"No, Matilda's Catholic. She won't divorce."

George was fairly getting through the highballs, and I wasn't far behind him. His brown eyes floated shiny and liquid as he told me how he had written to tell his uncle of his plight. "Except, of course, I didn't say we were married, that would have been too much for him. He's a prejudiced hardened old colonial. I only said I'd had a child by a colored woman and was expecting another, and he perfectly understood. He came at once by plane a few weeks ago. He's made a settlement on her, providing she keeps her mouth shut about her association with me."

"Will she do that?"

"Oh, yes, or she won't get the money."

"But as your wife she has a claim on you, in any case."

"If she claimed as my wife she'd get far less. Matilda knows what she's doing, greedy bitch she is. She'll keep her mouth shut."

"Only, you won't be able to marry again, will you, George?"

"Not unless she dies," he said. "And she's as strong as a trek ox."

"Well, I'm sorry, George," I said.

"Good of you to say so," he said. "But I can see by your chin that you disapprove of me. Even my old uncle understood."

"Oh, George, I quite understand. You were lonely, I suppose."

"You didn't even ask me to your twenty-first. If you and Skinny had been nicer to me, I would never have lost my head and married the woman, never."

"You didn't ask me to your wedding," I said.

"You're a catty bissom, Needle, not like what you were in the old times when you used to tell us you wee stories."

"I'll have to be getting along," I said.

"Mind you keep the secret," George said.

"Can't I tell Skinny? He would be very sorry for you, George."

"You mustn't tell anyone. Keep it a secret. Promise."

"Promise," I said. I understood that he wished to enforce some sort of bond between us with this secret, and I thought, "Oh well, I suppose he's lonely. Keeping his secret won't do any harm."

I returned to England with Skinny's party just before the war.

I did not see George again till just before my death, five years ago.

After the war Skinny returned to his studies. He had two more exams, over a period of eighteen months, and I thought I might marry him when the exams were over.

"You might do worse than Skinny," Kathleen used to say to me on our Saturday morning excursions to the antique shops and the junk stalls.

She too was getting on in years. The remainder of our families in Scotland were hinting that it was time we settled down with husbands. Kathleen was a little younger than me, but looked much older. She knew her chances were diminishing but at that time I did not think she cared very much. As for myself, the main attraction of marrying Skinny was his prospective expeditions to Mesopotamia. My desire to marry him had to be stimulated by the continual reading of books about Babylon and Assyria; perhaps Skinny felt this, because he supplied the books and even started instructing me in the art of deciphering cuneiform tablets.

Kathleen was more interested in marriage than I thought. Like me, she had racketed around a good deal during the war; she had actually been engaged to an officer in the U.S. Navy, who was killed. Now she kept an antique shop near Lambeth, was doing very nicely, lived in a Chelsea square, but for all that she must have wanted to be married and have children. She would stop and look into all the prams which the mothers had left outside shops or area gates.

"The poet Swinburne used to do that," I told her once.

"Really? Did he want children of his own?"

"I shouldn't think so. He simply liked babies."

Before Skinny's final exam he fell ill and was sent to a sanatorium in Switzerland.

"You're fortunate after all not to be married to him," Kathleen said. "You might have caught T.B."

I was fortunate, I was lucky . . . so everyone kept telling me on different occasions. Although it annoyed me to hear, I knew they were right, but in a way that was different from what they meant. It took me very small effort to make a living; book reviews, odd jobs for Kathleen, a few months with the publicity man again, still getting up speeches about literature, art and life for industrial tycoons. I was waiting to write about life and it seemed to me that the good fortune lay in this, whenever it should be. And until then I was assured of my charmed life, the necessities of existence always coming my way and I with far more leisure than anyone else. I thought of my type of luck after I became a Catholic and was being confirmed. The Bishop touches the candidate on the cheek, a symbolic reminder of the sufferings a Christian is supposed to undertake. I thought, how lucky, what a feathery symbol to stand for the hellish violence of its true meaning.

I visited Skinny twice in the two years that he was in the sanatorium. He was almost cured, and expected to be home within a few months. I told Kathleen after my last visit.

"Maybe I'll marry Skinny when he's well again."

"Make it definite, Needle, and not so much of the maybe. You don't know when you're well off," she said.

This was five years ago, in the last year of my life. Kathleen and I had become very close friends. We met several times each week, and after our Saturday morning excursions in the Portobello Road very often I would accompany Kathleen to her aunt's house in Kent for a long weekend.

One day in the June of that year I met Kathleen especially for lunch because she had phoned me to say she had news.

"Guess who came into the shop this afternoon." she said.

"Who?"

"George."

We had half imagined George was dead. We had received no letters in the past ten years. Early in the war we had heard rumors of his keeping a night club in Durban, but nothing after that. We could have made inquiries if we had felt moved to do so.

At one time, when we discussed him, Kathleen had said,

"I ought to get in touch with poor George. But then I think he would write back. He would demand a regular correspondence again."

"We four must stick together," I mimicked.

"I can visualize his reproachful limpid orbs." Kathleen said.

Skinny said, "He's probably gone native. With his coffee concubine and a dozen mahogany kids."

"Perhaps he's dead," Kathleen said.

I did not speak of George's marriage, nor of any of his confidences in the hotel at Bulawayo. As the years passed we ceased to mention him except in passing, as someone more or less dead so far as we were concerned.

Kathleen was excited about George's turning up. She had forgotten her impatience with him in former days; she said,

"It was so wonderful to see old George. He seems to need a friend, feels neglected, out of touch with things."

"He needs mothering, I suppose."

Kathleen didn't notice the malice. She declared, "That's exactly the case with George. It always has been, I can see it now."

She seemed ready to come to any rapid new and happy conclusion about George. In the course of the afternoon he had told her of his wartime night club in Durban, his game-shooting expeditions since. It was clear he had not mentioned Matilda. He had put on weight, Kathleen told me, but he could carry it.

I was curious to see this version of George, but I was leaving for Scotland next day and did not see him till September of that year, just before my death.

While I was in Scotland I gathered from Kathleen's letters that she was seeing George very frequently, finding enjoyable company in him, looking after him. "You'll be surprised to see how he has developed." Apparently he would hang around Kathleen in her shop most days, "it makes him feel useful" as she maternally expressed it. He had an old relative in Kent whom he visited at weekends; this old lady lived a few miles from Kathleen's aunt, which made it easy for them to travel down together on Saturdays, and go for long country walks.

"You'll see such a difference in George," Kathleen said on my return to London in September. I was to meet him that night, a Saturday. Kathleen's aunt was abroad, the maid on holiday, and I was to keep Kathleen company in the empty house.

George had left London for Kent a few days earlier. "He's actually helping with the harvest down there!" Kathleen told me lovingly.

Kathleen and I planned to travel down together, but on that Saturday she was unexpectedly delayed in London on some business. It was arranged that I should go ahead of her in the early afternoon to see to the provisions for our party; Kathleen had invited George to dinner at her aunt's house that night.

"I should be with you by seven," she said. "Sure you won't mind the empty house? I hate arriving at empty houses, myself."

I said no, I liked an empty house.

So I did, when I got there. I had never found the house more likeable. A large Georgian vicarage in about eight acres, most of the rooms shut and sheeted, there being only one servant. I discovered that I wouldn't need to go shopping, Kathleen's aunt had left many and delicate supplies with notes attached to them: "Eat this up please do, see also fridge" and "A treat for three hungry people see also 2 bttles beaune for yr party on back kn table." It was like a treasure hunt as I followed clue after clue through the cool silent domestic quarters. A house in which there are no people—but with all the signs of tenancy—can be a most tranquil good place. People take up space in a house out of proportion to their size. On my previous visits I had seen the rooms overflowing as it seemed, with Kathleen, her aunt, and the little fat maidservant; they were always on the move. As I wandered through that part of the house which was in use, opening windows to let in the pale yellow air of September, I was not conscious that I, Needle, was taking up any space at all, I might have been a ghost.

The only thing to be fetched was the milk. I waited till after four when the milking should be done, then set off for the farm which lay across two fields at the back of the orchard. There, when the byreman was handing me the bottle, I saw George.

"Hallo, George," I said.

"Needle! What are you doing here?" he said.

"Fetching milk," I said.

"So am I. Well, it's good to see you, I must say,"

As we paid the farm-hand, George said, "I'll walk back with you part of the way. But I mustn't stop, my old cousin's without any milk for her tea. How's Kathleen?"

"She was kept in London. She's coming on later, about seven, she expects."

We had reached the end of the first field. George's way led to the left and on to the main road.

"We'll see you tonight, then?" I said.

"Yes, and talk about old times."

"Grand," I said.

But George got over the stile with me.

"Look here," he said. "I'd like to talk to you, Needle."

"We'll talk tonight, George. Better not keep your cousin waiting for the milk." I found myself speaking to him almost as if he were a child.

"No, I want to talk to you alone. This is a good opportunity."

We began to cross the second field. I had been hoping to have the house to myself for a couple more hours and I was rather petulant.

"See," he said suddenly, "that haystack."

"Yes," I said absently.

"Let's sit there and talk. I'd like to see you up on a haystack again. I still keep that photo. Remember that time when—"

"I found the needle," I said very quickly, to get it over.

But I was glad to rest. The stack had been broken up, but we managed to find a nest in it. I buried my bottle of milk in the hay for coolness. George placed his carefully at the foot of the stack.

"My old cousin is terribly vague, poor soul. A bit hazy in her head. She hasn't the least sense of time. If I tell her I've only been gone ten minutes she'll believe it."

I giggled, and looked at him. His face had grown much larger, his lips full, wide and with a ripe color that is strange in a man. His brown eyes were abounding as before with some inarticulate plea.

"So you're going to marry Skinny after all these years?"

"I really don't know, George."

"You played him up properly."

"It isn't for you to judge. I have my own reasons for what I do."

"Don't get sharp," he said, "I was only funning." To prove it, he lifted a tuft of hay and brushed my face with it.

"D'you know," he said next, "I didn't think you and Skinny treated me very decently in Rhodesia."

"Well, we were busy, George. And we were younger then, we had a lot to do and see. After all, we could see you any other time, George."

"A touch of selfishness," he said.

"I'll have to be getting along, George." I made to get down from the stack.

He pulled me back. "Wait, I've got something to tell you."

"O.K., George, tell me."

"First promise not to tell Kathleen. She wants it kept a secret so that she can tell you herself."

"All right. Promise."

"I'm going to marry Kathleen."

"But you're already married."

Sometimes I heard news of Matilda from the one Rhodesian family with whom I still kept up. They referred to her as "George's Dark Lady" and of course they did not know he was married to her. She had apparently made a good thing out of George, they said, for she minced around all tarted up, never did a stroke of work, and was always unsettling the respectable colored girls in their neighborhood. According to accounts, she was a living example of the folly of behaving as George did.

"I married Matilda in the Congo," George was saying.

"It would still be bigamy," I said.

He was furious when I used that word bigamy. He lifted a handful of hay as if he would throw it in my face, but controlling himself meanwhile he fanned it at me playfully.

"I'm not sure that the Congo marriage was valid," he continued. "Anyway, as far as I'm concerned, it isn't."

"You can't do a thing like that," I said.

"I need Kathleen. She's been decent to me. I think we were always meant for each other, me and Kathleen."

"I'll have to be going," I said.

But he put his knee over my ankles, so that I couldn't move. I sat still and gazed into space.

He tickled my face with a wisp of hay.

"Smile up, Needle," he said; "let's talk like old times."

"Well?"

"No one knows about my marriage to Matilda except you and me."

"And Matilda," I said.

"She'll hold her tongue so long as she gets her payments. My uncle left an annuity for the purpose, his lawyers see to it."

"Let me go, George."

"You promised to keep it a secret," he said, "you promised."

"Yes, I promised."

"And now that you're going to marry Skinny, we'll be properly coupled off as we should have been years ago. We should have been—but youth!—our youth got in the way, didn't it?"

"Life got in the way," I said.

"But everything's going to be all right now. You'll keep my secret, won't you? You promised." He had released my feet. I edged a little further from him.

I said, "If kathleen intends to marry you, I shall tell her that you're already married."

"You wouldn't do a dirty trick like that, Needle? You're going to be happy with Skinny, you wouldn't stand in the way of my—"

"I must, Kathleen's my best friend," I said swiftly.

He looked as if he would murder me and he did. He stuffed hay into my mouth until it could hold no more, kneeling on my body to keep it still, holding both my wrists tight in his huge left hand. I saw the red full lines of his mouth and the white slit of his teeth last thing on earth. Not another soul passed by as he pressed my body into the stack, as he made a deep nest for me, tearing up the hay to make a groove the length of my corpse, and finally pulling the warm stuff in a mound over this concealment, so natural-looking in a broken haystack. Then George climbed down, took up his bottle of milk and went on his way. I supposed that was why he looked so unwell when I stood, nearly five years later by the barrow in the Portobello Road and said in easy tones, "Hallo, George!"

The Haystack Murder was one of the notorious crimes of that year.

My friends said, "A girl who had everything to live for."

After a search that lasted twenty hours, when my body was found, the evening papers said, " 'Needle' is found: in haystack!"

Kathleen, speaking from that Catholic point of view which

takes some getting used to, said, "She was at Confession only the day before she died—wasn't she lucky?"

The poor byre-hand who sold us the milk was grilled for hour after hour by the local police, and later by Scotland Yard. So was George. He admitted walking as far as the haystack with me, but he denied lingering there.

"You hadn't seen your friend for ten years?" the Inspector asked him.

"That's right," said George.

"And you didn't stop to have a chat?"

"No. We'd arranged to meet later at dinner. My cousin was waiting for the milk, I couldn't stop."

The old soul, his cousin, swore that he hadn't been gone more than ten minutes in all, and she believed it to the day of her death a few months later. There was the microscopic evidence of hay on George's jacket, of course, but the same evidence was on every man's jacket in the district that fine harvest year. Unfortunately, the byreman's hands were even brawnier and mightier than George's. The marks on my wrists had been done by such hands, so the laboratory charts indicated when my post-mortem was all completed. But the wrist-marks weren't enough to pin down the crime to either man. If I hadn't been wearing my long-sleeved cardigan, it was said, the bruises might have matched up properly with someone's fingers.

Kathleen, to prove that George had absolutely no motive, told the police that she was engaged to him. George thought this a little foolish. They checked up on his life in Africa, right back to his living with Matilda. But the marriage didn't come out—who would think of looking up registers in the Congo? Not that this would have proved any motive for murder. All the same, George was relieved when the inquiries were over without the marriage to Matilda being disclosed. He was able to have his nervous breakdown at the same time as Kathleen had hers, and they recovered together and got married, long after the police had shifted their inquiries to an Air Force camp five miles from Kathleen's aunt's home. Only a lot of excitement and drinks came of those investigations. The Haystack Murder was one of the unsolved crimes that year.

Shortly afterwards the byre-hand emigrated to Canada to start afresh, with the help of Skinny who felt sorry for him.

After seeing George taken away home by Kathleen that Saturday in the Portobello Road, I thought that perhaps I might be seeing more of him in similar circumstances. The next Saturday I looked out for him, and at last there he was, without Kathleen, half-worried, half-hopeful.

I dashed his hopes. I said, "Hallo, George!"

He looked in my direction, rooted in the midst of the flowing market-mongers in that convivial street. I thought to myself, "He looks as if he had a mouthful of hay." It was the new bristly maize-coloured beard and mustache surrounding his great mouth which suggested the thought, gay and lyrical as life.

"Hallo, George!" I said again.

I might have been inspired to say more on that agreeable morning, but he didn't wait. He was away down a side street and along another street and down one more, zig-zag, as far and as devious as he could take himself from the Portobello Road.

Nevertheless he was back again next week. Poor Kathleen had brought him in her car. She left it at the top of the street, and got out with him, holding him tight by the arm. It grieved me to see Kathleen ignoring the spread of scintillations on the stalls. I had myself seen a charming Battersea box quite to her taste, also a pair of enamelled silver earrings. But she took no notice of these wares, clinging close to George, and, poor Kathleen—I hate to say how she looked.

And George was haggard. His eyes seemed to have gotten smaller as if he had been recently in pain. He advanced up the road with Kathleen on his arm, letting himself lurch from side to side with his wife bobbing beside him, as the crowds asserted their rights of way.

"Oh, George!" I said. "You don't look at all well, George."

"Look!" said George. "Over there by the hardware barrow. That's Needle."

Kathleen was crying. "Come back home, dear," she said.

"Oh, you don't look well, George!" I said.

They took him to a nursing home. He was fairly quiet, except on Saturday mornings when they had a hard time of it to keep him indoors and away from the Portobello Road.

But a couple of months later he did escape. It was a Monday.

They searched for him in the Portobello Road, but actually he had gone off to Kent to the village near the scene of the Haystack Murder. There he went to the police and gave himself up, but they could tell from the way he was talking that there was something wrong with the man.

"I saw Needle in the Portobello Road three Saturdays running," he explained, "and they put me in a private ward but I got away while the nurses were seeing to the new patient. You remember the murder of Needle—well, I did it. Now you know the truth, and that will keep bloody Needle's mouth shut."

Dozens of poor mad fellows confess to every murder. The police obtained an ambulance to take him back to the nursing home. He wasn't there long. Kathleen gave up her shop and devoted herself to looking after him at home. But she found that the Saturday mornings were a strain. He insisted on going to see me in Portobello Road and would come back to insist that he'd murdered Needle. Once he tried to tell her something about Matilda, but Kathleen was so kind and solicitous, I don't think he had the courage to remember what he had to say.

Skinny had always been rather reserved with George since the murder. But he was kind to Kathleen. It was he who persuaded them to emigrate to Canada so that George should be well out of reach of the Portobello Road.

George has recovered somewhat in Canada but of course he will never be the old George again, as Kathleen writes to Skinny. "That Haystack tragedy did for George," she writes. "I feel sorrier for George sometimes than I am for poor Needle. But I do often have Masses said for Needle's soul."

I doubt if George will ever see me again in the Portobello Road. He broods much over the crumpled snapshot he took of us on the haystack. Kathleen does not like the photograph, I don't wonder. For my part, I consider it quite a jolly snap, but I don't think we were any of us so lovely as we look in it, gazing blatantly over the ripe cornfields, Skinny with his humorous expression, I secure in my difference from the rest, Kathleen with her head prettily perched on her hand, each reflecting fearlessly in the face of George's camera the glory of the world, as if it would never pass.

Felisberto Hernández

THE CROCODILE

Translated from the Spanish by Esther Allen

One autumn night when it was hot and humid I went to a city that was almost unknown to me; what little light there was in the streets was muted by the humidity and the few leaves left on the trees. I went into a cafe near a church, sat down at a table in the back and thought about my life. I knew how to isolate the hours of happiness and enclose myself within them. First, with my eyes, I stole anything left carelessly out on the street or inside a house, then bore it back to my solitude. Going over it in my head gave me such pleasure that if people had known they would have hated me. But there might not be many happy times left to me. I'd once toured cities like this one, giving piano concerts; my hours of pleasure had been few since I lived in the anguish of having to assemble a group of people who wanted to lend their support to a concert. I had to coordinate them, influence each one, and try to find an active man among them. It was almost always like having a fight with slow, distracted drunks. Just as I managed to bring one person in, another would slip away. On top of that I had to practice and write my newspaper articles.

But for some time I hadn't had to worry about that any

more, having managed to obtain a position with a large company that sold women's stockings. I figured that stockings were more necessary than concerts and would be easier to market. A friend of mine told the manager that as a concert pianist I had many female contacts and had visited many cities, and could make use of the influence of my concerts to peddle stockings.

The manager made a face but hired me. It wasn't only my friend's influence that made him accept me: my advertising slogan for the stockings had won second prize. The brand name was *Illusion*, and my slogan was "Nowadays, who doesn't cherish their Illusions?" But selling stockings also turned out to be very hard, and every day I expected to be called back to headquarters and have my travel allowance cut off. At first, I made a tremendous effort. (Selling stockings had nothing to do with my concerts—the only people I had to negotiate with were shopkeepers.) When I happened to run into old acquaintances, I told them that as the representative of a large company I could travel independently and no longer had to oblige my friends to sponsor concerts when the time was not ripe for them. The time had never been ripe for my concerts. In that very city, they'd made some rather unusual excuses: the Club president, annoyed because I took him away from his card game, told me that someone who had a lot of relatives had just died and half the city was in mourning. This time, I simply announced that I would be spending a few days there, to see if the desire for a concert arose of its own accord. But a concert pianist who sold stockings made a bad impression. As for the stockings, every morning I worked myself up to sell them and every night I was let down: it was like getting dressed and undressed. This constant replenishment of the brute force I needed to keep going at the shopkeepers, who were always very busy, took a lot out of me. But now, resigned to being fired, I was trying to enjoy myself for as long as my travel allowance lasted.

Suddenly I noticed that a blind man with a harp had come into the cafe; I'd seen him that afternoon. I decided to leave before I lost my will to enjoy life, but as I walked out I saw him again; the brim of his hat was crumpled and his eyes rolled towards the heavens as he struggled to play. A few of the harp's strings had been clumsily repaired, and covering the pale wood of the instrument and the man's whole body was a grime such as I had never seen before. I thought of myself and felt depressed.

When I switched on the light in my hotel room, I saw the bed that was my bed for those few days. The sheets were turned down, and the nickel-plated bars made me think of a young madwoman, yielding herself to every passer-by. Once I was in bed I turned the light off but couldn't sleep. I switched it back on. The bulb peeked out from under its shade like an eyeball from beneath a dark lid. I turned it off at once and tried to think about the stocking business, but in the darkness I still saw the lampshade a moment longer. Fading to a lighter color, its shape began shifting to one side, melting into the darkness as if it were the soul of the shade, departing for Purgatory. All this happened in the time it would take a blotter to absorb some spilled ink.

The next morning, after dressing and working myself up for the day, I went to see if the night train had brought bad news. There was no letter or telegram for me. I decided to visit every business on one of the main streets. There was a store at the top of the street. Going in, I found myself in a room crammed to the ceiling with trinkets and rags. There was only one naked dummy, made of red cloth with a black knob for a head. I clapped my hands and all the rags instantly swallowed up the sound. From behind the dummy appeared a girl of about ten who said rudely, "What do you want?"

"Is the owner here?"

"There is no owner. My mama's the one in charge."

"She's not here?"

"She went to see Doña Vicenta and she's coming right back."

Then a boy of about three appeared. He clung to his sister's skirt and they stood there a while, all in a row—dummy, girl, boy. "I'll wait," I said.

The girl said nothing. I sat down on a box and started playing with her little brother. Remembering I still had one of the chocolates I'd bought at the movies, I dug it out of my pocket.

The little boy quickly came and took it away from me. I covered my face with my hands and pretended to sob. My eyes were covered, but in the dark hollow of my hands I opened my fingers a crack and began watching the boy. He observed me without moving, and I cried harder and harder. Finally he decided to put the chocolate on my knee. Then I laughed and gave it to him. At that moment I realized that my face was wet.

I left before the owner came back. Passing a jewelry shop, I looked at myself in a mirror and my eyes were dry. After lunch I was sitting in the café but left immediately when I saw the blind man with the harp rolling his eyes. Then I walked to a solitary plaza in a deserted area and sat down on a bench facing a wall covered with vines. There I thought about the morning's tears. I was intrigued by the fact that they had come, and I wanted to be alone, as if I'd gone off to play in secret with the toy I'd accidentally switched on a few hours earlier. It shamed me a little, in my own eyes, to start crying for no reason, even if it was only in fun, as it had been that morning. With some hesitation I wrinkled up my eyes and nose to see if the tears would arrive, but then thought that I shouldn't just go looking for tears, like someone wringing out a rag. I'd have to give myself over to it with real sincerity. I buried my face in my hands. There was something serious about that position; unexpectedly I was moved. I felt a kind of pity for myself and the tears began to flow.

I'd been crying for a while when I saw two female legs clad in semi-sheer *Illusion* stockings climbing down from the top of the wall. Then I noticed a green skirt that was hard to see against the vines. I hadn't heard the ladder being set down. The woman was on the bottom rung and I quickly dried my tears but hung my head low, as if I were pensive. The woman slowly walked over and sat next to me. She'd climbed down with her back to me and I didn't know what her face looked like. Finally she said, "What's wrong? You can trust me . . ."

A few moments went by. I knotted my brow as if to hide behind it and wait there. I'd never adopted this expression before and my eyebrows were quivering. Then I made a gesture with my hand as if to begin speaking, though what I might say to her had not yet occurred to me. She spoke once more. "Talk to me, just talk. I have children. I know what heartache is."

I'd already imagined a face for that woman and that green skirt. But when she said this about heartache and children, I imagined a different one. At the same time, I said, "I have to think a little bit."

"With this kind of thing, the more you think the worse it gets," she replied.

I thought a wet rag had suddenly fallen nearby. But it turned out to be a large banana leaf, heavy with moisture. After a short pause, she picked up the conversation again, "Tell me the truth. What's she like?"

At first this struck me as funny. Then a girlfriend I once had came into my mind. Whenever I didn't feel like taking a walk with her along a stream—where she'd strolled with her father when he was alive—this girlfriend of mine would weep silently. Then, even though it bored me to be forever going to the same place, I indulged her. Thinking of her, I had the idea of saying to the woman now at my side, "She was a woman who often wept."

This woman placed her hands, which were large and reddish, on her green skirt and told me, laughing, "You men always believe in a woman's tears."

I thought of my own tears, a bit disconcerted. I stood up from the bench and said, "I believe you're mistaken. But thank you for comforting me all the same."

And I left without looking at her.

The next day, late in the morning, I went into one of the largest shops. The owner laid my stockings out on the counter and stroked them for some time with his stumpy fingers. He seemed not to hear my words. His sideburns were shot through with gray, as if he'd left shaving cream on them. Meanwhile, several women came in; before attending to them, he signaled me with one of the fingers that had caressed the stockings that he was not going to buy them. I didn't move and thought about persisting. Maybe later, when no one else was around, I could start up a conversation with him; I'd tell him about an herb which, when dissolved in water, could dye his sideburns. The women weren't leaving and I felt unusually impatient; I longed to leave that shop, that city, that life. I thought about my country and about many other things. And suddenly, just as I was beginning to calm down, I had an idea. What would happen if I started crying right in front of all these people? It struck me as a very violent thing to do, but I'd been wanting to do something out of the ordinary, to put the world to the test, for a long time. I also needed to prove to myself that I was capable of great violence. And before I could change my mind I sat down in a little chair backed up against the counter and with all those people around me I put my hands to my face and began emitting sobbing noises. Almost simultaneously, a woman let out a loud cry and said, "A man is weeping."

Then I heard a hubbub of voices and snatches of conversation: "Don't go near him, little girl . . ." "Maybe he just got some bad news . . ." "The train came in only a little while ago, there hasn't been time for the mail . . ." From between my fingers I saw a fat woman saying, "To think how the world is now. If my children couldn't see me, I'd be crying too!" At first the tears didn't come and I was desperate; I was even afraid they'd think I was playing a joke on them and have me arrested. But finally I choked up from my anguish and the tremendous effort I was making, and the first tears were possible. I felt a heavy hand settle on my shoulder, and when I heard the owner's voice I recognized the fingers that had stroked the stockings. He said, "But *compañero*, a man's got to have some spirit . . ."

Then I stood up, as if some mechanism had been activated, took my two hands away from my face, removed the third one that was on my shoulder, and said, my face still wet, "I'm fine, really. I have lots of spirit! It's just that sometimes this comes over me; it's like a memory . . ."

Through the expectant silence that fell around my words, I heard a woman say, "Ay! He's weeping over a memory . . ."

"That's all for now, señoras," the owner announced.

I smiled and dried my face off. Then the knot of people that had formed began milling around and a small woman with mad eyes appeared and said, "I know you. I think I've seen you some-where else, when you were agitated."

I thought she must have seen me in a concert, flinging my-self around during the finale, but I kept my mouth shut. Con-versation broke out among the women and some began to leave. The one who recognized me stayed there with me. Another one came over and said, "I know you sell stockings. By chance, some friends and I . . ."

The owner intervened. "Don't worry, señora," he said, adding (to me), "Come back this afternoon."

"I'm leaving town after lunch. Do you want two dozen?"

"No, half a dozen should be . . ."

"A dozen is the minimum order the company will accept. . . ."

Without going any closer to the owner, I took out my sales book and began filling out the order form, writing against a glass door, and surrounded by women talking loudly. I was afraid the owner would change his mind. Finally he signed the order and I went outside with everyone else.

Word soon got out that I had "this thing" that would come over me, which at first was like a memory. I wept in other stores and sold more stockings than usual. By the time I'd wept in several cities, my sales figures were comparable to any other salesman's.

Once they called me to company headquarters—I'd wept my way across the entire north of the country at that point — and as I was waiting my turn to speak to the manager I could hear an-other travelling salesman saying in the next room, "I do all I can, but I'm not going to start crying just so they'll buy from me!"

And the sickly voice of the manager replied, "You've got to do whatever it takes, even cry for them. . . ."

The salesman interrupted, "But I can't get the tears to come!"

After a silence, the manager said, "What? Who told you about that?"

"Yes! There's one guy who gushes tears . . ."

The sickly voice began laughing with some difficulty, be-tween bouts of coughing. Then I heard mumbling and footsteps moving away.

After a while, they called me in and had me cry in front of the manager, the supervisors, and all the other employees. When the manager first had me come in and the situation was explained, he laughed painfully until tears came to his eyes. He asked me, in the most courteous way, for a demonstration. Hardly had I accepted when a number of employees who'd been waiting outside the door came in. There was a lot of commotion and they asked me not to cry yet. "Hurry up! One of the travelling salesmen is going to cry," I heard someone say, from behind a screen.

"But why?"

"How should I know!"

I was sitting beside the manager at his big desk; they had phoned one of the company's owners but he couldn't come. The men weren't quieting down, and one shouted out, "Think of your sweet mama, that'll make you cry!"

"When they stop talking, I'll cry," I told the manager.

He threatened them in his sickly voice, and after a few moments of relative silence I looked out a window at the crown of a tree—we were on the second floor—buried my face in my hands and tried to cry. I was a little dismayed. Whenever I'd cried before, the people around me hadn't been aware of my real feelings, but these men knew I was going to cry and that inhibited me. When the tears finally came, I took one hand away from my face, both to get my handkerchief out and so they could see that my face was wet. Some laughed and others looked serious; then I shook my face violently and they all laughed. But then they were silent until they began to laugh again. I wiped my tears away as the sickly voice repeated, "Very good, very good." Maybe they were all disappointed. And I felt like an empty bottle, still dripping. I wanted to react; I was in a bad mood and felt like behaving badly. Catching up to the manager, I said, "I don't want any of the others using the same technique to sell stockings. I want the company to acknowledge my . . . my initiative and grant me a certain period of exclusivity."

"Come back tomorrow and we'll talk about it."

The next day the secretary had the document already drawn

up and read it aloud: "The company hereby pledges to refrain from using, and to enforce respect for, the system of advertising which consists of weeping . . ." Then they both laughed and the manager said that was no good. While he edited the document, I strolled out to the front desk. Behind it was a girl who watched me as she talked to me; her eyes looked as if they were painted on from the inside.

"So you cry because you like crying?"

"Yes."

"Then I know more than you do —you don't even know you have a sorrow of some kind."

I was pensive a moment, then said, "Look: I may not be the happiest person around, but I know how to make do with my misfortune. I'm almost lucky."

As I walked away—the manager was calling me—I stole a look at her gaze: she'd placed it on me, as if laying a hand on my shoulder.

On my next sales trip, I was in a small city. It was a sad day and I didn't feel like crying. I'd rather have been alone in my room, listening to the rain and thinking how the water was separating me from everyone. I travelled hidden behind a mask painted with tears, but my face was tired.

Suddenly I noticed that someone had approached me and was asking, "What's wrong?"

Then, like an employee caught in a moment of idleness, I felt I had to go back to my task. Putting my hands over my face I began making sobs.

That year I cried until December, stopped crying for January and part of February, and started crying again after Carnival. The break did me good and I went back to crying with renewed vigor—I'd missed the success my weeping brought. A certain pride in crying had been born within me. There were a lot of salesmen around. But I was an actor who could inhabit his role on the spur of the moment, convincing the public with his tears . . .

That year, I starting weeping in the west and reached a city where my concerts had been successful. The second time I played there, the public had greeted me with a long, affectionate ovation; I thanked them, standing next to the piano, and they wouldn't let me sit down to begin the concert. This time I would undoubtedly be giving at least a brief recital. The first time I wept there, I was in the most luxurious hotel, at lunchtime on a radiant day. I'd eaten and had a cup of coffee, when, elbows on the table, I covered my face with my hands. A few moments later, some friends I'd just greeted came over; I let them stand there, and meanwhile a poor old woman—I don't know where she came from—sat down at my table and I watched her from between my fingers which were already wet. She lowered her head and said nothing, but she had a face so sad it made you feel like bursting into tears. . . .

The day I gave my concert I was feeling a nervousness brought on by fatigue. As I played the last piece in the first half of the program, I took one of the movements too fast. I tried to slow down but grew clumsy and didn't have sufficient balance or strength; all I could do was go on, but my hands were getting tired, I was losing clarity, and I realized I wasn't going to make it to the finale. Then, before I could think, I'd taken my hands from the keyboard and put them on my face. It was the first time I wept onstage.

There were murmurs of surprise, and someone, I don't know why, tried to applaud, but other people were mumbling and I stood up. I covered my eyes with one hand, and groping along the piano with the other I tried to walk offstage. A few women cried out, thinking I was about to fall into the orchestra pit. I was halfway through a door in the wing when someone shouted from the upper tier, "Crooo-co-diiiiile!"

I heard laughter, but went to the dressing room, washed my face, reappeared immediately, and finished the first part of the program with fresh, clean hands. Afterwards, many people came to say hello to me and the cry of "crocodile" sparked much comment. "It seems to me that the person who shouted that is correct," I said. "I really don't know why I cry; weeping comes over me and I can't do anything about it. It may be as natural for me as it is for the crocodile. After all, I don't know why the crocodile weeps, either."

One of the people I'd just been introduced to had a long face, and since his hair was cut short and stood on end, his head looked like a brush. Another person in the circle pointed him out and told me, "Our friend here is a doctor. What do you say, doctor?"

I blanched. He looked at me with a police detective's eyes and asked, "Tell me one thing: do you cry more by day or by night?"

I remembered that I never cried at night because I never went out selling at night, and answered, "I cry only in the daytime."

I don't remember his other questions. But in the end he advised me, "Don't eat any meat. Your system has been poisoned for a long time."

A few days later a party was thrown for me at the town's finest club. I rented a dress coat with an immaculate white vest and when I looked at myself in the mirror, I thought, "Well, they can't say this crocodile doesn't have a fine white belly. Why, I believe that beast even has a double chin, just like mine—and it's voracious, too. . . ."

Not many people were at the Club when I got there, and I realized I'd arrived too early. I saw a gentleman from the committee and told him I would like to work a little at the piano. That way I'd have a pretext for my early arrival. We went through a green curtain and I found myself in a large, empty hall set up for dancing. Opposite the curtain, at the other end, was the piano. The gentleman from the committee and the porter walked me over, and as they were opening the piano, the gentleman—he had black eyebrows and white hair—told me that the party would be a great success, and that the head of the literary society, a friend of mine, would give a very lovely speech, which he had heard. He tried to recall a few phrases but then decided it was best not to tell me anything about it. I put my hands on the piano and they left. As I played, I thought, "Tonight I won't cry . . . that would be very ugly . . . the head of the literary society may want me to weep as evidence of the success of his speech. But I won't cry for anything in the world."

For a while I'd noticed the green curtain moving, and suddenly a tall girl emerged from among its folds, her hair hanging loose; her eyes were narrowed, as if to see across a distance. She was looking at me, and came towards me, carrying something in one hand; behind her appeared a maid who caught up with her and began speaking in her ear. I took the opportunity to look at her legs and realized she had only one stocking on. She kept gesturing to indicate that the conversation was over, but the maid went on talking and the two of them returned to their subject as if to a tempting delicacy. Still playing the piano while they conversed, I had time to think "What can she want with the stocking . . .? Was there some problem with it . . . and knowing that I represent the company —and right now, during a party!"

Finally she came over and said, "Excuse me, I'd like you to autograph a stocking."

At first I laughed; then I tried to react as if the request had been made of me before. I began explaining why the stocking wouldn't hold up under a pen; on other occasions I'd solved that problem by signing a label which the woman in question then glued to her stocking. But in giving these explanations, I displayed the experience of a former dry goods salesman who later became a pianist. Anguish was stealing over me when she sat down on the piano bench and said, as she put the stocking on, "It's too bad you're such a liar . . . you should have thanked me for the idea."

I had placed my eyes on her legs. Then I took them away and my thoughts became embroiled. There was a displeased silence. She bent her head and let her hair fall forward, and beneath that blond curtain her hands moved as if they were fleeing. I said nothing, and she took forever. Finally, the leg made a dancing movement, and as she stood up, the foot, its toes pointed, slipped on the shoe; the hands pulled back the hair, and waving at me silently she left.

When people started coming in, I went to the bar. It occurred to me to order a whisky. The bartender named all the different brands, and since I didn't know any of them I said, "Give me that last one."

I climbed onto a barstool, trying not to wrinkle the tails of my dress coat. I must have looked more like a black parrot than a crocodile. I was silent, thinking about the girl with the stocking; the memory of her busy hands was disturbing.

I felt myself guided into the auditorium by the head of the literary society. The dance stopped for a moment and he gave his speech. Several times he uttered the words "vicissitudes" and "necessity." When they applauded, I raised my arms like an orchestra conductor about to "attack" and once they were silent I said, "Now that I should be crying, I can't. I can't speak, either, and I don't want to keep apart any longer the couples who will now join together to dance." I concluded with a bow.

I turned around to embrace the man from the literary society and saw the girl with the stocking over his shoulder. Smiling at me, she raised the left side of her skirt a little to show me the place on her stocking where she'd pasted a small portrait of me cut out of the program. I smiled, full of gladness, but then blurted out a piece of idiocy which everyone repeated, "Very good, very good: the leg of the heart."

And yet I felt fortunate, and went to the bar. I climbed onto a stool again and the bartender asked me, "White Horse Whisky?"

And I answered, with the gesture of a musketeer drawing his sword, "White Horse or Black Parrot."

In a short while a boy walked over with one hand hidden behind his back.

"Chubby told me it doesn't bother you when they call you 'Crocodile'."

"That's true. I like it."

Then, taking his hand from behind his back, he showed me a caricature of a big crocodile that looked a lot like me; it had one small hand in its mouth, where its teeth were a keyboard, and from the other hand dangled a stocking it was using to wipe away its tears.

When my friends took me back to my hotel I thought about all the weeping I'd done in that country and took malevolent pleasure in having deceived them; I considered myself a bourgeois of anguish. But when I was alone in my room, something unexpected happened. First I looked at myself in the mirror; I had the caricature in my hand and started looking at the crocodile and at my own face, in succession. Suddenly, though I had no intention of imitating the crocodile, my face began to weep, all on its own. I watched, as if I were looking at a sister whose unhappiness I knew nothing about. My face had new wrinkles and the tears trickled across them. I turned off the light and lay down. My face went on weeping; the tears slid along my nose and onto the pillow. I fell asleep like that. When I woke up I felt the prickle of dried tears. I wanted to get out of bed and wash my eyes, but I was afraid my face would start crying again. I lay still, rolling my eyes in the dark, like that blind man who played the harp.

LEONID TSYPKIN

from SUMMER IN BADEN-BADEN
Translated from the Russian by ROGER KEYS and ANGELA JONES

I was on a train, travelling by day, but it was winter-time—late December, the very depths—and to add to it the train was heading north—to Leningrad—so it was quickly darkening on the other side of the windows—bright lights of Moscow stations flashing into view and vanishing again behind me like the scattering of some invisible hand—each snow-veiled suburban platform with its fleeting row of lamps melting into one fiery ribbon—the dull drone of a station rushing past, as if the train were roaring over a bridge—the sound muffled by the double-glazed windows with frames not quite hermetically sealed into fogged-up, half-frozen panes of glass—pierced even so by the station-lights forcefully etching their line of fire—and beyond, the sense of boundless snowy wastes—and the violent sway of the carriage from side to side—pitching and rolling—especially in the end corridor—and outside, once complete darkness had fallen and only the hazy whiteness of snow was visible and the surburban dachas had come to an end and in the window along with me was the reflection of the carriage with its ceiling-lights and seated passengers, I took from the suitcase in the rack above me a book I had already started to read in Moscow and which I had brought especially for the journey to Leningrad, and I opened it at the page held by a bookmark decorated with Chinese characters and a delicate oriental drawing—and in my heart of hearts I had no intention of returning the book borrowed from my aunt who possessed a large library, and because it was very flimsy and almost falling apart, I had taken it to a binder who trimmed the pages so that they lay together evenly and enclosed the whole thing in a strong cover on which he pasted the book's original title-page—the *Diary* of Anna Grigor'yevna Dostoyevskaya produced by some liberal publishing-house still possible at that time—either "Landmarks," or "New Life," or one of those—with dates given in both Old Style and New Style and words and whole phrases in German or French without translation and the *de rigueur* "Mme" added with all the diligence of a grammar-school pupil—a transliteration of the shorthand notes which she had taken during the summer following her marriage abroad.

The Dostoyevskys had left Petersburg in mid-April 1867, arriving in Vilna by the following morning where they were constantly pestered by loathsome little Jews thrusting their services upon them on the hotel stairs and even going as far as chasing after the horse-cab in which Anna Grigor'yevna and Fyodor Mikhaylovich were travelling, trying, until they were sent packing, to sell them amber cigarette-holders—and the same Jews with flowing uncut curls framing their brows could be seen in the evening walking their Jewish wives around the narrow old streets—and then a day or two later, off to Berlin and then to Dresden where they began to look around for an apartment, because Germans, and especially German women—all of these Fräulein-proprietors of boarding-houses and even of simple furnished rooms—ruthlessly overcharged and underfed newly arrived Russians—waiters cheated them out of their small change, and not just waiters either—the German race was a dim-witted bunch, as it seemed collectively incapable of explaining to Fedya how to get to any street whatsoever, invariably pointing in the wrong direction—it seemed almost deliberate—and Anna Grigor'yevna was an old hand at Jew-spotting from when she had first visited Fedya while he was writing *Crime and Punishment* at the Olonkin house, which, as Anna Grigor'yevna was to observe later, immediately reminded her of the house in which Raskol'nikov lived—and Jews could be nosed out there, too, scurrying up and down the stairs among the other tenants—but, to be quite fair, it should be stated that in the *Memoirs* which Anna Grigor'yevna wrote not long before the Revolution, perhaps even after she got to know Leonid Grossman, there is no mention at all of loathsome little Jews on stairs.

The photograph pasted into the *Diary* shows Anna Grigor'yevna still quite young at the time, her glowering face both possessed and pious, but Fedya, already getting on in years, not very tall and with such short legs that it seemed, if he were to get up from the chair on which he was sitting, he would not appear very much taller—he had the face of a man of the common people, and it was obvious that he liked to have his photograph taken and that he was a fervent man of prayer—so why had I rushed around Moscow shaking with emotion (I am not ashamed to admit it) with the *Diary* in my hands until I found someone to bind it?—Why, in public on a tram, had I avidly leafed through its flimsy pages, looking for places which I seemed to have glimpsed before, and then why, after seeing it bound, had I carefully placed the book, which had now become heavy, on my desk like the Bible, keeping it there day and night?—Why was I now on my way to Petersburg—yes, not to Leningrad, but precisely to *Petersburg* whose streets had been walked by this shortlegged, rather small individual (no more so, probably, than most other inhabitants of the nineteenth century) with the face of a church-warden or a retired soldier?—Why was I reading this book *now*, in a railway-carriage, beneath a wavering, flickering, electric light-bulb, glaring brightly at one moment, almost extinguished the next according to the speed of the train and the performance of the diesel locomotives, amid the slamming of doors at either end of the carriage by people constantly coming through balancing glasses full of water for children or for washing fruit, leaving for a smoke, or simply to go to the toilet, whose door would bang shut immediately afterwards?—amid the banging and slamming of all these doors, with the rolling motion jogging my book now to one side, now to the other, and the smell of coal and steam engines which somehow still lingered although they had stopped running long ago.

They eventually rented a room from Mme Zimmermann, a tall, angular Swiss, but on the very day of their arrival they booked in at a hotel on the main square and immediately made their way to the picture-gallery.

An enormous line converging on the Pushkin Museum in Moscow—small groups only being admitted at a time—the "Sistine Madonna" hanging on a landing somewhere between floors, a militiaman in situ beneath—and years later at the same museum the "Mona Lisa" displayed herself, strategically lit, behind double, bullet-proof panes of glass—the queue of "connected" people snaking its way towards the painting or, rather, to the glass armour-plating—an embalmed corpse in a sarcophagus, Madonna in a landscape background—a truly enigmatic smile or, perhaps, just the effect of public opinion—and beside the picture, another militiaman, urging the queue forward with a "Take your leave *now*, take your leave!" in decorous fashion, as they all, of course, were art experts or special guests—trying to linger as long as they could beside the painting and, when they had passed it by, catching up with the people who had gone on ahead, continuing to peer back at the picture, cricking their necks, revolving their heads nearly a hundred and eighty degrees—the "Sistine Madonna," hung on a wall between two windows, the light falling from the side—the day was cloudy and the painting seemed veiled with a kind of haze—the Madonna floated in clouds which seemed like the airborne hem of her dress or perhaps the two things melted together—and somewhere down below to the left an apostle looked piously up—with six fingers on one hand—really six, I counted them myself—and a photograph of this picture was given to Dostoyevsky for his birthday many years after his visit to Dresden and shortly before his death, by someone supposing that this was his favorite picture (although it was probably "Christ in the Sepulchre" by Holbein the Younger)—and anyway the photograph of Raphael's "Sistine Madonna," in a wooden frame, hangs in the Dostoyevsky Museum in Leningrad above the leather couch on which the writer died—an airborne Madonna holding an equally airborne half-seated child in her arms, perhaps offering him her breast like a gypsy woman, in front of anyone—her expression as enigmatic as the Mona Lisa's—a photograph just like that, a little smaller and probably not as good as a modern print, can be found on a shelf in my aunt's glass-fronted book-case, positioned with a somewhat deliberate carelessness.

The Dostoyevskys would visit the art gallery every day in the same way as people in Kislovodsk drop into the kursaal to take the waters, for a rendezvous or simply to stand about observing the comings and goings, and then go to lunch—looking for a cheaper-style restaurant, but a place which would provide them with good food and trustworthy waiters—always the Dostoyevskys found they were cheated out of two or three silver groschen as all Germans were undeniably unscrupulous—after the usual gallery visit they once chose the Brühlsche Terrasse, placed picturesquely over the Elbe—the waiter had been spotted on a previous visit and dubbed the "diplomat," as he looked like one—and into the bargain they had caught him charging twice the price for a cup of coffee—five groschen instead of two and a half—but they outsmarted him when Anna Grigor'yevna had slipped him the two and a half groschen, given them as change, back to him as a tip in place of five—but this time they were very hungry, especially Fedya, and instead of attending their table, the "diplomat" busied himself with a later arrival, some Saxon officer with fleshy red nose and yellowish eyes, his whole appearance that of a drinker—and although Fedya called to the waiter, he continued, with imperturbable expression, to serve the officer who was adjusting the starched napkin behind his tight military collar—revenge by the "diplomat" for their last encounter—Fedya tapped his knife on the table—and finally the "diplomat" arrived, but only, of course, in passing, to say that he could in fact hear them and there was no need to drum on the table—chicken again for Fedya and veal cutlets—much later one portion only of chicken arriving—"What is the meaning of this,"—and the "diplomat" replied with excessive politeness that only one portion was ordered—and the same thing again with the veal cutlets—and four waiters sat playing cards in the next dining-room, and in the room where the Dostoyevskys ate there were few customers—he must have done it on purpose—red blotches sprouted on Fedy's face, and loudly to his wife he said that, if he had been there alone, he would have shown them, and he even began to shout at her as if it were her fault that the two of them had gone there together—and with knife and fork poised he purposely hurled them down with a great crash, nearly smashing the plate—people began to stare—and they left without looking around, Fedya having thrown a whole thaler onto the table instead of the twenty-three groschen they owed—and, slamming the door so hard that the panes of glass shook, they set off down the chestnut-lined avenue—he walking resolutely ahead, she behind, scarcely able to keep up—without her, he could have seen the business through and insisted on his own way, but in fact he was now walking away humiliated by that villainous waiter, because all waiters were, of course, villains—the embodiment of the basest features of human nature—but, alas! the remnants of this cursed waiter-strain linger in all of us—had he himself not stared sycophantically into the yellow-lynx eyes of that drunk, red-nosed swine of a commandant in the convict prison?—yes! that was the one brought to mind by the Saxon officer just now—the one who, drunk and chaperoned by guards, had burst into their wooden barrack and, spotting a prisoner in gray-black jacket backed with its yellow ace of diamonds, spotting him lying down there on the bunk because he felt unwell that particular day, unable to work, had bellowed with all the strength of his bullish throat: "Up, you! Over here!"—and he had been that prisoner, the man now walking down a chestnut-lined avenue away from that restaurant and that terrace, so picturesquely placed over the Elbe—and even then, in the convict-prison, he had seen it all only from the side, as if it happened in a dream, or to someone else, not to him at all—and being present in the guard-house once, when corporal punishment was being applied—the victim lying motionless as he was beaten with birch-rods, leaving bloody weals on his back and buttocks—just as silently the prisoner slowly rose to his feet, carefully fastened each button on his jacket and left the room, without so much as a glance at Krivtsov who stood there beside him—would *he* have managed to keep so silent and leave the guard-room with such dignity?—jumping up off his bunk and with feverishly shaking hands adjusting the grey-black jacket, he walked towards Krivtsov who stood in the doorway—walked with head lowered—no, not walked, but almost ran—humiliating in itself—and when he reached the officer, he stared at him, not a firm, hard look, but with pleading eyes—realizing this from the way Krivtsov's pupils dilated like a predator's, the pupils of those yellow, lynx-eyes of his—lynx-like not only through their animal shape, but because of that hunting look, searching for the next victim—the thought running through his mind even as he stood before him, and that he could think of such a thing at such a moment had struck him at the time as strange—and what was this to do with servility?!—this fear, this simple fear—but fear gives rise to servility, does it not?

Anna Grigor'yevna managed to catch him up and, placing her hand with its worn glove beneath his elbow, looked guiltily into his eyes—without her, *he* would have shown that waiter what's what, *he* would have put them all in their place!—his eyes moving slowly away from her face, staring at the hand which lay on his shoulder—"It does not befit a neatly dressed woman to be seen in such gloves," he said slowly, distinctly, transferring his gaze to her face once again—with lips trembling and eyelids strangely swelling up, she continued to walk by his side, but only through inertia and because she thought that his words could not apply to her: he would not have said that to *her*—with quickening pace she left him, almost at a run, turning into some side-street, also lined with chestnut trees—she looked around briefly and, through the leaves and her tears, could make out his figure marching down the avenue, resolute as ever, wearing the dark-gray almost black suit, bought in Berlin—at the time the thought had not occurred to him to suggest that she might buy herself some new gloves, although the ones she had already had frayed at the seams, and twice on the journey she had had to sew them up—in his presence—and now *he* reproached *her* for *that*, *and* the money for their journey had been obtained by pawning her mother's things—walking down the street, almost running, she kept close to the walls of the buildings, veil raised so that no one could see her tear-swollen face—coming towards her, the occasional respectable bowler-hatted German out for a walk with his German wife, and their faces looked pink and self-satisfied—holding the hands of their children, clean and neatly dressed—and *they* didn't worry over paying for the day's lunch or dinner, and *they* didn't raise their voices at each other—and yet Fedya had shouted at her in the restaurant—slipping in through the door of their house she tried to avoid being seen—and first she entered the big room they used as a dining room, oleographs on the wall depicting some river—the Rhine, probably—trees reflected in it, or castles perched on mountains against backgrounds of false blue skies—then the second room, their bedroom with two cumbersome beds, and then the third, a tiny room, Fedya's, with a desk and lying on it, a neat white paper pile and some *papirosa* cigarettes with tobacco spilling out—and she suddenly realized she had come in here in the secret hope that he had overtaken her and would be waiting for her—then she left for the post-office where Fedya often called in, and he was not there and there were no letters, and she went back home again—surely he must be home by now?—Mme. Zimmermann on the stairs told her that Fedya had come in and gone out somewhere—outside again, running onto the street, and suddenly she saw him—coming towards her, pale and smiling guiltily, even pleadingly—and so it turned out he had gone back to the terrace, thinking she would have returned there, demonstrating her independence, and then he had gone to look in the reading-room—and so they went indoors for a moment to change clothes because it was coming on to rain—pouring down in bucketfuls as they emerged again, but they did, after all, have to have lunch—three courses at the Hotel Victoria cost them two thalers and ten silbergroschen—a terrible price seeing that each cutlet cost twelve silbergroschen—have you ever seen the like!—a thoroughly unlucky day!—it was eight o'clock at night when they left the restaurant, dark and wet—so she opened her umbrella, but not in the prudent German way—it brushed against a passing German—and Fedya shouted because her clumsiness could be misinterpreted—and her eyes began to swell again, and in the darkness nobody noticed, thank God!— home again, side by side, not talking, as if they were strangers, and at home they tried to quarrel over tea, though it had all been said already, and then she mentioned his projected trip to Bad Homburg, and he started shouting again, and in reply she shouted back and went into the bedroom—he locked himself in his study, but later came to kiss her goodnight—a nightly habit, especially after a quarrel or disagreement—the gentle awakening to caress or kiss her, because she was his and within his power was her happiness or misery—his awareness of total power over this ingénue, playing with her at will, was probably like the feeling which I have towards sleek young dogs who, at the sight of a hand stretched out for a stroke, wag their tails in a nervous, pleading way, flatten themselves against the ground and begin to tremble—it began with the kiss, then his lips on her breasts, then the swimming began—swimming with large strokes, thrusting their arms in unison from the water to take great gulps of air into their lungs, further and further from the shore, towards the deep-blue arch of the sea—but inevitably he found he was swept into counter-currents bearing him away at an angle, almost back on himself, and he could not keep up, as her arms continued to thrust from the water, still in rhythm, to vanish into the distance—and he felt that he no longer swam but floundered about in the water, his feet reaching for the bottom—and strangely this current, bearing him away, preventing him from moving with her, seemed to turn into the yellow eyes of the commandant with dilated predator pupils and into the rushed unbuttoning of his convict's jacket in order to prostrate himself over the low oak table in the centre of the guardhouse polished by thousands of bodies, and into the groans he could not suppress when the blows of the birch rods rained down, as if someone tightened a red-hot wire across his muscles and bones, and into the spasms of pain which began after the beating, and into the mocking or pitying faces of the onlookers, and into the satisfied smile of the commandant as he ordered the doctor to be summoned, turning sharply on his heels to march out of the guard-room—and the same thing happened with other women because, like Anya, they had all been invisible witnesses, peering through the metal grilled windows, or through the guard-house door, as they struggled to enter to plead on his behalf, but they were barred—all witnesses of his humiliation, and he hated them for that because it denied him experience of the full flight of his feelings—and today as well was added the insulting impudent look of that waiter and the face of the Saxon officer, so like that of the commandant.

A while back he had noticed a particular chair in the gallery where the "Sistine Madonna" hung, a soft chair with a curved back which seemed to be set apart from the others which were placed there for visitors to rest or to sit on and admire one of the pictures—and nobody seemed to sit on this one chair—perhaps meant for the attendant or possessing some historical value—and the first time the thought became tangible, a shiver ran down his spine, it seemed so audacious, so inconceivable—preparing himself for action, he passed the chair and once almost placed his foot on it, but a lot of people were in the room, and the bored-looking attendant dressed in his uniform jacket was leaning against the wall—and perhaps he should have done exactly that in front of everyone, the attendant in particular, as preventing this kind of thing was precisely an attendant's job—approaching the chair, his heart would stop, and after a second of hesitation, as if pondering which way to walk around the chair, he would pass by, peering at the Madonna with exaggerated interest—but that night, as Anya swam away so distantly and he floundered somewhere near the shore, unable to reach the bottom—that night he made a solemn vow to do exactly that—and so, entering the gallery as usual next morning, he headed immediately for the room where the "Sistine Madonna" hung, the beat of his heart echoing in his ears, a crowd jostling in front of the painting—some standing or sitting a slight distance away with opera-glasses (easier to look with *them* as your eyes were concentrated on the painting and did not wander)—and at first not seeing the chair and, from the way his heart stopped jumping and fluttering, realizing he was inwardly glad—but the chair was simply hidden by people—and there was the attendant, in full livery with gilded buttons—a purposeful walk to-wards the chair, even pushing his way through the visitors—Anna Grigor'yevna, who had entered the room with him, standing somewhere to one side, apparently having taken a pair of opera-glasses—and he stepped on to the chair with one foot, eyes closed—or perhaps for that moment he was simply sightless—and then he placed his other foot on it: shoes sinking deep into the soft seat—and above the heads of the crowd, the painting could be seen to particular advantage, the Madonna floating in the clouds with the child in her arms, the apostle looking piously up at her from below, and the angels above—and this was the reason, all things considered, for standing up on the chair, because he did have to think of some explanation for the lackey who would try to drag him off—"Fedya, are you mad!"—Anna Grigor'yevna stood beside him, looking up at him with startled eyes from below—even giving a discreet tug at this sleeve—and he was raised above all others—they were all pygmies, and one of the pygmies was rushing towards him—the attendant—and in place of the painting there appeared the face of the commandant with his bull-neck and Gargantuan chin, held in by the tightly fitting collar of his dress-uniform—smiling in a meek and even pleading sort of way, and not just the face, but there was his whole figure, strangely frail and cringing—and where the visitors had been, in place of their heads was a sea, and he and his wife swam into the deep-bluish distance, thrusting their arms up rhythmically, gulping in the air, moving further and further from the shore—and the prison commandant had nearly faded, his pitiful, bent figure scarcely visible somewhere in the distance, the figure of a beggar, asking for alms—"Standing on chairs is forbidden in this gallery, sir,"—staring reprovingly at the well-dressed person standing on a chair was the attendant, who then moved forward and lifted his arm as though offering support to the person on the chair, who stepped down, almost jumping, pushing aside the attendant's hand, and saw Anna Grigor'yevna standing in the corner of the room, having had time to move away and who was now pretending to be minutely examining a picture through her opera-glasses, but her hands, as she held the glasses, trembled—"For heaven's sake, let's get away from here," she said when he came up to her, her voice hoarse with agitation—visitors were looking around at them and whispering together about something—and taking him by the arm, she led him towards the door leading into the next room.

He should have remained standing on the chair to the bitter end, in spite of the lackey's reprimand, but he had given in and stepped down—appearing now in the wide window of the room, the commandant's face smiled contemptuously, and his fat, fleshy hand rakishly smoothed his mustache in a gesture of victory—and people stared through the guardroom windows, friends of the prisoner and women, too, their eyes full of pity and concern, and he lay across the table with his trousers down, and the guard methodically lashed him— Anna Grigor'yevna's arm was brusquely shaken away and, with lowered head, she resolutely walked into the next room—the chair should not have been left empty—it was unnatural, an empty chair—heading quickly for the center of the room, his feet sinking again into something soft and springy—to stand as long as he liked now—to overcome in himself that humiliation in the face of a servant—could he never cross that boundary?—the crowd had fallen silent, as they do before the curtain rises—and the commandant's face, once again in the place of the painting, winked at him arrogantly—swinging his arm, he slapped his cheek, and the face disappeared, slumping probably with the rest of the commandant's body, which lay on the floor next to the polished table—the prisoner he had tried to punish standing in a triumphant pose, leg placed firmly on the commandant's stomach, and the audience staring in through the windows clapped him loudly, and the women, especially the intimate ones, looked at him with delight and blew him kisses—unhurriedly stepping from the chair—not jumping but carefully stepping—he headed deliberately towards the next room—in the doorway bumping into the attendant who it seemed had been out of the room somewhere, and the lackey politely let him pass.

That night, when he went to kiss Anya, they swam away again together, rhythmically thrusting out their arms from the water and raising their heads to take in gulps of air—and the current did not sweep him away—they swam towards the receding horizon, into the unknown, deep-blue distance, and then he began to kiss her again—a dark triangle appeared, upturned—its apex, its peak, pointing downwards, forever inaccessible, like the inverted peak of a very high mountain disappearing somewhere into the clouds—or rather the core of a volcano—and this peak, this unattainable core, contained the answer both terrible and exquisite to something nameless and unimaginable and, throughout his life, even in his letters to her, he maintained the incessant struggle to reach it, but this peak, this core, remained forever inaccessible—and had he really stood on that chair for as long as he actually wanted to?—the attendant, after all, had been absent when he stood on it for the second time, so it could not be said he had been standing there in defiance of the attendant's will, even though he had resolved to remain in that position until he was led away—and if they had led him away, the attendant and maybe even a policeman—they would have dragged him across the whole room in full view of everyone including Anya, and everything would have thundered down as if from a high mountain—quickly, very quickly, and no longer could he have raised himself up from the polished table on which they had beaten him, and the commandant's face would have hung over him like a flushed red ball, like the gorged abdomen of a blood-sated mosquito, and his whole life would have become exquisite torment, because such humiliation was literally breathtaking—but neither thing had happened—

he had stepped down—voluntarily, without waiting for the attendant to return—and he had not, in fact, brought the business to a scandalous conclusion—the triangle's forbidden peak, both hidden in the clouds and disappearing into the depths of the earth, perhaps to the very center of the earth where the molten rock was constantly boiling, this peak had remained inaccessible.

[. . .]

The morning after he had visited the hotel, when they were just on the point of drinking their tea, Marie brought them a thick, glossy visiting-card announcing in flawless copperplate all too familiar a surname—the early hour having been chosen by Turgenev on purpose, of course, as a polite insult—whoever calls on people at *that* time?—and was it for this he had danced the cancan at his hotel?—and for a moment he pictured Turgenev's face to himself with its characteristic expression of feigned astonishment—no!—the face had not worn its customary expression that last time!—Turgenev's eyes had followed him through the lorgnette extremely intently, as if the lorgnette's owner were afraid he would be bitten by a mad dog at any moment—and this thought pleased him so much he even smiled—and in their rooms it was cool and dark, even peaceful, the workmen in the smithy probably being at their lunch, and the children having spent all night and morning emitting piercing shrieks, now asleep—and he wanted to take off his heavy frock-coat briefly and lie down for a while, but Anna Grigor'yevna had opened the windows and shutters, which she was always so careful to lock whenever they went out, being afraid of burglars, fire, and thunderstorms, and together with the fragrance of acacia blossom and bright sun, sounds from the street entered the room—the clattering of horses' hooves on the cobblestones, the occasional loud remark exchanged by women in the courtyard, the rumbling of carts delivering water or beer—no, he could not permit himself to do that now—he *had* to go—and Anna

Grigor'yevna, compelled by his imperative look, took her bag with a sigh and extracted a few gold coins from it which he stuffed with a trembling hand into his waistcoat pocket, although he did have a purse—it was quicker that way, and much more convenient for him when gambling, as he could bet more easily when he did not know how much he had left, undistracted by thoughts of how much remained and the game undisturbed by having to engage in unnecessary calculations.

He walked with his body bent slightly forward, his shadow gliding along behind him as the sun was now shining from the front—and he would ply between their lodgings and the Kurhaus several times a day, deviating from his route only to look in at the post-office (but money from the publisher Katkov never arrived), or a shop, or the market to buy fruit and flowers for Anna Grigor'yevna on his way back from the casino, whenever he had won—and in general, he would be on an upward climb, despite the smell of perfume wafting from some of the ladies, chance visitors staking one coin at a time, and also despite Jews and Poles who would block his view—on an upward climb, even if he sometimes stumbled or, against all expectation, began suddenly to fall, thinking each time that it was all over, but it would turn out to be only a foothill on the route to the summit which would slowly but surely draw closer, sometimes even visible through breaks in the cloud, covered in virgin snow, gleaming silver in the rays of the sun or even reflecting gold—and for the others—Turgenev, Goncharov, Panayev, Nekrasov—they all remained below at the foot of the mountain, hand in hand in some kind of round-dance, enveloped in the fetid mists of the lowlands, prancing about, full of empty vanity, and craning their necks to look enviously up at him as he climbed towards the unattainable peak, unconscious of the all-consuming sense of liberation which he felt, just as they were ignorant of the passion which compelled him to go on—he *had* to, he was obliged to cross the threshold.

As he approached the casino, he began to take smaller

steps so that the number of paces from their lodgings should add up to exactly 1457 as, according to earlier calculations, that number was his most successful, and it always led to his winning—not that there was anything strange about that, the last figure being a seven and all the figures together adding up to seventeen (yet another seven)—and there was something special about seven, and unremittingly odd number, divisible by nothing except itself and one, and this was true of it not only in its pure form, but as a unit of two-figure numbers as well—17, 34, 47, 67 etc.—it was a very special number—and now he had almost reached the bottom of the steps leading into the building and had to make his steps really tiny—almost mincing steps, managing all the same to make them finally add up to his figure of 1457!

He walked across the broad entrance-hall with its fountain surrounded by a few Frenchmen engaged in animated conversation, and up the wide staircase with its tasteless classical statues to the first floor, ready to begin, as always, with the middle, and largest, hall, his heart pounding as if he were about to have an assignation—and, feeling his waistcoat to make sure that he had not lost any of the money, he pushed his way through the crowd of curious onlookers around the table and announced he was placing three gold coins on *impair*, because three was an odd number—and now he was calm—the main thing having been to push his way through this crowd of alien and hostile people, to push his way through without anyone insulting him, or without it *appearing* that anyone had insulted him, and no less important had been the need to begin the game, in other words, to declare himself—and whenever he tried to shout out his stake and position, it seemed that the eyes of all those sitting or standing at the table were turned towards him and that they all believed he was gambling for the money, out of necessity, and so he always tried to announce his bet as clearly and carelessly as possible, but always managed to sound either too pleading or too defiant, so that people must still be thinking that some extremely special, pressing reasons were com-

pelling him to gamble—and now all this was behind him—
and he went on to win, and on the seven as well—double luck
and a good omen—and, having won three gold pieces, he
now placed all six on *impair*—and won again though on the
nine this time—he must switch to *manque* as *passe* had already
come up three times in a row—and he staked five of the nine
gold coins he had won—he was winning time after time—on
passe, manque, rouge, noir, and even twice on zero—the coins
were piling up before him—and someone obligingly placed a
chair behind him, but he did not sit down in case he altered
the tempo of his game and, in any case, he was probably quite
unaware of the chair and what he was supposed to do
with it—and everything around him spun in a kind of mad
vortex—nothing was visible except the piles of coins before
him and the tiny ball, rolling round and finishing in the sec-
tor he had divined—and he was betting over and over again,
raking in with his hands the coins he had won and adding
them to the pile which shone with a reddish-gold gleam—
and the peak of the mountain had suddenly emerged from
the clouds, which remained somewhere below—he was now
so high he could not even see the earth—all was covered with
white cloud, and he strode across the cloud and, strangely, it
supported him and even lifted him up towards the reddish-
gold, unconquered peak which until quite recently had
seemed unattainable.

[. . .]

JENNY ERPENBECK

HALE AND HALLOWED

Translated from the German by SUSAN BERNOFSKY

In the little vestibule off to the right as you enter the church, beside the plaque with the names of all those who lost their lives in the First World War, you can see the many crutches left behind by the ones who were healed, along with artificial legs hanging on the wall or simply propped against it. Jesus Scourged, for whom the church is named, is said to have performed the acts of healing borne witness to by these now superfluous makeshift limbs, and although these artificial limbs—many of the prostheses are no more than sticks with bands of cloth nailed to them, while others display marvelous wooden joints such as no one would know how to make any more—that is, although these artificial limbs have a decidedly antiquated appearance and have acquired a film of dust over the course of several renovations, the people who live in the region still make pilgrimages to this church, worshipping these dusty relics as a way of giving expression to their hope that such miracles will never cease.

Maria Kainbacher caught a ride with one of the other women from her village, the two of them intend to light candles in the church, the woman from the village for her deceased husband,

and Maria Kainbacher for her son, who came into this world fifty years ago today. Here in this region, this day is known as Holy Innocents' Day, and it is a local custom for the children to go from house to house carrying little bundles of twigs, they touch the adults with their twigs and wish them a "hale and hallowed" new year. "Hale and hallowed, hale and hallowed, a long life and good health!" After the two women have lit their candles and placed them before the altar, they turn to go, they leave the crutches behind them and step outside. When they are standing before the church, Maria Kainbacher announces that she'd like to return home on foot, and she only smiles and shakes her head when the other woman objects, saying this isn't possible, that she cannot allow it, it's much too far to walk, and she reminds Maria Kainbacher how, just the other week, during Milli's funeral, she had gotten dizzy and fallen down. But Maria Kainbacher only laughs and thanks her, and now she lifts her hand to wave goodbye, and the other woman doesn't know what to say, she looks at this five-fingered thing fashioned of skin and bones hovering in the air and shakes her head in disapproval, it isn't right for me to let you go, she says, but then she can't think of anything else to say. So she, too, briefly lifts her hand and then gets into her car all alone, she starts the engine and lets the car roll ever so slowly away from the snow-covered church square, quietly, quietly, almost without making any sound at all, and as she drives off, she watches in the rear-view mirror as Maria Kainbacher turns around and begins to place one foot in front of the other.

Maria Kainbacher omitted to say that she wanted to pay a visit before returning home. In the church, as she was lighting the candle for her son, she had suddenly felt the urge to see a friend of hers again with whom she had once shared a hospital room. This friend of hers had said she was from this region, and so now the old woman begins to circle the church, going from house to house, at every door she knocks and, when the door is opened, asks whether anyone knows her friend. She says, for instance: Listen, I'm looking for Gertrud, maybe she's married now, but her name used to be Möstl. Oh yes, the Möstls live down that way, one person says to her, but I couldn't tell you if there's a Gertrud living there. Another says: Oh, Gertrud, sure, I know her, but she doesn't live here anymore, and I'm not sure whether her name was Möstl before she got married. And another one says: There was a woman who used to live down there, but then she moved up to town, and it might well be that her name was Gertrud.

Little by little, however, without it being possible to say precisely how this comprehension comes about, the answers given by all these strangers who don't even know for certain whom Maria Kainbacher is looking for, these answers that in part even contradict one another begin to reveal the path the old woman must follow if she wishes to reach her friend. This path winds its way between the houses out into the fields, it leads slightly downhill, and the rocks and shards with which it is paved are now slippery beneath the thin dusting of snow. The old woman has slipped several times during the past year, stumbling or even falling, the last time during Milli's funeral, but none of her bones has ever snapped in two, and so she knows that her bones are more durable than those of other people, and it doesn't surprise her that a body, growing older, begins to gravitate toward the earth in which it will soon be buried. And so she trudges down this slippery downhill path without fear, until she comes to the pigsty that the people she asked for help described to her. The large white house diagonally across from the pigsty, they said, is where this Gertrud lives, this Gertrud who once, before her marriage, had borne the name Möstl. This information was the result derived from adding together all the various, in part mutually contradictory, responses.

When her friend opens the door, Maria Kainbacher begins to smile, but her friend does not smile, she simply says hello and seems not to know who is standing there on her doorstep. Then Maria bends over, picks up a twig from the ground, and begins, in jest, to beat time with the twig in her hand and recite the verse children always say to adults on this day: *Hale and hallowed, hale and hallowed, a long life and good health!* She brushes the twig against her friend's hip, as is customary here on this day, which is called Holy Innocents' Day, as though in this way she might awaken the memory that has obviously gone to sleep inside her friend. She herself still remembers perfectly well how she and this friend used to laugh together when the two of them were sharing the hospital room. But her friend doesn't remember their laughter in the hospital room, and so she still isn't laughing.

The woman who opened the door doesn't know who this shriveled old woman is who is reeling off these lines ordinarily spoken only by children in her quavering voice as if she's lost her wits and knocking the twig against her hip in jest, she doesn't know who this visitor is who is continuing to smile, who keeps standing there smiling, even after she has finished reciting her verse and now seems only to be waiting for her, Gertrud, to give her a proper welcome. Don't you remember? Maria finally asks when she realizes that the other woman doesn't know what to say. Don't you remember when we shared the hospital room? Aha, Gertrud thinks, but she cannot remember. Seven years ago, the stroke. Then the stomach operation. Last year the artificial hip. She remembers all the hospital rooms she has lain in, she can even remember the one or the other woman who shared a room with her and joined her in lamenting the frailties of age. But this woman who is standing here before her—this woman she cannot remember. Well, Gertrud, the woman says, shaking her head in bewilderment, do you really not remember? But Gertrud doesn't remember at all, and is only surprised that this woman who is a stranger to her appears to know her name.

Don't you remember when my Luis was born, my son, and you gave birth to Franz? Gertrud knows that fifty years ago she gave birth to her oldest son whose name is Franz and who now owns the pigsty across the way, Franz who is married and who cut off one of his fingers half a year ago while sawing wood. Franz is the president of the local curling league, and every Saturday after the game he goes to drink a beer at the Kreuzwirt Inn. There is a Franz, her son, that much Gertrud knows, but she still doesn't know who this woman is standing on her doorstep. Nevertheless she retreats a step, perhaps only out of curiosity, and in this way invites the stranger to enter her home.

Maria Kainbacher is now sitting in the kitchen of this farmwife who generously fills out her flowered apron and who, unlike Maria, wears her hair not hidden in a small flat knot at the nape of her neck, but rather in a fashionable cut, dyed and pinned up. But her legs are nonetheless adorned with blue veins just like the legs of Maria, and they bend in on themselves, almost with a crease, from the heavy weight that has been pressing down on them for a lifetime now. The farmwife places a bottle of apple juice on the table and a dish with Christmas cookies, two glasses, two plates, and then she sits down, ready to listen. But Maria just asks questions. She asks how Gertrud's sister Elfi is, whether she is still alive, this Elfi who was the very first person to visit Gertrud in the hospital, even before the father of her newborn child, Elfi who had brought a bouquet and had shared her sister's joy that the child had been born healthy. She also asks about Karl, Gertrud's husband, whether he is still alive, Karl who had held the child so awkwardly and had been so silent, she asks whether she gave birth to any more children after that—yes, two, Gertrud says, and immediately falls silent again—and whether she had had an easier time with her later deliveries than when Franz was born, when she had screamed so with pain and it had taken fourteen hours, during which time her son, Luis, was born, whether she still remembered how the doctor had finally come and said they would have to cut the child out and how she hadn't wanted that and in the end had given birth to Franz in the usual way. Whether she still remembered how the nurses had once mixed their children up and placed each woman's baby at the other's breast and she didn't notice until they were drinking, because Luis, who never wanted to drink, had suddenly become so greedy, because he was really Franz. How they had laughed that day, how they had always laughed, did she remember? She, Maria Kainbacher, can hardly think of a single person who liked to laugh as much as she did, Gertrud, her friend, with whom she had lain side by side fifty years ago when her son was born.

Suddenly Gertrud sees her kitchen filling up with people, she sees Elfi, her sister, standing at the sink putting water in a vase to freshen an enormous bouquet, she sees her husband Karl sitting at the table in front of a glass of beer, right next to Maria, staring silently into his glass, and now Franz comes in, he's still very small, just a child, and he goes to get a knife and a cutting board out of the drawer, he says he just wants to cut himself a piece of sausage, but Gertrud sees that the sausage is his own left thumb, she sees him cutting off his own thumb before she can cry out to stop him, his thumb which he has mistaken for a piece of sausage, but he cannot blame her for this, she brought him, Franz, into the world with all his parts intact, he had two thumbs when he was born, fifty years ago. Gertrud sees them all, she sees everything, she holds her breath and looks, not leaving anything out, until the complete memory drops into her lap, as complete as Franz was when he was born, and then she begins to breathe again.

Gertrud can now remember the young face of this old woman who has appeared before her, and she realizes that an entire piece of her lifetime which she herself had so thoroughly forgotten that she was not even able to regret forgetting it has been preserved inside this woman like a cake in a cool, dark pantry. Like a blind person she has had to rely on Maria Kainbacher to lead her into this far-distant period of her own life, but now she begins to respond. Starting with this beginning which Maria has given back to her, she now tells all her stories to the end, tells of her children and grandchildren, cousins, marriages and christenings, tells of funerals, illnesses, and travel. Now and then she goes to one of the drawers, so as to dig among the lottery tickets and rubber bands, the wooden spoons and greasy scraps of paper on which she has jotted down recipes, to pull out the photos that go with the stories. Then Gertrud, who had still been named Möstl when her oldest was born and married only later, with her infant on her arm, and her friend Maria, who fifty years later has come visiting on Holy Innocents' Day to wish her a "hale and hallowed" new year, bend over the pictures and reassure themselves as to the names, the resemblances between the different family members and all the things that have happened.

And because both clans, the Möstls and the Auers into which Gertrud married, were very fruitful and brought forth many offspring, as a result of which there were numerous christenings, birthdays, marriages, but also funerals that took place over the years, events whose photographic documentation now requires explanation, it doesn't occur to Gertrud until quite late, when it has already grown dark outside, to ask about Luis, her friend's son whom she gave birth to fifty years before and who therefore, without himself having had the least inkling of this, joined together the lives of these two woman to the present day.

He shot himself, that's all, Maria says.

RODRIGO REY ROSA

from THE GOOD CRIPPLE

Translated from Spanish by ESTHER ALLEN

II.

Juan Luis Luna was kidnapped one cool November morning when the Guatemalan sky, swept by the north wind, was at its purest and bluest. He was kidnapped for money, but not his own money, for though he lacked nothing he was not a rich man. His father, however, was.

There were five kidnappers, but he only recognized three of them: Barrios the Tapir, Bunny Brera, and Guzmán, a.k.a. El Horrible. As a boy he'd made friends with them, then broken off the friendship. The other two, who must have been a little older and looked as though they were just following orders, answered to the nicknames Carlomagno and the Sephardi. Carlomagno was a bulky man with Mayan features; the Sephardi was tall and lean, with an aquiline nose and curly hair.

They lowered him on a nylon rope down a deep, dark hole that was lined with rusted metal and reeked of gasoline. They left him there with a Rayovac flashlight, a copy of Dante's *Divine Comedy* translated into Spanish by the Conde de Cheste, and a plastic bucket for a toilet. Juan Luis had a very bad feeling about the whole thing. He knew many stories about kidnappings. He knew that if the Tapir, Bunny, and El Horrible hadn't bothered to conceal their faces it was because they weren't planning to let him out of there alive.

He remembered the Tapir and Bunny from when they were all in school together, the two of them standing at the door of a fancy house in La Cañada where a birthday party to which neither one had been invited was going on. He remembered them so clearly that for a moment he forgot what they had since become. Illuminated by a powerful floodlight, they stood at the house's grand entrance in their awkward polyester suits, their long hair still wet, the Tapir with an enormous pimple on his forehead, Bunny with his precocious adolescent stare, arguing with the portero who wouldn't let them in.

When the kidnappers got in touch with Don Carlos, he paid no attention. He did not place an advertisement in the daily papers as they requested, or give any sign of wishing to negotiate.

Juan Luis was given no food for two days. On the third day, Carlomagno opened the hatch and the hole filled with light and warmth. Dazzled, Juan Luis raised his eyes and saw the silhouette of the Tapir, who was standing at the edge of the hole with his arms crossed, looking down.

"Your old man doesn't want to play along," he said. "So you're going to have to help us out if you don't want us to start getting drastic."

El Horrible's silhouette appeared next to the Tapir's.

"You're going to write him a nice letter from his prodigal son, sí?"

[. . .]

Ana Lucía, Juan Luis's girlfriend, had spent another bad night. When she woke up, she remembered guiltily that while she was turning this way and that in the dark between the sheets, she'd felt anger—only a very slight anger, true—at Juan Luis. It was a complicated anger. She couldn't help him, not only because the kidnappers hadn't communicated with her, but also because she was not in a position to do anything. If only he'd agreed to marry her about a year before . . . But he was very stubborn and a little arrogant, too. Even so, she was sure he loved her. He was opposed to marriage, but he had brought her to live with him and practically made her his wife.

There was a time when Juan Luis's father had looked on her favorably, perhaps as a possible ally. Because deep down inside Don Carlos had not given up the fight, and believed that it was not too late to make an honorable man of his son. But that was not how she saw it—not when "honorable" was synonymous with being married and in business—and she'd been unwise enough to say, in the old man's presence, that she would leave Juan Luis the day he decided to play that game. After that, Don Carlos, without ever being at all rude, stopped inviting her to have lunch in his house, as he often used to; whenever they met he always seemed to be extremely busy or would come up with some excuse to keep from talking to her.

Over the course of her life with Juan Luis, father and son had quarreled several times; she knew that an old hostility persisted between them.

When she learned that Juan Luis had been kidnapped—the doorman witnessed the capture, which took place as he was driving away from the apartment building where they lived—Ana Lucía had called his father's house immediately.

"Well," said the old man, "it had to happen someday. Remember what he told me once, about a year ago, when we were talking about precisely this possibility? That he didn't expect me to pay any ransom for him."

"He was just saying that to say it, Don Carlos, for the love of God."

"Everyone says everything just to say it, amiga mía."

And the old man said goodbye and hung up. Ana Lucía hadn't managed to speak to him again. Once the housekeeper answered and said Don Carlos had had an accident and was in the hospital, and a few days later she dialed the number several times but no one answered.

All that time she had felt powerless to do anything. She often caught herself squeezing her hands together in anguish, immobilizing one of them with the other and exerting a futile force that ultimately exhausted her but gave her some relief from the oppression of her not at all irrational fears. She tried to breathe deeply, but it seemed as if there was never enough air to fill up her lungs.

He'd been kidnapped a week ago. It was a cold morning; when she got out of bed she put a sweater on underneath her robe, and some flannel pajama bottoms that belonged to Juan Luis. She went from the bedroom to the kitchen and put some water on to boil for coffee. While it was heating up, she went into the living room and sat down on a woolen ottoman. Perhaps the hardest thing to bear during those days, even worse than the fear and the anguish, had been the loneliness. She wondered if Don Carlos distrusted her. He was an old paranoid, that much was sure; he may even have been suspicious of Juan Luis himself. Resignedly she went back to the kitchen, where the water for the coffee was now boiling. Someone knocked at the door. Ana Lucía poured the last drops of boiling water into the paper filter, mechanically passed her hands over her head, and, as she crossed the living room towards the door, tightened the belt of her bathrobe. The door had no chain, and she opened it only a crack, with some apprehension.

A young man of good appearance with a friendly smile was standing there, tall, slender, and light-skinned, a nervous young man who was none other than Bunny.

"Forgive me," he said, "I have an urgent message."

Ana Lucía guessed what he was there for and her legs began trembling.

"Yes?" she managed to choke.

Bunny stretched out his arm to give her the package, which was surprisingly heavy. For a moment she thought she'd made a mistake, that this had nothing to do with Juan Luis's kidnapping. But Bunny told her, "This is for Don Carlos. Take it to him immediately. And please forgive me for troubling you." He turned rapidly on his heel and in no time was at the elevator, whose door he had propped open, and had disappeared.

Nauseated, Ana Lucía felt the bundle. She shut the door,

leaned her back against it and slipped down, sinking further and further until she was sitting on the cold tile floor, almost numb. She looked at the ceiling's granular plaster and it made her think of a patch of sand turned upside down. Meanwhile, her fingers felt the shape of a foot, cut off at the ankle, through the black plastic. She doubled over, her forehead almost touching the floor, and felt like vomiting. But there was nothing in her stomach. She lost all desire to drink coffee.

Not long after that she stood up, went to the kitchen, and set the envelope on the counter. She drank a glass of tap water. She sat down on one of the stools, exhausted. She surprised herself watching one of the bricklayers at the construction site across the street cleaning the panes of a window, and she breathed deeply before forcing herself to lower her gaze and look again at the bundle that contained Juan Luis's foot.

It was like an electric shock. She leaped to her feet and went to the telephone.

"Don Carlos?"

Silence.

"I think they've just brought me one of Juan Luis's feet. I'm not sure because it's inside a black plastic bag. They've asked me to take it to you. There's also a letter for you. Don Carlos?"

"I'm here." Both his voice and the silence that followed sounded cavernous. "A foot?"

"I'm bringing it to you right now."

Another silence.

"Yes. Come."

[. . .]

Don Carlos Luna was unusually vital and ruddy for a man of almost seventy. He was still a lustful man, and an element of sensuality was evident in all he did. On the strength of his money and his affability, he had emerged from a murky past into the most luminous social spheres. But after his wife died and he began to give up on his plans to make a worthy heir out of his son, he was overtaken by the lack of curiosity, the kind of apathy, that a belief in immortality engenders.

He left his bedroom, where he'd been organizing some papers—phone bills, all duly paid but it was a good idea to keep them around for a while; receipts from the veterinarian who had treated one of his mares; newspaper advertisements (land for sale, potter's wheels, winding frames) which his secretary had clipped—and went to the big living room to wait for Ana Lucía, thinking about two distinct aspects of the word *tiempo*. He felt a touch of vertigo, as if he were on the crest of the wave.

He would have to negotiate, he told himself. He thought with some aversion that he would have to write a letter asking them to settle for less. He still didn't know how much they wanted. But wasn't it only fair that he should pay less when they'd maimed the hostage?

"Crippled," he said in a low voice, like a man assuring himself that he's had the last word and come out ahead. He'd been staring fixedly at a patch of sky beyond the Surinam cherry trees in the garden when Ana rang the bell at the front gate and La Caya let her in.

She was driving the old BMW Juan Luis had inherited from his mother; she parked it under the balcony.

Ana Lucía hurried up the stairs and entered the living room through the balcony's glass door holding the black package she'd told him about.

"Here it is," she said, extending her arm.

Without any rush, he placed the package on a small, mosaic table, took the envelope, and opened it.

"Forgive me," he said, and began carefully reading the letter. Then he picked up the package and tried to untie it but the knot was impossible and he had to break the string. Inside he found what he'd been told to expect: his son's amputated foot wrapped in a piece of bloody gauze inside a zip-lock bag. He stared at it fixedly for a moment, then turned to look at her. He threw himself back in his armchair. He felt slightly dizzy.

Ana Lucía let out a moan that was inhuman, almost animal.

As he watched her, he started to recover a little.

"Are we sure it's his?"

She nodded, her eyes riveted to the foot.

It had the power to repel all gazes yet as soon as they stopped looking at it, it began acting as a powerful magnet, transforming their eyes into iron needles. Even if they didn't look directly at it, it weighed on the margin of their field of vision. And even glimpsed from the corner of an eye, its shape was apparent beneath the gauze.

The old man heard himself breathing. He saw a dark vein jumping in the woman's neck.

"We have to check to be sure," he said, but he didn't move. "But in his letter he asks us to freeze the foot, in case they can reattach it when he gets free."

It looked as if she were about to smile and an instant later she covered her face with her hands and started to cry.

"Come," he said. "Courage."

His blood was going cold. He stretched out his hands, bent over the table in all composure, and took the gauze off the foot to see if he recognized it. He touched it as if he were a blind man, then leaned back in his chair still looking at it.

The contact of his gaze with the place where the foot had been severed, where a circle of red flesh, now a little black along the edges, could be seen, with its concentric circle of white bone that was both milky and glassy, could not be compared to the contact of his pupils with other ordinary objects or with any work of art.

His Italo-Guatemalan businessman's mind was drawn to the bone marrow. It was crushed the way an object swallowed by a black hole in outer space would be; it was reduced to non-existence and what remained was darkness. A buzzing in his ears seemed so far off it might have originated in the sun. A dizziness brought him back to consciousness, and gave him the illusion that he had been on a journey through time. When he came back to himself he was no longer the same man. He was morose, because he knew he had just regressed. It was as if he'd been presented with an old invoice, benevolently forgotten for a very long time, which now transformed him from a millionaire into a poor man. He had a feeling of having walked down a very long road. He wrapped the foot back up in the gauze and put it back in its bag. He stood up and explained that he was going to put it in the freezer.

La Caya pulled various cuts of beef and a tray of ice cubes out of the freezer to make room for the foot, and then stood staring at the freezer door as if she could see through it. Don Carlos left her there, glued to the freezer door as if it were a TV.

[. . .]

Uwe Timm

from MORENGA

Translated from the German by Breon Mitchell

Warning Signs

On an afternoon in 1904, Farmer Kaempffer sends his houseboy
Jakobus, a Hottentot who's been with him for two years, to fetch
his youngest son Klaus to do his schoolwork. The faithful
Jakobus trots off at once. But neither he nor his son return.
Kaempffer finally tires of waiting. He leaves the house to look for
them. He finds his son quickly enough, playing near the kraal.
But Jakobus has disappeared. Kaempffer searches, calls out, asks
the other native workers. They claim they haven't seen him.
Kaempffer goes back to the house and returns to his desk. As he
sits down, he has the strange feeling that something has changed.
He's about to start working on his accounts again when he
glances up at the photograph of himself as a lieutenant in the Re-
serves and discovers a small cross in ink directly above his head.

Farmer Kruse steps from his farmhouse near Warmbad to assign
daily chores to the natives as usual.

There's not a man in sight.

He strides over to the native compound. All the pondoks

have been taken down overnight. A fire still smolders. Suddenly a flight of crowned lapwings whirs up from a stand of white thorn bushes. Kruse returns quickly to the house, bars the doors and windows, takes his gun from the wall, loads it, and places the remaining shells within easy reach on the table.

On the farm "German Soil," a black worker snatches the whip from Farmer Strohmeier, who uses it to make the men work faster. The native threatens Strohmeier with the whip. The farmer saddles his horse and rides off at once to the nearest police station.

A young Nama woman tells Frau Krabbenhöft: If there's a tap at your window in the night, it will be me, but then you must run fast.

In early June 1904 a telegram arrives at the Imperial Government headquarters in Windhoek: a band of armed Hottentots have attacked isolated farms in the southwestern part of the country, stealing cattle and weapons from white farmers. None of the farmers have been killed. The leader of the band is a man named Morenga.

Who is Morenga?

Information provided by the District Officer in Gibeon: A Hottentot Bastard (father: Herero, mother: Hottentot). Took part in the Bondelswart Rebellion in 1903. Said to have been reared in a missionary school. The name of school is unknown. Last employed in the copper mines of O'okiep in the northern part of Cape Colony.

Morenga rides a white horse that can go four days without water. Only a glass bullet polished by an African can kill him. He can see in the dark. He can shoot a hen's egg from a man's hand at a hundred meters. He wants to drive the Germans out. He can make rain. He turns into a zebra finch and spies on German soldiers.

Telegram: 30 August skirmish between Stempel's patrol and Morenga's band on Sjambok Mountain, Lieutenant Baron von Stempel and four men killed, four men wounded, one missing.

Von Burgsdorff, District Officer in Gibeon, tells Kries, a merchant: We've got to keep the Hottentots from rebelling until the Hereros are completely subdued.

The date is 1 October 1904.

On the afternoon of 3 October, two Witbooi Hottentots, Samuel Isaak and Petrus Jod, approach District Officer von Burgsdorff with a letter from their captain, Hendrik Witbooi, declaring war on the Germans.

Burgsdorff decides to ride at once to see Hendrik Witbooi. He's known him for ten years and hopes to change the man's mind. He tells his wife he'll be back tomorrow. Unarmed, he rides off toward Rietmont, accompanied by both Witbooi chiefs.

When he arrives in Mariental the following day, the assembled natives ask him if he received the captain's letter, and when he says yes, a Hottentot Bastard named Salomon Stahl shoots him in the back, killing him. (*The Battles of the German Colonial Guard in South West Africa*, ed. by the Office of the General Staff, Berlin, 1907, vol. 2, p. 13).

On 4 October 1904, the Hottentot (Nama) revolt breaks out in the German Protectorate in South West Africa, almost exactly eight months after the Herero uprising. Now the entire country is at war. The German general staff has to keep sending reinforcements.

BEYOND THE SURF

Veterinary Lieutenant Gottschalk was carried to shore by a black. In the distance, before the surf, the *Gertrud Woermann* lay at anchor. Black crew members paddled the soldiers through the surf. On the beach stood curious onlookers, among them several soldiers, as well as a few women holding parasols. It reminded Gottschalk of a beach resort named Norderney where he had once vacationed. Only the white bandages of the wounded disturbed the impression. When the boat ran aground in shallow water, Gottschalk mounted the shoulders of one of the waiting natives. The man wore nothing but a pair of ragged trousers. Gottschalk felt the perspiring black skin, smelled the sour sweat. He felt sick. With a gentle rotation he was deposited on the beach.

Gottschalk now stood on African soil. It seemed to sway beneath his feet.

Gottschalk had boarded the *Gertrud Woermann* almost three weeks earlier in Hamburg. On the afternoon of 28 September 1904, a fine drizzle set in. The horses had been brought aboard and were now sheltered in the forward hold. Crates of ammunition, guns, and provisions were still disappearing aft into the ship. At 6:30 p.m. the steam whistle wailed, releasing a white plume. It was time for visitors to return to shore. The hatches were closed and covered with tarps. On the dock below stood hundreds of people: relatives, friends, and curious onlookers; from the deck of the ship nothing could be seen but their black umbrellas. Gottschalk's parents had written to say they would stand on the dike at Glückstadt and wave, and that he should wave back from the ship, preferably with a white tablecloth. A military band from the 76th Regiment had assembled on the dock and was playing marches. The ship's pilot came on board. The gangway was drawn up and the ship was suddenly filled with a steady, throbbing drone that was to last almost three weeks; the deck planks vibrated gently, somewhere a flange banged. Black clouds billowed from the smokestack and, with no wind and the ship still docked, fell back to the deck beneath the rain. Small greasy coal smuts settled on Gottschalk's gray regimental cloak, leaving dark streaks when he tried to brush them away. Only now, with the hawsers cast off, did the band begin to play: *Muß i denn, muß i denn, zum Städtele hinaus*—faced with the black plume of smoke slowly rolling its sooty way across the ship, Gottschalk suddenly wished he could return to shore. He had no deep feelings about the war that was underway. How had he come up with the crazy idea of volunteering? On the other hand he'd been looking forward to being in South West Africa for the past few days. Summer was setting in there, while in Germany the days were growing shorter and colder. Gottschalk had been having a recurrent dream since childhood: there was no summer. Either he had slept through it, or for some unexplained reason it had never arrived. The officers and troops on board gave three cheers for the Kaiser. Gottschalk heard his own three hurrahs.

Two tugboats towed the steamer away from the dock and out into the river. The lights on the shore road to Ovelgönne were barely visible through the rainy gray twilight. Then the tugs cast off their lines and gave a farewell wail on their sirens.

Around ten the ship passed Glückstadt. Gottschalk stood alone on deck. The rain was falling more heavily now, and a gentle northwest wind had risen. The only thing Gottschalk could make out in the rain-drenched darkness was the navigational light at Glückstadt. Somewhere across the way his parents were standing on the dike with white bedsheets. They probably couldn't even see the lights of the steamer.

During the crossing Gottschalk shared a cabin with Medical Lieutenant Haring and an N.C.O. veterinarian named Wenstrup. The moment the steward showed Lieutenant Haring his bed, he placed a picture on the only table in the cabin. It was a photo, he told Gottschalk, of his wife and daughter, Lisa and Amelie. That very day Gottschalk discovered how complicated relationships were in the Haring family. Haring had married his cousin, although strictly speaking she wasn't really a cousin, since his uncle had adopted the girl. When Haring asked why Gottschalk wasn't married yet, he said he still hadn't found the right woman.

Wenstrup took no part in these conversations, even when

Haring tried to involve him on one occasion by remarking that one could easily ruin one's eyes given the poor light in the cabin. Wenstrup spent most of his time reading in bed.

Gottschalk would have liked to know what book Wenstrup was reading. But it was covered in a snakeskin dust jacket, and he didn't want to ask.

He'd brought along three books for the crossing himself. A textbook on immunology, a South African botany, and a novel by Fontane, *Die Stechlin.*

A few officers in his former regiment had teased Gottschalk at first about his reading habits. Once they even found him on maneuvers sitting in the shade of a wagon wheel with a book in his hand. What kept him from being known as an odd duck was his tendency to downplay his reading, referring to it as a necessary evil to keep up his medical knowledge. But there was no hiding the fact that he also read novels, and contemporary ones at that. Gottschalk had a reputation for getting badly hobbled horses quickly back on their legs. Regimental officers who thought they could wipe their boots on the horse doctor were in for an unpleasant surprise. Major von Consbruch chewed Gottschalk out on imperial maneuvers for advising the major to go easy on his horse, which was going lame. Later, when the troops broke into a gallop, the major had to switch to a side mount in the midst of the action. The battalion commander made a poor impression galloping along behind his troops. He received a personal reprimand from the commanding general. Such incidents became common knowledge, although Gottschalk never bragged about them.

Regulations for Saluting:
On ships a superior officer is saluted once a day, the first time he is encountered. A Veterinary N.C.O. salutes a Veterinary Lieutenant by touching the brim of his cap or hat. The Lieutenant gives an identical salute to a Medical Lieutenant. All three ranks, N.C.O., Veterinary Lieutenant, and Medical Lieutenant, must salute first, as indicated above, when meeting a Second Lieutenant.

The *Gertrud Woermann* had already passed through the English Channel before Gottschalk and Wenstrup began discussing personal matters.

The wind had risen and men were starting to get seasick. Wenstrup offered Gottschalk an anti-nausea pill. Gottschalk said he had been raised in Glückstadt, with ships practically at his doorstep. His father owned a store for colonial goods and his grandfather on his mother's side owned a herring lugger. He had sailed along to the Dogger Bank a few times during school holidays.

God save us from fire on the high seas was one of the inane phrases Gottschalk's grandfather repeated at every opportunity in his awkward High German.

Wenstrup said he was a landlubber from Berlin, so he'd made a point of bringing the pills along.

It was only later that Gottschalk recalled something strange: Wenstrup offered the pills to him, but not to Second Lieutenant von Schwanebach, who was suffering mightily, nor to the chief supply officer, Captain von Tresckow.

At breakfast von Tresckow maintained that cavalry men didn't get seasick all that easily, there were too many parallels between horses and ships. He skipped the noon meal. By afternoon he was standing on deck, clutching the railing and staring off into the distance, which one of the crewmen had told him would help. His monocle dangled on its cord, clinking against the steel railing with each roll of the ship. Shortly before supper Wenstrup entered the cabin and told Gottschalk to visit the head and check the battle readiness of the Cavalry Guard.

Gottschalk found Captain von Tresckow on the floor, embracing the toilet stool, his green face propped on the white porcelain rim. When Gottschalk asked if he could help, Tresckow said, thanks, comrade, without lifting his head.

Gottschalk's diary during the crossing consists almost entirely of daily notes on longitude and latitude, along with standard references to the weather: dull, overcast, sunny, rainy. Only three days show somewhat more extensive entries:

Tropic of Cancer. Awnings unfurled on deck. Horsehair everywhere. The animals are shedding their winter coats with the
change in climate.

10 October 1904
At night just above the horizon, the Southern Cross. Longing to
be alone; instead, desultory conversations in the mess. A feeling
of inner tension. W. keeps his distance.

13 October 1904
The ship crossed the equator. At twelve noon, standing upright,
you could cover your shadow with a cap.

Wenstrup, who was growing a beard, let himself be shaved
with a huge wooden knife by one of Neptune's minions (played
by Sergeant Ro., a veteran of the Colonial Guard) as part of the
crossing-the-line ceremony.

Wenstrup maintained a deadly serious expression throughout, as if he were about to be decapitated. Everyone laughed.
Including me.

Once Wenstrup asked Gottschalk why he had volunteered for
South West Africa. Gottschalk's reply: various reasons.

A photograph: Gottschalk is sitting beside a supply wagon in a
worn khaki uniform, a peaked cap on his head. Four spokes of
the six-foot-high wooden wheel are visible to the right. Gottschalk's left arm rests on a wooden table. On this table lie a field
canteen, sheets of paper, pencils, a pocketknife, and an oil-cloth
notebook (his diary). Dark eyes, a dark beard that he has apparently left untouched for the past few days, a softly curved
mouth. A keepsake photo for folks back home in Glückstadt,
that's the pose he's assumed. He gives the impression, gazing
into the camera, that he's holding his breath.

By the way, what does your father do, Lieutenant von Schwanebach asks him at supper.

Sells colonial goods.

The table erupts in laughter. They think Gottschalk has allowed himself a little joke.

The scales dangled from the ceiling above the shop counter. When his father weighed out 100 grams of saffron, he used copper weights of various sizes that nestled inside one another like small pots. What little Gottschalk could never understand was why he couldn't eat all the dates, figs, dried bananas, and almonds he wanted. (His playmates at school couldn't believe it either). His mother had to negotiate with his father for her cooking needs, and whatever she used was entered into the accounts. There was an invisible border between the shop and the apartment on the first floor, which could only be reached by a narrow staircase from the shop itself. The rules below were different and stricter than those above, and they were sharply drummed into little Gottschalk when he once took a handful of almonds from a glass jar on the shelf. Everything in the shop waited in glass jars, sacks, and boxes to be weighed out at some point, but only in exchange for money; then it was transferred to a new owner. The family seemed to live in a state of waiting.

On 11 October the *Gertrud Woermann* dropped anchor in Monrovia. A diplomatic secretary came on board with news that a Hottentot rebellion had broken out in South West Africa. Then we can kill two birds with one stone, said a lieutenant.

Fifteen black crew were taken on board. They were supposed to paddle the soldiers to land when the steamer reached Swakopmund. Dr. Haring was ordered to examine the natives, who were kept in the forward area of the ship.

Strictly speaking, that's a task for our two veterinarians, said Second Lieutenant Schwanebach. Everyone laughed, except Wenstrup. (Dr. Haring's reaction: the man has no sense of humor). Gottschalk felt he had laughed far too loudly. Strictly speaking, he hadn't felt like laughing at all.

Six days later the steamer reached Swakopmund. That night Gottschalk heard a loud splash and then the rattle of the anchor chain. But something else had awakened him. It took a moment to realize what it was: the steady, throbbing drone had ceased, along with the gentle vibration of the planks, cabin walls and bedstead. Gottschalk thought about going outside and taking a look at the coastline, but hearing voices on deck and seeing that Dr. Haring was already there, he stayed in bed.

When he emerged the next morning, he was astonished to find everything wrapped in a thick milky fog. He couldn't even make out the stern of the ship. Only the steady, recurrent boom and roar of the surf on the shore indicated the direction of the coast. Around eleven the fog began to disperse. A gray-brown desert landscape came into view.

On the coast lay a few scattered brick houses, shacks, corrugated tin huts, tents. No palms, no trees, not a speck of green. Although Gottschalk already knew what to expect from the landscape, he was still disappointed.

After the black crew paddled the soldiers to shore in the landing boats, the horses were unloaded. They were hoisted from the hold with a deck winch one by one in leather girths and then lowered onto flat wooden rafts. The rafts were towed to the surf by steam launch, where whip-cracking crew members drove the horses into the water. They swam to shore in small clusters.

Wenstrup arrived in the last boat. He had stayed on board to supervise the loading of the horses. When the boat ran aground in shallow water it could be seen he was barefoot. He declined to be carried ashore by a native. With boots, sword, and socks in hand, he waded onto land.

Captain von Tresckow, who stood beside Gottschalk watching the horses thrash wildly as men from the cavalry depot slowly herded them together, said dryly: Those nags can kick and bite all they want, they'll wind up pulling a wagon again, with a coachman or rider holding the reins and a whip.

In Swakopmund Gottschalk discovered he was not to proceed as expected to the Northern Division in Hereroland, but had been assigned instead to the 8th Regiment in the south.

Things are looking pretty bad down there, Lieutenant Ahrens said.

Two locomotives pulled the narrow-gauge train through the desert. Gottschalk could have easily trotted along beside the train, except for the extreme heat. He sat on bags of oats like the others. Tarps had been spread over the open boxcars to protect the men from the sun.

Captain Tresckow was the only one still wearing his uniform jacket with his pistol strapped on.

Is he going to mount the train and ride it, Wenstrup asked Gottschalk as they pulled out, pointing to the cavalry officer's riding crop. Gottschalk pretended not to understand. Later, with the train on its way, they learned he had a small gold cigarette lighter set in the handle of his riding crop, made to order by a whip factory in Allgäu.

Very handy, said Tresckow, the exact words a Hottentot was to say five months later, when he found the crop after a skirmish with a patrol.

Handy because you could light a cigarette before an attack without having to rummage around in your pockets. Gottschalk was sitting in the open door of the boxcar. He hoped the airstream would cool him a little, but it was like sitting in front of an open stove. Outside in the flickering heat lay a dreary, barren landscape from which fissured rocks rose now and again, with occasional immense gravel screes seemingly dumped at random.

Twice a year Gottschalk's father packed a sailcloth bag and took the train to Hamburg. Business trips he called them. In the sailcloth bag was his order book, in which he noted what and how much he needed to reorder from the colonial goods importer.

Little Gottschalk looked forward to these occasions, to these five or six days a year when he could play in the store. His mother would take the glass tops off the fat-bellied jars on the shelves and let him reach in: cinnamon, pieces of brown bark from Ceylon; vanilla, shriveled brownish-black pods from Guatemala; nutmeg, fluted gray kernels from Cameroon; the sweet, heavy fragrance of cloves, thick-stemmed buds from the Spice Islands in the Molucca Sea.

Those words: Spice Islands.

What do you think of when you hear the words Spice Islands, Gottschalk asked Wenstrup once during the crossing. Wenstrup ruminated a moment, as if savoring something, then said: Mulled wine, and to Gottschalk: I think it was the great Moltke who once said: the Prussian army has no room for Jews or dreamers.

The train stopped in the night at a small corrugated tin hut barricaded behind a wall of sandbags. Beside it stood a water tank, a mound of coal and a wooden cross. The station master had been shot by Hereros at the outbreak of hostilities. The station was now manned by six soldiers from the Railway Detachment. Sentries were posted. Gottschalk slept in the open for the first time, and had difficulty getting to sleep. They were awakened at five, coffee was poured, and there was zwieback from the ship. Around six the train pulled out again. They couldn't travel at night, the engineer said, scattered bands of Hereros still threatened the region.

Four hours into the journey the landscape changed: now it was hilly with a few dry bushes.

Dr. Haring and Lieutenant Ahrens discussed how one might go about cultivating the land some day.

Not long afterward the train stopped. The tracks were covered by sand drifts. A troop of Herero prisoners cleared them with shovels. They were chained together in pairs. Two sentries stood by. One was smoking a pipe.

One of the captive Hereros wore a tattered stiff collar—presumably to keep his neck from being chafed by the iron.

[. . .]

The train arrived at Waldau, the station in ruins. On the pale brown façade, above the empty windows, sooty traces of fire were visible. Next to the ruins three wooden crosses were stuck in the ground.

[. . .]

As von Tresckow observed, Gottschalk had adopted one of Wenstrup's characteristic gestures during the three-week voyage. When asking a question or offering a criticism, Wenstrup had a habit of grimacing and running a finger around inside his collar, as if he were having trouble breathing. One day Gottschalk began tugging at his own collar.

Gottschalk was well aware, by the way, that he tended to pick up certain turns of phrase, intonations, and gestures from others, possibly even personality traits, and he did so unwillingly, for he considered it a sign of immaturity, a weakness of character. He too noticed that he was running his finger inside his collar like Wenstrup, and stranger still, that this gesture immediately put him in a critical frame of mind; inserting his finger in such a way seemed to make him want to raise objections. It all struck Gottschalk as odd, but that didn't keep it from happening.

Although he was already thirty-four years old, Gottschalk still had no fixed physical traits, except for the way he walked, a rapid, jerky gait he'd developed even before joining the military, totally unlike the limping slouch of his father, which even as a boy on their Sunday strolls through Glückstadt he found unbearable.

Gottschalk's diary,
21 October 1904
(in the evening, on the troop train to Windhoek)

A herd of startled antelope raced along beside the train for a moment, then disappeared into the bush.

Tr. says that the entire Herero region will be annexed by the crown, i.e.—opened for settlement. The best land in South West Africa supposedly, good pastures and relatively abundant water.

It's a fine thought that at some point there will be eyes in this wilderness reading Goethe, ears listening to Mozart. They call the streams *rivier*.

Windhoek, the colonial capital: a military barrack with a small village attached. General Trotha on horseback. Line of command field officers. The fortress on the hill was supposedly built with bare hands by Captain von Françoise's troopers. The natives, black (Hereros) and brown (Hottentots), as well as numerous half-breeds, called Bastards, look like short, ragged Europeans, only black.

The next day Gottschalk reported to headquarters. Below the fort, near the soldiers' barracks, painted Hottentot women gestured to Gottschalk as he passed: poking a finger in their fists, or sticking out their tongues, trilling, and swaying their startlingly large hips.

The women are fantastic, said Captain Moll, the staff veterinarian, as he outlined Gottschalk's duties, completely immoral, total animals, but unfortunately syphilitic for the most part. Over twenty percent of the men were already infected.

The livestock were kept in large kraals on the outskirts of the village. Cattle, sheep and goats, taken from conquered Hereros. Unfortunately most of them died of thirst in the desert. They couldn't seize them from the Hereros without driving them out onto the sand flats. Now the cattle had to be inspected and checked for infectious diseases.

New animals were being brought in daily.

When Gottschalk asked how the livestock was used, Moll said it provided meat for the troops. The rest simply died. The German settlers protested of course, but those were the General's orders.

The cattle were a pitiful sight, totally emaciated, many injured by thorns or bullets, with festering wounds. Bodies of dead animals lay scattered everywhere. The stench of carrion filled the air.

A large area next to the kraal had been enclosed with barbed wire. Sentries were posted in front with fixed bayonets. Beyond the fence Gottschalk could see people, or rather skeletons, squatting—no, something halfway between humans and skeletons. They huddled together, mostly naked, in the piercingly hot sun.

What a sight, said Gottschalk, gazing at them.

That's our concentration camp, Moll explained, a new innovation based on the English experience in the Boer War.

But those are women and children, said Gottschalk.

Yes, they'd finally started separating the men from the women. Of course there weren't many men anyway. They were constantly coupling in broad daylight, though they received almost nothing to eat An insatiable urge to procreate. But now the death rate far exceeded new births.

The Spice Islands. They lie on the equator, at 130° longitude, in the Molucca Sea. Cloves grow there, blossoming with heavy, sweet fragrance in the fields of the interior, birds of paradise swirling about, the buds plucked by Malays, dried and carried by lines of native bearers through the screaming jungle, escorted at night by the velvet tread of the tiger. From the coast they are paddled rapidly by boat to a ship anchored beyond the reefs. White sails ascend the masts, billow out in the trade winds, drive the ship through the ocean, droop limply for weeks in the doldrums, explode like cannon in the Biscay. New sails propel the ship through the English Channel to the Elbe, past Glückstadt, on to Hamburg. The cloves, sewn up in sacks, are stacked in warehouses, until two are carried to Hannes Christiansen's barge and sail back to Glückstadt, where they fill the large glass jar on the shelf, are gradually weighed out into paper packets hand-twisted by his mother, and then delivered to homes, a task that falls mostly to little Gottschalk. There they are added to the gravy and the mulled wine, releasing at last upon the palate of Doctor Hinrichsen a flavor and fragrance that once merely drifted in the air on distant Spice Islands.

They die, Gottschalk later said to Wenstrup, from dysentery, typhus, and undernourishment. They starve to death.

No, said Wenstrup, they let them starve to death. That's a subtle but crucial distinction.

Gottschalk thought it was simply an administrative oversight on the part of lower-level bureaucrats.

Wenstrup, on the contrary, seriously maintained it was part of a systematic plan.

What plan?

The extermination of the natives. They want the land for settlement.

As Gottschalk rode out to the kraal the next day and passed by the camp, he saw hands stretched out toward him through the barbed wire.

Someone had lettered a sign and hung it on the fence: Please don't feed the animals.

Gottschalk had been ordered by Moll, the Chief Veterinarian, to find out why cattle were dying. He took blood samples, dissected a few of the dead bodies, and examined tissue samples under a microscope. The suspicion of rinderpest proved unfounded. A large number of Herero cattle had been immunized against the disease, as could be seen by checking their tails. A surprisingly simple but effective method had been employed, as one of the captured Hereros working for the Germans explained to Gottschalk. A strong thread was dipped in mucus from a cow that had died of the lung disease and then drawn through the skin of the tail with a needle. The thread was knotted and snipped off, so that part of it remained in the tail.

Gottschalk's report reached a simple conclusion: most of the cattle had starved to death.

Gottschalk's diary,
23 October 1904

Walking past the camp I saw white maggots as thick as my finger, as if they had mutated.

Yesterday in the officers' mess Haring said: Civilization is unthinkable without sacrifices.

That evening, Gottschalk told Wenstrup he was going to submit a petition to Colonial Guard headquarters requesting that the dead cattle be given to the starving prisoners.

Wenstrup said it wouldn't hurt to try, but he didn't see much likelihood of success.

Gottschalk expected Wenstrup to say just hide behind your pipe smoke instead. Gottschalk knew it wasn't smart to get mixed up in something that was already up and running, whether or not it was based on a specific order. The military bureaucracy was always temperamental when questions were raised, when someone asked why something already in place was being done that way. The only spot from which you can see everything is the top, Gottschalk's former regimental commander said, a military academy man: the front line soldier is blind precisely because he sees the whites of the enemy's eyes.

What upset Gottschalk was the absurd fact that human beings were starving to death while a few meters away cattle dropped to the ground and rotted away. He was convinced that the order to deny meat to the Hereros was meant to prevent cattle from being slaughtered for the prisoners and based on insufficient knowledge of the actual situation. In fact the animals were dying of starvation by the hundreds. They fell to the flat sandy plain and couldn't get up.

That night Gottschalk composed his petition.

He had two main points:

1. If used for food, the dead animals would not rot, thereby reducing the risk of plague for the Colonial Guard and the prisoners. 2. The lives of women and children would be saved.

Gottschalk couldn't get to sleep. Outside it was pouring rain.

The next morning Gottschalk reported to the office of Chief Veterinarian Moll. He was determined to follow official channels, going first through the Chief Veterinarian and then to headquarters. Gottschalk hoped Moll wouldn't start extolling the virtues of Hottentot women again.

What Gottschalk couldn't foresee was that Moll would be sitting at his desk in silent fury after a nasty dressing-down, a fury he hadn't been able to take out yet on his office orderly, a sergeant who simply hadn't given him an opportunity. Early that morning, Moll had been ordered to report to the base commander, Major von Redern, who normally spoke an easygoing Swabian dialect, but on this occasion chewed him out like a top-sergeant. Most of the oats, which had been stored in the open, had been soaked in last night's storm. No one had thought it would rain, nor were there any tarps to cover the sacks. Wet oats, possibly even fermented, Moll surely realized as a veterinarian, could disable an entire cavalry detachment. Colic turned even well-trained steeds into wildly thrashing mustangs. Moll had to face the worst of all reproaches: he was a dilettante, a bungler. It bordered on an insult to his honor. The Major shouted (what was humiliating was that Moll realized Redner had planned in advance to insult him by shouting). The Major said it smacked of sabotage, perhaps even collaboration. The insinuation that Moll might be in league with the kaffirs was the most outrageous insult of all. Moll tried to defend himself, but each time he tried to reply the Major cut him off: Keep your mouth shut! Don't say a word unless I say so. Then he dismissed Moll. On the way back to his office, Moll considered resigning. Collaboration. Moll chewed his lip as he read the petition, a fairly narrow lower lip on the thick peasant head so often found in North Germany: a broad jaw, with slightly protruding ears. Gottschalk, who had remained standing before Moll (Major von Redner kept Moll standing at noon too), watched those ears start to redden. While he read, Moll buttoned and unbuttoned his right breast pocket with a strange nervous twitch at odds with his massive body, then looked up at Gottschalk. Meanwhile his face took on the color of his ears. He stared at Gottschalk, and then a single phrase emerged from that hinged jaw: Jungle fever! At last Moll could shout.

That evening Wenstrup asked Gottschalk if denying food to prisoners had merely been a low-level bureaucratic oversight.

Gottschalk said those were the orders.

Wenstrup didn't ask Gottschalk if he had gone ahead with his petition.

On 3 November, Lieutenant Gottschalk received orders to proceed to Keetmanshoop, in the southern part of the Protectorate. He was to join the 5th Battery on its way toward Rehoboth. The route led through rebel Hottentot territory.

Two Positions

From General von Trotha's proclamation of 2 October 1904, to the Hereros: Within the German frontier every Herero with or without a rifle, with or without cattle, will be shot. I will not take over any more women or children. But I will either drive them back to your people or have them fired on. These are my words to the Herero people. The great General of the mighty German Kaiser. (Conrad R. Rust, *War and Peace*, Leipzig, 1965, p. 385)

Governor Colonel Leutwein is said to have worked for a negotiated peace even after the change of command, and described the Herero nation as a "necessary labor force." (German Colonial Archives 2089)

Imperial Chancellor von Bülow: The total, planned extermination of the Hereros would exceed any reasonable measure for the restoration of peace in South West Africa and of punishment. The natives are essential for farming, for raising livestock, and for mining. (German Colonial Archives 2089)

General von Trotha: I totally disagree. I believe the nation as such must be destroyed. (12 December 1904, GCA 2089)

Chief of the General Staff, Colonel-General Count Schlieffen: His assertion that the entire nation must be destroyed or driven from the country makes sense. After what has happened, it will be very difficult for blacks and whites to live together, unless the former are held in an extended state of forced labor, that is, a sort of slavery. The racial struggle that has erupted can only be brought to a close by the destruction of one side. (Schlieffen to the Colonial Office, 23 November 1904, GCA 2089)

Consequences: "Closing off of the sand flats with iron rigor for months," reports another combatant, "completed the task of destruction. The military dispatches of General von Trotha from that period include no reports of any special note. The drama took place on the darkened stage of the sand flats. But when the rainy season arrived, as the stage gradually brightened and our patrols pressed forward to the borders of Betschuanaland, the horrific image of troops who had died of thirst appeared before their eyes.

"The death rattles of the dying and the frenzied cries of those gone mad . . . faded into the exalted silence of infinity." (*The Battles of the German Colonial Guard in South West Africa*, edited by the Office of the General Staff, vol. I, p. 218)

Of approximately 80,000 Hereros, 15,130 survived.

[. . .]

RENÉ PHILOCTÈTE

from MASSACRE RIVER

Translated from the French by LINDA COVERDALE

Since five o'clock in the morning, a bird—to be honest, no one knows what it is—has been wheeling in the sky over Elías Piña, a small Dominican town near the Haitian border.

The children think it's the kite the local boss sometimes flies to kill time. The adolescents would love to straddle it for a joyride. The adults don't seem worried about it, but deep down, they're hoping the thingamajig will go away. Jaws jutting, eyelids blinking, the old folks slide sidelong glances at one another, spit three times on their chests, and cross themselves.

Suddenly, the bird hangs motionless, wings spread. Its shadow carves a cross that cuts Elías Piña into quarters. No sound leaves its throat. Not one twitter or chirp. The bird is mute. Dogs, cats, oxen, goats, donkeys, horses bite, claw, graze, browse its shadow set in the crystal of a Caribbean noon.

Señor Pérez Agustín de Cortoba, the boss, the government representative, is dozing, ensconced in a wicker armchair on his freshly whitewashed veranda, while a half-dozen flies buzz on his beige potbelly, bulging out from beneath a black sports shirt. In his siesta, he dreams of Emmanuela, his *negrita* who left more than a week ago for Cerca-La-Source, in Haiti. He clenches his fists: he strangles the unfaithful woman. The only distinct word among those disgorging from his gullet: *"¡Muerte!"*

Between a hiccup and a head-wobble, he opens a bloodshot right eye. The eye swivels toward the bird, smiles, closes. While the fingers squeeze . . . until they scrape his palms raw.

Meanwhile the bird takes life easy in the village sky. An elderly hunter armed with buckshot peppers it with a hail of pellets that rebound in an arc to the ground, squashed flat.

There is no blood in the bird.

Swallowing his spittle once, twice, thrice, the old hunter goes home, his head hanging. A loud report rattles the neighborhood. The old hunter has just blown his brains out.

No one attacks the machine with impunity. Pablo Ramírez tried once; he was thrown into the quagmires of Lake Enriquillo. The caymans ate him. Sonia del Sol and her four children (Miguel, Sunilda, Mario, Marco) hanged themselves in Barahona. Roberto Sánchez disappeared. Now his voice no longer lullabies the nights of Santiago de los Caballeros.

"Neighbor, do you know the story of Paco Moya? They say he was a sailor, in the capital between voyages, and died under suspicious circumstances, a starfish between his eyes."

"¡Verdad!"

"And the story of María, *la puta*? Of José, *el poeta*? Of Rafaelo, the baker? Of Juan, *el campesino*? Of García, the teacher? Of Enrico, the tailor?"

"Death lowered the drawbridge, the castle swallowed them up."

No, no one attacks the thing. Or else children waste away and women piss blood between their thighs.

The bird is a sorcerer.

With one fell swoop it plummets, head down, onto the trees. Leaves go flying, branches break, flowers catch fire. The impact against the trunks does not stem its fury. Everything collapses at its passage, leaving it free to maneuver.

The bird is blind.

Now it shoots skyward, wings folded, feet together, drilling the air. Struck head-on, the sun quivers, shrinks, caves in. No one dares to comment on the missile's acrobatics or even *try* to cast a counter-spell.

[. . .]

Only Roberto Pedrino, a vacationing sociology student visiting his cousin Antonia Felicia Salvador y López, tries to appease the creature's anger, by playing the mandolin. But his fingers on the instrument's strings shrivel up to their roots. Undaunted, with his teeth Roberto César Pedrino plucks chords from the instrument—any chords at all!—that tangle, squeak, whistle, flounder. And playing back-up to the notes of Roberto César Pedrino y Márquez, the corrugated-metal roofs of the houses begin to screech, cackle, cheep, and mew. The emboldened inhabitants of Elías Piña take up whatever comes to hand—drum, flute, saxophone—and troop through the streets to music that murmurs and neighs. The bells in the wooden chapel of Notre-Dame de la Conception quit their tower, calling and jostling one another with the rapid-fire sound of weddings.

How long does that last? Nobody in Elías Piña can say. Except that at six in the evening they are still parading around to the din of cymbals, the squealing of guitars, the thunder of drums, the moaning of saxophones, and the hysteria of the bells.

Enveloped in his ample black cassock and assisted by two peevish, toothless, verminous, and hunchbacked old women, José Ramírez, the Andalusian priest, even drenches the crowd with streams of water consecrated pronto to that purpose in the name of the Trinity and poured into big saffron-yellow earthenware basins.

No one wonders why José Ramírez Pepito y Biembo threw hundreds of bars of soap into the holy water. Nevertheless, strangely shaped, rainbow-hued bubbles slip hissing from everyone's mouth: green ones with gargoyle heads; pink ones rippling like parasols; crudely grimacing black ones; bubbles as white as sails, yellow as autumn, blue as the high seas, red as the fires of rose gardens and the waning moments of engagement balls. (A kind of fugue from the village orchestra.)

Meanwhile, after hounding the sun into a corner, the device reappears in the sky over Elías Piña. It buries its head under its left wing and sleeps, suspended between the fields and the first stars.

The beast is deaf.

No one knows where it comes from.

"Hey! Hey! Señor Pérez Agustín! Is this thing from around here?"

Of course! Don Pérez's red eye tumbles down his beige belly, disturbing five or six flies along the way, and stops at the huge navel to say "¡Claro!" Climbs back up, pops back into its socket. In the meantime his fingers, finishing their throttling of Emmanuela, fumble to caress her.

"Come, now!"

We are its guests, just possibly its children. Anoint! Anoint thy nation and thy bride, thy people and thy lamb! The old hunter tried to shoot thee down and brought about his own death. Carlos Fuentes rose against thee; the Sierra de Bahoruco smothered him. Angel Toya threatened thee; he rotted away in Macorís. The thing watches over us. So who fears it? It's a Dominican affair. *Una cabeza de la tierra. ¡La primera cabeza de la tierra! ¡La cabeza nuestra!** Let us kindle a blaze to warm its vigil. Saint, saint, saint, thrice-blessed Rafael Leónidas Trujillo y Molina!

And Don Agustín congratulates his eye.

On a binge, the bells peal out their arpeggios. Without any prompting, children gather dead branches and fragrant leaves. Men toss into the air lighted matches that fall in a luminous necklace onto firewood transformed into a mass of sparks, madly changing colors like chameleons, trembling, writhing, burning the night of Elías Piña. Women cut off their hair—cascading black braids gleaming like deep water, loose tresses smooth as corn silk—and toss it into the flames. Whirls of

*A homeland head. The first head in the land! Our head!

blue, green, pink smoke swirl away the charred odors of violets, chamomile, and basil, sowing them across the plowed land, strewing them beneath the stars. All while the thing broods a nightmare above Elías Piña.

On his candy-pink porch facing Don Pérez Agustín de Cortoba's veranda, the alcalde Preguntas Feliz, the number-two man in the village—light brown skin, a thin figure in clinging rust-red trousers, right hand holding aloft a late-eighteenth-century wrought-iron lantern, left hand over his heart—begins to sing a kind of slow merengue. Like an Adoration. His slippery voice paralyzes all others, vanishes in the distance and returns; spirit of the times, it seeps into everyone and everything (the springhead shivers; the butcher's dog curls up in a ball; the daughter of Don Miguel, the surveyor, has one of her fits), going deep, settling in. As on a throne. "By the eyes of the Madonna and the gold of the sierra, we hail thee, Lord of blood and horror!" shouts the alcalde Preguntas Feliz. "Lord of the dreadful blood!" bleat the villagers. A child starts sniveling after biting his tongue. With a menacing finger, Preguntas Feliz shows him the late-eighteenth-century lantern. The child chokes back his tears. The man of justice, left hand over his heart, holding the lantern out toward the villagers, fine-tunes his Adoration: "By the power of the agony we hail thee, Lord of demented death!"

Pérez Agustín de Cortoba, befogged until that moment in his noon siesta (and the flesh of Emmanuela), stretches, hiccups, reopens the red eye. Hiccups. Wipes away the thick drool on his beige belly with a hairy left hand. Stretches. Farts. Stands up, waves his arms around, sways from side to side on his crooked bowed legs, and to the tune of "The Blue Danube" sings: "For the head of a Haitian man, the accolade of Trujillo; for the body of a Haitian child, male or female, the smile of Trujillo; for a Haitian woman hacked in two, the gratitude of Rafael Leónidas Trujillo y Molina." Hiccups.

The villagers try to take up Don Agustín's song, but their voices seem stuck. Are they appalled? Just plain ashamed? Or afraid?

Slipping furtively along, Preguntas Feliz, slim as a stiletto, steps down from the candy-pink porch into the street and slices through the crowd. The lantern swings gently from his hand as he heads—chin up, eyes front—toward Don Agustín de Cortoba. Who, shambling heavily, leaves his whitewashed veranda to fall into the street (crushing people) and the arms of Preguntas. They huddle together in the center of the prostrate, frozen village. Their voices, one thin, the other booming, clump together, merging for the paroxysm of the Adoration: "The reign of the dagger is within heart's reach, announcing the loyalty of the people to the coming harvest of death." Their faces in the dirt, the villagers mumble: "Thou whose firmness hast taken precedence over our plans, thou who hast anointed us with the oil of obedience, mayest thou be truly welcome. O thou! Here, there, and everywhere, lord and master of the alliance, may the wine of solemn allegiance be served to thee!"

Elías Piña recites the glory of Trujillo. Recites until night stops up every throat and each mouth gapes mutely.

So it goes while the contraption, hovering between the fields and the stars, continues to brood a nightmare, and piled-up machetes lie resting, recuperating for the next onslaught on Haitian heads. The bells are quiet now.

Carefully bound and gagged, silence stands guard over Elías Piña.

Pedro Alvarez Brito, *el mulato dominicano*, a worker at the sugar factory in San Pedro de Macorís, who had neither sung nor wept nor spoken nor even looked at the bird-lord, the raptor-kite, the sign-bird, touches the right hand of his wife, Adèle Benjamin, *la chiquita negrita haitiana* from Belladère. And finds it freezing!

"Adèle!" says Pedro Brito tenderly.

"The day of blood is coming closer," murmurs the young woman.

"Yes, the signs are everywhere, they're obvious."

"The day of shame and scorn . . ."

"Is it possible?"

"What isn't possible when power turns stupid?" exclaims Adèle in exasperation.

[. . .]

Standing in the middle of the street, Don Agustín de Cortoba, the representative of order, tackles the air. Armed with *la couline*—a long, thin, flat, gleaming machete for combat—he whirls around, sweeping up in his rotation the village steeple, his whitewashed house, the trees, the dust, the candy-pink porch of Preguntas, the dead dog, the flies, his own drunkard's mug, his bristling mustache, his beige belly. A head rolls at his feet. Taken by surprise, the air rears back at first, then ripostes. An arm moans. Some teeth grimace. Two fingers poke themselves up Don Agustín's nostrils. The air doubles over, then pounces, hissing. Don Agustín pants for breath. A yellowish drool drips down his chin. Don Agustín hiccups, returns to the fray. The air retreats. Confident of victory, Don Agustín advances boldly. The machete cuts, cleaves, chops, carves, slices, dices. Guts tumble at the feet of Don Agustín. A palpitating liver sticks to the skin of his stomach. The machete speeds up. The air huddles, a porcupine caught in a corner. Take that, and that! The machete amputates, mutilates, decapitates. Don Agustín sings, shouts, bellows, Don Agustín howls in the battle. Writhing nerves twine around his hams. And snip goes the machete, and snap goes the machete. One! Two! Hack, hew! The air cowers. Don Agustín sweats, swaggers, dashes here, darts there, advances, retreats, leaps, bounds. Each time he strikes, Emmanuela's long, slender legs grip, girdle, press, squeezing his huge beige body dry. And the machete cuts capers, turns somersaults. The machete pirouettes. Snicker-snack! And slashes, sunders, severs, shears. A bladder bursts. The air, abruptly, unleashes a multiplication of entrechats and—big surprise—strikes home. Don Agustín whimpers. Don Agustín slobbers. Don Pérez Agustín de Cortoba y Blanco gabbles like a goose. A vagina foams, contracted in pain. Slack-jawed, heart pounding, Don

Agustín staggers around with Emmanuela's legs scraping his ribs. The machete snips, slits, struts its stuff. Princess, suzeraine, dowager, it visits its domain: bells, fields, houses, men's heads, women's hearts, and the laughter of children. Take that! Bisects, beheads. And that! Disjoints, dismantles, dismembers. A passing sunbeam is promptly chased down by Don Agustín and hanged from the top of a Spanish lime tree. Here are flowers, branches, fruits. Winded, Don Agustín stops, right in front of the house of Pedro Alvarez Brito, with heads clinging to his head, hands stuck to his hands, loins girdling his loins, two fingers up his nose, and hair in his left eye. And now here is my heart! Shivering, the air flings itself to the ground. Don Agustín is perspiring profusely as Emmanuela's long, slender legs go up and down him, lifting and rhythmically rocking him.

A rippling, rattling, crackling caterpillar of tufa, the main street of Elías Piña announces:

"Operation Haitian Heads has been going on now for over an hour. The scene is the Haitian-Dominican border; the characters: both peoples—more than 120,000 human beings interconnected through their languages, their pastimes, their dress, their customs, their environment—plus the machetes, of all shapes and sizes. Over by Dajabón, diligent machetes are cutting a current tally of more than thirty heads a minute; in Pedernales, a less hurried pace is racking up only eighteen. Here in Elías Piña, the machetes are in training with our head coach for Operation *Cabezas Haitianas*, Don Pérez Agustín de Cordoba, Grandmaster of the Clotted Blood. Be patient. We'll keep you informed of any new developments. Playing a bit part: the Haitian government. Enjoy refreshing Coca-Cola!"

And this unique radio—Elías Piña's main street—continues its broadcast with Tino Rossi singing "Under Paris Skies."

Don Agustín opens his mouth, releasing an endless stream of grasshoppers whose wings squeak "*¡Perejil!*" Ripped to rags, the air goes down for the count.

Don Preguntas Feliz arrives huffing and puffing, wiping his face with a putty-colored handkerchief. In great excitement, he whispers to Don Agustín. Then the two confederates turn their eyes to Adèle. She has almost finished rinsing the overalls, and now their smell of honest toil is really going to her head.

The representatives of power stare at me as if looks could kill. Can any human gaze be so inhuman? I saw Pablo Márquez fall in a burst of machine-gun fire last summer when Trujillo's Guardia crushed the workers' strike. The look he gave me held a flash of astonishment, but it was the look of a man. I saw Lucita Gómez clutch her abdomen as if to tear it open when the soldier brought the body of her son Renecito, a strapping young man, a journalist in Macorís, but the look she gave me was the dark, bewildered gaze of a grieving mother. There are lost, defeated eyes, buffeted by the four winds, the eyes of a lifer in prison; of a beggar mired in misery; the eyes of a dying patient turning away from the doctor; of a professional gambler who has placed a bad bet; the eyes of a startled child; the martyr's eyes of a simple plaster statue of Christ; the eyes of a rejected husband; of a fugitive tracked by the police; of a miser burning through his money. They're like the debris of human shipwrecks, but they are still the eyes of real people, hoping somehow to come safely into harbor . . .

[. . .]

Musing, Adèle goes inside the house. She can hear the pickax blows of Don Agustín digging a grave for the sunbeam he'd hanged by the neck until dead. Branches, fruits, pecked by birds. Outside: Elías Piña, deserted. "Hey, neighbor! Tell me—have you seen Don Pablo, *el profesor?*" Striking a rock, Don Agustín's pickax throws off sparks. Adèle lights the lamp to Our Lady, the Mater Dolorosa, in her portable shrine, and wonders why the Virgin hasn't smiled at her. And yet, the oil in the white china bowl is of good quality, and the yellow flame is burning blue at the wick. The smell of benjamin mingled with the scent of basil gives the room a taste of apples and flesh. Seized with terror, Adèle rushes out into the courtyard. "Neighbor! Have you seen *la santa? ¿La santa mía? ¿La mía santa? ¿Mía la santa?*" Don

Agustín's pickax claws in the black soil laced with pink earth-worms. Swaying its hips, the street performs conjuring tricks with long, flashing machetes—it curses, raves, murmurs, murders. Adèle rushes back into the bedroom like a whirlwind. The odor of apples and flesh stretches itself languorously; the flame in the white china bowl wavers, stands up, bows down, trembles, sputters, yellow burning blue at the wick. Adèle stares at the image of the Virgin. The image has lost its eyes. In place of the pale blue pupils quiver two indescribable little things. Two paws. Two chimneys. Two drops. Two.

Adèle races outside: "Hey! Neighbor! *Mira*, neighbor! Look! The Madonna's eyes are gone, off in my blue heaven, flown away home like black and yellow Our-Ladybugs. Neighbor, tell me! Where is my head? My *chiquita haitiana* from Belladère's head. My head where the fires of day break. My headless head. My calamity-head. My boring old not-happy-enough head!"

The body of the sunbeam drops into the grave. Limp. Pitiful.

Adèle is overcome by exhaustion. A kind of flight of all her limbs. Her right leg rolls in the dust beside the dog, now greenish-black with decay. Her left leg goes off to frolic around Don Agustín, who is tamping the sunbeam's body down into the soft ground. Adèle's left arm has snagged itself on something, she can't say what, but she has the feeling that it's barbed wire. An exasperating gnashing noise scrapes the air.

Channeling its radio, the street updates the news:

"In Azua Province, 908 heads; 819 in Santiago; in Peder-nales, a sudden access of national fervor: 1,217! Dajabón is the winner, with a current head count of 15,208! (Pause.) Here in Elías Piña, in view of the training program, we started with the children: 128 males between the ages of eight and nine, 237 fe-males between the ages of four and seven, nubile and pubescent, intended for the colonels. Unfortunately, we do not have a reli-able statistical summary for that category of children. In any case, we will keep you informed. The operation is proceeding smoothly. Definite progress. *¡Saludo!* Gillette, the long-lasting blade that gives a close shave."

And the unique radio of Elías Piña's main street offers for consideration by its listeners an extract from the latest speech by Francisco Franco on "The Respect of Peoples for Their Leaders."

The vault of the firmament cracks.

Splitting, exfoliating, Adèle becomes half a body. I'm slipping. Ah! My man! The rain was blue, and went on forever. From the sky tumbled birds so green they seemed like torrents of water. Songs came from everywhere. And there were bells, fried fish, guitars, watermelons, hats, plus endless palaver!

Adèle measures the pangs of absence.

The street strikes up again in strident tones:

"The children's flesh is so tender that the machetes can't sink in—they slide instead of slicing, causing more painful bruises than outright wounds from direct hits. Therefore, as a humanitarian gesture, the *Cabezas Haitianas* Committee has stipulated that the throats of children be chomped with bare teeth. The tally for the moment: 8,286 children of both sexes have perished at the claws and fangs of the Guardia. The venture is going better and better from moment to moment. This evening, at The Eldorado, the film that's all the rage in the capital: *La Joie de Vivre!* Tonight's weather: cool all across the island."

And the only radio goes on the fritz with static.

The child atop the steeple screams loud enough to wake the dead: "*¡Perejil!*" The pickax plops the last clods of dirt on the corpse of the sunbeam. The entire village surges into view, as if propelled out of the earth, the sky, the air. Adèle is almost sweating delirium. "Neighbor! Where is the Virgin? *¿La santa mía?* Neighbor, I'm leaving!" The village laughs. Peal after peal of laughter, echoing even louder than the mad tolling of the bells. "Neighbor, I'm locking myself in!"

[. . .]

Adèle buries her head in her hands. Her finger-joints crack: "*¡Perejil!*" Padre Ramírez's black cassock, the olive-drab truck, the young man with his fingers worn down by music, the crazy bells, the children with dusty eyes, the dead dog, soap bubbles,

flies, bonfire, the charred hanks of women's hair, the two toothless trollops, hunchbacked and verminous, the drums, holy
water, flutes, cymbals, the old suicide, the lost eyes of the Virgin
prance, dance, wriggle, cackle, gesture and grimace, embrace,
and parade down the street chanting: "*¡Perejil!*" Adèle vomits. At
her feet swarm countless unspeakable things shed by Don
Agustín, who has been standing unnoticed before her for some
time. And who orders her to say "*¡Perejil!*" Adèle stammers. The
l has fled into her uvula. The *e* has trod on the *i*. The *j* has frozen
up. The *p* is bumping into the *r*, stifling it. Adèle's mouth opens
painfully. An almost inhuman sound wobbles out. Don Agustín
swells, shoots upward, hoisted by Emmanuela's long, slender
legs, until his noggin is level with the raptor's. The two heads
confer. Then Don Agustín shrinks, descends between Emmanuela's legs. His enormous beige belly pops out from beneath
his black sports shirt. His teeth champ and gnash: "*¡Perejil!*"
Adèle mumbles "*¡Perejil!*" Her tongue coils. Her gums grow hot
and puffy. The whole word squeezes into her throat with a gur-
gle that must hurt. Then the young woman's limbs come to the
rescue of her voice. But the left leg has switched places with the
right one—and they're squabbling: "I'm going first." "Forget it,
me first!" Don Agustín bellows "*¡Perejil!*" Snarls "*¡Perejil!*" Adèle
tries one more time. The letters get mixed up, have a shoving
match, fall to pieces, down the hatch.

The sunbeam sags deeper into its grave. The child tolls the
bells, his rhizomatous fingers gripping the ropes that set them
pealing left and right in the tiny white wooden steeple. A
brazen, bone-rattling ringing wings out over the roofs. The sky
cracks. Elías Piña is once again in adoration of Trujillo: "Saint,
saint, saint, anoint thy people, thy nation, thy bride!"

The raptor (to be honest, no one knows what it is) has girded
itself with shadows, tipping the strutting sun and all its medals
into darkness.

Don Agustín is lapping noisily. Emmanuela is undulating.
The *negrita's* nipples stiffen. Don Agustín starts slobbering. Emmanuela wriggles. The *negrita's* belly snaps. Don Agustín stut-

ters. Emmanuela rears. The *negrita's* body leaps. Don Agustín collapses, pumped dry. Dazed, he rubs a flabby hand over his damp fly.

A crackling:

"Attention, please! There has been a request to speed up the operation. There is absolutely no call to poeticize the accumulation of heads, along the lines of 'falling petals' or 'falling stars'— typical naive metaphors we must banish from the Dominican nationalist vocabulary. Let them fall by the hundreds of thousands every second (mown down like hay, exactly): we remain unaffected. When you pull up weeds, you don't pay attention to the cicadas' song. Make way for the serenity of machetes, the spilling of blood! (Pause.) While we're on the subject: 18,203 heads in Dajabón. For children, teeth and claws; results, positive; *método: ¡Hasta luego!* Flash! After the death of Sanjurjo, General Francisco Franco has become the uncontested master of Spain. Today our president has sent him a message for the occasion. Listerine protects and whitens your teeth!"

And the only radio on the main street begins to prattle about the benefits of fluoride in dental hygiene.

Leaving Emmanuela's bed, Don Agustín roars: "*¡Perejil!*" As if abruptly inspired, he dashes toward a kitchen garden adjoining the old gray presbytery with the slate roof. In the twilight, the blowsy heads of cabbage throw out their chests; the leeks draw themselves up like soldiers. He's looking for something or other. The lettuces open their hearts. The pink-and-white radishes show off in the tender shade of the celery. Suddenly overjoyed, Don Agustín pulls up a bright green tuft of parsley and brandishes it like a trophy before dashing back. A rustle of wings sets the wild thyme shivering. *(Adèle sees the machete coming,)* Don Agustín waves the parsley, squeaking: "*¡Perejil!*" *(sees it teasing passersby,)* Chortling: "*¡Perejil!*" Mewing: "*¡Perejil!*" Farting: "*¡Perejil!*" Adèle's mouth opens. Elías Piña piles inside with a crash, the village's laughter still rolling over the roofs. *(sees it skipping rope,)* Don Agustín's machete rises, sucks up darkness, *(sees it slip between her breasts.)* and whirls around, carrying along in its windmilling the chiming bells, *(Adèle hears the machete talking to her,)* crawling, spinning spiders, blinding, stifling dust, *(telling her stories,)* the stretching, upsetting street, *(imitating the ocean.)* Father Ramírez, the whitewashed house, the blind Virgin, the fields, the stars, and the machete spins in circles, gets itself together, growing stronger from the darkness, and shoots all the way up to the thing, *(Adèle senses the machete is running out of breath,)* consults the object, swears to obey the orders to slice-and-dice, shrieks with laughter, savors its feast of flesh, *(sweating over its work.)* asks for a drink, carouses, gaily greets the entire village, which it demands bear witness to its redoubtable striking force and tempered steeliness, then pledges fresh allegiance to the System ("Anoint, anoint thy people, thy lamb!") and flits about, warming the hand of Don Agustín—to which the machete gives confidence, guarantees power, promises a role in the grand finale plus the conveyance of kind regards to the *Cabezas Haitianas* Committee—and, smelling blood, pirouettes, prances, swanks around, confers again with that flying thing, coordinates, plans, returns to earth, kicks up its heels, plays the fool, reassures Don Agustín's hand, observes, reasons, hesitates: "Am I cut out to cut off heads? What will the grass say? The boles of oaks? The old mango trees, sages of the Sierra?" Then, impulsively—"I am my own master, as I am of death"—the machete opts for the Reason of State, the purity of the Dominican nation, its authenticity, specificity, originality, remembers it's the champion of the *blancos de la tierra*, persuades itself that ocher must snuff out black, leach it out, so that from Bahoruco to Monte Cristi all will be yellow or white (mostly white) like the dawn rallying its people of light, white like the foaming crests of waves breaking into doves of water. And hop! The machete makes up its mind, *(Adèle imagines it as a train, a snake in the night, a dragon)* comes to a conclusion, and falls on the back of Adèle's neck! *(A vapor, a doll, a locust.)*

Aghast, the young woman's head opens eyes in which floats a blue rain, so blue it's misty, so misty it's blue. "Hey, neighbor! Have you seen my man? He went into the dawn. My man,

Pedro Brito, the worker at San Pedro de Macorís, the husband of the dawn! Did you watch him grow up? Neighbor, *¡Dime por favor!*"

The sunbeam is seeping deeper and deeper into the clayey soil, amid the pink miracle of the earthworms, the village's hearty laughter, the din of the bells rung by the spider recovering its human form: paws with dirty nails, a shaved head with mauve scabs, the swollen belly of a suckling pig.

Elías Piña's main street lets out a squeak:

"By mistake, the Dominican Guardia has killed more than five hundred of its own peasants on the banks of the Guayamuco River. Although we regret this incident, we must condemn all discontented rumors, as well as any hint of controversy. Buy Dominican: Bermudez, the macho rum!"

The sole radio hiccups as the power goes off for just a second.

[. . .]

Although Adèle tries hard to catch her head and attach it to her body, and though she relights the Virgin's lamp to plead and promise, and even freshens the scents of benjamin and basil to sweeten her request, the head darts off. Runs away.

Caught up in the breath of the emblem-sign-object, the head rises, falls, bounds, rebounds, hedge-hops, puddle-jumps, watched by the children doggedly throwing dust in one another's eyes. Adèle runs after it, calling and begging, but the jubilant head, curling its lips, enters the darkness of the System and remains there, allowing itself to be touched, weighed, squeezed: the extraordinary, intimate embrace between the executioner and the victim.

In vain Adèle reminds her head of the wonderful memories of Pedro: rain so blue it was misty, parrots from the sky, wedding night in Maïssade between the full moon and the cavalcade of wild mint . . . Her frisky head ferrets around, inquiring here and there: "Neighbor! What happened to Guillermo Sánchez? Neighbor! Who turned the fangs loose? Neighbor! Who unleashed these instincts, these passions, this madness?" The head stops to think, floats, oscillates. Then knocks on doors: "He went to see the others." Weeping, it knocks. "The workers had gathered together, to join forces." Now silent, it knocks.

The doors remain mute.

Pedro Brito falls to his knees in the dust. The dust moans. One can die of disappointment. As from hunger. Failure is a terrible starvation. No one has any guarantees against lost hope. Any insurance against it.

Adèle's head comes to huddle against the crumpled legs of Pedro Alvarez Brito y Molina. For just twenty seconds. Barely time enough to feel all funny, as at the touch of the orange shirt of coarse linen—a light deep in the thighs. Pivoting, the head returns to knocking on doors: "Neighbor! Hey, neighbor!"

Elías Piña cloisters itself in Elías Piña.

In the middle of the main street, where Chicha is displaying the body of the *negrita*, the rooster's remains, plus the petrified passengers on the ten rows of seats, Adèle's head grows drowsy. I'm done for. I was cut on the fly, on the sly, on the prowl by Don Pérez Agustín de Cortoba who—with Don Preguntas Feliz by his side, sweating in his tight, rust-red trousers—has been industriously chasing other heads, slicing-dicing with tongue and sword, spitting: "*¡Perejil! ¡Perejil!*" While I was washing your shirt, your work-smell possessed me. It's true that the Madonna lost her eyes, that the rain came back green in its verdigris setting, that Rosita Rochas's dog was underground up to its belly, that the children were terrorizing their sorrows, that the good Father Ramírez was too thin for his cassock, that the village had forgotten the springtime. All that is quite true, even the bells of the white wooden chapel that kept tolling, it seems, in my honor and still are, in fact! As though I were someone important, me, Adèle Brito, condemned along with so many others. But free in the wide blue yonder, beyond my body. "Neighbor! He thought he could wed the dawn. My head set out in his footsteps. *Mi cabeza loca* that mixes up what's happening with the public toilet, the birds, the hours."

[. . .]

CLARICE LISPECTOR

THREE CRÔNICAS

Translated from the Portuguese by GIOVANNI PONTIERO

IN FAVOR OF FEAR

I am convinced that at some time during the Stone Age I was definitely ill-treated by some man who loved me. Ever since then I have been haunted by a secret terror.

It so happened that one warm evening I was having polite conversation with a man of some breeding. He was dressed in a dark suit, with well-manicured hands. I was sitting there eating some guavas and feeling *completely relaxed*, as Sérgio Porto would say, when suddenly the man asked me: "Shall we go for a walk?"

No. I am going to be blunt. What he really said was: "Shall we take *a little stroll?*"

Why he should say *little stroll* I never did discover. Because suddenly, from a height of thousands of centuries, the first stone of an avalanche came tumbling down: it was my heart. Who could it have been? Who could have taken me for that *little stroll* in the Stone Age from which I never returned because I ended up staying there?

I do not know what element of terror exists in the monstrous delicacy of that expression *a little stroll*.

Once my first heart came rolling down and I had wickedly devoured those guavas, I felt foolish but terrified at the prospect of some improbable danger.

I can now say improbable, reassured as I am by civilized customs, by a strict police force, and my own ability to escape as fast as the most slippery of eels. Yet I should dearly love to know what I would have said in the Stone Age when, looking like a female ape, they shook me from my leafy arbor. Such nostalgia! I really must spend some time in the countryside.

Having swallowed my tiny guavas, I turned pale without the color draining altogether from my face: my fear was much too vertical in time to leave any traces on the surface. Besides, it was not fear. It was terror. It was my entire future disintegrating. This man, who was my equal, murdered me for love. For this is what they call love and they are right.

A little stroll? Those are the words the wolf used when he spoke to Little Red Riding Hood, who got wise only after the event. "Just in case of lurking danger, beneath the leaves I'll build my nest"—where had I heard these lines before? I cannot remember, but the people of Pernambuco know what they are talking about.

May the Man forgive me if he should recognize himself in this tale of fear. Let him take comfort from the fact that I was to blame. I should have accepted his invitation without suspicion, as well as the roses he sent beforehand: such kindness, the night was warm, his car waiting outside. And he should know that—in the simplistic division the centuries imposed on me between good and evil—I know that he was A GOOD MAN, LIVED IN A CAVE, ONLY HAS FIVE WIVES, DOES NOT BEAT ANY OF THEM, ALL FIVE WIVES LIVE CONTENTEDLY.

And I beg of him to try and understand—I appeal to his good humor—for I know that an indecisive man like him uses the expression *a little stroll* quite naturally while for me those words conveyed the terrible threat of sweetness. I must thank him for this expression. Never having heard those words before, they left me deeply shocked.

Being polite, I explained to the Man that I could not take *a*

little stroll. The centuries have prepared me and now I am as re-
fined as any woman even if I choose to take the precaution of
building my nest beneath the leaves to avoid any danger.

The Man did not insist, although it would not be true to say
he was pleased. We confronted each other for less than a fraction of a second—after thousands of years we have come to understand each other much better, and now it takes less than a
fraction of a second—we confronted each other and that no,
however mumbled, echoed loudly against the walls of the cavern
which have always been more favorable to the desires of Man.

After the Man's sudden retreat, here I am, safe but still shaken.
Have I escaped *a little stroll* which might easily have cost me my
life? Nowadays it is all too common to lose one's life by chance.

Once the Man had gone, I realized that I was overjoyed and
a completely new person. Oh, not because of his invitation.
For thousands of years we women have continually been invited
to go for a walk, we are used to it and happy to accept without
being pushed. I was happy and transformed—but out of fear.

Because I am in favor of fear.

For certain fears—if they are not demeaning and have inde-
structible roots—have given me my most incomprehensible reality. The illogical nature of my fears fascinates me, gives me an
aura which can be disconcerting. I can barely conceal beneath
this modest smile my extraordinary gift for succumbing to fear.

But in the case of this particular fear, I keep asking myself
what could possibly have happened to me in the Stone Age? It
was clearly something unnatural, otherwise I should hot have
been left with this tendency to look sideways, or have become so
discreetly invisible, cunningly assuming the color of the shadows and greenery, always keeping well into the side when walking along pavements and adopting a brisk pace. It had to be unnatural, otherwise it would never have frightened me, given my
nature and circumstances. Or could it have been that even in
that age when people lived in caves—where I continue to retire
in secrecy—could it have been that even then I invented this
neurosis about the motives behind that *little stroll?*

The answer is yes, but there is nothing wrong with having an oblique heart, it is a lighthouse, a compass, wisdom, sharp instinct, experience of death, the power to divine a disquieting but blissful lack of adjustment, because I am discovering that my own maladjustment stems from my origins. For everyone knows that mosquitoes are a sign of heavy rain, that to cut my hair under a new moon will give it greater strength, to mention a name I dare not utter will cause delays and great misfortune, and tying the devil with red string to the leg of a piece of furniture has at least tied up my demons. And I know in my heart—which has never dared expose itself in the center, and for centuries has kept well to the left under the cover of shadows—I know full well that Man is such a stranger, even unto himself, that innocence alone makes him natural.

No, this oblique heart of mine is right, even if the facts soon prove me wrong. *A Little Stroll* brings certain death, and the victim's startled face remains with glassy eyes staring up at that complacent moon.

SPAIN

It could scarcely be called singing, in so far as singing means using one's voice musically. It was scarcely vocal, in so far as the voice tends to utter words. Flamenco singing precedes utterance, it is human breathing. Sometimes, the odd word escaped, revealing how that mute singing was achieved. It was all about life, love, and death. Those three unspoken words were interrupted by laments and modulations. Modulations of breath, that initial vocal phase which captures the suffering in that opening lament and also the joy in that first outcry of sorrow. And pain. And then another piercing cry, this time of happiness at the outburst of that sorrow. The audience sit huddled round the dancers, looking swarthy and unwashed. After a lengthy modulation which dies away with a sigh, the audience, sounding as exhausted as the singer, murmurs an *olé*, an *amen*, a dying ember.

But there is also that impatient song which the voice alone does not express: then the nervous, insistent tapping of feet intervenes, the *olé* which continually interrupts the song is no longer a response; it is incitement, it is the black bull. The singer, almost clenching his teeth, gives voice to the fanaticism of his race, but the audience demands more and more, until that final spasm is achieved: this is Spain.

I could also hear the song that was absent. It consists of silence interrupted by cries from the audience. Within that circle of silence, a short, gaunt, swarthy little man, with inner fire, hands on hips and head thrown back, hammers out the incessant rhythm of that absent song with the heels of his shoes. This is not music. Not even dance. *Zapateado** predates the choreography of dancing—it is the body manifesting itself and manifesting us, feet communicating to a pitch of fury in a language which Spain understands.

The audience intensifies its wrath within its very silence. From time to time, you could hear the hoarse taunts of a gypsy, all charcoal and red tatters, in whom hunger has turned to passion and cruelty. It was not a spectacle, for there were no spectators: everyone present played as important a role as the dancer who was tapping his feet in silence. Becoming more and more exhausted, they can communicate for hours through this language which, were it ever to have possessed words, must have gradually lost them throughout the centuries—until the oral tradition came to be transmitted from father to son like the impetus of blood.

I watched two flamenco dancers partner each other. I have never witnessed any other dance in which the rivalry between a man and a woman becomes so naked. The conflict between them is so open that their wiles are of no importance: at certain moments the woman becomes almost masculine, and the man looks at her in amazement. If the Moor on Spanish soil is Moorish, his female counterpart has lost any languor she ever possessed when confronted with Basque severity. The Moorish woman in Spain is as proud as a peacock until love transforms her into a *maja.**

Zapateado: the tap-dancing peculiar to Spanish flamenco.
maja: low-class woman (especially in Madrid).

Conquest is arduous in flamenco dancing. While the male dancer speaks with insistent feet, his partner pursues the aura of her own body with her hands outspread like two fans: in this way she magnitizes herself, and prepares to become tangible and at the same time intangible. But just when you least expect it, she puts forward one foot and taps out three beats with her heel. The male dancer shudders before this crude gesture, he recoils and freezes. There is the silence of dance. Little by little, the man raises his arms once more, and cautiously—out of fear rather than modesty—attempts with splayed hands to shadow his partner's proud head. He circles her several times and at certain moments almost turns his back to her, thus exposing himself to the danger of being stabbed. And if he has avoided being stabbed, he owes his escape to his partner's unexpected recognition of his bravado: this then is her man. She stamps her feet, her head held high, with the first cry of love: at last she has found her companion and enemy. The two withdraw bristling with pride. They have acknowledged each other. They are in love.

The dance itself now begins. The man is dark-skinned, lithe, and defiant. She is severe and dangerous. Her hair has been drawn back, she is proud of her severity. This dance is so vital that it is hard to believe life will continue once the dance has ended: this man and woman must die. Other dances express nostalgia for their courage. But this dance *is* courage. Other dances are joyful. But the joy of this dance is solemn. Or missing. What matters here is the mortal triumph of living. The two dancers neither smile nor forgive. But do they understand each other? They have never thought of understanding each other. They have each brought themselves as their banner. And whoever is vaquished—in this dance both are vanquished—will not weaken in submission. Those Spanish eyes will remain dry with love and wrath. Whoever is vanquished—and both of them will be vanquished—will serve wine to the other like a slave. Even though that wine may prove fatal once jealous passion finally explodes. The partner who survives will feel revenged. But condemned to eternal solitude. For this woman alone was his enemy, this man alone was her enemy, and they chose each other for the dance.

The Princess (i)

If I were to be asked about Ofélia and her parents, I should reply with decorous honesty: I scarcely knew them. Before the same jury I should testify: I scarcely know myself—and to each member of the jury I should say, with the same innocent look of someone who has hypnotized herself into obedience: I scarcely know you. But sometimes I wake from a long sleep and turn submissively towards the delicate abyss of disorder.

I am trying to speak about that family which disappeared years ago without leaving any traces in me, and of which all that remains is a faded and distant image. My sudden willingness to know was provoked today when a little chick appeared in the house. It was brought by a hand which wanted to have the pleasure of giving me some living thing. Upon releasing the chick from its box, its charm overwhelmed us. Tomorrow is Christmas Day, but the moment of silence I await all year came on the eve of Christ's birth. Something chirping by itself arouses the most gentle curiosity which, beside a manger, becomes adoration. Well, whatever next, said my husband. He felt much too big and clumsy. Scruffy and with gaping mouths, the children approached. Feeling somewhat courageous, I gave in to feelings of happiness. As for the chick, it went on chirping. But tomorrow is Christmas, the older boy said self-consciously. We smiled, disarmed and curious.

But sentiments are like sudden water. Presently—just as water changes and loses some of its force when it attempts to devour a stone, and changes once more when we bathe our feet—presently there is no longer simply an aura and glow on our faces. Feeling good and anxious, we gathered around the distressed chick. Soft-heartedness leaves my husband cold and morose, something to which we have become accustomed; he tends to torment himself. For the children, who are much more serious, kindness is a passion. As for me, kindness inhibits me. Very soon the same water had changed, and we watched, ill at ease, entangled in our clumsiness as we struggled to be good. And now the water had changed, the expression on our faces gradually betrayed the burden of our desire, our hearts weighed down by a love which was no longer free. The chick's fear of us also made us feel uncomfortable; there we were, and not one of us worthy of appearing before a chick; with every chirp it was driving us away. With each chirp, it was reducing us to helplessness. Its persistent terror accused us of thoughtless mirth which by now was no longer mirth, but annoyance. The chick's moment had passed, and with increasing urgency it was expelling us without letting go. We adults quickly suppressed our feelings. But the children were silently indignant. They accused us of doing nothing for the chick or for humanity. The chick's persistent chirping had already left us, the parents, uncomfortably resigned: such is life. Only we had never said so to the children, for we were ashamed; and we postponed indefinitely the moment when we should summon them and tell them straight that this is how things are. It became increasingly difficult, the silence grew, and they were slow to respond to our anxiety to give them love in return. If we had never discussed such things before, all the more reason why we should hide from them now the smile that came to our faces as we listened to the desperate squawks coming from that beak; a smile as if it were up to us to bless the fact that this is the way things are, and we had just given them our blessing.

As for the chick, it was chirping. Standing on the polished table, it dared not make a move as it chirped to itself. I never realized there could be so much terror inside a creature made only of feathers. Feathers covering what? Half a dozen fragile little bones put together for what purpose? To chirp terror. Mindful of our inability to understand each other and out of respect for the children's revolt against us, we watched impatiently in silence. It was impossible to comfort the chick with words of reassurance, to console that tiny creature which was terrified just to have been born. How could we promise that everything would be all right? A father and a mother, we knew just how brief the chick's life would be. The chick also knew, in the way that living creatures come to know; through profound fear.

Meanwhile, there was the chick with all its charm, an ephemeral, yellow thing. I also wanted the chick to experience the joys of life, just as we were expected to experience them, for its only joy was to make others happy. That the chick should feel it was superfluous, unwanted—one of the chicks is bound to be useless—and had only been born for the greater glory of God and, therefore, for the happiness of mankind. But in loving our dear little chick, did we wish it to be happy simply because we loved it? I also knew that only a mother determines birth, and ours was the love of those who take pleasure in loving; I rejoiced in the grace of having devoted myself to loving; bells, bells were pealing because I know how to adore. But the chick was trembling, a thing of terror rather than beauty.

The younger boy could stand it no longer:

—Do you want to be its mummy?

Startled, I answered yes. I was the messenger assigned to that creature which did not understand the only language I knew: I was loving without being loved. My mission might founder and the eyes of four children waited with the intransigence of hope for my first real sign of love, I recoiled a little, smiling and aloof; I looked at my family and wanted them to smile. A man and four little boys were staring at me, incredulous and trusting. I was the mistress of that household, the provider. I could not understand the impassiveness of these five males. How often I would founder, so that, in my hour of fear, they would look at me. I tried to isolate myself from the challenge of those five males, so that I, too, might expect love from myself and remember what love is like. I opened my mouth, I was about to tell them the truth: exactly how, I cannot say.

But what if a woman were to appear to me in the night holding a child in her arms. And what if she were to say: Take care of my child. I would reply: How can I? She would repeat: Take care of my child. I would reply: I cannot. She would insist: Take care of my child. Then—then, because I do not know how to do anything and because I cannot remember anything and because it is night—I would then stretch out my hand and save a child. Because it is night, because I am alone in another's night, because this silence is much too great for me, because I have two hands in order to sacrifice the better of the two, and because I have no choice.

THE PRINCESS (II)

It was at that moment that I saw Ofélia again in my mind's eye. And at that same moment I recalled that I had been the witness of a little girl.

Later, I remembered how my neighbour, Ofélia's mother, had the dark complexion of an Indian woman. The dark shadows around her eyes made them very beautiful and gave her the sort of languorous appearance which caused men to take a second look. One day, when we were seated on a bench in the park, while the children were playing, she told me with that resolute expression of someone scanning the desert: "I have always wanted to take a course in confectionery." I remembered that her husband—who was also dark-skinned, as if they had chosen each other for their complexion—wanted to make a fortune in his particular line of business: he was the manager or perhaps even the owner of a hotel, I was never quite sure. This gave him an air of refinement but a distinct coolness. When we could not avoid meeting in the lift, he tolerated an exchange of words with that haughty tone of voice which he had acquired in greater battles. By the time we reached the tenth floor, the humility his cold manner had forced from me placated him a little: perhaps he might even arrive home a little more amiable. As for Ofélia's mother, because we lived on the same floor she feared we might become too intimate, and started avoiding me, unaware that I was also on my guard. The only intimacy between us had been that day on the bench in the park, where, with those dark shadows round her eyes and those thin lips, she had talked about learning how to decorate cakes. I did not know what to say and ended up by confiding, so that she might know that I liked her, that I, too, would like to take a course in confectionery. That one moment of mutual intimacy divided us even more, out of fear that any mutual understanding might be abused. Ofélia's mother was even rude to me in the lift: the next day I was holding one of my children by the hand, the lift was going down slowly and, feeling oppressed by the silence which gave the other woman strength—I said in an affable tone of voice, which I myself found repugnant even as I spoke:

—We're going to visit his grandmother.

Whereupon to my horror, she snapped in reply:

—No one asked you where you're going. I never poke my nose into other people's affairs.

—Well I never, I mumbled in a low voice.

This led me to believe there and then that I was being made to pay for that moment of intimacy on the park bench. This in turn made me think that she was afraid of having confided more than she actually had that day. And in turn made me wonder if she had not told me more, in fact, than either of us had realized. By the time the lift finally reached the ground floor, I had reconstituted that obstinate, languid air of hers on the park bench— and I gazed with new eyes at the proud beauty of Ofélia's mother. "I won't tell a soul that you want to learn how to decorate cakes," I thought to myself, giving her a furtive glance.

The father hostile, the mother keeping her distance. A proud family. They treated me as if I were already living in their future hotel and as if I had offended them by not paying my bill. Above all, they treated me as if I did not believe, nor could they prove, who they were. And who were they? I sometimes asked myself that question. Why was that slap imprinted on their faces and why was that dynasty living in exile? Nor could they forgive me for carrying on as if I had been forgiven. If I met them on the street, outside the zone to which I had been confined, it terrified me to be caught out of bounds: I would draw back to let them pass, I gave way as the dusky, well-dressed trio passed as if on their way to Holy Mass—a family that lived under the sign of some proud destiny or hidden martyrdom—purple as the flowers of the Passion. Theirs was an ancient dynasty.

But contact was made through the daughter. She was a most beautiful child with her long hair in plaits. Ofélia with the same dark shadows round her eyes as her mother, the same gums looking a little inflamed, the same thin lips as if someone had inflicted a wound. But how those lips could talk. She started coming to visit me. The door-bell would ring, I would open the spy-hole without seeing anyone, and then I would hear a resolute voice:

—It's me, Ofélia Maria dos Santos Aguiar.

Disheartened, I would open the door. Ofélia would enter. She had come to visit me, for my two little boys were far to small then to be treated to her phlegmatic wisdom. I was a grown-up and busy, but it was me she had to visit. She would arrive dispensing with any formalities, as if there were a time and place for everything. She would carefully lift her flounced skirt, sit down and arrange the flowers—and only then would she look at me. In the midst of duplicating my files, I carried on working and listening. Ofélia would then proceed to give me advice. She had very decided opinions about everything. Everything I did was not quite right in her opinion. She would say "in my opinion" in a resentful tone, as if I should have asked her advice and, since I had not asked, she was giving it. With her eight proud and well-lived years, she told me that, in her opinion, I did not rear my children properly: for when you give children an inch, they take a mile. Bananas should not be served with milk. It can kill you. But of course, you must do what you think is best: everyone knows their own mind. It was rather late for me to be wearing a dressing-gown: her mother dressed as soon as she got up, but everyone must live as they see fit. If I tried to explain that I still had to take my bath, Ofélia would remain silent and watch me closely. With a hint of tenderness and then patience, she added that it was rather late to be taking a bath. I was never allowed the last word. What last word could I possibly offer when she informed me: vegetable patties should not be covered. One afternoon in the baker's shop, I found myself unexpectedly confronting the useless truth: there stood a whole row of uncovered vegetable patties. "But I told you so," I could hear her say, as if she were standing there beside me. With her plaits and flounces, with her unyielding delicacy. She would descend like a visitation into my sitting-room, which was still waiting to be tidied up. Fortunately she also talked a lot of nonsense, which made me smile, however low I might be feeling.

The worst part of this visitation was the silence. I would raise my eyes from the typewriter and wonder how long Ofélia had been watching me in silence. What could possibly attract this child to me? Personally, I found myself exasperating. On one occasion, after another of her lengthy silences, she calmly said to me: you are a strange woman. And as if I had been struck on the face without any form of protection—right on the face which is our inner self and therefore extremely sensitive—struck full on the face, I thought to myself in a rage: you are about to see just how strange I can be. She who was so well protected, whose mother was protected, whose father was protected.

The Princess (iii)

However, I still preferred her advice and criticism. Much less tolerable was her habit of using the word *therefore* as a way of linking sentences into a never-ending chain. She told me that I bought far too many vegetables at the market—therefore—they would not fit into my small fridge and—therefore—they would go bad before the next market day. A few days later I looked at the vegetables, and they had gone bad. Therefore—she was right. On another occasion, she saw fewer vegetables lying on the kitchen table, as I had secretly taken her advice. Ofélia looked and looked. She seemed prepared to say nothing. I waited, standing there fuming but saying nothing. Ofélia said phlegmatically:

—It won't be long before there's another market day.

The vegetables had run out towards the middle of the week. How did she know? I asked myself bewildered. Probably she would reply with "therefore". Why did I never, never know? Why did she know everything, why was the earth so familiar to her, and here was I without protection? Therefore? Therefore.

On one occasion, Ofélia actually made a mistake. Geography—she said, sitting before me with her hands clasped on her lap—is a kind of study. It was not exactly a mistake, it was a slight miscalculation—but for me it had the grace of defeat, and before the moment could pass, I said to her mentally: that's exactly how it's done! just go on like that and one day it will be easier or more difficult for you, but that's the way, just go on making mistakes, ever so slowly.

One morning, in the midst of her conversation, she announced peremptorily: "I'm going home to get something but I'll be right back." I dared to suggest: "If you've got something to do, there's no need to hurry back." Ofélia looked at me, silent and questioning. "There is a very nasty little girl," I thought firmly to myself so that she might see the entire sentence written on my face. She kept on looking at me. A look wherein—to my surprise and dismay—I saw loyalty, patient confidence in me, and the silence of someone who never spoke. When had I ever thrown her a bone—that she should follow me in silence for the rest of my life? I averted my eyes. She gave a tranquil sigh. "I'll be right back." What does she want?—I became nervous—why do I attract people who do not even like me?

Once when Ofélia was sitting there, the door-bell rang. I opened the door and came face to face with Ofélia's mother. Protective and unbending, she had come in search of her daughter.

—Is Ofélia Maria here by any chance?

—Yes, she is, I said, excusing myself as if I had abducted her.

—Don't do that again—she said to Ofélia with a tone of voice that was meant for me: then turning to me, she suddenly sounded peevish: I'm sorry if you've been troubled.

—Not at all, your little girl is so clever.

The mother looked at me in mild surprise—but suspicion flickered across her eyes. And in her expression I could read: what do you want from her?

—I have already forbidden Ofélia to come bothering you, she now said with open distrust. And firmly grabbing the little girl by the hand to lead her away, she appeared to be protecting her from me. Feeling positively degenerate, I watched them through the half-opened spy-hole without making a sound: the two of them walked down the corridor leading to their apartment, the mother sheltering her child with murmured words of loving reproach, the daughter impassive with her swaying plaits and flounces. On closing the spy-hole, I realized that I was still in my dressing-gown and that I had been seen like this by the mother who dressed the moment she got up. I thought somewhat defiantly: Well, now that her mother despises me, at least there will be no more visits from the daughter.

But naturally, she came back. I was much too attractive for that child. I had enough defects to warrant her advice, I was apt terrain for exercizing her severity, I had already become the property of that slave of mine: of course, she came back, lifted her flounces and sat down.

As it happened, Easter was approaching, the market was full of chicks, and I had brought one home for the children. We amused ourselves with it, then the chick was put in the kitchen while the children went out to play. Soon afterwards, Ofélia appeared for her daily visit. I was typing and from time to time I would express assent, my thoughts elsewhere. The girl's monotonous voice, the singsong of someone reciting from memory, made me feel quite dizzy, her voice infiltrating between the words typed on the paper, as she talked and talked.

Then it struck me that everything seemed to have come to a sudden standstill. Aware that I was no longer being tortured, I looked at her hazily. Ofélia Maria's head was erect, her plaits transfixed.

—What's that? she asked.

—What's what?

—That! she said stubbornly.

—What?

We might have remained there forever in a vicious circle of "that!" and "what?," were it not for the extraordinary will-power of this child, who, without saying a word, but with an expression of intransigent authority, obliged me to hear what she herself was hearing. Forced into attentive silence, I finally heard the faint chirping of the chick in the kitchen.

—It's the chick.

—The chick? she said, most suspiciously.

—I bought a chick, I replied submissively.
—A chick! she repeated, as if I had insulted her.
—A chick.

The Princess (iv)

And there the matter would have rested had I not seen something which I had never noticed before.

What was it? Whatever it was, it was no longer there. A chick had flickered momentarily in her eyes only to disappear, as if it had never existed. And a shadow had formed. A dark shadow covering the earth. From the moment her trembling lips almost involuntarily mouthed the words: "I want one, too"—from that moment, darkness intensified in the depths of her eyes into remorseful desire which, if touched, would close up like the leaf of the opium poppy. She retreated before the impossible, the impossible which had drawn near, and which, in a moment of temptation, had almost become hers; the darkness of her eyes changed color like gold. Slyness crept into her face—and had I not been there, she would slyly have stolen something. In those eyes, which blinked with cunning knowledge, in those eyes there was a marked tendency to steal. She gave me a sudden look betraying her envy: you have everything; and censure: why are we not the same, then I would have a chick? and possessiveness—she wanted me for herself. Slowly I slumped into my chair, her envy was exposing my poverty and left my poverty musing: had I not been there, she would have stolen my poverty as well. She wanted everything. After the tremor of possessiveness subsided, the darkness of her eyes revealed her suffering. I was not only exposing her to a face without protection. I was now exposing her to the best of the world: to a chick. Without seeing me, her moist eyes stared at me with an intense abstraction, which made intimate contact with my intimacy. Something was happening which I could not understand at a glance. And desire returned once more. This time her eyes were full of anguish, as if they had nothing to do with the rest of her body, which had become detached and independent. And those eyes grew wider, alarmed at the physical strain as her inner being began to disintegrate. Her delicate mouth was that of a child, a bruised purple. She looked up at the ceiling—the dark shadows around her eyes gave her an air of sublime martyrdom. Without stirring, I watched her. I knew about the high incidence of infant mortality. The great question she was asking concerned me as well. Is it worthwhile? I do not know, my increasing composure replied, but it is so. There, before my silence, she surrendered to the process, and if she was asking me the great question, it must remain unanswered. She had to surrender—and without anything in return. It had to be so. And without anything in return. She held back, reluctant to surrender. But I waited. I knew that we are that thing which must happen. I could only be her silence. And, bewildered and confused, I could hear her heart, which was not mine, beating inside me. Before my fascinated eyes, like some mysterious emanation, she was being transformed into a child.

Not without sorrow. In silence, I watched the sorrow of her awkward happiness. The lingering colic of a snail. She slowly ran her tongue over her thin lips. (Help me, her body said, as it painfully divided into two. I am helping, my paralysis replied.) Slow agony. Her entire body became swollen and deformed. At times, her eyes became pure eyelashes, avid as an egg in the process of being formed. Her mouth trembling with hunger. Then I almost smiled, as if stretched out on an operating table, and insisting that I was not suffering much pain. She did not lose sight of me: there were footprints she could not see, no one had passed this way before, and she perceived that I had walked a great deal. She became more and more distorted, almost the image of herself. Shall I risk it? Shall I give way to feeling? she asked herself. Yes, she replied to herself, through me.

And my first yes sent me into rapture. Yes, my silence replied to her, yes. Just as when my first son was born and I had said: yes. I had summoned the courage to say yes to Ofélia, I who knew that one can die in childhood without anyone noticing. Yes, I replied enraptured, for the greater danger does not exist:

when you go, you go together, you yourself will always be there: this, this you will carry with you whatever may become of you.

The agony of her birth. Until then I had never known courage. The courage to be one's other self, the courage to be born of one's own parturition, and to cast off one's former body. And without being told whether it was worthwhile. "I," her body tried to say, washed by the waters. Her nuptials with self.

Fearful of what was happening to her, Ofélia slowly asked me:

—Is it a chick?

I did not look at her.

—Yes, it's a chick.

From the kitchen came a faint chirping. We remained silent, as if Jesus had just been born. Ofélia kept on sighing.

—A tiny little chick? she confirmed, with some uncertainty.

—Yes, a little chick, I said, guiding her carefully towards life.

—Ah, a little chick, she said pensively.

—A little chick, I repeated, trying not to be unkind.

For some minutes now, I had found myself in the presence of a child. The transformation had taken place.

—It's in the kitchen.

—In the kitchen? she repeated, pretending not to understand.

—In the kitchen, I repeated, sounding authoritarian for the first time, and without saying anything more.

—Ah, in the kitchen, said Ofélia, shamming and looking up at the ceiling.

But she was suffering. Feeling almost ashamed, I became aware that I was taking my revenge at last. Ofélia was suffering, shamming, looking up at the ceiling. Her mouth, those shadows around her eyes.

—Why don't you go into the kitchen and play with the little chick?

—Me . . .? she asked slyly.

—Only if you want to.

I know that I should have ordered her to go rather than expose her to the humiliation of such intense desire. I know that I should not have given her any choice, and then she could say that she had been forced to obey. At that moment, however, it was not out of revenge that I tormented her with freedom. The truth is that this step, this step, too, she had to take alone. Alone and without delay. It was she who had to go to the mountain. Why—I wondered—why am I trying to breathe my life into her purple mouth? Why am I giving her my breath? How can I dare to breathe inside her, if I myself . . . is it only that she may walk, that I am giving her these painful steps? Am I only breathing my life into her so that one day she may momentarily feel in her exhaustion that the mountain has come to her?

Perhaps I had no right. But there was no choice. This was an emergency, as if the girl's lips were becoming more purple by the minute.

THE PRINCESS (v)

—Go and see the little chick only if you want to, I then repeated with the extreme harshness of someone saving another.

We stood there facing each other, dissimilar, body separated from body; united only by hostility. I sat still and composed in my chair so that the girl might cause pain to some other being, unyielding so that she might struggle inside me; I felt increasingly strong as I saw Ofélia's need to hate me, her determination that I should resist the suffering of her hatred. I cannot live this for you—my coldness told her. Ofélia's struggle came ever closer and then inside me, as if that creature who had been born and endowed me with the most extraordinary strength were drinking from my weakness. In using me, she bruised me with her strength: she clawed me as she tried to cling to my smooth walls. At last the words came out in simmering rage:

—I'm off to see the chick in the kitchen.

—Yes, off you go, I said slowly.

She withdrew hesitantly, conscious of her dignity, even as she turned her back on me.

She re-emerged from the kitchen immediately—she looked startled, shamelessly holding out the chick in one hand and examining me from head to foot in her bewilderment.

—It's a little chick! she said.

She looked at the chick in her outstretched hand, then looked at me, then looked once more at her hand—and suddenly she became nervous and worried, which automatically made me feel nervous and worried.

—But it's a little chick! she said, and reproach flickered in her eyes at once as if I had not told her what was chirping.

I laughed. Ofélia looked at me, deeply offended. And suddenly—suddenly she laughed. Then we both laughed, somewhat stridently.

When we stopped laughing, Ofélia put the chick down on the floor to see it walking. When it ran, she went after it. She seemed to be giving the chick its freedom in order to provoke desire, but if it cowered, she rushed to its aid, pitying it for being subjected to her power: "Poor little thing, he's mine": and when she held the chick, it was with a hand deformed by delicacy.— Yes, it was love, tortuous love. He's very little and needs a lot of attention. One mustn't fondle him for that could be really dangerous; don't let people handle him unless they promise to be careful, and do as you think best, but corn is far too big for his little open beak; for he's very fragile, poor little thing, and so tiny; therefore, you shouldn't let your children play with him; I'm the only one who knows how to look after him; he keeps slipping all over the place, so the kitchen floor is clearly no place for a little chick.

For the last half hour I had been trying to get back to my typewriter in order to make up for lost time, while Ofélia's voice droned on. Little by little, she was only speaking to the little chick, and loving for love's sake. For the first time she had abandoned me, she was no longer me. I watched her, pure gold, and the chick, pure gold, and the two of them were humming like distaff and spindle. For me this also meant freedom at last and without any malice. Farewell. And I smiled with longing.

It was only much later that I realized that Ofélia was talking to me.

—I think—I think I'll put him in the kitchen.

—Off you go then.

I did not see her leave, nor did I see her return. At a given moment, quite by chance and somewhat distracted, I realized that there had been silence for some time. I suddenly looked at her. She was sitting with her hands folded on her lap. Without quite knowing why, I looked at her a second time.

—What is it?

—I . . .?

—Do you want to go to the lavatory?

—I . . .?

I gave up and carried on with my typing. Some time later, I heard a voice:

—I must go home now.

—Of course.

—If you don't mind.

I looked at her in surprise: Now then, if you wish . . .

—Well then, she said, I'll be going.

She walked away slowly and closed the door quietly behind her. I went on staring at the closed door. What a strange child you are, I thought to myself. I went back to my typing.

But I was stuck at the same sentence. Well—I thought impatiently, looking at my watch—now what's the matter? I sat there, searching restlessly in my mind, searching in my mind to discover what was troubling me. Just as I was about to give up, I saw that impassive face again: Ofélia. Something started to cross my mind, when to my surprise, that face was leaning over me in order to be able to hear what I was feeling. I slowly pushed away the typewriter. Reluctantly, I began moving chairs out of the way, until I came to a halt in the doorway of the kitchen. On the floor lay the dead chick. Ofélia, I impulsively called after the girl who had fled.

From an infinite distance, I saw the floor. Ofélia. From afar, I tried in vain to reach the heart of that silent girl. Oh, don't be so frightened! Sometimes people kill for love, but I promise you that one day you will forget everything. I promise you! People do not know how to love, do you hear me, I repeated as if I might reach her before she should proudly serve nothingness in refusing to serve the truth. I who had forgotten to warn her that without fear there was the world. But I swear that this is breathing. I was very tired. I sat down on the kitchen stool.

Where I am still sitting, slowly beating the mixture for tomorrow's cake. Sitting, just as if throughout all these years I had been patiently waiting in the kitchen. Beneath the table today's chick shudders. The same yellow, the same beak. As we are promised at Easter, He will return in December. It is Ofélia who has not returned: she grew up. She went away to become the Indian princess whose tribe awaited her in the desert.

César Aira

from AN EPISODE IN THE LIFE OF A LANDSCAPE PAINTER

Translated from the Spanish by Chris Andrews

Western art can boast few documentary painters of true distinction. Of those whose lives and work we know in detail, the finest was Rugendas, who made two visits to Argentina. The second, in 1847, gave him an opportunity to record the landscapes and physical types of the Río de la Plata—in such abundance that an estimated two hundred paintings remained in the hands of local collectors—and to refute his friend and admirer Humboldt, or rather a simplistic interpretation of Humboldt's theory, according to which the painter's talent should have been exercised solely in the more topographically and botanically exuberant regions of the New World. But the refutation had in fact been foreshadowed ten years earlier, during Rugendas's brief and dramatic first visit, which was cut short by a strange episode that would mark a turning point in his life.

Johan Moritz Rugendas was born in the imperial city of Augsburg on the 29th of March 1802. His father, grandfather and great-grandfather were all well-known genre painters; one of his ancestors, Georg Philip Rugendas, was famous for his battle scenes. The Rugendas family (although Flemish in origin) had emigrated from Catalonia in 1608 and settled in Augsburg, hoping to find a social environment more hospitable to its Protestant faith. The first German Rugendas was a master clockmaker; all the rest were painters. Johan Moritz confirmed his vocation at the age of four. A gifted draughtsman, he was an outstanding student at the studio of Albrecht Adam and then at the Munich Art Academy. When he was nineteen, an opportunity arose to join the expedition to America led by Baron Langsdorff and financed by the Czar of Russia. His mission was one that, a hundred years later, would have fallen to a photographer: to keep a graphic record of all the discoveries they would make and the landscapes through which they would pass.

[. . .]

Rugendas's second and final voyage to America lasted seventeen years, from 1831 to 1847. His industrious journeying took him to Mexico, Chile, Peru, Brazil again, and Argentina, and resulted in hundreds, indeed thousands of paintings. (An incomplete catalogue, including oil paintings, watercolors and drawings, numbers 3353 works.) Although the Mexican phase is the best represented, and tropical jungles and mountain scenes constitute his most characteristic subject matter, the secret aim of this long voyage, which consumed his youth, was Argentina: the mysterious emptiness to be found on the endless plains at a point equidistant from the horizons. Only there, he thought, would he be able to discover the other side of his art . . . This dangerous illusion pursued him throughout his life. Twice he crossed the threshold: in 1837, he came over the Andes from Chile, and in 1847, he approached from the east, via the Rio de la Plata. The second expedition was the more productive, but did not take him beyond the environs of Buenos Aires; on his first journey, however, he ventured towards the dreamed-of center and in fact reached it momentarily, although, as we shall see, the price he had to pay was exorbitant.

Rugendas was a genre painter. His genre was the physiognomy of nature, based on a procedure invented by Humboldt. The great naturalist was the father of a discipline that virtually died with him: *Erdtheorie* or *La Physique du monde*, a kind of artistic geography, an aesthetic understanding of the world, a science of landscape. Alexander von Humboldt (1769-1859) was an all-embracing scholar, perhaps the last of his kind: his aim was to apprehend the world in its totality; and the way to do this, he believed, in conformity with a long tradition, was through vision. Yet his approach was new in that, rather than isolating images and treating them as "emblems" of knowledge, his aim was to accumulate and coordinate them within a broad framework, for which landscape provided the model. The artistic geographer had to capture the "physiognomy" of the landscape (Humboldt had borrowed this concept from Lavater) by picking out its characteristic "physiognomic" traits, which his scholarly studies in natural science would enable him to recognize. The precise arrangement of physiognomic elements in the picture would speak volumes to the observer's sensibility, conveying information not in the form of isolated features but features systematically interrelated so as to be intuitively grasped: climate, history, customs, economy, race, fauna, flora, rainfall, prevailing winds . . . The key to it all was "natural growth," which is why the vegetable element occupied the foreground, and why, in search of physiognomic landscapes, Humboldt went to the tropics, which were incomparably superior to Europe in terms of plant variety and rates of growth. He lived for many years in tropical regions of Asia and America, and encouraged the artists who had adopted his approach to do likewise. Thus he established a circuit, stimulating curiosity in Europe about regions that were still little known and creating a market for the works of the traveling painters.

Humboldt had the highest admiration for the young Rugendas, whom he dubbed the "founding father of the art of pictorial presentation of the physiognomy of nature," a description that could well have applied to himself. He played an advisory role in the painter's second great voyage, and the only point on which they disagreed was the decision to include Argentina in the itinerary. Humboldt did not want his disciple to waste his efforts south of the tropical zone, and in his letters he was generous with recommendations such as the following: "Do not squander your talent, which is suited above all to the depiction of that which is truly exceptional in landscape, such as snowy mountain peaks, bamboo, tropical jungle flora, groups composed of a single plant species at different ages; filiceae, lataniae, feathery-fronded palms, cylindrical cactuses, red-flowered mimosas, the inga tree with its long branches and broad leaves, shrub-sized malvaceous plants with digitate leaves, particularly the Mexican hand plant (Cheirantodendron) in Toluca; the famous ahuehuete of Atlisco (the thousand-year-old Cupressus disticha) in the environs of Mexico City; the species of orchids that flower beautifully on the rounded, moss-covered protuberances of tree-trunks, surrounded in turn by mossy bulbs of dendrobium; the forms of fallen mahogany branches covered with orchids, banisteriae and climbing plants; gramineous species from the bamboo family reaching heights of twenty to thirty feet, bignoniaceae and the varieties of Foliis distichis; studies of pothos and dracontium; a trunk of Crescentia cujete laden with calabashes; a flowering Teobroma cacao with flowers springing up from the roots; the external roots of Cupressus disticha, up to four feet tall, shaped like stakes or planks; studies of a rock covered with fucus; blue water lilies in water; guastavia (pirigara) and flowering lecitis; a tropical jungle viewed from a vantage point high on a mountain, showing only the broad crowns of flowering trees, from which the bare trunks of the palms rise like a colonnade, another jungle on top of the jungle; the differing material physiognomies of pisang and heliconium . . ."

The excess of primary forms required to characterize a landscape could only be found in the tropics. Insofar as vegetation was concerned, Humboldt had reduced these forms to nineteen: nineteen physiognomic types that had nothing to do with Linnean classification, which is based on the abstraction and isolation of minimal differences. The Humboldtian naturalist was not a botanist but a landscape artist sensitive to the processes of growth operative in all forms of life. This system provided the basis for the "genre" of painting in which Rugendas specialized.

After a brief stay in Haiti, Rugendas spent three years in Mexico, from 1831 to 1834. Then he went to Chile, where he was to live for eight years, with the exception of his truncated voyage to Argentina, which lasted roughly five months. The original aim had been to travel right across the country to Buenos Aires, and from there to head north to Tucumán, Bolivia, and so on. But it was not to be.

He set out at the end of December 1837 from San Felipe de Aconcagua (Chile), accompanied by the German painter Robert Krause, with a small team of horses and mules and two Chilean guides. The plan was to take advantage of the fine summer weather to cross the picturesque passes of the Cordillera at a leisurely pace, stopping to take notes and paint whenever an interesting subject presented itself. And that was what they did.

In a few days—not counting the many spent painting—they were well into the Cordillera. When it rained they could at least make headway, with their papers carefully rolled up in waxed cloth. It was not really rain so much as a benign drizzle, enveloping the landscape in gentle tides of humidity all afternoon. The clouds came down so low they almost landed, but the slightest breeze would whisk them away . . . and produce others from bewildering corridors which seemed to give the sky access to the center of the earth. In the midst of these magical alternations, the artists were briefly granted dreamlike visions, each more sweeping than the last. Although their journey traced a zigzag on the map, they were heading straight as an arrow towards openness. Each day was larger and more distant. As the mountains took on weight, the air became lighter and more changeable in its meteoric content, a sheer optics of superposed heights and depths.

They kept barometric records; they estimated wind speed with a sock of light cloth and used two glass capillary tubes containing liquid graphite as an altimeter. The pink-tinted mercury of their thermometer, suspended with bells from a tall pole, preceded them like Diogenes' daylight lamp. The regular hoofbeats of the horses and mules made a distant-seeming sound; though barely audible, it too was a part of the universal pattern of echoes.

[. . .]

They took an old guide, a boy to cook for them, five horses, and two little mares (they had finally managed to get rid of the grumpy mules). The weather, still hot, became drier. In a week of unhurried progress, they left behind trees, rivers, and birds, as well as the foothills of the Andes. A ruse against Orphic disobedience: obliterate all that lies behind. There was no point turning around any more. On the plains, space became small and intimate, almost mental. To give their procedure time to adjust, they abstained from painting. Instead they engaged in almost abstract calculations of the distance covered. Every now and then they overtook a cart, and psychologically it was as if they had leapt months ahead.

They adapted to the new routine. A series of slight bumps indicated their way across the flat immensity. They began to hunt systematically. The guide entertained them with stories at night. He was a mine of information about the region's history. For some reason (no doubt because they were not practicing their art), Rugendas and Krause, in their daily conversations on horseback, hit upon a relation between painting and history. It was a subject they had discussed on many previous occasions. But now they felt they were on the point of tying up all the loose ends of their reasoning.

One thing they had agreed about was the usefulness of history for understanding how things were made. A natural or cultural scene, however detailed, gave no indication of how it had come into being, the order in which its components had appeared, or the causal chains that had led to that particular configuration. And this was precisely why man surrounded himself with a plethora of stories: they satisfied the need to know how things had been made. Now, taking this as his starting point, Rugendas went one step further and arrived at a rather paradoxical conclusion. He suggested, hypothetically, that, were all the storytellers to fall silent, nothing would be lost, since the present generation, or those of the future, could experience the events of the past without needing to be told about them, simply by recombining or yielding to the available facts, although, in either case, such action could only be born of a deliberate resolution. And it was even possible that the repetition would be more authentic in the absence of stories. The purpose of storytelling could be better fulfilled by handing down, instead, a set of "tools," which would enable mankind to reinvent what had happened in the past, with the innocent spontaneity of action. Humanity's finest accomplishments, everything that deserved to happen again. And the tools would be stylistic. According to this theory, then, art was more useful than discourse.

A bird flashed across the empty sky. A cart immobile on the horizon, like a midday star. How could a plain like this be re-made? Yet someone would, no doubt, attempt to repeat their journey, sooner or later. This thought made them feel they should be at once very careful and very daring: careful not to make a mistake that would render the repetition impossible; daring, so that the journey would be worth repeating, like an adventure.

It was a delicate balance, like their artistic procedure. Once again Rugendas regretted not having seen the Indians in action. Perhaps they should have waited a few more days . . . He felt a vague, inexplicable nostalgia for what had not happened, and the lessons it might have taught him. Did that mean the Indians were part of the procedure? The repetition of their raids was a concentrated form of history.

Rugendas kept delaying the beginning of his task, until one day he discovered that he had more reasons for doing so than he had realized. A casual remark made beside the campfire provoked a rectification from the old guide: No, they were not yet in the renowned Argentinean pampas, although the country they were crossing was very similar. The real pampas began at San Luis. The guide thought they had simply misunderstood the word. And in a sense, they must have, the German reflected, but the thing itself was involved as well; it had to be. He questioned the guide carefully, testing his own linguistic resources. Were the "pampas," perhaps, flatter than the land they were crossing? He doubted it; what could be flatter than a horizontal plane? And yet the old guide assured him that it was so, with a satisfied smile rarely to be seen among the members of his grave company. He discussed this point at length with Krause later on, as they smoked their cigars under the starry sky. After all, he had no good reason to doubt the guide. If the pampas existed (and there was no good reason to doubt that either), they lay some distance ahead. After three weeks of assimilating a vast, featureless plain, to be told of a more radical flatness was a challenge to the imagination. It seemed, from what they could understand of the old hand's scornful phrases, that, for him, the current leg of the journey was rather "mountainous". For them, it was like a well-polished table, a calm lake, a sheet of earth stretched tight. But with a little mental effort, now that they had been alerted, they saw that it might not be so. How odd, and how interesting! Needless to say their arrival in San Luis, which was imminent according to the expert, became the object of eager anticipation. For the two days following the revelation they pressed on steadily. They started seeing hills everywhere, as if produced by a conjurer's trick: the ranges of El Monigote and Agua Hedionda. On the third day they came to expanses resonant with emptiness. The sinister nature of the surroundings made an impression on the Germans, and, to their surprise, on the Gauchos too. The old man and the boy talked in whispers, and the man dismounted on a number of occasions to feel the soil. They noticed that there was no grass, not the least blade, and the thistles had no leaves: they looked like coral. Clearly the region was drought-stricken. The earth crumbled at a touch, yet a layer of dust did not seem to have formed, although they could not be sure, because the wind had dropped to nothing. In the mortal stillness of the air, the sounds of the horses' hooves, their own words and even their breathing were accompanied by menacing echoes. From time to time they noticed that the old guide was straining anxiously to hear something. It was contagious;

they started listening too. They could hear nothing, except perhaps the faint hint of a buzzing that must have been mental. The guide clearly suspected something, but a vague fear prevented them from questioning him.

For a day and a half they advanced through that terrifying void. Not a bird to be seen in the sky, no guinea pigs or rheas or hares or ants on the ground. The planet's peeling crust seemed to be made of dried amber. When they finally came to a river where they could take on water, the guide's suspicions were confirmed. He solved the enigma, which was especially perplexing there on the river banks: not only were they devoid of the least living cell of vegetation, the numerous trees, mainly willows, had been stripped of all their leaves, as if a sudden winter had plucked them bare for a joke. It was an impressive spectacle: livid skeletons, as far as the eye could see, not even trembling. And it was not that their leaves had fallen, for the ground was pure silica.

Locusts. The biblical plague had passed that way. That was the solution, revealed to them at last by the guide. If he had delayed doing so, it was only because he wanted to be sure. He had recognized the signs by hearsay, never having seen them with his own eyes. He had also been told about the sight of the swarm in action, but preferred not to talk about that, because it sounded fanciful, though, considering the results, fancy could hardly have outstripped the facts. Alluding to his friend's disappointment at having missed the Indians, Krause asked if he did not regret having arrived too late on this occasion too. Rugendas imagined it. A green field, suddenly smothered by a buzzing cloud, and, a moment later, nothing. Could a painting capture that? No. An action painting, perhaps.

They proceeded on their way, wasting no time. It was idle to wonder which direction the swarm had taken, because the area affected was too large. They had to concentrate on getting to San Luis, and try to enjoy themselves in the meantime, if they could. It was all experience, even if they had missed out by minutes. The residual vibration in the atmosphere had an apocalyptic resonance.

As it turned out, a number of practical problems made it hard for the painters to enjoy themselves. That afternoon, after two days of involuntary fasting, the horses reached the limits of their endurance. They became uncontrollable, and there was no choice but to stop. To make things worse, the temperature had continued to rise, and must have been near fifty degrees. Not at atom of air was moving. The barometric pressure had plummeted. A heavy ceiling of gray clouds hung over their heads, but without affording any relief from the glare, which went on blinding them. What could they do? The young cook was frightened, and kept clear of the horses as if they would bite him. The old man would not raise his eyes, ashamed of his failure as a guide. There were attenuating circumstances: this was the first time he had crossed an area stricken by a plague of locusts. The Germans conferred in whispers. They were in a lunar ocean, rimmed around with hills. Krause was in favor of grinding up some biscuits, mixing them with water and milk, patiently feeding the horses with this paste, waiting a few hours for them to calm down and setting off again in the cool of the evening. For Rugendas, this plan was so absurd it did not even merit discussion. He proposed something a little more sensible: heading off at a gallop to see what was on the other side of the hills. Accustomed to reckoning distance in paintings, they misjudged the remoteness of those little mountains; in fact they were almost among them already. So the vegetation on their slopes had probably not been spared by the mobile feast. They consulted the guide, but could not get a word out of him. All the same, it was reasonable to suppose that the hills had served as a screen to deflect the swarm, so if they went around to the other side they would find a field with its full complement of clover leaves. Rugendas already had a plan: he would ride south to the hills, while his friend would ride north. Krause disagreed. Given the state of the horses, he thought it reckless to make a dash. Not to mention the storm that was brewing. He categorically refused. Tired of arguing, Rugendas set off on his own, announcing that he would be back in two hours. He spurred his horse to a gallop and it responded with an explosion of nervous energy; horse and rider were drenched with sweat, as if they had just emerged from the sea. The drops evaporated before they hit the ground, leaving a wake of salty vapor. The grey cones of the hills, on which Rugendas fixed his gaze, kept shifting as he rode on in a straight line; without becoming noticeably bigger, they multiplied and began to spread apart; one slipped around behind him surreptitiously. He was already inside the formation (why was it called El Monigote: The Puppet?). The ground was still bare and there was no indication that there would be grass ahead, or in any direction. The heat and the stillness of the air had intensified, if that was possible. He pulled up and looked around. He was in a vast amphitheatre of interlayered clay and limestone. He could feel the horse's extreme nervousness; there was a tightness in his chest, and his perception was becoming abnormally acute. The air had turned a lead-grey color. He had never seen such light. It was a see-through darkness. The clouds had descended further still, and now he could hear the intimate rumbling of the thunder. "At least it will cool off," he said to himself, and those trivial words marked the end of a phase in his life; with them he formulated the last coherent thought of his youth.

What happened next bypassed his senses and went straight into his nervous system. In other words, it was over very quickly; it was pure action, a wild concatenation of events. The storm broke suddenly with a spectacular lightning bolt that traced a zig-zag arc clear across the sky. It came so close that Rugendas's upturned face, frozen in an expression of idiotic stupor, was completely bathed in white light. He thought he could feel its sinister heat on his skin, and his pupils contracted to pin-points. The thunder crashing down impossibly enveloped him in millions of vibrations. The horse began to turn beneath him. It was still turning when a lightning bolt struck him on the head. Like a nickel statue, man and beast were lit up with electricity. For one horrific moment, regrettably to be repeated, Rugendas witnessed the spectacle of his body shining. The horse's mane was standing on end, like the dorsal fin of a swordfish. From that moment on, like all victims of personalized catastrophes, he saw himself as if from outside, wondering, Why did it have to happen to me? The sensation of having electrified blood was horrible but very brief. Evidently the charge flowed out as fast as it had flowed into his body. Even so, it cannot have been good for his health.

The horse had fallen to its knees. The rider was kicking it like a madman, raising his legs till they were almost vertical, then closing them with a scissor-like clicking action. The charge was flowing out of the animal too, igniting a kind of phosphorescent golden tray all around it, with undulating edges. As soon as the discharge was complete, in a matter of seconds, the horse got to its feet and tried to walk. The full battery of thunder exploded overhead. In a midnight darkness, broad and fine blazes interlocked. Balls of white fire the size of rooms rolled down the hillsides, the lightning bolts serving as cues in a game of meteoric billiards. The horse was turning. Completely numb, Rugendas tugged at the reins haphazardly, until they slipped from his hands. The plain had become immense, with everywhere and nowhere to run, and so busy with electrical activity it was hard to get one's bearings. With each lightning strike the ground vibrated like a bell. The horse began to walk with supernatural prudence, lifting its hooves high, prancing slowly.

The second bolt of lightning struck him less than fifteen seconds after the first. It was much more powerful and had a more devastating effect. Horse and rider were thrown about twenty meters, glowing and crackling like a cold bonfire. The fall was not fatal, no doubt because of exceptional alterations to atomic and molecular structure, which had the effect of cushioning their impact. They bounced. Not only that, the horse's magnetized coat held Rugendas in place as they flew through the air. But once on the ground the attraction diminished and the man found himself lying on the dry earth, looking up at the sky. The tangle of lightning in the clouds made and unmade nightmarish figures. Among them, for a fraction of a second, he thought he saw a horrible face. The Puppet! The sounds all around him were deafening: crash on crash, thunderclap on thunderclap. The circumstances were abnormal in the extreme. The horse was spinning around on its side like a crab, cells of fire exploding around it in thousands, forming a sort of full-body halo, which moved with the animal and did not seem to be affecting it. Did they cry out, the man and his horse? The shock had probably struck them dumb; in any case their cries would have been inaudible. The fallen horseman reached for the ground with his hands, trying to prop himself up. But there was too much static for him to touch anything. He was relieved to see the horse getting up. Instinctively he knew this was a good thing: better the solitude of a temporary separation than the risk of a third lightning strike.

The horse did indeed rise to its feet, bristling and monumental, obscuring half the mesh of lightning, his giraffe-like legs contorted by wayward steps; he turned his head, hearing the call of madness . . . and took off . . .

But Rugendas went with him! He could not understand, nor did he want to—it was too monstrous. He could feel himself being pulled, stretching (the electricity had made him elastic), almost levitating, like a satellite in thrall to a dangerous star. The pace quickened, and off he went in tow, bouncing, bewildered . . .

What he did not realize was that his foot was caught in the stirrup, a classic riding accident, which still occurs now and then, even after so many repetitions. The generation of electricity ceased as suddenly as it had begun, which was a pity, because a well-aimed lightning bolt, stopping the creature in its flight, might have spared the painter no end of trouble. But the current withdrew into the clouds, the wind began to blow, rain fell . . .

It was never known how far the horse galloped, nor did it really matter. Whatever the distance, short or long, the disaster had occurred. It was not until the morning of the following day that Krause and the old guide discovered them. The horse had found his clover, and was grazing sleepily, with a bloody bundle trailing from one stirrup. After a whole night spent looking for his friend, poor Krause, at his wits' end, had more or less given him up for dead. Finding him was not entirely a relief: there he was, at last, but prone and motionless. They hurried on and, as they approached, saw him move yet remain face down, as if kissing the earth; the flicker of hope this aroused was quenched when they realized that he was not moving himself, but being dragged by the horse's blithe little browsing steps. They dismounted, took his foot from the stirrup and turned him over . . . The horror struck them dumb. Rugendas's face was a swollen, bloody mass; the bone of his forehead was exposed and strips of skin hung over his eyes. The distinctive aquiline form of his Augsburg nose was unrecognizable, and his lips, split and spread apart, revealed his teeth, all miraculously intact.

The first thing was to see if he was breathing. He was. This gave an edge of urgency to what followed. They put him on the horse's back and set off. The guide, who had recovered his guiding skills, remembered some ranches nearby and pointed the way. They arrived half way through the morning, bearing a gift that could not have been more disconcerting for the poor, isolated farmers who lived there. It was, at least, an opportunity to give Rugendas some simple treatment and take stock of the situation. They washed his face and tried to put it back together, manipulating the pieces with their fingertips; they applied witch hazel dressings to speed the healing and checked that there were no broken bones. His clothing was torn, but except for minor cuts and a few abrasions to his chest, elbow and knees, his body was intact; the major damage was limited to his head, as if it were the bearing he had rolled on. Was it the revenge of the Puppet? Who knows. The body is a strange thing, and when it is caught up in an accident involving non-human forces, there is no predicting the result.

He regained consciousness that afternoon, too soon for it to be in any way advantageous. He woke to pain such as he had never felt before, and against which he was defenseless. The first twenty-four hours were one long howl of pain. All the remedies they tried were useless, although there was not much they could try, apart from compresses and good will. Krause wrung his hands; like his friend, he neither slept nor ate. They had sent for the doctor from San Luis, who arrived the following night in the pouring rain on a horse flogged half to death. They spent the next day transporting the patient to the provincial capital, in a carriage sent by His Excellency the governor. The doctor's diagnosis was cautious. In his opinion the acute pain was caused by the exposure of a nerve ending, which would be encapsulated sooner or later. Then the patient would recover his powers of speech and be able to communicate, which would make the situation less distressing. The wounds would be stitched up at the hospital and the extent of the scarring would depend on the responsiveness of the tissue. The rest was in God's hands. He had brought morphine and administered a generous dose, so Rugendas fell asleep in the carriage and was spared the uncertainties of a night journey through quagmires. He woke in the hospital, just as they were stitching him up, and had to be given a double dose to keep him quiet.

A week went by. They took the stitches out and the healing proceeded rapidly. They were able to remove the bandages and the patient began to eat solids. Krause never left his side. The San Luis hospital was a ranch on the outskirts of the city, inhabited by half a dozen monsters, half-man half-animal, the results of cumulative genetic accidents. There was no way to cure them. The hospital was their home. It was an unforgettable fortnight for Rugendas. The sensations impinging on the raw, pink flesh of his head were recorded indelibly. As soon as he could stand and go out for a walk on Krause's arm, he refused to go back in. The governor, who had surrounded the great artist with attentions, offered his hospitality. Two days later Rugendas began to ride again and write letters (the first was to his sister in Augsburg, presenting his misfortunes in an almost idyllic light; by contrast, the picture he painted for his friends in Chile was resolutely grim). They decided to leave without delay. But not to follow their original route: the unknown immensity separating them from Buenos Aires was a challenge they would have to postpone. They would return to Santiago, the nearest place where Rugendas could receive proper medical treatment.

For his recovery, though miraculous, was far from complete. He had hoisted himself out of the deep pit of death with the vigor of a titan, but the ascent had taken its toll. Leaving aside the state of his face for the moment, the exposed nerve, which had caused the unbearable suffering of the first days, had been encapsulated, but although this meant the end of the acute phase, the nerve ending had reconnected, more or less at random, to a node in the frontal lobe, from which it emitted prodigious migraines. They came on suddenly, several times a day; everything went flat, then began to fold like a screen. The sensation grew and grew, overpowering him; he began to cry out in pain and often fell over. There was a high-pitched squealing in his ears. He would never have imagined that his nervous system could produce so much pain; it was a revelation of what his body could do. He had to take massive doses of morphine and the attacks left him fragile, as if perched on stilts, his hands and feet very far away. Little by little he began to reconstruct the accident, and was able to tell Krause about it. The horse had survived, and was still useful; in fact, it was the one he usually chose to ride. He renamed it Flash. Sitting on its back he thought he could feel the ebbing rush of the universal plasma. Far from holding a grudge against the horse, he had grown fond of it. They were fellow survivors of electricity. As the analgesic took effect, he resumed his drawing: he did not have to learn again, for he had lost none of his skill. It was another proof of art's indifference; his life might have been broken in two, but painting was still the "bridge of dreams." He was not like his ancestor, who had to start over with his left hand. If only he had been so lucky! What bilateral symmetry could he resort to, when the nerve was pricking at the very center of his being?

He would not have survived without the drug. It took him some time to metabolize it. He told Krause about the hallucinations it had caused during the first few days. As clearly as he was seeing his friend now, he had seen demonic animals all around him, sleeping and eating and relieving themselves (and even conversing in grunts and bleats!) . . . Krause undeceived him: that part was real. Those monsters were the poor wretches interned for life in the San Luis hospital. Rugendas was stunned by this, until the onset of the next migraine. What an amazing coincidence! Or correspondence: it suggested that all nightmares, even the most absurd, were somehow connected with reality. He had another memory to recount, different in nature, although related. When they took the stitches out of his face, he was vividly aware of each thread coming loose. And in his addled, semi-conscious state, he felt as if they were removing all the threads that had controlled the puppets of his feelings, or the expressions that manifested them, which came to the same thing. Averting his gaze, Krause made no comment and hastened to change the subject. Which was not so easy: changing the subject is one of the most difficult arts to master, the key to almost all the others. And in this case, change was a key part of the subject.

[. . .]

Victor Pelevin

THE LIFE AND ADVENTURES OF SHED NUMBER XII

Translated from the Russian by Andrew Bromfield

In the beginning was the word, and maybe not even just one, but what could he know about that? What he discovered at his point of origin was a stack of planks on wet grass, smelling of fresh resin and soaking up the sun with their yellow surfaces: he found nails in a plywood box, hammers, saws, and so forth—but visualizing all this, he observed that he was thinking the picture into existence rather than just seeing it. Only later did a weak sense of self emerge, when the bicycles already stood inside him and three shelves one above the other covered his right wall. He wasn't really Number XII then; he was merely a new configuration of the stack of planks. But those were the times that had left the most pure and enduring impression. All around lay the wide incomprehensible world, and it seemed as though he had merely interrupted his journey through it, making a halt here, at this spot, for a while.

Certainly the spot could have been better—out behind the low five-story prefabs, alongside the vegetable gardens and the garbage dump. But why feel upset about something like that? He wasn't going to spend his entire life here, after all. Of course, if he'd really thought about it, he would have been forced to admit that that was precisely what he was going to do—that's the way it is for sheds—but the charm of life's earliest beginnings consists in the absence of such thoughts. He simply stood there in the sunshine, rejoicing in the wind whistling through his cracks if it blew from the woods, or falling into a slight depression if it blew in from over the dump. The depression passed as soon as the wind changed direction, without leaving any long-term effect on a soul that was still only partially formed.

One day he was approached by a man naked to the waist in a pair of red tracksuit pants, holding a brush and a huge can of paint. The shed was already beginning to recognize this man, who was different from all the other people because he could get inside, to the bicycles and the shelves. He stopped by the wall, dipped the brush into the can, and traced a bright crimson line on the planks. An hour later the hut was crimson all over. This was the first real landmark in his memory—everything that came before it was still cloaked in a sense of distant and unreal happiness.

The night after the painting (when he had been given his Roman numeral, his name—the other sheds around him all had ordinary numbers), he held up his tar-papered roof to the moon as he dried. "Where am I?" he thought. "Who am I?"

Above him was the dark sky and inside him stood the brand-new bicycles. A beam of light from the lamp in the yard shone on them through a crack, and the bells on their handlebars gleamed and twinkled more mysteriously than the stars. Higher up, a plastic hoop hung on the wall, and with the very thinnest of his planks Number XII recognized it as a symbol of the eternal riddle of creation which was also represented—so very wonderfully—in his own soul. On the shelves lay all sorts of stupid trifles that lent variety and uniqueness to his inner world. Dill and scented herbs hung drying on a thread stretched from one wall to another, reminding him of something that never ever happens to sheds—but since they reminded him of it anyway, sometimes it seemed that he once must have been not a mere shed, but a dacha, or at the very least a garage.

He became aware of himself, and realized that what he was aware of, that is himself, was made up of numerous small individual features: of the unearthly personalities of machines for conquering distance, which smelled of rubber and steel; of the mystical introspection of the self-enclosed hoop; of the squeaking in the souls of the small items, such as the nails and nuts which were scattered along the shelves; and of other things. Within each of these existences there was an infinity of subtle variation, but still for him each was linked with one important thing, some decisive feeling—and fusing together, these feelings gave rise to a new unity, defined in space by the freshly painted planks, but not actually limited by anything. That was him, Number XII, and above his head the moon was his equal as it rushed through the mist and the clouds. . . . That night was when his life really began.

Soon Number XII realized that he liked most of all the sensation which was derived from or transmitted by the bicycles. Sometimes on a hot summer day, when the world around him grew quiet, he would secretly identify himself in turn with the "Sputnik" and the folding "Kama" and experience two different kinds of happiness.

In this state he might easily find himself forty miles away from his real location, perhaps rolling across a deserted bridge over a canal bounded by concrete banks, or along the violet border of the sun-baked highway, turning into the tunnels formed by the high bushes lining a narrow dirt track and then hurtling along it until he emerged onto another road leading to the forest, through the forest, through the open fields, straight up into the orange sky above the horizon: he could probably have carried on riding along the road till the end of his life, but he didn't want to, because what brought him happiness was the possibility itself. He might find himself in the city, in some yard where long stems grew out of the pavement cracks, and spend the evening there—in fact he could do almost anything.

When he tried to share some of his experiences with the

occult-minded garage that stood beside him, the answer he received was that in fact there is only one higher happiness: the ecstatic union with the archetypal garage. So how could he tell his neighbor about two different kinds of perfect happiness, one of which folded away, while the other had three-speed gears?

"You mean I should try to feel like a garage too?" he asked one day.

"There is no other path," replied the garage. "Of course, you're not likely to succeed, but your chances are better than those of a kennel or a tobacco kiosk."

"And what if I like feeling like a bicycle?" asked Number XII, revealing his cherished secret.

"By all means, feel like one. I can't say you mustn't," said the garage. "For some of us feelings of the lower kind are the limit, and there's nothing to be done about it."

"What's that written in chalk on your side?" Number XII inquired.

"None of your business, you cheap piece of plywood shit," the garage replied with unexpected malice.

Of course, Number XII had only made the remark because he felt offended—who wouldn't by having his aspirations termed "lower"? After this incident there could be no question of associating with the garage, but Number XII didn't regret it. One morning the garage was demolished, and Number XII was left alone.

Actually, there were two other sheds quite close, to his left, but he tried not to think about them. Not because they were built differently and painted a dull, indefinite color—he could have reconciled himself with that. The problem was something else: on the ground floor of the five-storey prefab where Number XII's owners lived there was a big vegetable shop and these sheds served as its warehouses. They were used for storing carrots, potatoes, beets, and cucumbers, but the factor absolutely dominating every aspect of Number 13 and Number 14 was the pickled cabbage in two huge barrels covered with plastic. Number XII had often seen their great hollow bodies girt with steel hoops surrounded by a retinue of emaciated workmen who were rolling them out at an angle into the yard. At these times he felt afraid and he recalled one of the favorite maxims of the deceased garage, whom he often remembered with sadness: "There are some things in life which you must simply turn your back on as quickly as possible." And no sooner did he recall the maxim than he applied it. The dark and obscure life of his neighbors, their sour exhalations, and obtuse grip on life were a threat to Number XII: the very existence of these squat structures was enough to negate everything else. Every drop of brine in their barrels declared that Number XII's existence in the universe was entirely unnecessary: that, at least, that was how he interpreted the vibrations radiating from their consciousness of the world.

But the day came to an end, the light grew thick, Number XII was a bicycle rushing along a deserted highway and any memories of the horrors of the day seemed simply ridiculous.

It was the middle of the summer when the lock clanked, the hasp was thrown back, and two people entered Number XII: his owner and a woman. Number XII did not like her—somehow she reminded him of everything that he simply could not stand. Not that this impression sprang from the fact that she smelled of pickled cabbage—rather the opposite: it was the smell of pickled cabbage that conveyed some information about this woman, that somehow or other she was the very embodiment of the fermentation and the oppressive force of will to which Numbers 13 and 14 owed their present existence.

Number XII began to think, while the two people went on talking:

"Well, if we take down the shelves it'll do fine, just fine. . . ."

"This is a first-class shed," replied his owner, wheeling the bicycles outside. "No leaks or any other problems. And what a color!"

After wheeling out the bicycles and leaning them against the wall, he began untidily gathering together everything lying on the shelves. It was then that Number XII began to feel upset.

Of course, the bicycles had often disappeared for certain periods of time, and he knew how to use his memory to fill in the gap. Afterwards, when the bicycles were returned to their places, he was always amazed how inadequate the image his memory created was in comparison with the actual beauty that the bicycles simply radiated into space. Whenever they disappeared the bicycles always returned, and these short separations from the most important part of his own soul lent Number XII's life its unpredictable charm. But this time everything was different—the bicycles were being taken away forever.

He realized this from the unceremonious way that the man in the red pants was wreaking total devastation in him—nothing like this had ever happened before. The woman in the white coat had left long ago, but his owner was still rummaging around, raking tools into a bag, and taking down the old cans and patched inner tubes from the wall. Then a truck backed up to his door, and both bicycles dived obediently after the overfilled bags into its gaping tarpaulin maw.

Number XII was empty, and his door stood wide open.

Despite everything he continued to be himself. The souls of all that life had taken away continued to dwell in him, and although they had become shadows of themselves they still fused together to make him Number XII: but it now required all the willpower he could muster to maintain his individuality.

In the morning he noticed a change in himself. No longer interested in the world around him, his attention was focused exclusively on the past, moving in concentric rings of memory. He could explain this: when he left, his owner had forgotten the hoop, and now it was the only real part of his otherwise phantom soul, which was why Number XII felt like a closed circle. But he didn't have enough strength to feel really anything about this, or wonder if it was good or bad. A dreary, colorless yearning overlay every other feeling. A month passed like that.

One day workmen arrived, entered his defenseless open door, and in the space of a few minutes broke down the shelves. Number XII wasn't even fully aware of his new condition before his feelings overwhelmed him—which incidentally demonstrates that he still had enough vital energy left in him to experience fear.

They were rolling a barrel towards him across the yard. Towards him! In his great depths of nostalgic self-pity, he'd never dreamed anything could be worse than what had already happened—that this could be possible!

The barrel was a fearful sight. Huge and potbellied, it was very old, and its sides were impregnated with something hideous which gave out such a powerful stench that even the workers angling it along, who were certainly no strangers to the seamy side of life, turned their faces away and swore. And Number XII could also see something that the men couldn't: the barrel exuded an aura of cold attention as it viewed the world through the damp likeness of an eye. Number XII did not see them roll it inside and circle it around on the floor to set it at his very center—he had fainted.

Suffering maims. Two days passed before Number XII began to recover his thoughts and his feelings. Now he was different, and everything in him was different. At the very center of his soul, at the spot once occupied by the bicycles' windswept frames, there was pulsating repulsive living death, concentrated in the slow existence of the barrel and its equally slow thoughts, which were now Number XII's thoughts. He could feel the fermentation of the rotten brine, and the bubbles rose in him to burst on the surface, leaving holes in the layer of green mold. The swollen corpses of the cucumbers were shifted about by the gas, and the slime-impregnated boards strained against their rusty iron hoops inside him. All of it was him.

Numbers 13 and 14 no longer frightened him—on the contrary, he rapidly fell into a half-unconscious state of comradery with them. But the past had not totally disappeared; it had simply been pushed aside, squashed into a corner. Number XII's new life was a double one. On the one hand, he felt himself the equal of Numbers 13 and 14, and yet on the other hand, buried somewhere deep inside him, there remained a sense of terrible injustice about what had happened to him. But his new existence's center was located in the barrel, which emitted the constant gurgling and crackling sounds that had replaced the imagined whooshing of tires over concrete.

Numbers 13 and 14 explained to him that all he had gone through was just a normal life change that comes with age.

"The entry into the real world, with its real difficulties and concerns, always involves certain difficulties," Number 13 would say. "One's soul is occupied with entirely new problems."

And he would add some words of encouragement: "Never mind, you'll get used to it. It's only hard at the beginning."

Number 14 was a shed with a rather philosophical turn of mind. He often spoke of spiritual matters, and soon managed to convince his new comrade that if the beautiful consisted of harmony ("That's for one," he would say) and inside you— objectively speaking now—you had pickled cucumbers or pickled cabbage ("That's for two"), then the beauty of life consisted in achieving harmony with the contents of the barrel and removing all obstacles hindering that. An old dictionary of philosophical terms had been wedged under his own barrel to keep it from overflowing, and he often quoted from it. It helped him explain to Number XII how he should live his life. Number 14 never did feel complete confidence in the novice, however, sensing something in him that Number 14 no longer sensed in himself.

But gradually Number XII became genuinely resigned to the situation. Sometimes he even experienced a certain inspiration, an upsurge of the will to live this new life. But his new friends' mistrust was well founded. On several occasions Number XII caught glimpses of something forgotten, like a gleam of light through a keyhole, and then he would be overwhelmed by a feeling of intense contempt for himself—and he simply hated the other two.

Naturally, all of this was suppressed by the cucumber barrel's invincible worldview, and Number XII soon began to wonder what it was he'd been getting so upset about. He became simpler and the past gradually bothered him less because it was growing hard for him to keep up with the fleeting flashes of memory. More and more often the barrel seemed like a guarantee of stability and peace, like the ballast of a ship, and sometimes Number XII imagined himself like that, like a ship sailing out into tomorrow.

He began to feel the barrel's innate good nature, but only after he had finally opened his own soul to it. Now the cucumbers seemed almost like children to him.

Numbers 13 and 14 weren't bad comrades—and most importantly, they lent him support in his new existence. Sometimes in the evening the three of them would silently classify the objects of the world, imbuing everything around them with an all-embracing spirit of understanding, and when one of the new little huts that had recently been build nearby shuddered he would look at it and think: "How stupid, but never mind, it'll sow its wild oats and then it'll come to understand. . . ." He saw several such transformations take place before his own eyes, and each one served to confirm the correctness of his opinion yet again. He also experienced a feeling of hatred when anything unnecessary appeared in the world, but thank God, that didn't happen often. The days and the years passed, and it seemed that nothing would change again.

One summer evening, glancing around inside himself, Number XII came across an incomprehensible object, a plastic hoop draped with cobwebs. At first he couldn't make out what it was or what it might be for, then suddenly he recalled that there were so many things that once used to be connected with this item. The barrel inside him was dozing, and some other part of him cautiously pulled in the threads of memory, but all of them were broken and they led nowhere. But there was something once, wasn't there? Or was there? He concentrated and tried to understand what it was he couldn't remember, and for a moment he stopped feeling the barrel and was somehow separate from it.

At that very moment a bicycle entered the yard and for no reason at all the rider rang the bell on his handlebars twice. It was enough—Number XII remembered:

A bicycle. A highway. A sunset. A bridge over a river.

He remembered who he really was and at last became himself, really himself. Everything connected with the barrel dropped off like a dry scab. He suddenly smelt the repulsive stench of the brine and saw his comrades of yesterday, Numbers 13 and 14, for what they really were. But there was no time to think about all this, he had to hurry: he knew that if he didn't do what he had to do now, the hateful barrel would overpower him again and turn him into itself.

Meanwhile the barrel had woken up and realized that something was happening. Number XII felt the familiar current of cold obtuseness he'd been used to thinking was his own. The barrel was awake and starting to fill him—there was only one answer he could make.

Two electric wires ran under his eaves. While the barrel was still getting its bearings and working out exactly what was wrong, he did the only thing he could. He squeezed the wires together with all his might, using some new power born of despair. A moment later he was overwhelmed by the invincible force emanating from the cucumber barrel, and for a while he simply ceased to exist.

But the deed was done: torn from their insulation, the wires touched, and where they met a purplish-white flame sprang into life. A second later a fuse blew and the current disappeared from the wires, but a narrow ribbon of smoke was already snaking up the dry planking. Then more flames appeared, and meeting no resistance they began to spread and creep towards the roof.

Number XII came round after the first blow and realized that the barrel had decided to annihilate him totally. Compressing his entire being into one of the upper planks in his ceiling, he could feel that the barrel was not alone—it was being helped by Numbers 13 and 14, who were directing their thoughts at him from outside.

"Obviously," Number XII thought with a strange sense of detachment, "what they are doing now must seem to them like restraining a madman, or perhaps they see an enemy spy whose cunning pretence to be one of them has now been exposed—".

He never finished the thought, because at that moment the barrel threw all its rottenness against the boundaries of his existence with redoubled force. He withstood the blow, but realized that the next one would finish him, and he prepared to die. But time passed, and no new blow come. He expanded his boundaries a little and felt two things—first, the barrel's fear, as cold and sluggish as every sensation it manifested; and second, the flames blazing all around, which were already closing in on the ceiling plank animated by Number XII. The walls were ablaze, the tarpaper roof was weeping fiery tears, and the plastic bottles of sunflower oil were burning on the floor. Some of them were bursting, and the brine was boiling in the barrel, which for all its ponderous might was obviously dying. Number XII extended himself over to the section of the roof that was still left, and summoned up the memory of the day he was painted, and more importantly, of that night: he wanted to die with that thought. Beside him he saw Number 13 was already ablaze, and that was the last thing he noticed. Yet death still didn't come, and when his final splinter burst into flames, something quite unexpected happened.

The director of Vegetable Shop 17, the same women who had visited Number XII with his owner, was walking home in a foul mood. That evening, at six o'clock, the shed where the oil and cucumbers were stored had suddenly caught fire. The spilled oil had spread the fire to the other sheds—in short, everything that could burn had burned. All that was left of hut Number XII were the keys, and huts Number 13 and 14 were now no more than a few scorched planks.

While the reports were being drawn up and the explanations were being made to the firemen, darkness had fallen, and now the director felt afraid as she walked along the empty road with the trees standing on each side like bandits. She stopped and looked back to make sure no one was following her. There didn't seem to be anyone there. She took a few more steps, then glanced round again, and she thought she could see something twinkling in the distance. Just in case, she went to the edge of the road and stood behind a tree. Staring intently into the darkness, she waited to see what would happen. At the most distant visible point of the road a bright spot came into view. "A motorcycle!" thought the director, pressing hard against the tree trunk. But there was no sound of an engine.

The bright spot moved closer, until she could see that it was not moving on the surface of the road but flying along above it. A moment later, and the spot of light was transformed into something totally unreal—a bicycle without a rider, flying at a height of ten or twelve feet. It was strangely made; it somehow looked as though it had been crudely nailed together out of planks. But strangest of all was that it glowed and flickered and changed color, sometimes turning transparent and then blazing with an unbearably intense brightness. Completely entranced, the director walked out into the mid-dle of the road, and to her appearance the bicycle quite clearly responded. Reducing its height and speed, it turned a few circles in the air above the dazed women's head. Then it rose higher and hung motionless before swinging round stiffly above the road like a weather vane. It hung there for another moment or two and then finally began to move, gathering speed at an incredible rate until it was no more than a bright dot in the sky. Then that disappeared as well.

When she recovered her senses, the director found herself sitting in the middle of the road. She stood up, shook herself off, completely forgetting. . . . But then, she's of no interest to us.

László Krasznahorkai

from WAR AND WAR
Like a Burning House

Translated from the Hungarian by George Szirtes

1.

I no longer care if I die, said Korin, then, after a long silence, pointed to the nearby flooded quarry: *Are those swans?*

2.

Seven children squatted in a semi-circle surrounding him in the middle of the railway footbridge, almost pressing him against the barrier, just as they had done some half an hour earlier when they first attacked him in order to rob him, exactly so in fact, except that by now none of them thought it worthwhile either to attack or to rob him, since it was obvious that, on account of certain unpredictable factors, robbing or attacking him was possible but pointless because he really didn't seem to have anything worth taking, the only thing he did have appearing to be some mysterious burden, the existence of which, gradually, at a certain point in Korin's madly rambling monologue—which "to tell you the truth," as they said, "was boring as shit"—became apparent, most acutely apparent in fact, when he started talking about the loss of his head, at which point they did not stand up and leave him babbling like some halfwit, but remained where they were, in the positions they had originally intended to adopt, squatting immobile in a semi-circle, because the evening had darkened around them, because the gloom descending silently on them in the industrial twilight numbed them, and because this frozen dumb condition had drawn their most intense attention, not to the figure of Korin which had swum beyond them, but to the one object remaining the rails below.

3.

Nobody asked him to speak, only that he should hand over his money, but he didn't, saying he had none, and carried on speaking, hesitantly at first, then more fluently, and finally continuously and unstoppably, because the eyes of the seven children had plainly scared him, or, as he himself put it, his stomach had turned in fear, and, as he said, once his stomach was gripped by fear he absolutely had to speak, and furthermore, since the fear had not passed—after all, how could he know whether they were carrying weapons or not—he grew ever more absorbed in his speech, or rather he became ever more absorbed by the idea of telling them everything from beginning to end, of telling someone in any case, because, from the time that he had set out in secret, at the last possible moment, to embark on his "great journey" as he called it, he had not exchanged a word, not a single word, with anyone, considering it too dangerous, though in any case there were few enough people he could engage in conversation, since he hadn't so far met anybody sufficiently harmless, nobody, at least, of whom he was not wary, because in fact there really was nobody harmless enough, which meant he had to be wary of everyone, because, as he had said at the beginning, whoever it was he set eyes on it was the same thing he saw, a figure, that is, who, directly or indirectly, was in contact with those who pursued him, someone related intimately or distantly, but most certainly related, to those who, according to him, kept tabs on his every move, and it was only the speed of his movements, as he later explained, that kept him "at least half a day" ahead of them, though these gains were specific to places and occasions: so he had not said a word to anyone, and only did so now because fear drove him, because it was only under the natural pressure of fear that he ventured into these most important areas of his life, venturing deeper and deeper still, offering them ever more profound glimpses of that life in order to defeat them, to make them face him so that he might purge his assailants of the tendency to assail, so he should convince all seven of them that someone had not only given himself up to them, but, with his giving, had somehow outflanked them.

4.

The air was full of the sharp, nauseous smell of tar that cut through everything, nor did the strong wind help because the wind, that had chilled them through to the bone, merely intensified and whipped the smell up without being able to substitute anything else for it in return, the whole neighborhood for several kilometers being thick with it, but here more than anywhere else, for it emanated directly from the Rákos railway yard, from that still visible point where the rails concentrated and began to fan out, ensuring that air and tar would be indistinguishable, making it very hard to tell what else, apart from soot and smoke, that smell—composed of the hundreds and thousands of trains that rumbled through, the filthy sleepers, the rubble, and the metallic stench of the rails—comprised, and it wouldn't be just these but other, more obscure, almost indiscernible ingredients, ingredients without name, that would certainly have included the weight of human futility ferried here by hundreds and thousands of railway cars, the scary and sickening view from the bridge of the power of a million wills bent to a single purpose and, just as certainly, the dreary spirit of desolation and industrial stagnation that had hovered about the place and settled on it decades ago, in all of which Korin was now endeavoring to locate himself, having originally determined simply to cross over to the far side as quickly, silently, and inconspicuously as possible in order to escape into what he supposed to be the city center, instead of which he was having, under present circumstances, to pull himself together at a cold and draughty point of the world, and to hang on to whatever incidental detail he could make out, from his eye-level at any rate, whether this was barrier, curb, asphalt or metal, or appeared the most significant, if only so that this footbridge, some hundred meters from the railway yard, might become a passage between the non-existing to the existing section of the world, forming therefore an important early adjunct, as he later put it, to his mad life as a fugitive, a bridge that, had he not been detained, he would have rushed obliviously across.

5.

It had begun suddenly, without preamble, without presentiment, preparation, or rehearsal, at one specific moment on his forty-fourth birthday, that he was struck, agonizingly and immediately, by the consciousness of it, as suddenly and unexpectedly, he told them, as he was by the appearance of the seven of them here, in the middle of the footbridge, on that day when he was sitting by a river at a spot where he would occasionally sit in any case, this time because he didn't feel like going home to an empty apartment on his birthday, and it really was extremely sudden, the way it struck him that, good heavens, he understood nothing, nothing at all about anything, for Christ's sake, nothing at all about the world, which was a most terrifying realization, he said, especially in the way it came to him in all its banality, vulgarity, at a sickeningly ridiculous level, but this was the point, he said, the way that he, at the age of forty-four, had become aware of how utterly stupid he seemed to himself, how empty, how utterly blockheaded he had been in his understanding of the world these last forty-four years, for, as he realized by the river, he had not only misunderstood it, but had not understood anything about anything, the worst part being that for forty-four years he thought he had understood it, while in reality he had failed to do so; and this in fact was the worst thing of all that night of his birthday when he sat alone by the river, the worst because the fact that he now realized that he had not understood it did not mean that he understood it now, because being aware of his lack of knowledge was not in itself some new form of knowledge for which an older one could be traded in, but one that presented itself as a terrifying puzzle the moment he thought about the world, as he most furiously did that evening, all but torturing himself in the effort to understand it and failing, because the puzzle seemed ever more complex and he had begun to feel that this world-puzzle that he was so desperate to understand, that he was torturing himself trying to understand, was really the puzzle of himself and the world at once, that they were in effect one and the same thing, which was the conclusion he had so far reached, and he had not yet given up on it, when, after a couple of days, he noticed that there was something the matter with his head.

6.

By this time he had lived alone for years, he explained to the seven children, he too squatting now and leaning against the barrier in the sharp November wind on the footbridge, alone because his marriage had been wrecked by the Hermes business (he gestured with his hand as if to say he would explain about it later), after which he had "badly burned his fingers with a deeply passionate love affair" and decided: never, never again, would he even so much as get close to a woman, which did not mean, of course, that he led an entirely solitary life, because, as Korin elaborated, gazing at the children, there was the occasional woman on the occasional difficult night, but essentially he was alone, though there remained the various people he came into contact with in the course of his work at the records office, as well as the neighbors with whom he had to maintain neighborly relations, the commuters he bumped into while commuting, the shoppers he met while shopping, the barflies he'd see in the bar and so forth, so that, after all, now he looked back at it, he was in regular contact with quite a lot of people, even if only on the most tenuous of terms, occupying the furthermost corner of the community, at least until they too started to melt away which probably dated from the time that he was feeling increasingly compelled to regale those he met at the records office, on the staircase at home, in the street, at the store and in the bar, with the regrettable news that he believed he was about to lose his head, because, once they understood that the loss was neither figurative nor symbolic but a genuine deprivation in the full physical sense of the word, that, to put it plainly, his head, alas, would actually be severed from his neck, they eventually fled from him as they might flee from a burning house, fleeing in their droves, and very soon every one of them had gone and he stood alone, very much like a burning house in fact: at first it being just the matter of a few people behaving in a more distant fashion, then his colleagues at the records offices ignoring him, not even returning his greeting, refusing to sit at the same table and finally crossing the street when they saw him, then people actually avoiding him in the street, and can you imagine, Korin asked the seven children, how painful this was? how it hurt me most, more than anything, he added, especially with what was happening to the vertebrae in his neck, and this was just when he most needed their support, he said, and while it was plain to see that he would have been pleased to explore this matter in the most intricate detail, it was equally obvious that it would have been wasted on the seven children because they would not have been able to respond in any way, being bored of the subject, particularly at the point when "the old fart started going on about losing his head" which meant "fuck all" to them, as later they would tell their friends, and looked at one another while the oldest nodded in agreement with his younger companions as if to say, "forget it, it's not worth it," after which they simply continued squatting, watching the confluence of rails as the occasional freight train rattled by below them, though one did ask how much longer they were going to stay there as it was all the same to him, and the blond kid next to the senior one consulted his watch and replied merely that he'd tell them when it was time, and until then he should shut the fuck up.

7.
Had Korin known that they had already arrived at a decision, and specifically at this particular decision; had he in fact noted

the meaningful gesture, nothing would have turned out as it did, but, since he hadn't noted it, he wasn't to know and, as a result, his perception of reality was incorrect; for to him it seemed that his current predicament—squatting on the ground with these children in the cold wind—was increasingly fraught with anxiety precisely because nothing was happening, and because it wasn't made clear to him what they wanted, if indeed they wanted anything at all, and since there was no explanation forthcoming as to why they were refusing to let him go or just leave him there, having succeeded in convincing them that the whole thing was pointless because he really had no money, he still felt that there should have been an explanation, and indeed had found one, albeit the wrong one as far as the seven children were concerned, he being aware of exactly how much money was sewn into the lining on the right side of his coat, so their immobility, their numbness, their failure to do anything, in fact the utter lack of any animation whatsoever on their part, took on an ever greater, ever more terrifying significance, though if he had looked at it another way he might have found it progressively more reassuring and less significant; which meant that he spent the first half of each moment preparing to spring to his feet and make a dash for it and the second half remaining precisely where he was, apparently content to stay there and to keep talking, as if he had only just begun his story; in other words, he was equally disposed to escape or remain, though every time he had to make a decision he chose, in fact, to remain, chiefly because he was scared of course, having constantly to assure them how happy he was to have found such sympathetic listeners and how good it all felt, because he had so much, it was extraordinary quite how much, to tell them, really and truly, because when you took time to think about it, "extraordinary" was absolutely the right word to describe the complex details of his story which, he said, he should tell so it would be clear to them, so they should know how it was that Wednesday, at what precise time he could not remember but it was probably some thirty or forty hours ago, when the fateful day arrived and he realized that he really did have to embark on his "great journey," at which point he understood that everything, from Hermes down to his solitary condition, was driving him in one direction, that he must already have started on the journey because it was all prepared and everything else had collapsed, which is to say that everything ahead of him had been prepared and everything behind him had collapsed, as tended to be the way with all such "great journeys," said Korin.

8.

The only street lights burning were those at the top of the stairs and the light they gave out fell in dingy cones that shuddered in the intermittent gusts of wind that assailed them because the other neon lights positioned in the thirty or so meters between them had all been broken, leaving them squatting in darkness, yet as aware of each other, of their precise positions, as of the enormous mass of dark sky above the smashed neon, the sky which might have glimpsed the reflection of its own enormous dark mass as it trembled with stars in the vista of railway yards spreading below it, had there been some relationship between the trembling stars and the twinkling dull red semaphore of lights sprinkled among the rails, but there wasn't, there was no common denominator, no interdependence between them, the only order and relationship existing within the discrete worlds of above and below, and indeed of anywhere, for the field of stars and the forest of signals stared as blankly at each other as does each and every form of being, blind in darkness and blind in radiance, as blind on earth as it is in heaven, if only so that a long moribund symmetry among this vastness might appear in the lost glance of some higher being, at the center of which, naturally, there would be a miniscule blind spot: as with Korin . . . the footbridge . . . the seven kids.

9.

A total shithead, they told a local acquaintance the next day, a total shithead in a league of his own, a loser they really should have got rid of because you never knew when he'd squeal on you, cause he'd had a good look at everybody's face, they added to each other, and could have made a mental note of their clothes, their shoes, and everything else they were wearing that late afternoon, so, yeah, that's right, they admitted the next day, they should have got rid of him, only it didn't occur to any of them at the time to do so, everyone being so relaxed and all, so laid back, like a bunch of dopes on the footbridge while ordinary people carried on leading ordinary lives beneath them as they gazed at the darkening neighborhood above the converging rails and waited for the signals for the six-forty-eight in the distance so that they might rush down to the cuttings, taking up their positions behind the bushes in preparation for the usual ritual, but, as they remarked, none of them had imagined that the ritual might have ended in some other fashion, with a different outcome, that it might be completed entirely successfully, triumphantly, right on target, in other words with a death, in which case of course even a pathetic twerp like him would be an obvious danger because he might squeal, they said, might get into a funk and, quite unexpectedly, squeal on them to the cops, and the reason it worked out differently, as it did in fact, leaving them to think the thoughts they had just thought, was that they hadn't been concentrating, and can't have been, otherwise they'd have realized that this was precisely the kind of man who presented no danger because, later, he couldn't even remember what, if anything, had happened at about six-forty-eight, as he had fallen ever deeper under the spell of his own fear, the fear that drove his narrative onwards, a narrative that, there was no denying, apart from a certain rhythm, lacked all sense of shape or indeed anything that might have drawn attention to his own person, except perhaps its copiousness, which was the result of him trying to tell them everything at once, in the way he himself experienced what had happened to him in a kind of simultaneity that he first noticed added up to a coherent whole that certain Wednesday morning some thirty or forty hours before, two-hundred-and-twenty kilometers from here in a travel agent's, at the point when he arrived at the front of the line and was about to ask the time of the next train for Budapest and the cost of the ticket, when, standing at the counter, he suddenly felt that *he should not ask that question here*, at the same moment recognizing in the reflection in the glass over one of the posters above the counter, two employees of the District Psychiatric Unit, disguised as a pair of ordinary idiots, really, two of them, and behind him, at the entrance, a so-called nurse whose aggressive presence made his skin prickle and break into a sweat.

10.

The men from the District Psychiatric Unit, said Korin, never explained to him what he had wanted to know, which was the reason he had attended the unit to start with, and that was the matter of how the whole system that held the skull in place, from the first cervical vertebra through to the ligaments (the Rectus capitis), actually functioned, but they never explained it, because they couldn't, chiefly because they themselves had not an inkling, their minds being shrouded in a wholly impenetrable darkness that resulted in them first staring at him in astonishment, as if to indicate that the question itself, the mere asking of it, was so ludicrous that it provided direct and incontrovertible proof of his, Korin's, madness, then giving each other significant glances and little nods whose portent was (was it not?) perfectly clear, that they had dismissed the subject, as a consequence of which he made no further enquiries regarding the matter but, even while steadfastly bearing the enormous weight of the problem, literally, on his shoulders, tried to solve the problem himself by asking what that certain first cervical vertebra and the Rectus capitis actually were, how (sighed Korin) they performed their crucial functions and how it was that his skull was simply propped on the topmost vertebra of his spinal column, though when he thought about it at the time, or so he told them now, the idea of his skull being fixed to his spine by cerebro-spinal ligaments, which were the only things holding the lot together, was enough to send shivers down him when he thought of it, and still did send shivers down him, since even a brief examination of his own skull demonstrated the patent truth that this arrangement was so sensitive, so brittle, so vulnerable, in fact one of the most frail and delicate physical structures imaginable,

that he concluded it must have been here, at this particular junc-
ture, that his problems had begun and would end, for if the doctors were incapable of coming to any worthwhile conclusion
after looking at his X-rays, and things had turned out as they
had done so far, then, having steeped himself to some degree at
least in the study of medicine, and having conducted an endless
self-examination based on this study, he had no hesitation in declaring that the pain he was in had its root cause here, in that
arrangement of tissue and bone, where vertebra met ligament,
and that all attention should be focused on this point, on the
ligaments, on which precise point he was not yet certain though
he was certain enough about the sensation that spread through
his neck and back, week by week, month by month, constantly
increasing in intensity, knowing that the process had started and
was proceeding irresistibly, and that this whole affair, if one considered it objectively, he said, was bound to lead to the terminal
decay of the union of skull and spine, culminating in a condition, *not to beat around the bush*, for why should one, said Korin,
pointing to his neck, whereby this frail piece of skin finally gave
out when he would inevitably lose his head.

11.
One, two, three, four, five, six, seven, eight, nine sets of rails
could be distinguished from the vantage point of the footbridge,
and the seven of them could do little but count them over and
over again, concentrating their attention on the confluence of
rails in the perceptibly deepening darkness that was accentuated
by the red lights of the signals while waiting for the six-forty-
eight to appear at last in the distance, for the tension that had
suddenly appeared on everyone's hitherto relaxed countenance
was occasioned by nothing more at this stage than the impending arrival of the six-forty-eight, the mark they had set out to
rob having failed, after their first couple of attempts, to provide
sufficient entertainment in the short period of their waiting, so
that within fifteen minutes of having cornered him, even if they
had wanted to, they would have remained incapable of listening
to a single word more of the seamless and endless monologue

that, even now, cornered as he was, flowed unstoppably from him, because he kept on and on regardless, as they explained the next day, and it would have been unbearable had they not ignored him, because, they added, if they had continued to pay attention to him they would have had to do him in if only to preserve their own sanity, and they had, unfortunately, ignored him for the sake of their sanity, even though this resulted in them missing the chance of eliminating him, for they really should have eliminated him good and proper, or so they kept repeating to themselves, particularly since the seven of them would normally have been perfectly aware what failing to eliminate a witness might cost them, a witness like him, who would never completely vanish in the crowd, not to mention the fact that they had begun to get a reputation in certain important places as cutthroats, a reputation they had to protect, and killing him would not have been difficult, nor indeed a new proposition to them, and this way they would have been taking no chances.

12.

What had happened to him—Korin shook his head as if he still could not believe it—was, at the beginning, almost inconceivable, nigh unbearable, because even at first glance, following an initial survey of the complex nature of what was involved, one straight look told him that from now on he'd have to abandon his "sick hierarchical view of the world," explode the illusion of an orderly pyramid of facts and liberate himself from the extraordinarily powerful and secure belief in what was now revealed as merely a kind of childish mirage, which is to say the indivisible unity and contiguity of phenomena, and beyond that, the unity's secure permanence and stability; and, within this permanence and stability, the overall coherence of its mechanism, that strictly-governed interdependence of functioning parts which gave the whole system its sense of direction, development, pace, and progress, in other words whatever suggested that the thing it embodied was attractive and self-sufficient, or, to put it another way, he now had to say No, an immediate and once-and-for-all No, to that entire mode of life; but some hundred yards on he was forced to reconsider certain aspects of what he had originally termed his rejection of the hierarchical mode of thinking because it seemed to him that he had lost nothing by rejecting a particular order of things that he had elevated into a pyramid structure, a structure that self-evidently needed correcting or rejecting in perpetuity as misleading or inappropriate, no, strange to say, he had lost nothing by the rejection, for what had actually happened that certain night of his birthday, could not be accounted loss as such but rather gain, or at least as a first point gained, an advance in the direction of some all-but-inconceivable, all-but-unbearable end— and in the gradual process of walking the hundred paces from the river to the point where the struggle had begun, and having been granted a glimpse of the terrible complexity ahead, he saw that while the world appeared not to exist, the totality of that-which-had-been-thought-about-it did in fact exist, and, furthermore, that it was only this, in its countless thousands of varieties, that did exist as such, that what existed was his identity as the sum of the countless thousand imaginings of the human spirit that was engaged in writing the world, in writing his identity, he said, in terms of pure word, the doing word, the Verb that brooded over the waters, or, to put it another way, he added, what became clear was that most opinions were a waste of time, that it was a waste thinking that life was a matter of appropriate conditions and appropriate answers, because the task was not to choose but to accept, there being no obligation to choose between what was appropriate and what was inappropriate, only to accept that we are not obliged to do anything except to comprehend that the appropriateness of the one great universal process of thinking is not predicated on it being correct, for there was nothing to compare it with, nothing but its own beauty, and it was its beauty that gave us confidence in its truth—and this, said Korin, was what struck him as he walked those hundred furiously-thinking paces on the evening of his birthday: that is to say he understood the infinite significance of faith and was given a new insight into what the ancients had long known, that it was faith in its existence that had both created and maintained the world; the corollary of which was that it was the loss of his own faith that was now erasing it, the result of which realization being, he said, that he experienced a sudden, utterly numbing, quite awful feeling of abundance, because from that time on he knew that whatever had once existed, existed still and that, quite unexpectedly, he had stumbled on an ontological place of such gravity that he could see—oh but how, he sighed, how to begin—that Zeus, for instance, to take an arbitrary example, was still "there," now, in the present, just as all the other old gods of Olympus were "there," as was Yahweh and The Lord God of Hosts, and there alongside them, the ghosts of every nook and cranny, and that this meant they had nothing and yet everything to fear, for nothing ever disappeared without trace, for the absent had a structure as real as the structure of whatever existed, and so, in other words, you could bump into Allah, into the Prince of the Rebel Angels, and into all the dead stars of the universe, which would of course include the barren unpopulated earth with its godless laws of being as well as the terrifying reality of hell and pandemonium which was the domain of the demons, and that was reality, said Korin: thousands upon thousands of worlds, each one different, majestic or fearsome; thousands upon thousands in their ranks, he continued, his voice rising, in a single absent relationship, that was how it all appeared to him then, he explained, and it was then, when he had got so far, continually reliving the infinite capacity of the process of becoming, that the trouble with his head first started, the predictable course of which process he had already outlined, and possibly it was the sheer abundance, the peculiar inexhaustibility of history and the gods that he found hard to bear, for ultimately he didn't know, nor to this very day was it clear to him, precisely how the pain that started suddenly and simultaneously in his neck and his back, began: the forgetting, subject by subject, random, ungovernable and extraordinarily rapid, first of facts such as where he had put the key that he had only just now been holding in his hand, or what page he had got to in the book he had been reading the previous night, and, later, what had happened on Wednesday, three days ago, in the time between morning and evening, and after that, whatever was important, urgent, dull, or insignificant, and finally, even his mother's name, he said, the scent of apricots, whatever made familiar faces familiar, whether he had in fact completed tasks he had set himself to complete—in a word, he said, there was literally nothing that stayed in his head, the whole world had vanished, step by step, the disappearance itself having neither rhyme nor reason in its progress, as if what there was left was somehow sufficient, or as if there were always something of greater importance that a higher, incomprehensible force had decided he should forget.

13.

I must somehow have drunk of the waters of Lethe, Korin explained, and while disconsolately wagging his head as if to convey to them that the understanding of the manner and consequence of events would probably always lie beyond him, he brought out a box of Marlboros: *Anyone got a light?*

14.

They were roughly the same age, the youngest being eleven, the oldest perhaps thirteen or fourteen, but every one of them had at least one slip-cased razor-blade nestling by his side, nor was it just a matter of nestling there, for each of them, from the youngest to the oldest, was capable of handling it expertly, whether it was of the simple singleton kind or the triple sort they referred to as "the set," and not one of them lacked the ability to yank the thing forth in the blink of an eye and slip it between two fingers into the tense palm without the merest flickering of outward emotion while gazing steadily at the victim so that whichever of them happened to be in the right position could, quick as a flash, find the artery on the neck, this being the skill they had most perfectly mastered, a skill which rendered them, when all seven of them were together, so exceptionally dangerous that they had begun to earn a genuinely well-deserved reputation, only through constant practice, of course, the practice that enabled them to achieve their current level of performance and involved a carefully planned course of training that they carried through at constantly changing venues, repeating the same moves a hundred times, over and over again, until they could execute the moves with inimitable, blinding speed and such perfect coordination that in the course of an attack, they knew instinctively, without saying a word to each other, not only who would advance and who would stand, but how those standing would form up, nor was there any room for boasting, you couldn't even think of it, so faultless was their teamwork, and in any case, the sight of gushing blood was enough to stop their mouths and render them dumb, disciplined and solemn, perhaps even too solemn, for the solemnity was something of a burden to them, leaving them with a desire for some course of action that would lead rather more playfully, more fortuitously, that is to say entailing a greater risk of failure, to the fact of death, since this was what they all sought, this was the way things had developed, this was what interested them, in fact it was the reason they had gathered here in the first place, the reason they had already spent a good many afternoons, so many weeks of afternoons and early evenings, passing the time right here.

15.
There was absolutely nothing ambiguous about the way he moved, said Korin next day in the MALEV tourist office, the whole thing being so completely normal, so ordinary, the reaching for his cigarettes so perfectly innocent and harmless that it was merely a kind of instinct, the result of an on-the-spur-of-the-moment notion that he might lessen the tension and thereby ease his own situation by a friendly gesture such as the offering of cigarettes, for really, no exaggeration, it was just that and nothing more, and while he expected almost anything to happen as a result, what he did not expect was to find another hand holding his wrist by the time his had reached the Marlboros in his pocket, a hand that did not grip the way a pair of handcuffs would, but one that rendered him immobile and sent a flood of warmth lapping across his wrist, or so he explained the next day, still in a state of shock, while at the same time, he con-

tinued, he felt his muscles weaken, only those muscles that were grasping the pack of Marlboros, and all this happened without a word being exchanged and, what was more—apart from the child nearest to him, who had responded so nimbly and with such breath-taking skill to the gesture he had misinterpreted—the group did not move an inch, but merely glanced at the falling Marlboro pack, until one of them eventually lifted it up, opened it, drawing out a cigarette, and passed it on to the next, and so forth to the end while he, Korin, in his terror, behaved as though nothing had happened, nothing significant at least, or, if anything had happened it was only by accident so minor and so unworthy of mention as to be laughable, an accident that left him gripping his wounded wrist with his blameless hand, not quite understanding what had happened, and even when he did eventually realize, he merely pressed his thumb against the tiny nick, for that was all it was, he told them, a miniscule cut, and when the expected rush of panic, with its attendant throbbing, trembling, and loud noises in the head began to die away, an icy calm had lapped about him in much the same way as the blood had lapped about his wrist, in other words, as he declared the next day, he was utterly convinced that they were going to kill him.

16.
The work in the records office, he continued in a quavering voice, having waited for the last of the children to light his cigarette, did not involve, as did that of so many others, at least as far as he personally was concerned, a process of humiliation, blackmail, of wearing people down; no, not in his case, he stressed: on the contrary, he was bound to say, that after "the sad turn of events in his social life," it was precisely his work that remained most important to him, that was his sole consolation both in the obligatory and voluntary after-hours areas of his specialization; it was the one thing, in the fundamental and, as far as he was concerned, fateful, process of the last few months of coming to terms with a reality which involved acknowledging the not-so-much bitter as amusing evidence that showed history and truth had nothing to do with each other, that demonstrated

to him that everything he, in his capacity as a local historian, had done to explore, establish, maintain and nurture as history, had in fact given him an extraordinary freedom and raised him to a state of grace; because once he was capable of considering how any particular history served as a peculiar—if one regarded its origins, accidental, and if one considered its outcomes, cynically concocted and artificially articulated—blend of some remaining elements of the truth, of human understanding and the imaginative re-creation of the past, of what could and could not be known, of confusion, of lies, of exaggerations, of both fidelity to—and misuse of—given data, of both proper and improper interpretations of evidence, of inklings, suggestions and of the marshalling of a sufficiently imposing body of opinion, then the work in the records office, the labor of what was referred to as the classifying and ordering of archive material and indeed all such enterprises, represented nothing less than freedom itself, *for it did not matter in the least* what task he was currently engaged in, whether the classification was within general, median, or specific categories, whether it was filed under this or that heading; whatever he did, whichever section of that almost two-thousand-meters' length of archival corridor he dealt with, he was simply keeping history going, if he might put it that way, while knowing, at the same time, that he was entirely missing the truth, though the fact that he knew, even while he was working, that he was missing it, rendered him calm and equable gave him a certain sense of invulnerability, the kind that comes to a man who recognizes that what he is doing is as pointless as it is meaningless, and furthermore that, precisely because it lacks point and meaning, it is accompanied by an entirely mysterious yet quite inimitable sweetness—yes, that was the way it was, he said, he really did find freedom through work, and there was just one problem, which was that this freedom wasn't quite enough, for, having tasted it these last few months and having realized how rare and precious it was, it suddenly seemed insufficient, and he had started to sigh and pine for a greater, an absolute freedom, and thought only of how and where he might find it, until the whole issue became a burning obsession that disturbed him in his work in the records office, because he had to know where to seek it, where absolute freedom might reside.

17.

All this, of course, indeed his whole history, originated in the distant past, said Korin, as far back as the time he first announced the fact that though an utterly mad world had made a madman of him, pure and simple, it didn't mean that that is entirely what he was, for while it would have been stupid to deny that sooner or later, naturally enough, that was how he'd "finish up," or rather, sooner or later, reach a state resembling madness, it was obvious that whatever might in fact happen, madness was not a particularly unfortunate condition that one should fear as being oppressive or threatening, a condition one should be frightened of, no, not in the least, or at least he personally was not scared of it, not for a moment, for it was simply a matter of fact, as he later explained to the seven children, that one day the straw actually did "break the camel's back," for now that he recalled it, the story did not begin beside that certain river but much earlier, well before the riverside events, when he was suddenly seized by a hitherto unknown and unfathomably deep bitterness that resonated through his entire being, a bitterness so sudden that one particular day it simply struck him how bitter, how deathly bitter he was about that which he used to refer to as "the state of things," and that this was not the result of some mood that quickly appeared then disappeared but of an insight that illuminated him like a bolt of lightning, something, he said, that branded him for ever and would remain burning, a lightning-insight that said there was nothing, but *nothing* worthwhile left in the world, not that he wanted to exaggerate, but that was how it was, there really was nothing worthwhile in his circumstances, nor would there be anything lovely or good ever again, and though this sounded childish, and indeed he recognized that the essential element of that which he had distilled from his entire history, was, as he was content to acknowledge, childish, he began to peddle this insight regularly in bars, hoping to find someone that, in his "general state of despair," he might regard as one of those "angels of mercy," seeking such a one constantly, determined to tell him everything or to put a pistol to his own head, as he did, he said, without success, thank heaven; so, in other words, though the whole thing was perfectly idiotic, no doubt, that was how it started, with this sense of bitterness that created a whole "new Korin," from which point on he began to ponder over matters such as how things fitted together, and if their condition were such and such what the implications might be for him personally, and once having understood that there were absolutely no personal implications, and furthermore, having grasped that he had reached his absolute limit, he then decided that he would resign himself to it, to say OK, fine, that's how things are, but then, if that was the case, what should he do, give up? disappear? or what? And it was precisely this question, or rather the fact that he approached this question in such a "so-what's-the-point-of-it-all" manner, that led directly to the fateful day, meaning that certain Wednesday morning when he concluded that there was nothing for it but to take immediate action, this being the direct conclusion he had reached, albeit by a dauntingly difficult route, and the seven of them here were witnesses, he said, still squatting in the middle of the footbridge, to the daunting difficulty of it, right from the time by the river when he first understood the complexity of the world, then by developing an ever-deepening comprehension which in someone like him, a local historian of some godforsaken place, involved getting to grips with the inordinate wealth and complexity of possible thought about a world that didn't exist, as well as with the strength to be derived from the creative power of blind faith, and all this while forgetfulness and the constant terror of losing his head crept up on him, so that the taste of freedom he had enjoyed in the records office might carry him through to the end of his quest, after which there would be nowhere left to go and he would have to decide, and indeed declare, that he himself would no longer allow matters to proceed as they might have wanted to proceed, but mount the stage "as an actor," not as others around him tended to do, did but quite differently, by, for instance, after one enormous effort of thinking, simply leaving, yes, leaving, abandoning the place allotted to him in life, leaving it for ever, not simply in order to be in an indeterminate elsewhere, but, or so the idea came to him, to locate *the very center of the world*, the place where matters were actually decided, where things happened, a place such as Rome had been, ancient Rome where decisions had been made and events set in motion, to find that place and *then* quit everything; in other words he decided to pack up his things and seek such a "Rome"; for why, he asked himself, why spend his time in an archive some two hundred kilometers southwest of Budapest when he could be sitting at the center of the world, since one way or the other, it would be his last stop on Earth? and the idea having come to him it began to crystallize in his constantly aching head and he had even begun to study foreign languages, when, one late afternoon, having stayed behind in the records office, vaguely checking the shelves, as he put it, utterly by chance, he arrived at a shelf he had never before explored, took down from it a box that had never been taken down, not at least since the Second World War, that was for sure, and from this box labeled "Family Papers of No Particular Significance" took out a fascicule headed IV.3 / 1941-42, opened it and, in doing so, changed his life for ever, for there he discovered something that decided for once and for all what he should do if he still wanted to "carry his plan through" and to make "his last good-byes"; something that finally determined him to put all those years of thinking, proposing and doubting behind him, to let those years go, to let them rot in the past, and not to let them determine his future but to act right now, for the fascicule headed IV.3 / 1941-2 had left him in no doubt what should be done, what to do in order to recover the dignity and meaning whose loss he had been mourning, what important thing there remained for him to do, and above all, where he should seek that which he so much lacked: that peculiar, furiously desired, greatest, very last freedom that earthly life was capable of offering.

18.

The only things that interested them, they said the next day while hanging about in front of the Bingo Bar, were the feeding-catapults, the kind used by anglers for bait, not the mind-numbingly idiotic claptrap the old fart spewed continuously, without any prospect of an end, for he was incapable of stopping, so that eventually, after an hour or so of it, it became clear that it was his own repulsive gabble that had turned him into a head-case, though as far as they were concerned, they said, it didn't add up to anything, so it was completely pointless for him to talk himself into a frazzle, since the old fart meant as much to them as the wind on the footbridge, wind, that, like him, just kept blowing because it was impossible to shut either of them up, not that they gave it a thought, why would they? since he wasn't worth it, let him talk, the only things that mattered being the three feeding-catapults, how they worked and how they would employ them when the six-forty-eight arrived, and that was what they'd all been thinking about just before this creep arrived, of the three professional model ground-baiting catapults they had got as a bargain, for nine thousand forints, at the Attila József flea market, the three professional *German* ground-baiting catapults they had tucked under their bomber jackets, and they wondered how these would perform, for people said their projectile power was vastly greater than that of the Hungarian sort, and, of course, far superior to that of hand-held missiles, some people even claiming that this German gear was not only more powerful but almost ensured that your aim was one hundred-percent effective, and that it was, according to its reputation, no argument about it, the best on the market, chiefly because of the track-device, attached to the handle below the fork, that steadied your hand in case it accidentally trembled, thereby reducing the uncertainty factor to a minimum by holding the arm firm all the way to the elbow, or so it was said, they declared, or so they say, but not in their wildest dreams would they have imagined what really happened after that, since this piece of goods was genius, its capacity absolutely unbelievable, they said, or so said the four of them who were not among the first to use it, absolutely unbelievable, they said.

19.

Another long freight train rumbled by below them and the footbridge shook gently along its whole length until the train was gone—leaving two blinking red lights in its wake—when the noise of the very last car began to fade along with the rattling of wheels, and, in the newly settled silence, after the two red lights disappearing in the distance, just above the rails, no more than a meter high, a flock of bats appeared and followed the train towards the Ràkosrendezö, utterly silent, without the least sound, like some medieval battery of ghosts, in close order, at even pace, indeed at a mysteriously even pace, swooping strictly between the parallel lines of the rails, suggesting somehow that they were being drawn towards Budapest or riding in the slipstream of the train as it went, the train that was showing them the way, carrying them, drawing them, sucking them on so that they could travel perfectly effortlessly, with steady, spread wings, reaching Budapest, at a precise height of one meter above the rails.

[. . .]

Dubravka Ugrešić

from THE MUSEUM OF UNCONDITIONAL SURRENDER

Translated from the Croatian by Celia Hawkesworth

In the Berlin zoo, beside the pool containing the live walrus, there is an unusual display. In a glass case are all the things found in the stomach of Roland the walrus, who died on 21 August 1961. Or to be precise:

> a pink cigarette lighter, four ice-lolly sticks (wooden), a metal brooch in the form of a poodle, a beer-bottle opener, a woman's bracelet (probably silver), a hair grip, a wooden pencil, a child's plastic water pistol, a plastic knife, sunglasses, a little chain, a spring (small), a rubber ring, a parachute (child's toy), a steel chain about 18 ins in length, four nails (large), a green plastic car, a metal comb, a plastic badge, a small doll, a beer can (Pilsner, half-pint), a box of matches, a baby's shoe, a compass, a small car key, four coins, a knife with a wooden handle, a baby's dummy, a bunch of keys (5), a padlock, a little plastic bag containing needles and thread.

The visitor stands in front of the unusual display, more enchanted than horrified, as before archaeological exhibits. The visitor knows that their museum-display fate has been determined by chance (Roland's whimsical appetite) but still cannot resist the poetic thought that with time the objects have acquired some subtler, secret connections. Caught up in this thought, the visitor then tries to establish semantic coordinates, to reconstruct the historical context (it occurs to him, for instance, that Roland died one week after the Berlin Wall was erected), and so on and so forth.

The chapters and fragments which follow should be read in a similar way. If the reader feels that there are no meaningful or firm connections between them, let him be patient: the connections will establish themselves of their own accord. And one more thing: the question as to whether this novel is autobiographical might at some hypothetical moment be of concern to the police, but not to the reader.

PART ONE: *ICH BIN MÜDE*

1.

"*Ich bin müde*," I say to Fred. His sorrowful, pale face stretches into a grin. *Ich bin müde* is the only German sentence I know at the moment. And right now I don't want to learn any more. Learning more means opening up. And I want to stay closed for a while longer.

2.

Fred's face reminds one of an old photograph. Fred looks like a young officer driven by unhappy love to play Russian roulette. I imagine him some hundred years ago spending whole nights in Budapest restaurants. The mournful scraping of Gypsy violins doesn't provoke so much as a quiver on his pale face. Just occasionally his eyes shine with the gleam of the metal buttons on his uniform.

3.

The view from my room, my temporary exile, is filled with tall pine trees. In the morning I open the curtains to reveal a romantic stage set. The pines are at first shrouded in mist like ghosts, then the mist disperses in wisps, and the sun breaks through. Towards the end of the day the pines grow dark. In the left-hand corner of the window a lake can just be seen. In the evening I close the curtains. The stage set is the same each day, the stillness of the scene is broken occasionally by a bird, but all that ever really changes is the light.

4.
My room is filled with a silence as thick as cotton wool. If I open the window, the silence is shattered by the twittering of birds. In the evening, if I go out of my room into the hall, I hear the sound of a television (from Kira's room on my floor) and the sound of a typewriter (the Russian writer on the floor below me). A little later I hear the uneven tapping of a stick and the scrape of the invisible German writer's small footsteps. I often see the artists, a Romanian married couple (from the floor below me), they pass silently like shadows. The silence is sometimes disturbed by Fred, our caretaker. Fred cuts the grass in the park, driving the pain of his love away with the noisy electric mower. His wife has recently left him. "Zy vife ist crazy," Fred explained. That's the only English sentence he knows.

5.
In the nearby town of Murnau there is a museum, the house of Gabriele Münter and Wassily Kandinsky. I am always a little troubled by the traces of other people's lives, they are at once so personal and yet impersonal. When I was there I bought a postcard showing a painting of the house, *Das Russen-Haus*. I often look at this postcard. I sometimes feel that the tiny human form at the window, that dark-red dot, is me.

6.
On my desk there is a yellowed photograph. It shows three unknown women bathers. I don't know much about the photograph, just that it was taken at the beginning of the century on the river Pakra. That is a little river that runs not far from the small town where I was born and spent my childhood.

I always carry the photograph around with me, like a little fetish object whose real meaning I do not know. Its matte yellow surface attracts my attention, hypnotically. Sometimes I stare at it for a long time, not thinking about anything. Sometimes I plunge attentively into the reflections of the three bathers mirrored in the water, into their faces which are looking straight at mine. I dive into them as though I am about to solve a mystery, discover a crack, a hidden passage through which I shall slip into a different space, a different time. Usually I prop up the photograph in the left-hand corner of the window, where the end of the lake can be seen.

7.

I sometimes have coffee with Kira from Kiev, a retired literature teacher. "*Ya kamenshchitsa*,"* says Kira. Kira is passionate about every kind of stone. She tells me that she spends every summer in the Crimea, in a village where the sea throws all kinds of semi-precious stones up onto the shore. She is not alone, she says, other people come there as well, they are all *kamenshchiki*. Sometimes they meet up, make a fire, cook borsch and show one another their "treasures." Here, Kira passes the time painting copies of various subjects. She has made a copy of the archangel Michael, although, she says, she prefers—threading. She asks whether I have a broken necklace, she could mend it, she says, re-thread the beads. "You know," says Kira, "I like threading things." She says it as though she were apologizing.

8.

In nearby Murnau, there is a museum commemorating Odön von Horváth. Odön von Horváth was born on 9 December 1901 in Rijeka, at 16.45 (according to some other documents it was 16.30). When he had attained a weight of some 16 kilograms, he left Rijeka, and spent some time in Venice and some more in the Balkans. When he reached a height of 1 meter 20 he moved to Budapest and lived there until he was 1 meter 21. According to

* '*I am a pebble-lover.*'

Odön von Horváth's own account, Eros awoke in him when he was 1 meter 52. Horváth's interest in art, and particularly literature, appeared at a height of 1 meter 70. When the First World War started Odön von Horváth measured 160cm, and when the war ended he was a whole 180cm. Odön von Horváth stopped growing when he reached a height of 184cm. Horváth's biography measured in centimetres and geographical points is confirmed by museum photographs.

9.
There is a story told about the war criminal Ratko Mladić, who spent months shelling Sarajevo from the surrounding hills. Once he noticed an acquaintance's house in the next target. The general telephoned his acquaintance and informed him that he was giving him five minutes to collect his "albums," because he had decided to blow the house up. When he said "albums," the murderer meant the albums of family photographs. The general, who had been destroying the city for months, knew precisely how to annihilate memory. That is why he "generously" bestowed on his acquaintance life with the right to remembrance. Bare life and a few family photographs.

10.
"Refugees are divided into two categories: those who have photographs and those who have none," said a Bosnian, a refugee.

11.
"What a woman needs most is air," says my friend Hannelore as we walk towards the nearby Andechs monastery.

"What a woman needs most is a butler," I reply to Hannelore as I buy a cheap plastic ball with a guardian angel in it in the souvenir shop at the monastery.

Hannelore laughs inaudibly. When the ball is given a little shake, snow falls on the guardian angel. Hannelore's laughter rustles like polystyrene snow.

12.

Before I came here, I spent a few days on the Adriatic, in a house beside the sea. Occasional bathers came to the little beach. They could be seen and heard from the terrace. One day my attention was drawn to a woman's strikingly loud laughter. I looked up and saw three elderly bathers in the sea. They were swimming with naked breasts, right by the shore, in a small circle, as though they were sitting at a round table, drinking coffee. They were Bosnian (judging by their accent), probably refugees, and nurses. How do I know? They were recalling their distant schooldays and gossiping about a fourth who had confused the words "anamnesis" and "amnesia" at her final examination. The word "amnesia" and the story about the exam were repeated several times and each time they provoked salvoes of laughter. At the same time, all three waved their hands as though they were brushing invisible crumbs from a non-existent table. All at once there was a shower, one of those short, sudden summer ones. The bathers stayed in the water. From the terrace I watched the large shining drops of rain and the three women: their laughter was increasingly loud, with increasingly short intervals, now they were doubled-up with laughter. In the pauses I could make out the word "falling" which they kept repeating, meaning, presumably, the rain . . . They spread their arms, splashed the water with their hands, now their voices were like birds' cawing, as though they were competing as to whose voice would be throatiest and loudest, and the rain too, as though it had gone mad, was ever heavier and warmer. Between the terrace and the sea a misty, wet, salty curtain fell. All at once the curtain absorbed all the sound and the three pairs of wings continued flapping magnificently in the glistening silence.

I made an inner "click" and recorded the scene, although I don't know why.

13.

"What a woman needs most is water," says Hannelore as we rest after swimming in the luxurious atmosphere of the Müllersche Volksbads.

14.

From the start, my acquaintance S.'s life didn't go well. But still, she managed to complete her nursing training and get a job in a hospital for mentally retarded children on the edge of town. "It won't end well. I absorb other people's misfortune like blotting paper," she said. In the hospital she found her little personal happiness, a male nurse, much younger than her, an exceptionally small man (when I met him I couldn't take my eyes off his little lacquered shoes) who even had a surname that was diminutive. At a relatively advanced age, she fell pregnant. She decided to go ahead with the pregnancy despite the fact that they were both diabetic. She carried the pregnancy (twins!) to term, and then, the day before they were due, the unborn babies suffocated. My acquaintance fell apart like wet blotting paper. She spent some time in the psychiatric wing, recovered and moved with her little husband to a smaller town. One day she suddenly appeared in my house. Everything was "normal," we talked about her work, about her husband, about this and that, and then my acquaintance took a little plastic bag out of her handbag and spread her "treasures" before me. These were two or three insignificant little shiny objects, so insignificant that I don't remember what they were. She fiddled with her trinkets for a long time. Then, catching sight of a miniature spray of dried flowers on my shelf, she said that she really liked the spray, that it was wonderful, simply wonderful, and asked me to give it to her. She shoved the little spray into the plastic bag, and then departed with her pathetic magpie's treasure.

15.

Over coffee, Kira tells me something about the other inhabitants of the villa. "You know, we're all alike in a way, we are all looking for something . . . As though we had lost something . . . ," she says.

16.

An exile feels that the state of exile is a constant, special sensitivity to sound. So I sometimes feel that exile is nothing but a state of searching for and recollecting sound.

In Munich where I had gone to meet Igor, I stopped for a moment near Marienplatz, drawn to the sound of music. An elderly Gypsy was playing Hungarian Gypsy songs on a violin. He caught my passing glance, gave me a smile that was both deferential and brazen at the same time, recognising me as "one of his". Something caught in my throat, for a moment I couldn't breathe, and then I lowered my eyes and hurried on, realising a second later that I had set off in the wrong direction. A couple of paces further on I caught sight of a life-saving telephone box and joined the queue, pretending that I had to make a phone call, what else?

There was a young man standing in front of me. Tight black leather jacket, tight jeans, high-heeled boots, a kind of insecurity and impudence on his face at the same time, like colors running into each other. A second later I knew that he was "one of us," "my countryman." The way he slowly and persistently dialed the number—looking neither to right nor left, like a waiter in a cheap restaurant—filled me with a mixture of anger and pity and put me on the side of the people in the queue. And then the young man finally got through (yes, "one of us," of course!). My countrymen's habit of talking for a long time, about nothing, as though coddling, pampering, mutually patting each other's backs and jollying each other along, that habit filled me again with a sudden mixture of anger and pity. The violin was still whining sorrowfully, the young man was talking to a certain Milica, and in my head, as at an editing table, I was mixing the whine with the young man's babbling. The black-eyed violinist was staring persistently in my direction. For a moment I wanted to leave the queue, but I didn't, that would have given me away, I thought. That is why, when the young man finished his conversation and smoothed his hair with his hand (a gesture which filled me with the same mixed feelings as before, because of its unexpectedness), I telephoned Hannelore, who was the only person I could have telephoned, thinking up some urgent, practical question.

I was late for my meeting with Igor. We went to a Chinese restaurant and, as we chatted brightly waiting to be served, I observed that I was restless, absent, that my eyes were wandering, I felt as though I was covered with a fine film, like spectacles on a winter's day. And then I became aware of a sound I had not at first registered. There was Chinese or Korean pop-music playing, or at any rate pop-music from that part of the world. It was a soft, elegiac, sweet crooning, a love song presumably, which could have been from my home, or from Igor's Russian home. Just then there was a sudden downpour of rain which streamed down the restaurant window behind Igor, and finally I broke, let myself go, reacted properly, precisely, following an ancient, well-practised reflex, of which I had not been conscious until that moment. In a word, I salivated at the sound of the bell, that universal, sweet whine, the same whine no matter where it came from . . . I struggled inwardly, resisted, grumbled, almost glad that I was in its power, almost physically satisfied, weakened, softened, I splashed about in the warm invisible puddle of tears . . .

"What's happening, Igor . . .?" I asked him, as though apologizing.

"The glint of the button on your blouse is making your eyes shine," said my friend, a Russian Jew from Chernoviats, an exile.

I looked dully down at the button. It was an opaque, plastic-goldish color.

17.

"I have no desire to be witty. I have no desire to construct a plot. I am going to write about things and thoughts. To compile quotations," wrote a temporary exile a long time ago. His name was Viktor Shklovsky.

18.

"*Ich bin müde,*" I say to Fred. His pale sorrowful face stretches into a grin. *Ich bin müde* is the only German sentence I know at the moment. And right now I don't want to learn any more. Learning more means opening up. And I want to stay closed for a while longer.

In the silence of my room, with the romantic stage set in the windows, I arrange my bits and pieces, some I have brought with me, without really knowing why, some I found here, all random and meaningless. A little feather I picked up while walking in the park gleams in front of me, a sentence I read somewhere rings in my head, an old yellowing photograph looks at me, the outline of a gesture I saw somewhere accompanies me, and I don't know what it means or who made it, the ball containing the guardian angel shines before me with its plastic glow. When I shake it, snow falls on the angel. I don't understand the meaning of all of this, I am dislocated, I am a weary human specimen, a pebble, I have been cast by chance onto a different, safer shore.

19.
"What a woman needs most are air and water." says Hannelore instructively as we sit in a bar, blowing the froth from the beer in our mugs.

20.
The exile feels that the state of exile has the structure of a dream. All at once, as in a dream, faces appear which he had forgotten, or perhaps had never met, places which he is undoubtedly seeing for the first time, but that he feels he knows from somewhere. The dream is a magnetic field which attracts images from the past, present and future. The exile suddenly sees in reality faces, events, and images, drawn by the magnetic field of the dream; suddenly it seems as though his biography was written long before it was to be fulfilled, that his exile is therefore not the result of external circumstances nor his choice, but a jumble of coordinates which fate had long ago sketched out for him. Caught up in this seductive and terrifying thought, the exile begins to decipher the signs, crosses, and knots and all at once it seems as though he were beginning to read in it all a secret harmony, a round logic of symbols.

21.
"*Nanizivat', ya lyublyu nanizivat',*"* says Kira as though apologising for something, and smiles the pale smile of a convalescent.
    "Threading, I like threading things."

*"Threading, I like threading things."

22.

In the glass studio at the end of our park, the Romanian couple is preparing an exhibition. The young woman uses an axe to shape pieces of wood she has been collecting around the park for days. Meanwhile, the man pins little pieces of thin, almost transparent, paper to a huge white board. On each one a bird's head is painted in soft, bright, grey water-colors. The young woman hits the wood rhythmically with her axe. At first the little pieces of paper are still, and then an invisible current slowly stirs them. The birds' heads quiver as though they were going to fall.

[. . .]

ENRIQUE VILA-MATAS

from BARTLEBY & CO.

Translated from the Spanish by JONATHAN DUNNE

I never had much luck with women. I have a pitiful hump, which I am resigned to. All my closest relatives are dead. I am a poor recluse working in a ghastly office. Apart from that, I am happy. Today most of all because, on this day 8 July 1999, I have begun this diary that is also going to be a book of footnotes commenting on an invisible text, which I hope will prove my reliability as a tracker of Bartlebys.

Twenty-five years ago, when I was very young, I published a short novel on the impossibility of love. Since then, on account of a trauma that I shall go into later, I had not written again, I stopped altogether, I became a Bartleby, and that is why I have been interested in them for some time.

We all know the Bartlebys, they are beings inhabited by a profound denial of the world. They are named after the scrivener Bartleby, a clerk in a story by Herman Melville, who has never been seen reading, not even a newspaper; who for long periods stands looking out at a pale window behind a folding screen, upon a brick wall in Wall Street; who never drinks beer, or tea and coffee, like other men; who has never been anywhere, living as he does in the office, spending even his Sundays there; who has never said who he is, or where he comes from, or whether he has any relatives in this world; who, when he is asked where he was born or given a job to do or asked to reveal something about himself, responds always by saying,

"I would prefer not to."

For some time now I have been investigating the frequent examples of Bartleby's syndrome in literature, for some time I have studied the illness, the disease, endemic to contemporary letters, the negative impulse or attraction towards nothingness that means that certain creators, while possessing a very demanding literary conscience (or perhaps precisely because of this), never manage to write: either they write one or two books and then stop altogether or, working on a project, seemingly without problems, one day they become literally paralyzed for good.

The idea of investigating the literature of the No, that of Bartleby & Co., came about last Tuesday in the office when I thought I heard my boss's secretary say to somebody on the phone,

"Mr Bartleby is in a meeting."

I chuckled softly to myself. It is difficult to imagine Bartleby in a meeting with somebody, immersed, for example, in the heavy atmosphere of an assembly of directors. But it is not so difficult—it is what I propose to do in this diary or book of footnotes—to assemble a good number of Bartlebys, that is to say a good number of writers affected by the disease, the negative impulse.

Of course I heard "Bartleby" where I should have heard my boss's surname, which is very similar. But undoubtedly this mistake could not have been more propitious, since it made me strike out and decide, after twenty-five years of silence, finally to start writing again, writing about the last secrets of some of the most conspicuous cases of creators who gave up writing.

It is my intention, therefore, to make my way through the labyrinth of the No, down the roads of the most disquieting and attractive tendency of contemporary literature: a tendency in which is to be found the only path still open to genuine literary creation; a tendency that asks the question, "What is writing and where is it?" and that prowls around the impossibility of the same and tells the truth about the grave, but highly stimulating, prognosis of literature at the end of the millennium.

Only from the negative impulse, from the labyrinth of the No, can the writing of the future appear. But what will this literature be like? Not long ago a work colleague, somewhat maliciously, put this question to me.

"I don't know," I said. "If I knew, I'd write it myself."

I wonder if I can do this. I am convinced that only by tracking down the labyrinth of the No can the paths still open to the writing of the future appear. I wonder if I can evoke them. I shall write footnotes commenting on a text that is invisible, which does not mean it does not exist, since this phantom text could very well end up held in suspension in the literature of the next millennium.

1.

Robert Walser knew that writing that one cannot write is also writing. Among the many minor positions that he held—bookshop assistant, lawyer's clerk, bank employee, worker in a factory that made sewing machines, and finally major-domo of a castle in Silesia—Robert Walser would from time to time retire to Zurich, to the "Chamber of Writing for Unoccupied Persons" (the name could not be more Walserian, but it is genuine), and there, seated on an old stool, in the evening, in the pale light of an oil lamp, he would make use of his graceful handwriting to work as a copyist, to work as a "Bartleby."

Both his occupation as a copyist and Walser's whole existence remind us of the character in Melville's story, the scrivener who spent twenty-four hours a day in the office. Roberto Calasso, referring to Walser and Bartleby, has remarked that in such beings who have the appearance of ordinary and discreet men there is, however, to be found an alarming tendency to negate the world. All the more radical the less it is observed, the blast of destruction is frequently ignored by people who consider the Bartlebys to be gray, good-natured beings. "For many, Walser, the author of *Jakob von Gunten*," writes Calasso, "is still a familiar figure and it is possible to read even that his nihilism is middle class and good-natured like the Swiss. And yet he is a remote character, a parallel path of nature, an almost indiscernible knife-edge. Walser's obedience, like Bartleby's disobedience, presupposes a total break [. . .]. They copy, they transcribe texts that pass through them like a transparent sheet. They make no special pronouncements, no attempt to modify. 'I do not develop,' says Jakob von Gunten in *Jakob von Gunten*. 'I would prefer not to make any change,' says Bartleby. Their affinity reveals the similarity between silence and a certain decorative use of language."

Of the writers of the No, what we might call the scriveners' section is one of the strangest and the one that perhaps affects me the most. This is because, twenty-five years ago, I personally experienced the sensation of knowing what it is to be a copyist. And I suffered terribly. I was very young at the time and felt very proud to have published a book on the impossibility of love. I gave my father a copy without foreseeing the troublesome consequences that this would have for me. A few days later, my father, annoyed at what he perceived in my book to be a record of offences against his first wife, obliged me to write a dedication to her in the copy that I had given him, which he himself dictated. I resisted such an idea as best I could. Literature was precisely—the same was true for Kafka—the only means I had to try to become independent of my father. I fought like a madman not to have to copy what he wanted to dictate to me. But finally I gave in, it was dreadful to feel that I was a copyist under the orders of a dictator of dedications.

This incident had such a negative impact on me that I did not write anything for twenty-five years. Not long ago, a few days before hearing that Mr Bartleby was in a meeting, I read a book that helped reconcile me to my condition as a copyist. I believe that the laughter and enjoyment I derived from reading *Institute Pierre Menard* helped pave the way for my decision to be rid of the old trauma and go back to writing.

Institute Pierre Menard, a novel by Roberto Moretti, is set in a secondary school whose pupils are taught to say "no" to over a thousand proposals, ranging from the most ludicrous to the most attractive and difficult to turn down. The novel is written in a jocular vein and is a very clever parody of Robert Walser's *Jakob von Gunten*. In fact Walser himself and the scrivener Bartleby are among the school's pupils. Nothing much happens in the novel, except that, by the time they have completed their studies, all the pupils have been transformed into consummate and cheerful copyists.

I laughed a lot while reading this novel, I am still laughing. Right now, for example, I laugh while I write because it occurs to me that I am a scrivener. To fix the image better in my mind, I take one of Robert Walser's books and pick a sentence at random, which I copy down: "Over the now darkened landscape treks a solitary figure." I copy this sentence down and proceed to read it aloud with a Mexican accent, and chuckle softly to myself. And this reminds me of a story of copyists in Mexico: that of Juan Rulfo and Augusto Monterroso; for years they worked as clerks in a gloomy office where, as I understand, they behaved like pure Bartlebys, always afraid of their boss who was in the habit of shaking hands with his employees at the end of each day's work. Rulfo and Monterroso, copyists in Mexico City, would frequently hide behind a pillar because they thought that what their boss wanted was to say goodbye to them for good.

This fear of a handshake now brings to mind the story of the composition of *Pedro Páramo*, which its author, Juan Rulfo, explained in the following terms, revealing his human condition as a copyist: "In May 1954 I bought a school exercise book and jotted down the first chapter of a novel which for years had been taking shape inside my head. I still do not know where the intuitions that gave rise to *Pedro Páramo* came from. It was as if someone dictated it to me. Suddenly, in the middle of the street, an idea would occur to me and I would note it down on scraps of green and blue paper."

After the success of the novel that he wrote as if he were a copyist, Rulfo wrote nothing else in thirty years. His case has often been compared to that of Rimbaud, who, having published his second book at the age of nineteen, abandoned everything and went off in search of adventure, until his death two decades later.

For a time, the panic he felt that his boss's handshake might mean the sack coexisted with the fear of people coming up to him to tell him that he had to publish again. When they asked him why he no longer wrote, Rulfo would say,

"Well, my Uncle Celerino died and it was he who told me the stories."

His Uncle Celerino was no fabrication. He existed in real life. He was a drunk who made a living confirming children. Rulfo frequently accompanied him and listened to the fabulous stories he related about his life, most of which were invented. The stories of *El llano en llamas* almost had the title *Los cuentos del tío Celerino* (Tales of Uncle Celerino). Rulfo stopped writing shortly before his uncle's death. The excuse of his Uncle Celerino is one of the most original I know among all those concocted by the writers of the No to justify their abandonment of literature.

"You ask why I do not write?" Juan Rulfo was heard to remark in Caracas in 1974. "It is because my Uncle Celerino died and it was he who told me the stories. He was always chatting to me. But he was full of lies. Everything he told me was pure lies and so, naturally, what I wrote was pure lies. Some of the things he chatted to me about had to do with the misery in which he had lived. But Uncle Celerino was not so poor. Given that he was a respectable man, in the opinion of his local archbishop, he was appointed to tour the different towns confirming children. These were dangerous lands and the priests were afraid of them. I frequently accompanied Uncle Celerino. Each place we arrived in, he had to confirm a child and then he charged for the confirmation. I have yet to write all of this down, perhaps I'll eventually get around to doing it. It's interesting how we moved from town to town confirming children, bestowing God's blessing on them and so on, don't you think? Especially considering he was an atheist."

But Juan Rulfo did not only have the story of his Uncle

Celerino to justify his not writing. Sometimes he would resort to smokers of pot.

"Now," he would comment, "even smokers of pot publish books. There've been a lot of very strange books recently, don't you think? I have preferred to keep silent."

Concerning Juan Rulfo's mythical silence, Monterroso, his good friend in the office of Mexican copyists, has written an ingenious fable, "The Wisest Fox." In it, there is a certain Fox, who produced two successful books and with good reason was prepared to stop there, and the years went by and he did not publish any more. The others started to gossip and to wonder out loud what had happened to the Fox and when they met him at a cocktail party they would go up to him and tell him that he had to publish again. "But I've already published two books," the Fox would say wearily. "And they're very good," they would answer, "which is why you should publish another." The Fox would not say so, but he thought that what people really wanted was for him to publish a bad book. But, because he was the Fox, he refused.

Transcribing Monterroso's fable has finally reconciled me to the good fortune of being a copyist. Farewell, trauma brought about by my father. There is nothing horrible about being a copyist. When one copies something, one belongs to the line of Bouvard and Pécuchet (Flaubert's characters) or of Simon Tanner (with his creator Walser in the shadows) or of Kafka's anonymous court officials.

To be a copyist is also to have the honor of belonging to the constellation of Bartleby. Filled with joy, I lowered my head a few moments ago and became lost in other thoughts. I was at home, but I fell half asleep and was transported to an office of copyists in Mexico City. Desks, tables, chairs, armchairs. In the background, a large window through which, rather than being seen, fell a fragment of the Comala landscape. And further back, the exit door with my boss extending his hand. Was it my boss in Mexico or my real boss? Brief confusion. I was sharpening pencils, and I realized that it would take me no time at all to hide behind a pillar. The pillar reminded me of the folding screen behind which Bartleby continued to hide after the Wall Street office in which he lived had already been dismantled.

I said to myself suddenly that, if someone were to discover me behind the pillar and want to find out what I was doing there, I would cheerfully tell them that I was the copyist who worked with Monterroso, who in turn worked for the Fox.

"Is Monterroso, like Rulfo, a writer of the No as well?"

I thought I could be asked this question at any time and so I was ready with the answer:

"No. Monterroso writes essays, cows, fables and flies. He doesn't write much, but he writes."

Having said this, I woke up. I was then overcome by a huge desire to record my dream in this book of footnotes. A copyist's happiness.

That is enough for today. I shall carry on with my footnotes tomorrow. As Walser wrote in *Jakob von Gunten*, "I must stop writing for today. It excites me too much. The letters flicker and dance in front of my eyes."

[. . .]

3.

"I grew used," writes Rimbaud, "to simple hallucination: I saw very clearly a mosque in place of a factory, a school of drummers formed by angels, carriages on the highways of the sky, a salon at the bottom of a lake."

At the age of nineteen, Rimbaud, with amazing precociousness, had already completed his works and fell into a literary silence that would last until the end of his days. Where did his hallucinations originate from? I believe they came to him simply from a very powerful imagination.

Less clear is where the hallucinations of Socrates came from. Although it has always been known that he had a delirious and hallucinatory character, a conspiracy of silence has ensured that this was kept in the dark for centuries. The fact that one of the pillars of our civilisation should have been an unbridled eccentric was not an easy pill to swallow.

Until 1836 no one dared to recall the real personality of Socrates; it was Louis Francisque Lélut in a beautiful essay, "Du démon de Socrate," who, basing his essay scrupulously on the testimony of Xenophon, dared to redress the image of the Greek sage. Sometimes one could almost be looking at a portrait of the Catalan poet Pere Gimferrer: "He wore the same coat in all seasons, he walked barefoot on the ice and on the earth warmed by the Greek sun, he danced and jumped frequently on his own, with no motive, as if on a whim, in short, owing to his conduct and manners, he gained the reputation of being such a misfit that Zeno the Epicurean nicknamed him 'the Attic buffoon,' what today we would term an 'eccentric.'"

Plato offers a rather disturbing account of Socrates' delirious and hallucinatory character in the Symposium: "On the way Socrates fell into his own private thoughts and kept dropping behind. I stopped to wait for him, but he told me to go on ahead. 'No,' I said to the others, 'leave him. He does this very often, he suddenly comes to a halt and stands there.' 'I perceived,' Socrates said suddenly, 'that divine sign which is familiar to me, the appearance of which always stops me in my tracks. The god governing me has not allowed me to talk to you of it until now, and I was waiting for his permission.'"

"I grew used to simple hallucination" is something Socrates could have written as well, were it not for the fact that he never wrote a single line; his mental excursions of a hallucinatory nature may have had a lot to do with his rejection of writing. No one can derive much pleasure from the task of making a written inventory of their own hallucinations. Rimbaud did it, but after two books he grew tired, perhaps because he sensed that he was going to lead a very bad life if he spent all his time recording his incessant visions one by one. Rimbaud may have been aware of that story by Asselineau, "The Musician's Hell," which tells of the terrible hallucination endured by a composer condemned to hear all his compositions performed both well and badly on all the pianos in the world simultaneously.

There is an evident relationship between Rimbaud's refusal to continue making an inventory of his visions and the perpetual literary silence of a hallucinating Socrates. However, we might, if we wish, see Rimbaud's emblematic decision to stop writing as simply repeating the historic gesture of a silent Socrates, who did not bother to write books like Rimbaud, but went straight to the point, and from the start declined to write down all his hallucinations as if heard on all the pianos in the world.

The following words of Victor Hugo could well be applied to this relationship between Rimbaud and his illustrious predecessor Socrates: "There are some mysterious men who can only be great. Why are they great? Even they do not know. Might He who has sent them know? They possess a terrible vision in their eyes that never abandons them. They have seen the ocean like Homer, the Caucasus like Aeschylus, Rome like Juvenal, the Inferno like Dante, Paradise like Milton, man like Shakespeare. Drunk with fantasy and intuition in their almost unconscious advance over the waters of the abyss, they have crossed the strange line of the ideal, which has penetrated them for ever . . . A pale shroud of light covers their countenance. Their soul emerges through their pores. What soul? God."

Who sends these men? I do not know. Everything changes except God. "In six months even death changes fashion," Paul Morand observed. But God never changes, I tell myself. It is well known that God keeps quiet, is a master of silence, hears all the pianos in the world, is a consummate writer of the No, and for that reason He is transcendent. I could not agree more with Marius Ambrosinus, who said, "In my opinion, God is an exceptional person."

[. . .]

24.

Last Sunday in July, rainy. It reminds me of a rainy Sunday Kafka recorded in his *Diaries*: a Sunday when the writer, because of Goethe, feels invaded by a complete inability to write and spends the day staring at his fingers, in the grip of Bartleby's syndrome.

"So the peaceful Sunday goes by," writes Kafka, "so the rainy Sunday goes by. I am sitting in the bedroom and I have silence to spare, but instead of settling down to write, an activity that the day before yesterday, for example, I would have thrown myself into with everything I've got, for a while now I've been staring at my fingers. I think this week I've been totally under the influence of Goethe, I think I have exhausted the energy of this influence and that is why I've become useless."

Kafka writes this on a rainy Sunday in January 1912. Two pages further on, in an entry dated 4 February, we discover that he is still trapped by the Evil One, by Bartleby's syndrome. We receive full confirmation that Kafka's "Uncle Celerino," at least for a good number of days, was Goethe: "the uninterrupted enthusiasm with which I read things about Goethe (conversations with Goethe, years as a student, hours with Goethe, a visit by Goethe to Frankfurt) and which prevents me from doing any writing."

There is the proof, if anyone was in doubt, that Kafka suffered from Bartleby's syndrome.

Kafka and Bartleby are two fairly unsociable characters I have tended to associate for some time. Of course I am not the only one to have felt tempted to do this. In fact Gilles Deleuze, in *Bartleby or the Formula*, says that Melville's copyist is the very image of the Bachelor, spelt with a capital letter, who appears in Kafka's *Diaries*, the Bachelor for whom "Happiness is the understanding that the ground on which he has stopped cannot be bigger than the area covered by his feet," the Bachelor who knows how to resign himself to a space that for him is growing smaller; the Bachelor the exact measurements of whose coffin, when he dies, will be just what he needs.

Along the same lines, I am reminded of other descriptions of the Bachelor, by Kafka, which also seem to be building up the very image of Bartleby: "He walks about with his jacket securely fastened, with his hands in his pockets, which are too high, his elbows sticking out, his hat pulled over his eyes, a false smile, innate by now, which must be to protect his mouth, just as his glasses protect his eyes; his trousers are tighter than is aesthetically pleasing on a pair of spindly legs. But everyone knows what is happening to him and can enumerate all his sufferings."

From the cross between Kafka's Bachelor and Melville's copyist I can picture a hybrid whom I am going to call Scapolo (*bachelor* in Italian) and who is related to that curious animal—"half kitten, half lamb"—inherited by Kafka.

Do we know what is happening to Scapolo? Well, I would say that a blast of coldness blows from within him, where he shows the sadder side of his double countenance. This blast of coldness derives from an innate and incurable disorder of the soul. It lays him at the mercy of an extreme negative impulse that causes him always to pronounce a resounding NO that is as if he were drawing it in capital letters in the quiet air of any rainy Sunday afternoon. This blast of coldness means that the more Scapolo withdraws from the living (for whom he works at times as a slave, at others as a clerk), the less space others consider necessary for him.

Scapolo seems good-natured like the Swiss (like the lackadaisical Walser) and he resembles the classic man without qualities (like Musil), but we have already seen that Walser only appeared to be good-natured and that the appearances of the man without qualities are not to be trusted. In reality Scapolo is frightening, because he walks straight through a terrible zone, a zone of shadows which is also where the most radical of denials has its home and where the blast of coldness, in short, is a blast of destruction.

Scapolo is a stranger to us, half Kafka and half Bartleby, living on the edge of the horizon of a very distant world: a bachelor who says now that he would prefer not to, now, in a voice trembling like that of Heinrich von Kleist before his lover's grave, something as terrible and at the same time as simple as this:

"I'm not from here any more."

This is Scapolo's formula, quite an alternative to Bartleby's. I say this to myself while listening to the rain this Sunday blustering against the glass.

"I'm not from here any more," Scapolo whispers in my ear.

I smile at him with a certain fondness, and recall Rimbaud's "I am really from beyond the grave." I look at Scapolo and invent my own formula, and I also whisper in his ear, "I'm alone, bachelor." And then I can't help seeing myself as rather comical. Because it is comical to realize that one is alone while addressing another person.

[. . .]

26.

"Art is a stupidity," said Jacques Vaché, and then he killed himself, choosing the quick way to become an artist of silence. There won't be much room in this book for suicide Bartlebys, I'm not too interested in them, since I think that taking one's own life lacks the nuances, the subtle inventions of other artists—the game, in short, which is always more imaginative than a shot in the head—when called on to justify their silence.

I include Vaché in this book of footnotes, for him I make an exception, because I love his remark that art is a stupidity, and because it was he who revealed to me something that Susan Sontag discusses in her book *Styles of Radical Will*: "The choice of permanent silence doesn't negate [the artist's] work. On the contrary, it imparts retroactively an added power and authority to what was broken off—disavowal of the work becoming a new source of its validity, a certificate of unchallengeable seriousness. That seriousness consists in not regarding art as something whose seriousness lasts for ever, an 'end,' a permanent vehicle for spiritual ambition. The truly serious attitude is one that regards art as a 'means' to something that can perhaps be achieved only by abandoning art."

So I make an exception for the suicide Vaché, paradigm of the artist without works; he is listed in all the encyclopedias, though he wrote only a few letters to André Breton and nothing else.

And I'd like to make another exception for a genius of Mexican literature, the suicide Carlos Díaz Dufoo Jr. For this strange writer art is also a false path, an idiocy. In the epitaph from his bizarre *Epigrams*—published in Paris in 1927 and supposedly composed in this city, though later research shows that Carlos Díaz Dufoo Jr never left Mexico—he affirmed that his actions were dark and his words insignificant and he asked to be imitated. This out-and-out Bartleby is one of my greatest literary weaknesses and, despite committing suicide, he had to take his place in this book of footnotes. "He was a complete stranger among us," Christopher Domínguez Michael, the Mexican critic, has said of him. One has to be very strange indeed to appear strange to the Mexicans, who—at least so it seems to me— are so strange themselves.

I shall finish with one of his epigrams, my favorite epigram by Dufoo Jr: "In his tragic desperation he brutally tore the hairs from his wig."

[. . .]

49.
In his biography of Joyce, Richard Ellmann describes the following scene, which took place when Joyce was fifty and Beckett twenty-six, and which could have come straight from the theatre of the No:

"Beckett was addicted to silences, and so was Joyce; they engaged in conversations which consisted often of silences directed towards each other, both suffused with sadness, Beckett mostly for the world, Joyce mostly for himself. Joyce sat in his habitual posture, legs crossed, toe of the upper leg under the instep of the lower; Beckett, also tall and slender, fell into the same gesture. Joyce suddenly asked some such question as, 'How could the idealist Hume write a history?' Beckett replied, 'A history of representation.'"

[. . .]

56.
Today is Monday. At sunrise this morning, I was reminded of Michelangelo Antonioni, who once had the idea of making a

film while looking at "the evilness and great capacity for irony," he said, "of the sun."

Shortly before reaching this decision, Antonioni had been mulling over these verses (worthy of any noble branch of the art of denial) in *Autumn Journal*, a poem by Louis MacNeice, the great Belfast poet, who today is half-forgotten: "Think of a number, double it, treble it, square it / And sponge it out."

Antonioni knew straight away that these verses could be turned into the heart of a dramatic but slightly humorous film. He then thought of another quote—this from *An Introduction to Mathematical Philosophy* by Bertrand Russell—which also had a certain comic tone: "The number 2 is a metaphysical entity about which we can never feel sure that it exists or that we have tracked it down."

All of this led Antonioni to think of a film that would be called *The Eclipse* and would be about a couple's feelings drying up, becoming eclipsed (as writers are, for example, when they unexpectedly abandon literature), so that all their old relationship disappears.

Since a total eclipse of the sun was imminent, he went to Florence, where he saw and filmed the phenomenon, and wrote in his diary, "The sun has gone. Suddenly, ice. A silence different from other silences. And a light distinct from any other light. After that, darkness. Black sun of our culture. Complete immobility. All I can manage to think is that during the eclipse feelings will probably dry up as well."

The day *The Eclipse* was first shown, he said that he would always be left with the doubt whether he should not have headed his film with these two verses by Dylan Thomas in *Out of the Sighs*: "There must, be praised, some certainty, / If not of loving well, then not."

It seems that for me, tracker of Bartlebys and literary eclipses, Dylan Thomas' verses are very easy to modify: "There must, be praised, some certainty, / If not of writing well, then not."

[. . .]

NOTES ON THE CONTRIBUTORS

The Argentinian writer CÉSAR AIRA was born in 1949 in Coronel Pringles. Described as "the most original and shocking, the most exciting and subversive" Spanish-language writer (Ignacio Echeverri), and one of the most prolific writers in Argentina, with more than 30 books published, Aira has lived in Buenos Aires since 1967, working as an editor and translator and teaching at the University of Buenos Aires (on Copi and Rimbaud) and at the University of Rosario (on Constructivism and Mallarmé). Roberto Bolaño hailed Aira as an "excellent" writer, "whose position in contemporary Hispanic literature is equal in complexity to that of Macedonio Fernández at the beginning of the 20th century." Aira's next novel with New Directions, *How I Became a Nun*, will be published soon.

　　CHRIS ANDREWS is a lecturer in the School of Languages at the University of Melbourne. His translation of Roberto Bolaño's *Distant Star* won the 2005 TLS Vallé-Inclan Prize and he also won a 2005 PEN Translation Fund Award for Bolaño's *Last Evenings on Earth*. In addition to Bolaño and César Aira, Chris Andrews has also translated Luis Sepulveda and Ana Briongos.

Born in Santiago, Chile, in 1953, ROBERTO BOLAÑO moved to Mexico City with his family in 1968. He went back to Chile in 1973 to "help build socialism" (as he wrote in his story "Dance Card"), but less than a month after his return, the army seized power. Bolaño was arrested and imprisoned in Concepción. After his release, he returned to Mexico, working as a literary journalist and teacher, before moving to Paris (which he thought "the most beautiful city in the world") and then on to Barcelona. He took on a series of casual jobs (as dishwasher, night watchman, waiter, salesman) while writing steadily and sending in his work to provincial literary competitions in Spain. The 1996 appearance of *Nazi Literature in the Americas* first brought his work to wide public attention, and his publications maintained a fierce pace. Winner of many prizes, including the Premio Herralde de Novela and the Premio Rómulo Gallegos, Bolaño is "his generation's premier Latin American writer. . . . Bolaño's reputation and legend are in meteoric ascent." (*The New York Times*) He wrote nine novels, two story collections, and five books of poetry. He died on July 15, 2003, at the age of 50.

CHRIS ANDREWS: please see entry for César Aira.

Chinese author CAN XUE (whose real name is Deng Xiaohua) was born in 1953 in Changsha City, in Hunan province, and is the only woman associated with a male-dominated avant-garde school that emerged in China around 1985 and includes such authors as Mo Yan, Yu Hua, and Su Tong. Can Xue suffered when her parents were condemned as ultra-rightists in 1957, and during the Cultural Revolution, she was raised by her grandmother and was often on the brink of starvation. Can Xue's formal education ceased after just completing primary school. Formerly a tailor by trade, Can Xue (the name means "the dirty snow that refuses to melt") only began to write fiction seriously in 1983. She learned English on her own and has written books on Borges, Shakespeare, and Dante. A prolific writer of short stories, novellas, novels, and critical commentaries, Can Xue's first Chinese work was published in 1985 and her books previously published in the U.S. are *The Embroidered Shoes*, *Old Floating Cloud*, and *Dialogues in Paradise*. Robert Coover has called her "a new world master."

KAREN GERNANT, Professor Emerita of Chinese History, now divides her time between homes in Fuzhou, China, and Talent, Oregon. CHEN ZEPING, professor of linguistics at Fujian Teachers' University, has taught for extended periods at Southern Oregon University and Ehime University. Together they have translated contemporary Chinese fiction writers Alai, Yan Lianke, Zhang Kangkang, Zhu Wenying, Su Tong, Bei Cun, Lin Bai, Guo Xuebo, and Wei Wei.

Born in 1935 on the eastern coast of Jutland in the town of Vejle where her father was a tailor, prolific Danish poet and novelist INGER CHRISTENSEN is considered the foremost experimentalist of her generation. Central to her work is the distance between language and experience, reality and words: "I have attempted to tell about a world that does not exist in order to make it exist." In 1954, Christensen moved to Copenhagen and began publishing her poems and in 1964 became a full-time writer: her numerous prizes include the Nordic Prize of the Swedish Academy, Der österreichische Staatspreis für Literatur, and the Grand Prix des Biennales Internationales de Poésie. A member of the Danish Academy, she became a member of Académie

Européenne de Poésie in 1995. She is frequently mentioned as a candidate for the Nobel Prize in literature. Called "marvelous" by Bei Dao, "seductive" by *The Boston Review*, and "visionary" by *The Chicago Review*, Christensen's work is like no other poet's. New Directions has published *Alphabet* and *Butterfly Valley: A Requiem; for Azorno* and *it* are forthcoming.

DENISE NEWMAN was born in New Jersey and studied comparative literature at the University of Copenhagen. Her books of poetry include *Blood Flower, Why Pear?*, and *Human Forest*, and she also translated Christensen's novel *The Painted Room*.

JENNY ERPENBECK was born in East Berlin in 1967. After apprenticing as a bookbinder, she studied theater in Berlin, before working in the props and costume departments at the Staatsoper. She has since become a director of several opera and musical productions, in addition to writing stories, novels, and plays. *Die Zeit* has praised her gift for "sustained feats of verbal economy." Her story "Siberia" won the Jury Prize at the Ingeborg Bachmann Competition, and Nicole Krauss selected *The Old Child and Other Stories* as a Best Book of 2005 in *The Los Angeles Times*: "I haven't read anything this good—this bracing, unflinching and alive—for a long time. . . ."

SUSAN BERNOFSKY is the author of *Foreign Words: Translator-Authors in the Age of Goethe* and has translated books by Robert Walser, Gregor von Rezzori, Yoko Tawada, and others. Her current projects are a retranslation of Hermann Hesse's *Siddhartha*, a critical biography of Robert Walser, and, for New Directions, translations of Walser's novels *The Assistant* and *The Tanner Family*, which have never appeared in English.

FELISBERTO HERNÁNDEZ was born in Montevideo, Uruguay, in 1902. A talented pianist, he was playing in the silent-screen movie theaters when he was twelve years old; in his twenties he toured the small concert halls of Uruguay and Argentina before becoming a government employee. He married four times, spent two years writing in Paris, published seven books, and died, impoverished, in 1964. Although he never enjoyed commercial success of any kind, Hernández was immensely inspiring for his fellow writers: Gabriel García Marquez has stated, "If I hadn't read the stories of Felisberto Hernández, I wouldn't be the writer I am today."

ESTHER ALLEN has translated books by José Martí, Jorge

Luis Borges, Javier Marías, Antonio Muñoz Molina, Rodrigo Rey Rosa, Juan Bonilla, and a number of other writers. She is an Assistant Professor at Seton Hall University and co-Director of PEN World Voices: the New York Festival of International Literature.

Born in Romania in 1938, YOEL HOFFMANN, when he was just a year old, escaped to Palestine with his parents, where his mother died and he spent some time in an orphanage. A professor of Philosophy and East Asian Religious Studies at the University of Haifa for many years, Hoffmann has had a lifelong engagement with Western philosophy and Japanese Buddhism. He lived for two years in a Zen monastery, which inspired his translation *Japanese Death Poems*, and his book about the secrets of zen koans, *The Sound of One Hand Clapping*. Hoffmann has published seven fiction books, including *Katschen & The Book of Joseph*, *The Christ of Fish*, *Bernhard*, *The Heart Is Katmandu*, and *The Shunra and the Schmetterling* (New Directions). Winner of the first Jewish Book Prize from the Koret Foundation as well as the Bialik Prize, Hoffmann is acclaimed "Israel's celebrated avant-garde genius" *(Forward)*, and viewed by Amos Oz with "awe" and acclaimed as "miraculous" by A. B. Yehoshua. He now lives in Galilee.

PETER COLE's most recent book of poems is *Hymns & Qualms*. He has translated widely from medieval and modern Hebrew and has received numerous awards for his work, including a Guggenheim Foundation fellowship and the 2004 PEN Translation Fund Award. *The Dream of the Poem: Hebrew Poetry from Muslim and Christian Spain, 950–1492* is forthcoming from Princeton University Press.

Swiss-born FLEUR JAEGGY writes in Italian and has lived in Milan since 1968. She has won many European prizes (including Italy's prestigious Viareggio-Rèpaci, the Bagutta, and Boccaccio Europa), and is the author of six books. *Sweet Days of Discipline*, *Last Vanities*, and *SS Proleterka* are available from New Directions, and have been acclaimed here as "small-scale, intense, and impeccably focused" (*The New Yorker*): of her style, *The Los Angeles Times Book Review* commented: "Nothing rivals its intensity." Jaeggy has also written on Keats, Robert Walser, De Quincey, and Marcel Schwob, and translated into Italian Schwob's *Imaginary Lives* and De Quincey's *Last Days of Immanuel Kant*.

British novelist TIM PARKS's eleven novels include *Europa*, *Destiny*, *Judge Savage* and *Rapids*, as well as three non-fiction accounts of life in northern Italy, where he has lived for many years (most recently *A Season with Verona*). His many translations from the Italian include works by Moravia, Calvino, and Calasso, and for New Directions, Tabucchi and Jaeggy. He lectures on literary translation in Milan and has published a book, *Translating Style*.

JOHN KEENE, Associate Professor of English and African American Studies at Northwestern University, was born in St. Louis in 1965 and has been the recipient of fellowships from the Artists Foundation of Massachusetts, the *New York Times* Foundation, Yaddo, the Bread Loaf Writer's Conference, and, most recently, was awarded a Whiting. Keene, who has a B.A. from Harvard and an M.F.A. from New York University, is a longtime member of the Dark Room Collective and a graduate fellow of Cave Canem. His first novel, *Annotations* (New Directions, 1995), was selected as a Critic's Choice by *The San Francisco Review of Books* and a Best Book of the Year by *Publishers Weekly*; a starred *Kirkus* review called it "a dense, intelligent, poetic highly allusive word-tapestry . . . tiny and filled with enormous themes: a tour de force of intelligence, wordsmithing, and passion." He is currently working on poems, a collection of short stories, and a novel.

ALEXANDER KLUGE, born in Germany in 1932, is a world-famous filmmaker who once studied with Fritz Lang. His 23 movies include *Yesterday Girl, The Female Patriot*, and *The Candidate*. He is a lawyer, an associate of Theodor Adorno and the Frankfurt School, and also a media magnate of independent television in Germany. Susan Sontag remarked that "Kluge is a gigantic figure in the German cultural landscape. He exemplifies—along with Pasolini—what is most vigorous and original in the European idea of the artist as intellectual, the intellectual as artist." Winner of Germany's highest literary award, the Georg Büchner Prize, Kluge displays in his books as in his films a profound interest in montage and history. *The Devil's Blind Spot* was selected by *Artforum* as a Best Book of 2005.

MARTIN CHALMERS lives in London where he writes extensively on German literature, film, and history; he is the translator of the Klemperer diaries as well as works by Jelinek, Enzensberger, and Fichte. Poet MICHAEL HULSE has translated more than fifty books (by authors such as Goethe, Sebald, Botho Strauss) and is now running the Writing Program of the University of Warwick, as well as serving as the editorial director of the Leviathan Press.

Born in 1926 in Osaka, KONO TAEKO's childhood was scarred by World War II, which also ruined her family financially. She graduated from the University of Osaka, and, after surviving tuberculosis, she devoted herself exclusively to writing in 1960. Her fiction, which is influenced by Tanizaki and Emily Brontë, has won all of Japan's major literary prizes—including the Akutagawa, the Tanizaki, the Noma, and the Yomiuri. Shusaku Endo stated that "her unsparing gaze penetrates the depths of human nature; and she sets forth what she finds there with absolute precision." And Kenzaburo Oe has saluted her as "at once the most carnally direct and the most lucidly intelligent woman writing in Japan."

Associate Professor at the University of Hawaii Manoa, LUCY LOWER is a scholar of modern Japanese literature and film, and has also translated the poetry of Makato Ooka.

Born in 1954, LÁSZLÓ KRASZNAHORKAI lives in Pilissentlászló, Hungary. Author of eleven books, he is widely regarded as his country's foremost experimental fiction writer and won Hungary's highest literary award, the Kossuth Prize, in 2005. *The Melancholy of Resistance* was selected as Best Book of the Year in Germany in 1993. W.G. Sebald stated that Krasznahorkai's "vision rivals that of Gogol's *Dead Souls* and far surpasses all the lesser concerns of contemporary writing." And Imre Kertes remarks: "I love Krasznahorkai's books, his long meandering sentences enchant me, and even if his universe appears gloomy, we always experience the transcendence which Nietzsche identified as metaphysical consolation." Two of Krasznahorkai's novels have been made into award-winning films by the renowned filmmaker Béla Tarr.

GEORGE SZIRTES was born in Budapest in 1948 and came to England as a refugee in 1956. He has written many books of poetry (and won the 2005 T.S. Eliot Prize), and his award-winning translations include works by Dezsö Kosztolányi, Sándor Márai, and Agnes Nemes Nagy.

Born in the Ukraine in 1925, CLARICE LISPECTOR was barely two months old when her family settled in Recife. At the age of 19, Lispector published her first novel, *Near to the Wild Heart*, which was a watershed in Brazilian literature, catapulting it into modernism. She went on to write nineteen more books, becoming "the premier Latin American woman prose writer of the twentieth century" (*The New York Times*) and arguably Brazil's greatest twentieth-century writer. The *crônica*, or chronicle, a literary genre peculiar to the Brazilian press, allows poets and novelists (and soccer stars) to address a wide readership on any theme they like. Lispector's Saturday column from 1967 to 1973 in Rio's leading newspaper, the *Jornal do Brasil*, was, even by the Brazilian standards, extraordinarily free-ranging and intimate—astonishingly so to readers of U.S. newspapers. She died in 1977.

GIOVANNI PONTIERO, who also died in 1977, was reader in Spanish and Portuguese Literature at the University of Manchester, England. A foremost translator from the Portuguese, he was for years the principal voice in English for Lispector and José Saramago, and he won the Teixiera-Gnomes Prize for Portuguese Translation for Saramago's *The Gospel According to Jesus Christ*.

JAVIER MARÍAS was born in Madrid in 1951, the son of anti-fascist intellectuals, and published his first novel at the age of 19. He held various academic posts in Spain, the U.S. (as a visiting professor at Wellesley), and the U.K. (as a lecturer in Spanish at Oxford), and has gone on to write 28 books. As well as contributing a weekly newspaper column to *El País*, and in addition to his own busy career as "one of Europe's most intriguing contemporary writers" (*TLS*), he has translated into Spanish a vast range of English-language authors (from Ashbery and Auden to Conrad, Hardy, and Laurence Sterne). He is, additionally, King Xavier I of Redonda and runs the publishing program Reino de Redonda. Translated into forty languages, his own work (called by *The New York Times Book Review* "a rare gift") has won a dazzling range of prizes, and five million copies of his books have been sold worldwide.

MARGARET JULL COSTA has translated many Spanish, Portuguese, and Latin American authors—amongst them Bernardo Atxaga, Eça de Queiroz, and Juan José Saer—and has won prizes for her translations of Fernando Pessoa's *Book of Disquiet* and José Saramago's *All the Names*. For Javier Marías's *A Heart So White* she won the International IMPAC Dublin Literary Award.

Born in 1962 in Moscow, VICTOR PELEVIN was educated as an engineer, before establishing his reputation as the most brilliant Russian writer of his generation: "A psychedelic Nabokov for the cyber age" (*Time*). In 1993 he won the little Russian Booker for his story collection *The Blue Lantern*. New Directions also publishes *The Yellow Arrow*,

Omon Ra, Four by Pelevin, and *A Werewolf Problem in Central Russia.*
Pelevin's latest novel is *Homo Zapiens.* "To paraphrase Churchill, post-
Soviet Russia is a riddle, wrapped in a mystery inside a Pelevin" *(The
New York Times)*. A practicing Buddhist, Pelevin spends considerable
time in monasteries in Asia and tries to avoid literary conferences and
festivals "because such events make me wish I had never been born."

ANDREW BROMFIELD has translated many books by Vic-
tor Pelevin, Boris Akunin, Vladimir Voinovich, Irina Denezhkina, and
Leonid Latynin.

Acclaimed Haitian poet and scholar RENÉ PHILOCTÈTE published
many books and was a founder of the group Haiti Littéraire and the
Spiraliste literary movement. He remained in Haiti during the dangerous Duvalier years and was widely respected for his fearless rejection of
all forces of oppression. Born in Jérémie on November 16, 1932, during
the first American occupation of Haiti, Philoctète died on July 17, 1995,
with American soldiers once again in his beloved homeland. "An
extraordinary writer" (Edwidge Danticat), and deeply revered by his
countrymen, a true citizen of the world, René Philoctète has been called
by Lyonel Trouillot "the Haitian writer par excellence."

LINDA COVERDALE is the translator of over forty
books, including works by Roland Barthes, Annie Ernaux, and Patrick
Chamoiseau. Her translation of Tahar Ben Jelloun's *This Blinding
Absence of Light* won the 2004 International IMPAC Dublin Literary
Award.

Born in Guatemala in 1958, RODRIGO REY ROSA is the author of
eight books. He settled in the United States for a time, after leaving
Guatemala due to the atmosphere "of violence." On his first trip to
Morocco he met Paul Bowles, who translated Rey Rosa's first three
works into English. In addition to writing novels and stories, he is a
filmmaker and has also translated into Spanish literary authors including Bowles. Rey Rosa's style has been hailed as "a marvel of poetic effi-
ciency and power" *(The San Francisco Chronicle)*, "fiercely impressive"
(WorldView), and "compelling in the extreme" *(Blitz)*.

ESTHER ALLEN: please see entry for Felisberto Hernández.

W.G. SEBALD was born in 1944 in Wertach im Allgäu, Germany.
Alienated by the academic atmosphere of West Germany at the time,

he studied German language and literature in Switzerland and Britain. Beginning in 1970 he taught at the University of East Anglia in Norwich, England, and from 1989 to 1994 was the first director of The British Centre for Literary Translation. His books *The Emigrants, The Rings of Saturn, Vertigo, Austerlitz, The Natural History of Destruction,* and *After Nature* won many international awards, including *The Los Angeles Times* Book Award for Fiction, the National Book Critics Circle Award, and the Berlin Literature Prize. "Is literary greatness still possible?" Susan Sontag asked in the London *Times Literary Supplement,* and then replied: "One of the few answers . . . is the work of W.G. Sebald." When he died in December 2001, he was eulogized as "one of the great writers of our time" (*The New York Review of Books*).

MICHAEL HULSE: please see entry for Alexander Kluge.

The magisterial Scottish writer Dame MURIEL SPARK was born in Edinburgh in 1918 and was educated at the James Gillespie's School for Girls—an experience mined in *The Prime of Miss Jean Brodie*. In 1938 she married, and after working in intelligence in WWII, she began her literary career. She edited *The Poetry Review,* wrote studies of Mary Shelley, John Masefield, and the Brontë sisters, and published her first poetry collection. Winning the 1951 Observer prize for short fiction finally inspired her to write fiction full-time. Written three years after Spark converted to Roman Catholicism, her first published novel *The Comforters* (1957) was an enormous hit. Enjoying the success of her early novels, Spark moved between Rome and New York, before taking up residence in Tuscany where she now resides. She is currently at work on her 22nd novel, following the success of her latest, *The Finishing School*.

One of the most renowned voices in the European literature and the foremost Italian writer of his generation, ANTONIO TABUCCHI was born in Pisa in 1943. The author of novels, short stories, essays, and plays, he holds the Chair of Literature at the University of Siena. A champion of Portuguese literature, Tabucchi is the chief Italian translator of Pessoa. Translated into more than forty languages, his books have won prestigious prizes including the PEN Club Prize, the Campiello, the Viareggio-Rèpaci, the Prix Médicis Etranger, the Prix Européen de la Littérature, the Prix Méditerranée, the Aristeion, the Nossack, the Europaeischer Staatspreis, the Hidalgo, and the Francisco Cerecedo. As *World Literature Today* stated,

"By now the appearance of a new novel by Antonio Tabucchi is a literary event."

JANICE M. THRESHER won the 1983 PEN Renato Poggioli Award for her translations of the early works of Giovanni Verga.

Educated at Waseda University and the University of Hamburg, YOKO TAWADA was born in Tokyo in 1960. In 1982 she took the Siberian Express from Japan to Hamburg, where she worked for a time as a bookseller, and settled there. She made her debut as a writer with *Missing Heels*, which was awarded the Gunzo Prize for New Writers in 1991. In 1993, she received the prestigious Akutagawa Prize for *The Bridegroom Was a Dog* (which was translated by Margaret Mitsutani and published in English in 2003). She writes in both Japanese and German, and in 1996, she won the Adelbert von Chamisso Prize, a German award granted to foreign writers for their contribution to German culture. *Where Europe Begins*, a collection of stories translated from both languages by Yumi Selden and Susan Bernofsky, was selected by Marjorie Perloff as a 2005 *TLS* Best Book of the Year: she called it "astonishing . . . exhilarating"; a new collection is forthcoming.

SUSAN BERNOFSKY: please see entry for Jenny Erpenbeck.

UWE TIMM was born in Hamburg in 1940. Though first apprenticed to a furrier, he went on to study philosophy and philology in Munich and Paris, and after working as an editor for a decade, he became a full-time writer of remarkable range (novels, stories, plays, children's books). To date, Timm has been translated into more than twenty languages and has published 22 titles, including *Headhunter*, *The Invention of Curried Sausage*, *Midsummer Night*, *Morenga*, and *The Snake Tree* (available from New Directions). *The New Yorker* hailed Timm as "an extraordinary storyteller."

BREON MITCHELL, Professor of Germanic Studies and Comparative Literature at Indiana University, where he also serves as Director of The Lilly Library, has recently translated a new version of Franz Kafka's *The Trial*, *The Silent Angel* by Heinrich Böll, the collected short stories of Siegfried Lenz, and Marcel Beyer's *Spies*. He has won the ATA German Literary Prize, the ALTA Translation Prize, the Theodore Christian Hoepfner Award, and the Helen and Kurt Wolff Prize (for Uwe Timm's *Morenga*).

LEONID TSYPKIN was born in Minsk in 1926 of Russian-Jewish parents, both physicians. *Summer in Baden-Baden*, his last book, was the culmination of a passionate clandestine literary vocation; a distinguished medical researcher, Tsypkin wrote strictly for the desk drawer and never had a measure even of "underground" fame. He was twice denied permission to leave the Soviet Union with his family. Instead, he was demoted professionally, treated very badly, and died of a heart attack in Moscow in 1982. "Although its publication comes almost twenty years after the death of its author," *The Washington Post* commented, "and although his name continues to go unrecognized in Russia, this [*Summer in Baden-Baden*] volume stands to change the way we think of 20th-century Russian fiction." Sontag ranked the book among literature's "most beautiful, exalting and original achievments." Two more of his books have been discovered and will be published by New Directions.

ROGER KEYS AND ANGELA JONES collaborated on a variety of translations while they were married in the 1970s and 80s. Roger is still a lecturer in Russian at the University of St. Andrews in Scotland. He is a specialist in Russian Symbolism and has written key works on the author Andrei Belei. Angela has moved on to learn Spanish, and has helped to translate the works of local poets in Castilla-La-Mancha, Spain.

DUBRAVKA UGREŠIĆ was born and raised in what used to be Yugoslavia. In 1993, she left Croatia for political reasons. She has taught in several American and European universities. She has been awarded various international prizes for her writing, including the Swiss Charles Veillon European Prize, the Austrian Europaeischer Staatspreis, the Dutch Resistance Prize, and the German SudWest Funk Prize. Ugrešić has been hailed by Susan Sontag as "brilliant . . . a writer to cherish" and by Charles Simic as the "philosopher of evil and exile . . . utterly original." She is also the author of *Lend Me Your Character, Ministry of Pain*, and *Thank You for Not Reading*.

CELIA HAWKESWORTH is Senior Lecturer in Serbian and Croatian at the School of Slavonic and East European Studies, University College, London. In addition to numerous translations, including several works by Ivo Andric, she has published *Ivo Andric: Bridge between East and West* and *Voices in the Shadows: Women and Verbal Art in Serbia and Bosnia*.

ENRIQUE VILA-MATAS was born in Barcelona in 1948 and in 1968 moved to Paris where he rented an apartment from Marguerite Duras. His dozen books have been translated into eleven languages and honored by many prestigious literary awards, including the Prize of the City of Barcelona, the Premio Herralde de Novela, the Premio Rómulo Gallegos, and the *Prix Médicis Etranger.* He has been called "the most important living Spanish author" by Bernardo Atxaga. *The Los Angeles Times* greeted his first book to be translated into English, *Bartleby & Co.*, as: "Perfect, beautiful . . . exquisite, exhilarating." In a starred review, *Kirkus* called the book "a wry, mind-bending delight: Borges and Calvino would have welcomed Vila-Matas as a kinsman."

JONATHAN DUNNE was born in Kingston-upon-Thames, England in 1968 and educated at King's College School, Wimbledon, and at Oxford University, where he read Classics. A poet (author of *Even Though That)*, he translates literature from Bulgarian, Catalan, Galician, Portuguese, and Spanish, including the authors Tsvetanka Elenkova, Carme Riera, Manuel Rivas, Rafael Dieste, and Enrique Vila-Matas.